A CHOSEN WAR

REUTS PUBLICATIONS

A CHOSEN WAR

CARLY ELDRIDGE

Cover design by Ashley Ruggirello
Edited by Kisa Whipkey, Rae Oestreich
Book design by Ashley Ruggirello

Electronic ISBN: 978-1-942111-42-9
Paperback ISBN: 978-1-942111-41-2

REUTS Publications
www.REUTS.com

MAIA STARED AT her mother's favorite rare rosebush. It was dying. Slowly and quietly, it succumbed to an indomitable illness no amount of tears, anger, love, or determination could defeat.

Just like him.

Disease marred its velvety flesh. Withered leaves drooped around the curled, lavender-brown remnants of petals and buds that had once glistened with morning dew, had once caused passersby to stop and exhale in wonder.

Maia wished, for a brief moment, that the garden was hers to create and destroy as she saw fit. She'd put that little rose out of its damn misery. But unfortunately, the garden belonged to her mother, and Beth refused to give up hope, clinging instead to the idea that the rose could be saved. Just like him.

Maia sometimes wondered if her mom loved that rose more than she loved her, but a tiny voice in the back of her mind echoed: "*Ignorant child. You know that's not true.*" The voice sounded strangely like her Nanna—a voice she thankfully hadn't heard in nearly seven years. Nanna had made the overzealous, religious mother in *Carrie* look positively heathen.

Goose bumps bloomed across her skin at the memories, and she wrapped her arms tightly around her waist, holding in the fear her grandmother's indoctrination had caused. You can only be told you're destined to grow up a failure so many times before you start to believe it.

Maia shivered. It wasn't exactly cold this morning, but she was wearing only a faded, long-sleeved Seahawks t-shirt and Beth's gardening clogs. Summer had come early to Portland. In fact, it was already sixty-eight degrees at the ungodly hour of six a.m., and Maia had been rationed yet another blessed—but wasted—hour of sleep before her alarm was set to wake her for her summer job. She wasn't the only one to have given up on sleep so soon, though. Her street was already abuzz with activity. The uncharacteristic heat had driven some neighbors to get their morning jogs in early, while others were setting sprinklers into motion. The ripping sound of a lawnmower coughing to life tore through the friendly greetings between neighbors as small animals scurried for the cool shade of brush. For most residents on the quiet Portland street, the strange weather was the most interesting topic. But Maia wasn't most people.

She rubbed her nose with a sleeve-covered wrist. The sharp scent of the fertilizer Beth had lovingly patted around the base of the rose last night stung, burning its way through her sinuses and threatening to bloom into a headache.

The rose bush had been a gift. The kind only given by one who knows all of your secrets, has shaken hands with the skeletons in your closet, has sifted through the mess of your life and unloaded the baggage to determine that what they have found is treasure. Only now, after twenty-five years and despite constant attention, the rose was slowly dying. Beth had worked feverishly—at times obsessively—over the past few months, trying to bring it back to life. Often, late at night, the sounds of her cajoling sniffles would join the croaking melody of the garden frogs' night-song as she tended the tiresome thing. Maia would inevitably tug her tangled ear-buds out from under one of her bed's many pillows, pop them back in, and play another hypnosis track on her phone in the hope of being lulled back to sleep.

Her heart clenched over Beth's constant sorrow, for it was a pain she couldn't ease, no matter what sacrifices she made. Her mother's tear-streaked face this morning as she left for another grueling shift at the ER vindicated Maia's stare down with the stumpy bush at this God-awful, dawn-hued hour. Maia was going to be twenty in three months, but was she off at one of the many prestigious art schools that had courted her for her photography skills? Did she take that internship at the fashion magazine in Milan? Was she out embarking on sexual excursions in an effort to "discover herself" and prove that her gender really could "have it all"?

No. She still lived at home, the parent to both of hers.

Maia pulled in a shaky breath that rattled through her lungs. It wasn't just the rose Beth cried for. Her mother's ob-session over the dying plant had nothing to do with the fact that it was rare, or the sentimentality of its origin. Instead, it was an outlet. She couldn't save *him* any more than she could save the rose.

Maia's father had pancreatic cancer, and despite multiple forms of treatment—including surgery—he, like the rose, was gradually declining. Just two minutes ago, he'd left for yet another meeting with his oncologist to "discuss what could be done." Maia rolled her eyes and huffed annoyance, gritting her teeth. Nothing could be done. They all knew it.

Maia hugged herself tighter, digging her fingers into her sides to hold herself together. If she relaxed, she'd somehow shatter—an unfixable glass vase. She clenched her eyes shut as a tiredly familiar thought marched through her mind: *I can only control me.*

Maia hunched until her shoulders nearly touched her ears before she forced her eyes open again, glaring at the rose. She knew it wasn't the plant's fault, but that didn't stop her anger from simmering as she chewed on the inside of her cheek until a slight copper tang filled her mouth. It had become a relentless habit and, by now, the taste of blood was more familiar than any food. She wanted to throttle the damn rose.

In a haze of blurred, worry-fueled anger, Maia rushed forward until she was so close to the rose that the edge of her shirt brushed against the tips of its dried-up twigs. Her fingers curled around the decaying plant, and an instant surge of energy sizzled through her veins. The leaves and petals crackled in her crushing grip. The air filled with the concentrated scent of rose. A sudden lightheadedness dropped Maia to her knees, but she barely registered the impact with the moist dirt. Focusing on the plant before her, Maia willed her fingers to let go; they ignored her command. She could only hold on and sway in place. Her head throbbed as saliva pooled in her mouth, accompanying the churning of her nauseated stomach. She blinked rapidly against the mounting fear of a full blackout.

Then, between the space of two heartbeats, the strange sensations were gone. Her breath came in ragged gasps as her grip finally relaxed, releasing its victim, and she stared at her upturned palms, flexing her fingers.

What the hell had just happened? Maia squeezed her eyes shut a few times, still lightheaded. She tried focusing on the sounds and smells of normalcy around her: birds in a nearby tree defending their nest, her neighbor's annoying Yorkipoo barking at one of the many outdoor cats patrolling his territory, the smell of the drying dirt beneath her mixed with the hot smell of dryer sheets as someone's outdoor vent exhaled into the side yard. Gulping, she licked her suddenly dry lips, trying to regulate her breathing. Hysterical giddiness bubbled within her chest as she glanced up at the rose bush. Nothing was particularly funny, but that didn't stop the surge of laughter that caused her muscles to quiver in stressful release.

A moment later, she found herself curled into a ball, cackling madly. Maia couldn't remember the last time she'd laughed like this. It felt good, like stretching tight, unused muscles.

Finally, though, her sides stopped heaving and the laughter subsided. Still lying in a ball, Maia relaxed, face resting against the grass beneath her, palms open to the sun peeking out from the wispy clouds in the sky. Peace settled deep within her bones, and she closed her eyes, reveling in the brief moment of pure relaxation. This was better than any drug. Not that she was highly experienced in those. She was no neophyte to escapism, either.

A prick of guilt from her busy day ahead shattered the peaceful moment and, with a sigh, Maia stood, dusting dirt off her long bare legs. They made her look like a skittish colt rather than the ballerina her inner five-year-old still yearned to blossom into.

A shiver of premonition ran down her spine as she scrubbed at a particularly stubborn patch of mud on her calf and she froze. Slowly, she lifted her head to stare at the rose bush once more.

It was thriving. The tea rose before her was no longer the diseased, brittle plant she'd touched mere moments ago. In fact, it didn't look anything like it ever had; at least, to her memory. Even on its best day, it had never looked so healthy. And to make matters worse, the vibrant plant was now sharing its good fortune with whatever flora its roots could touch. The surrounding foliage flourished and transformed before her eyes, stems stretching, flowers blossoming, fruit ripening . . . all in an instant. Brilliant, shimmering colors that glittered in the morning sunlight bounced off the waxy perfection of the plants around her, as if someone had Photoshopped the tiny little section of reality she stood before.

Something brushed against the tips of her fingers, delivering a tiny electrical shock. Yelping, Maia jumped back, shoving the abused digits into her mouth to suck away the pain. Only then did she notice the azalea bush beside her. It had been completely barren this morning, well past its bloom. Now, it erupted in fresh blossoms, red and white florets competing for space among the plant's normal dark pink flowers. Maia's heart faltered.

Choking back a scream, she ran into the house, images of Disney-movie magic scampering along in her mind. Taking the first right turn, Maia careened past her homemade dark room and down the hallway to her bedroom. Slamming the door behind her with the kick of a muddy foot, the clogs abandoned halfway down the hall, Maia stood in the middle of her artistically chaotic—some would argue messy—sanctuary, staring at her fingers. Maia shook them out, tilting her head back until it met the door behind her with a thud. What was going on? Maia's chest tightened as she started to hyperventilate, and her stomach responded with another wave of nausea. She hadn't eaten anything yet that morning, and she shuddered to think what her stomach would produce.

"Get a grip," Maia muttered. "Get a freaking grip. I can only control me."

Placing her hands on her knees, Maia tried to sort through the facts, the solid things that made up her life. Number one: her father's illness. Two: Beth's grief and absurd work schedule. Three: the long list of missed opportunities on a promising career, and now . . . this? How was she supposed to handle it all? She was expecting to hear back on some possible freelance contracts in the next few days. What she really needed was money and exposure, not hallucinations. Sure, crazy made for good art, but Maia wasn't into avant-garde. Whatever had happened in the garden had to be a fluke.

Yeah. Maia nodded to herself. *No big deal. Life's been hectic. It's probably just stress.* Beth blamed every physical upset she had on stress, so why couldn't Maia? Licking dry lips, she gathered in a steadying breath. She glanced around, looking for the stick of Burt's Bees she was always misplacing as she nodded again to herself. *Yeah*. Stress sounded like a perfectly good rationale.

A chuckle echoed off the walls, and it took Maia a moment to realize the phantom noise had come from her own lips. Startled at the strange sound of her lonely laughter, Maia fought another wave of nausea that curled her body further inward.

It's not like I can heal anything. She grasped at any rational thought she could to calm her nerves. But . . . what if? The next deep breath ended in a squeaky hiccup.

What if she *could* heal things? Why now? Why had this new "power," or whatever it was, suddenly decided to show up? Maia's inner cynic was fully on its high horse now, whispering that she was being ridiculous, that this was just a childish daydream. Besides, wasn't this sort of thing supposed to happen when she hit puberty, or on a harvest moon, or when she turned a significant age, like twenty-one or something? If Maia was going to believe in magic, she may as well do it right. Maia could feel the hysterical laughter from earlier welling up again. *This is it. I've cracked. I'm going crazy.*

Grasping for any sense of normalcy to ground her, Maia's gaze traveled over the room, as if her many art posters and photographs could provide an answer. Instead, she noticed the bright red analog numbers of her alarm clock, blinking at her from her nightstand. The haze in Maia's brain cleared, and she straightened. Great, she was late for her job at the state park down the road.

It was just the dose of reality she needed. The real world was still out there, waiting on her to get to Tryon Creek and do her job. With a groan of obligation, Maia grabbed a work polo and some jeans off the floor, heading for the bathroom down the hall. She felt a small burst of gratitude that her family had shaved their heads a year ago in support of Greg losing his hair to chemo. Now, she sported a wavy, dirty-blonde pixie cut that suited her petite features. It also meant she didn't have to mess with fixing her hair every morning, which was perfect for days like this.

Moments later, Maia returned to her room, running her fingers through damp, curling locks before grabbing her maroon

Converse. Hopping in place, she struggled into the sneakers while reaching over to the nightstand to check her phone. She was hoping for a message from her parents, but when her fingers pressed the button, she got a nasty surprise instead. The sleek little rectangle outdid itself in a magnificent display of fireworks, bursting into vicious white and blue flames.

With a shriek, Maia toppled onto her backside, scrambling backward over the piles of clothes and books littering the floor. Patting around, she flicked through cloth and paper until her fingers finally hit something cool and solid, curling around the neck of a forgotten bottle of Arizona Iced Tea.

Maia flung the contents of the bottle onto the burning phone and watched as it settled into a timid sizzle. It let out one last *pop* before going quiet as the charred stench of plastic and the metallic tang of burnt wire filled the room.

Maia snorted, staring at the pitiful device on her blackened nightstand. "I don't know what sort of third dimension I woke up in," Maia whispered through clenched teeth, "but I've had it." She chucked the empty bottle into her waste basket with a satisfactory thump and glanced at the bed. If she burrowed under the downy blue blankets and fell asleep, would she wake up to normalcy?

Maia sighed in resignation before grabbing her bag and heading downstairs, trying to ignore the flashes of hot and cold that traveled over her skin. Was this what it felt like to go into shock?

No. Maia gave herself a mental shake. This could be the big break she was waiting for. Maybe the universe was tired of dealing her one crappy hand of karma after another. Maybe, just maybe . . . nah. She shook her head before the thought could fully form. Inner Cynic was right. That was ridiculous. Only in fairy tales did one get magical powers to heal their dying father. This was reality. The sight of the garbage truck in front of her house, dumping waste into its dank cavity, convinced her. Maia blew out a calming breath and instantly regretted it; her next breath was destined for less pleasant smells.

As the familiar foes of cynicism and anxiety battled in her head, tightening the muscles around her heart, Maia swung her leg over her bike and set off for work.

MAIA PUMPED THE pedals of the bike as fast as she could, hoping the trembling that had overtaken her body would not affect her balance. She was late, very late. Her heart thrashed about in her chest, and she squeezed the handle bars of the bike until the rubber nubs of the grips dug into her palms. She wanted to let go emotionally and wear her internal battle on her sleeve, but instead, she sailed past the austere buildings of Lewis and Clark College and stuck her tongue out at the brick- and ivy-covered campus. The morning ritual brought a small sense of normalcy back. Knowing her future most likely did not include a fancy private college—or any school, for that matter—she reveled in the tiny display of rebellion, however pathetic. A paintball gun would have been more apropos. *Less second grade, more Banksy*, she thought smugly to herself.

Clenching her teeth in a grimace, she stood on the bike's pedals and coasted down the hill, thankful for the burn in her thighs distracting her from her suddenly raw throat. The morning's irritations continued to pile up around her, but she had to keep a cool head. Beth worked long hours as an ER nurse, and would often be gone for days at a time, only to come home and sleep for nearly as long. If she could handle that, Maia could handle this. *I can only control myself. I am an island of one.*

Maia pedaled furiously, trying to expend the adrenaline still coursing through her and finally calm her nerves. The thick tires of her bike crunched across scattered pine needles and gravel as she turned into the entrance of the park.

Locking the brakes, she skidded to a stop near the bike rack and stuffed her hands into the pocket of her hoodie, searching around for something to wipe her nose with. Triumphantly, she pulled out a clean but wadded tissue and buried her nose into it. The cold undertone of Portland's air always made her nose run, even on this early summer day. Maia sniffed loudly a few times before crumpling the tissue again and tossing it into a nearby trash can. With a determined set of her shoulders, she shoved down the hollow feeling in her chest and slapped on her trademark carefree smile. It was the only thing that convinced others that she was "fine." Too bad it never worked on the shame spiral she constantly drowned in.

Depression lies.

Maia rolled her eyes as the mantra skipped through her mind, this one in the chirpy voice of the affirmation app Beth made the entire family listen to.

As Maia fumbled to lock up her bike and helmet, her fingers numbed from the chilly ride, she focused on the upcoming day. A full day of escorting snotty-nosed daycare kids on a tour of the park while attempting to convince them that nature was more interesting than their iPads had little appeal. Still, the meager pay was enough to cover her few bills, and she loved any part of the city that allowed her to get lost in the wilderness. She could never explain why she felt more at home among the trees and the wildness of exposed earth, but it was why she loved photography, why she had plastered her walls with pictures of landscapes and spider webs gleaming in morning dew. If she couldn't physically bring the beauty of nature inside, then pictures would serve as a compromise—at least to her mother's sanity. A fond memory of her first camera and the deal made with her parents to abstain from bringing the outside in eased some of the morning's irritation.

Finished with the bike, she stood and started rolling the building tension from her shoulders. Something tickled along her calf. Absently, Maia brushed the sensation away, but when the flutter against her skin returned, she glanced down to see the ferns around the base of the bike rack curling and stretching their long fronds in her direction. Maia backed away quickly, her heart racing up her throat once more.

No. She shook her head so hard her ears rang and stars burst in her vision. *What happened this morning was a fluke.* Maia stared at the fern's waving tendrils. Maybe it was the breeze? But not even logic could argue with the fact that there wasn't a wisp of wind present. She closed her eyes tight, but when she opened them, the ferns were still straining in her direction and thoughts of impending insanity slipped into her mind again. At this point, trying to sort the plausible from the implausible was heralding a migraine.

A pair of thin, strong arms snaked around her chest in a vice grip, lifting Maia off the ground, her surprised shriek quickly swallowed by the surrounding forest.

With a throaty chuckle that matched a jazz singer's smoky-rich voice, Hayley released her from the biggest hug she'd ever experienced. Maia fought the prickles of irritation that raced across her skin. She hated being touched, by anyone—a point which Hayley regularly enjoyed challenging.

"Damn, girl," she drawled, her thick Portuguese accent adding exotic appeal to every turn of phrase that fell from her lips. "I guess I just don't know my own superhuman strength." She struck a dramatic pose, making a show of kissing her biceps.

Maia spun around with a laugh that quickly became a snort, feeling slightly embarrassed for overreacting, and came face-to-clavicle with her best friend's perfectly toned body. Hayley's skin seemed to shimmer with the rays of a thousand summers and disgustingly put every Brazilian model to strut a Victoria's Secret runway to shame.

"So?" Maia wiggled her eyebrows, hoping to distract herself from the shiver coursing over her as she shook off the feeling of Hayley's touch. "How's Terrance? Or is it Jemal? Or, no, don't tell me"—she held up her hand as the taller girl fought to hold back a canary-eating grin—"Marcus?"

Hayley's lips twitched in amusement as Maia slung a mock punch at her shoulder and they headed down the dirt path toward the Nature Center's front door. She let out an exaggerated sigh. "You know, Maia, I just can't decide. But, really, why?"

Maia scoffed. "Why what?"

"Why choose? Isn't there some song that says, 'let it be'?" Hayley's already wide-eyed grin widened further. "Yeah, that's it! I heard it in a commercial yesterday. Cool, huh?"

Maia rolled her eyes. "Oh my God. I know you didn't just—"

Hayley interrupted with a pout. "Hey, what happened to you this morning? I tried to pick you up, but you weren't home. You didn't answer your phone, either." Hayley punctuated her sentences with an airiness that didn't quite reach her eyes, or the slight crease between her dark brows.

"You were worried?" That would be news to Maia. The most Hayley ever worried about was which nail color to use next.

"A little," Hayley admitted with a wink, just as they reached the door. She stopped short of actually opening it, though.

Maia rolled her eyes before wrenching it open for Her Royal Majesty. Hayley was an impossible germophobe, but Maia suspected it was most likely an act—an act that worked. She rarely did anything for herself that she couldn't get someone else to do for her.

"My phone died this morning," Maia replied, allowing the Nature Center's familiar scent of reclaimed wood to wash over her as she stepped inside, hoping it could return a sense of security. "Besides, you know I'd rather ride my bike than be in that road-kill maker."

Hayley sailed through the door behind her with a mock gasp, her hand fluttering over her substantial chest as she drawled in a horrible, fake Georgian accent, "How could you say that about my baby? You'll hurt his feelings, Maia. Mac!" She quickly pounced as their coworker emerged from the hallway, shrugging into his favorite black jacket which never allowed enough room for the cords of muscle that snaked around his arms. "Did you hear what Maia said about my baby?"

Mac scratched his frizzy auburn curls as a shy smile tilted across his strong features. "Well, if she was insulting that bedazzled tank you call a car, I'm on her side."

Maia's eyes narrowed as she tucked an errant curl behind her ear. She still couldn't quite figure him out. Mac was the only male Hayley's charms failed to attract, though Maia caught him staring at her often. For some reason, though, he never tried to make a move, and his gaze seemed more cautious than admiring. His only mistake had been mentioning during their last trip to the movies that he found the lead actress's Georgian accent endearing. Ever since, Hayley had added horrible attempts at being a Southern belle into her exhaustive repertoire for hooking him. Maia noticed, with raised brows, that it still had not worked, leaving them all to the mercy of Hayley's perseverance. She didn't take kindly to losing.

Mac headed for the door, clearly on his way to check the trails designated for the kids' nature walk, and Hayley shadowed his every step. Normally, Maia would have left them to it, as there was plenty of prep work to be done before the gaggle of sticky grade-schoolers arrived—those juice and raisin boxes weren't going to pair up by themselves, after all— but before the door could close behind them, Mac pinned her with a pained look, tugging on her sympathy. Despite being nearly six feet tall, built like a boxer, and moving with the confident grace of an athlete, he was a big baby when it came to dealing with Hayley's effusiveness. So, with a quiet, annoyed groan, Maia trudged after them.

The crunch of gravel underfoot and the call of wildlife flitting through the trees did nothing to deter Hayley from dramatically expounding upon the finer points of the new Range Rover her daddy had bought her for her twenty-first birthday. And since Hayley was focused on her favorite topic—herself—she never noticed that Mac had dropped back to walk beside Maia instead. The two exchanged their childhood elbow bump in a silent oath to de-Hayley the situation. This morning's tactic? Distraction.

Mac went first with a horrible fox call that sounded more like a drowning cat. Maia winced, lifting a condescending eyebrow that quickly faltered under the giggle she smothered beneath her hand. Maia tried a simple sparrow call, but if Mac's strangled fox call didn't break Hayley's concentration, they were going to have to up the ante.

The next five minutes were spent shuffling loudly through the verdant, lush Pacific Northwest forest behind Hayley, who led the conversation easily, as undeterred as ever. So far, they had passed a few morning joggers, a sweet old couple with knotted hands intertwined and wispy, gray-haired heads close together, and a young man being walked by his exuberant pack of three lab mixes. But despite life happening all around, the animal-call impersonations by Mac and Maia, and the fresh outburst of laughter heinously snorted through failed cover-ups, Hayley kept up her diatribe on her second favorite topic: celebrity gossip.

They had come to the halfway point of the walk-through when the breast pocket of Mac's jacket began to vibrate. Pulling a sleek phone out, he glanced at the display before roughly shoving it back into his pocket, his brows bunched together in concern.

"Can you girls finish checking the paths?" He had to raise his voice to a near-shout to break into Hayley's chatter. Finally realizing someone else was trying to speak, Hayley paused mid-sentence. "I need to run back to the office."

"Is everything all right?" Maia searched his face, trying to read the fine lines tightening around the edges of his green eyes. It was unusual for him to treat a call with such urgency, and his hand was still inside his pocket, clutching his phone as if it would run away if he let go.

Mac shuffled backward down the trail. "Yup! Everything's fine." With that, he spun on his heel and set off, nearly sprinting back to the office.

3

AFTER MAC'S ABRUPT departure, Maia and Hayley followed the path in unusual silence, finishing their rounds
before Hayley finally piped up again.

"Man, I hope it wasn't his mom or anything."

She punctuated her words with little kicks of her wedge-
heeled boots in the dirt, a not-so-subtle hint for Maia to take
the bait. The sun streaming in through the canopy of trees
brought out the copper highlights in her hair, enveloping her
head in a halo of fire.

"What do you mean?" Maia's hand hovered over a tram-
pled plant, and she watched in horrified wonder as it slowly
began to heal itself. Quickly, she looked up, guilt burning

through her cheeks as a jolt of adrenaline flashed through her heart. Had Hayley seen that? Maybe if she kept her talking, the other woman wouldn't notice.

"Well . . ." Hayley drew the word out slowly, as only an expert gossiper could, and Maia instantly regretted having neglected the dangers of egging Hayley on. "She was taken to the hospital last night after she collapsed on the stairs. I asked him this morning why he wasn't still with her, but you know . . ."

Relief escaped Maia in a puff of breath, and she followed as Hayley continued to trot down the path like it was a runway. Maia shook her head in good-natured amusement. Hayley was new to the job, but Summer Camp Counselor for a state park in no way meant that one had to dress like they were strutting down Park Avenue. She chuckled at the memory of Hayley's first day, how she had boldly shown up in five-inch stilettos paired with a jersey jumpsuit and a large, bauble necklace. Even with her ridiculous choice of footwear, the woman had been incredible. Her heels never sank into the earth, creating the illusion that she floated instead of walked, and she had somehow remained spotless throughout the entire day.

"Witchcraft," Maia muttered.

"What's that?" Hayley asked, tossing the words over her shoulder as Maia finally caught up. Damn, the woman could walk fast.

"Nothi—"

"Hey, do you guys work here?"

A young man cut through the brush behind them, leaves and branches crunching under his hiking boots as he hopped over a fallen log, the branches he'd pushed aside clinging to his thin, long-sleeved t-shirt and scratching at his neck and hands. He must have cut through the forest from the trail that ran parallel to theirs.

"*Ladies*," Hayley said.

"Come again?" The young man ducked under a branch that blocked his way and stepped out onto their path.

"We aren't 'guys.' We are *ladies*." Hayley looked him up and down, condescension practically dripping from her.

Maia stole a quick glance at the tense line of Hayley's jaw, and then cleared her throat in rebuke. "It's fine," she said, frowning as Hayley's upper lip curled slightly with disgust. Her friend huffed and crossed her arms, turning slightly away as the young man approached.

Finally focused on the figure in front of them, Maia stiffened, the reassuring smile she'd been about to offer dying on her lips. He had to be well over six feet tall, and he had wavy, gold-streaked brown hair that curled low on his forehead but was buzzed on the sides. Sun and laughter lines creased the edges of his blue eyes—eyes that put the myriad blues of the Bali Sea to shame. His looks weren't what terrified her, though; good-looking guys were a dime a dozen. No, what terrified her was that she knew him. Not *knew* him, knew him, but knew him in a way that made about as much sense as anything else that had happened that morning. Ever since she was little, she had dreamt of a man with preternaturally blue eyes—the same eyes that were now staring into her own.

Maia couldn't quite remember exactly when the dreams had started. At first, they were just visions of eyes that were a uniquely brilliant blue. They were always kind, and warm with mirth, but that was all she'd had to go on. By the time Maia was thirteen, the rest of his face had formed, too. Sheepishly, she remembered Googling the color of those eyes with every adjective she could pull from her father's old college thesaurus, hoping to find the man's picture. But she never could.

Every few years, more of the man had emerged in her dreams, and the dreams themselves had become more and more frequent, until finally, last year, Maia was privy to not only his strong neck and broad shoulders, but his sculpted torso and, well . . . she felt the burn of embarrassment return to her cheeks at that thought.

Maia flicked a quick glance over the man's powerful form, no longer in her dreams, but standing right in front of her, and was glad that he was too busy brushing the curious petals of nearby wildflowers away from his calves to notice her gawking. As of a few weeks ago, she had not only seen everything there was to see about him, but also . . . memories of their tangled limbs—her hair wrapped tight around his fingers, the salty taste of his skin, the feel of his body on hers—flashed through her mind and senses. The tips of her fingers found their way to her lips, and Maia gulped in confusion at the gut-tightening emotions flooding through her. Suddenly, she found her dirty shoe laces to be the most interesting thing in the forest.

"Righto." The man nodded. "Sorry, ladies." His Australian accent caressed the vowels of each word he spoke, finishing with a lazy drawl. Maia glanced up again, hoping her cheeks weren't as flushed as they felt. She'd never heard his voice before, only felt . . . she quickly shoved the memory of the dream from her mind.

The man attempted a weak grin, thankfully oblivious to her pathetic ogling, but the concern etched across his face halted the smile's progress. "I was hoping you might be able to help me. I was hiking with my dog, and he was attacked. I really don't want to leave him alone." He turned back toward the forest, his expression a mix of pleading worry.

"Of course," Maia blurted, still feeling the gravitational pull of her dreams incarnate. She took a step toward him, ready to follow.

"No," Hayley huffed. "We're busy. Sorry." Her acidic tone invalidated the apology.

Maia snorted in disbelief at her rudeness as she looked back at her friend's rigid form, standing still on the path behind them.

"Yes, we *can*," Maia said pointedly. "We work here. It's what we *do*." Maia turned to follow, well, her dream man— quite literally, she realized—and groaned inwardly at the cliché as they headed toward the green haze of the moss-strewn forest.

"Forget it," Hayley insisted, nearly shouting at their retreating backs. "We deal with kids, not strange dudes who can't control their dogs."

Maia flinched as Hayley's tone grew sharper. What had gotten into her? She hadn't known her long—they had become fast best friends—but she had never seen her so derisive. She wasn't just annoyed or put out; this was something more.

"Well, ladies . . ." the guy said as he ducked under a branch, loud enough for Hayley to hear. "My name is Blake. Not Dude or Duderino." He chuckled slightly at his own joke. "And my dog didn't do anything. He was the one attacked."

Maia could have sworn the leaves were stretching toward Blake's face as he passed, their fragile stems quivering with effort and anticipation. She blinked furiously, pinching the bridge of her nose. *Get a grip, Maia.* When she reopened her eyes, no doubt looking like an absurd little barn owl woken too early, Blake was swatting at a leaf seemingly snuggling against his cheek. Weird.

"So you say," Hayley answered from behind her.

Maia gave a little start at Hayley's sudden proximity, wondering how delusional she must be to have not heard her friend approach. Shaking her head, Maia rubbed her forehead vigorously. She needed to focus. Yes, this morning had been . . . well, strange, to put it lightly, but she needed to maintain a firm grip on what was real. I can only control me. I am an island of one. Her shoulders settled into a more confident position as she slowly straightened her back. Maia knew who and what she could depend upon, and that reminder grounded her in the moment, in reality.

"Just a few more steps and we're there, ar'right?" Blake said.

"Fine," Hayley growled, stomping after him.

Maia quickly positioned herself between the two as they sidestepped stumps and the spindly fingers of searching branches. The tension was beginning to make her skin crawl.

"So, what exactly attacked your dog?"

Blake grimaced. "You're probably gonna laugh." He gave a lighthearted shrug. "He was attacked by a fox."

"That's . . . odd." Maia stumbled over a rock hidden in the carpet of leaves coating the forest floor. "Foxes usually mind their own business, unless your dog came upon it while it was eating, or he got too close to its den."

"Yeah-nah." Blake shook his head and paused to lift a tree branch out of Hayley's way. The branch's leaves stretched to the extent of their lengths in an attempt to touch his face; he absently swatted them away. Hayley returned his kindness with an ungracious harrumph before kicking through a pile of leaves on the ground. "Leo was on a leash, and we were on the path. The fox came out of nowhere, as if it was running from something, and it just jumped on my dog."

"I guess that explains it," Maia answered, incredulous. "But it's still rather odd."

Her steps faltered as they finally approached the other trail, and she clamped down on a squeak of shock at what lay before them. The most beautiful husky she'd ever seen lay shivering just off the far side of the path, covered in a mixture of dirt, matted white and pale brown fur, and blood.

"Oh, poor thing," she whispered. Her heart clenched as she rushed forward, dropping to her knees by the dog's side. Maia gently cradled the creature's head, placing it in her lap and rubbing his soft ears. He whined faintly, and her throat ached with a sudden rawness. Desperate for a distraction, Maia rubbed two fingers gently between the dog's eyes and felt him relax.

"Hey, his eyes are green. I've never seen that on a husky," Maia said, sniffing away the threat of tears. "Normally they're blue, or two different colors. Is he purebred?"

"You know what I find odd?" Sarcasm bled through Hayley's tone as she hovered over Maia. "Such a big dog—especially a husky—should have been able to survive an attack by a fox. Aren't they known for eating cats and small children?"

Blake frowned, concern tightening the corners of his eyes as he knelt near Maia and Leo. He cradled the dog's paw in his fingers, as though he were holding the hand of an injured friend. Leo's labored panting slowed.

Maia glared at Hayley before turning to Blake. "Your dog's lost a lot of blood, but fortunately, we have Portland's best vet on call for our park. Dr. Connor will take good care of him, don't worry." Maia patted her pockets. "Crap. I forgot.

My phone died this morning. Hayley, do you mind going back and calling the vet for him?"

"What *did* happen to your phone?"

Maia flinched as Hayley's nasty tone was directed now at her. Remembering the tiny fireworks display from this morning, she gave a shaky laugh. "It just died. Okay? Simmer down."

Hayley sighed. "Just wrap the dumb thing up. He'll be fine." She nudged the dog, none too gently, with the tip of her boot, and Maia slapped her foot away.

"That's a bit harsh, Hayley. What's your problem, anyway?"

"Fine, whatever." Hayley threw up her hands. "I'll be back." She pointed a finger at Blake, closing one eye like she was aiming a gun. "Just don't have too much fun until I return, kiddies." Then she spun on her heel and flounced off, giving him a few more glares over her shoulder before she rounded the corner of the path.

Maia's shoulders slumped slightly in embarrassment over Hayley's unusual attitude. "I'm very sorry about that. I don't know what's gotten into her. You don't have a cell phone, do you? I forgot to ask."

"Didn't bring one," Blake said. He rubbed the back of his neck with a wry smile. "I purposely leave it behind on hikes." He shrugged, and Maia pressed her lips together, just to be sure she wasn't gaping dumbly at him as he continued, nodding toward the place Hayley had disappeared from view. "Doesn't *she* have a phone?"

Maia shook her head, standing. "She's always losing it. Here." She gestured for Blake to take her spot on the ground next to Leo. "Put his head in your lap and sit with him. We need to keep him calm, but alert, and put pressure on the wound near his neck." Maia peeled off her hoodie and was shoving it into a ball when he gently stilled her hands. She froze under his touch, not daring to so much as even breathe as her heart pounded with absurd volume. Slowly, Blake withdrew his hands, as though she were a skittish animal preparing to bolt.

"Yeah-nah." His words were barely a rough whisper as he looked up at her. "I couldn't do that to you. Your sweater'll get all bloody." He stuck the edge of his t-shirt between his teeth and proceeded to rip off the hem.

Maia looked away the instant his hard, golden-tan stomach made an appearance. "Or you could do that, I guess," she mumbled. Her voice shook as awkwardness rocked her stomach. She closed her eyes in a long blink, grounding herself. How often did one actually meet their sex-dream fantasy, let alone talk to them? This was absurd. Then again, this whole day was absurd. She was starting to doubt whether or not she'd actually gotten out of bed at all. A dream would certainly be preferable to the alternative.

Commotion in the shrubs behind them drew their attention as the plants beside the path began to quiver and shake. Seconds later, a dust-colored pygmy rabbit exploded from the brush, pummeling toward them. Maia knew that most wild animals would give you a wide berth rather than engage. So even though the critter was headed right for her, Maia was confident it would alter its direction and most likely bury itself in a nearby tree or bush.

Except, it didn't.

Instead, it skidded to a stop in front of her sneakers, pawing furiously at the laces with frightened little squeaks.

Maia stared at the shaking creature in bewilderment, careful not to startle it as she looked over her shoulder at Blake and the prone husky. Leo would certainly register the activity of prey in the vicinity, and she expected him to at least growl, no matter how hurt he was. Instead, he lay calmly, making no sound at all. His green eyes stared keenly at the rabbit, but instead of predatory, he looked almost worried.

Leo let out a small whine, and Blake rubbed between his ears, giving her an expectant, knowing look. Maia frowned at him as the fear of incompetence and embarrassment—its partner-in-crime—threatened the situation. In response to her confusion, Blake raised his eyebrows, as if trying to telepathically communicate something that Maia should already know.

Not wanting to scare the rabbit, she mouthed, "What?" Blake nodded toward the tiny creature as Maia realized that more bushes, and even the branches of the trees above them, were trembling with the disturbance of wildlife. Returning her gaze to the rabbit, she discovered it had somehow multiplied into three more of its kin, all now busily attempting to dig beneath her sneakers.

Maia let out a soft gasp and began to lift her feet, until a shushing noise gave her pause.

Blake was shaking his head, pointing to the sky. The unusually clear day had turned cloudy, as was typical of Portland weather. Yet it wasn't clouds that had obscured the sun.

It was birds. Hundreds of them, maybe thousands. All shapes, and colors, and species, they blanketed the sky in their loud, verbal escape. Maia had seen migrations before, but not this kind of chaotic and loud mass exodus.

Finally realizing that they couldn't make a new place of refuge beneath her sneakers, the rabbits abandoned their project and ran in the same direction the birds were flying. Within seconds, they were joined by a herd of other animals, both predator and prey, co-mingling without regard for each other.

A gray fox and a coyote scampered next to beavers and white-tailed deer, while red tree voles leapt from branch to branch alongside burrowing owls. Even though these creatures were known to Maia as forest regulars, an awed and terrified gasp escaped her as a black bear lumbered by. Its midnight-colored coat glinted in the shafts of sunbeams that escaped the blanket of feathers coating the sky. The bear paid her no mind as his roar rang in her ears, and the scent of his breakfast assaulted her nose. He was so close Maia could have easily reached out to run her fingers through his coarse fur. Hot on the bear's heels, a snarling wolverine ignored her just as equally.

As the wildlife made their retreat, a fine mist settled upon the forest, dissolving fur and feathers into foliage and stone.

Swallowing the dryness that fear had left in her mouth, Maia asked, "What *was* that?"

Blake tilted his head toward the sky, breathing deeply until a crease formed between his eyes. "I'm not usually the best one to ask about this," he said. "But . . ." He looked down at the bloody mass of fur in his lap, as if asking for confirmation of his thoughts. Leo responded with a lick to his face. A smirk stretched across Blake's features as he said, "Something's about to happen. Something big."

"Like what, exactly?"

Blake opened his mouth to reply, but instead of words, the rumble of an approaching motor filled the air. Relieved, Maia saw a tiny John Deere Gator trundling down the path, carrying Mac and Dr. Connor's wife/assistant, Samantha. Sam's chin-length russet bob swayed with the motion of the golf cart-sized vehicle; perched on the edge of its bed, she gazed at the sky in amazement as the Gator skidded to a stop a few feet before them.

"Good, you're here," Maia said.

"Maia." Sam's nodded greeting was all business as she focused on her patient with clinical alacrity. "Mac told me what happened." She gave Maia's shoulder a reassuring squeeze before turning to Blake and kneeling near the dog with a makeshift stretcher. "Where's he injured?"

"What happened to Hayley?" Maia looked to Sam first, but she was too busy wrapping Leo's injuries to answer. "Mac?" she asked, turning to him instead. "Mac? What's wrong?"

He was frozen in his seat, his knuckles white as he clutched the steering wheel, his expression unreadable as he stared past Maia to Blake and the dog sitting on the trail.

"Mac?" Maia snapped her fingers before his face and waved. "What's going on? Where's Hayley?"

He blinked a few times, somehow managing to unhinge his clenched jaw enough to answer. "Couldn't say. After she told me what happened, she disappeared. So I called the Connors." He tilted his head slightly toward Sam, his eyes never leaving Blake, who was helping the vet's assistant bring Leo over on the stretcher.

"Okay . . ." Maia hemmed. Sure, Hayley had been acting strange, but she hadn't expected her to just run off. "What do you think is stirring the wildlife?" Maia gestured to the bushes and trees, where the sounds of frantic scurrying could still be heard.

Mac gave an odd look to Blake as the young man climbed into the cramped Gator bed with Sam and a bandaged up, tucked in Leo. "I can't be sure, but something bad." His look turned accusatory when Blake made eye contact with him and gave him a curt nod. "Something very bad."

Clambering into the Gator, Maia plopped down on the bench next to Mac. He wheeled the vehicle around, none too gently, before forcing it at top speed back to the Nature Center.

"Careful, Mac! You'll overturn our patient," Sam admonished, giving the back of Mac's head a stern look. She placed her hands protectively across Leo in an effort to keep him from bouncing out of the small bed. Mac ignored her warning as he catapulted the Gator over potholes and took several more rough turns, kicking the trail's gravel into clouds of dust. Maia was thankful the Gator couldn't go as fast as Mac clearly intended, but just like Hayley's sudden mood swing, she couldn't account for his sudden intensity. His exchange with Blake had been uncharacteristic, and she couldn't help looking back and forth between the two men. Something was going on here. First Hayley, and now these two. They looked as though they were ready to throw down with each other, or anyone else who crossed their paths. Blake opened and closed his fists, his eyes darting about with paranoid quickness. His movements were sharp and focused, and his rigid posture resembled a coiled spring ready to be released. Curiosity soon got the best of her. Something was off, and she needed to know what.

"Do you guys . . . know each other?" she asked.

"Old school friend." Mac shrugged as they pulled up to the back of Dr. Connor's rusty green Suburban. Dr. Connor said a quick hello, accompanied by his always strained, yet patient smile, as he helped Blake and Sam put Leo in the back of his vehicle. Nothing creates an opportunity for getting answers like a good distraction, and Leo's heart-piercing whimpers were just what Maia needed to find out more.

"Mac, you've been my next-door neighbor my entire life. I know *all* of your friends." She poked his ribs gently in an attempt to ease whatever was bothering him. Mac was the most laid-back person she knew, having only seen him angry a handful of times. He'd always been like the big brother she'd never had, but this? This was a new level of intensity.

"I met him at college."

Ouch. She'd forgotten about that. Mac often took great pains to never bring it up, knowing the C-word was a sensitive subject, but he was right; Maia didn't know who he'd met there.

With Leo safely bandaged and ensconced in the back of the old Suburban, the usual sentiments occurred: good-byes were made, along with assurances that the dog would be looked after, and that they had done the right thing in calling. During it all, though, Maia felt numb and slightly out of body. She could hear everything, and knew that words were leaving her mouth, but she couldn't begin to comprehend what was being said. It must have been proper, because no one looked at her strangely. But it wasn't until Blake's sharp blue eyes entered her vision that reality snapped back into place.

"Maia." Blake folded her hand into both of his, some-how turning the handshake intimate. Comforting. Her skin grew warm at his touch, as though a blanket fresh from the dryer was wrapped around their grasped hands. Maia suddenly worried that the handshake would turn soggy with her sweat, and her bout of social anxiety quickly turned into irritation at his impertinence. Who did he think he was, being so forward with her personal space? She'd known guys like him before, ones who would take liberties with touching in the name of flirting, hoping that one thing would ultimately lead to another. It didn't matter that he was literally the man of her dreams. She hadn't given him permission to touch her.

"Thank you ever so much for aiding us," he said as she subtly pulled her hand from between his. "I don't know what's going on with the weather, but when animals act like this?" He looked up at the sky for a moment before his sorrowful gaze returned to her eyes. Maia waited for the moment to turn uncomfortable, for that time when social norms would dictate that one or the other look away. The moment failed to show up, though, and he continued. "When animals act like this, it usually precedes a natural disaster of some sort."

"Cascadia Fault," Mac muttered beside her.

Blake's eyes flickered to him for a moment, almost as if in warning, before he returned his attention to her. "Go home, Maia. Get your family to a safe place, and be careful. Promise?"

"S-sure," Maia stuttered, hardly able to deny that plea, or those eyes. Goodness, what was happening to her? Promise or no, she hadn't the slightest clue how she was going to accomplish that feat. Her parents were stubborn homebodies whenever their busy schedules allowed.

Blake smiled, seemingly relieved at her words, and after another shielded glance at Mac, he hopped into the back of the Suburban and closed the door.

Mac stood beside her in silence long after the diesel SUV had turned the corner and they had lost sight of it, its green paint easily blending with the surrounding foliage.

"Mac?" Maia couldn't find the words to ask what she wanted, knowing that everything she wanted to say sounded ridiculous. "Mac—"

"I think you should go home, Maia."

"But what about the park, the kids?"

Mac was still staring at the road, that same unreadable look on his face. She'd never seen his face so devoid of emotion before. It made her squirm. He looked . . . dangerous.

"I don't think anyone's coming today," he said. "I'll make a few calls. Close the park . . ." A wave of his hand finished his thought.

"Oh, okay. I'll see you tomorrow, then?"

Mac barely spared her a glance as he walked back into the office. "Just find a safe place for your family."

The glass door closed behind him, hiding him from view. The only words her jumbled brain could put together were some of Blake's last.

"'Thank you ever so much'?" Maia whispered. "'Aiding'? Who in the hell talks like that?"

4

AS THE PALE green, two-story cottage came into view, Maia half rode her bike, half ran up the driveway of the only home she'd ever known. Both of her parents' cars were parked in the drive. Dropping the bike on its side on the lawn, she rushed through the open garage packed nearly to the ceiling with all the things her parents couldn't bear to part with. Maia hurriedly picked her way through a makeshift path, stumbling over paint cans and shoving crinkly blue tarps out of the way with a few choice words. After earning a couple of new bruises on her shins and knees, she finally burst through the door and into the house, stripping her sneakers off as the aroma of Greg's favorite meal hit her—chicken marsala. Maia dropped her sneakers in the shoe bin, closing the door softly behind her, and struggled to calm her racing heart. Chicken marsala meant good news.

A giggle from the kitchen was all the encouragement Maia needed to place one foot in front of the other, until she found herself at the end of the dark hallway, standing in the fluorescent glare of the kitchen's long ceiling light. The sight of her mother wrapped in her father's thin arms, his nose nestled in her hair, made Maia's heart nearly burst with happiness. Two half-empty glasses stood on the counter next to an open bottle of wine, but it was whatever Greg was whispering into his wife's ear that caused Beth's cheeks to turn a darker shade of pink than even wine could conjure.

"Ugh! That is so gross, you two. Get a room!" Maia's sarcasm was marred by the huge grin changing the shape of her face. Beth and Greg turned their smiling, tear-streaked faces toward her.

For a moment, nobody said anything. Nobody had to. Maia rushed into their outspread arms, not even pausing to care about the stack of medical reports and bills sprawled on the already set table. They stood huddled like that for a long moment, clasped together in the best three-way hug Maia was sure had ever existed.

Beth was the first to pull away, snatching a spoon off the stove and stirring as she turned the gas burner down.

"Don't want dinner to burn!" she said, sniffling lightly and dabbing at her damp cheeks.

A few tiny sparks jumped from the outlets in the wall to Maia's right. She froze. The clocks on the stove and microwave blinked erratically, and then died. Gut clenching, she edged backward, using her hands to feel along the table until she found a chair. Maia collapsed with a soft thud, her eyes never leaving the clocks and outlets, nervously licking her lips before plastering a grin on her face. She didn't want to ruin this rare moment. Her gaze shifted to her parents, still giddy in whatever bubble of happiness the latest news from the doctor had provided.

"Beth, trust me," Greg said with a good-natured, reassuring grin. "Nothing can ruin this night!" He picked up his wineglass, swirling the crimson liquid around casually as he leaned against the chipped Formica counter.

"I thought you guys were saving that stuff for your thirtieth anniversary." Maia nodded at the wine bottle as she grabbed a glass from the table and moved to the sink, filling it with water. The water's coolness calmed her nerves as it slipped down her tense throat, and she was grateful for the much-needed sense of serenity the fresh liquid gave. *Good God, that water tasted amazing.* Like a desert wanderer, she rushed to fill the glass again before quickly draining it down a second time. She was on her third glass when she felt a gentle touch on her arm.

"Are you okay, sweetie?" Greg's green eyes were round with concern.

Maia sputtered and coughed as the water went down the wrong pipe. "Oh, yeah." Greg thumped her back. "I just . . . forgot to drink enough water today." Conspicuously clearing her throat, she grasped for a way to get the night back on track. "So, the wine?"

"Yeah." Greg shrugged lightly, twisting the bottle around and examining the subtly majestic label of the *Avignonesi Occhio di Pernice*. "This seemed like a good occasion to use it, too. Here."

He exchanged a half-worried look with Beth before grabbing another wineglass and pouring Maia a drink. Maia pretended not to notice the exchange. Greg pulled out a chair and handed her the glass, motioning for her to join him. Maia sat down across from him, noticing how the color had already begun to return to his pale face. As she scooped the papers covering the plates and silverware into a neat pile, she ventured, "Is everything okay? I mean, what, exactly, did the doctor say?"

"Oh, well . . . it's gone. For sure, we think, but you know . . . things happen." Her father readjusted the already perfectly set tableware with his long fingers. A thousand questions buzzed through Maia's thoughts. She knew what he meant. Her dad may have a clean bill of health now, but the cancer had returned before. This news wasn't exactly new, or permanent.

"Remember, guys, the more grateful we are, the more we'll have to be grateful for." Beth's soft voice shook slightly as she brought the completed meal to the table, and the smile she offered was a fragile one. Maia glanced at her mom's pinched face. Despite always looking younger than her age, the worry lines between her brows and around her mouth made her look tired, aged. Maia hoped that the sparkle in her blue eyes would return soon. She missed the woman who couldn't clean the house without turning the vacuum into an unwilling dance partner, warbling along while Lionel Ritchie or Rod Stewart crackled from the old stereo speakers. She missed the horrible puns that were groan worthy, but also quite clever. She missed the way she'd made the best smoothies from the fruit grown in her garden. And, more than anything, she missed the way she'd always smelled faintly of fresh dirt and morning dew. Her garden had become neglected over the past few years, except for that stupid rose. She worked too many hours now, cried too many nights, and never danced anymore. A lump formed in Maia's throat as she bit the inside of her cheek to stem the tears, her earlier encounter with the rose playing on a loop in her memory, like a bad one-night stand.

Greg's voice interrupted, pulling Maia back to the topic at hand. "Yeah, you know we always try to remain realistic, though. Everything's fine!" He waved a hand as though shooing away a fly, flashing a quick grin that oddly reminded Maia of Blake.

Maia flushed, becoming extremely interested in the process of scooping floppy pieces of marsala-drowned chicken and mushrooms onto her plate. She really wanted to forget what had happened at the park, but the way Blake had looked at her, and his archaic choice of words . . . they pulled on her somehow. It was almost as if he had jolted an old memory she hadn't realized she'd forgotten, but every time her brain tried to grasp it, the thought would slip away like a fine silk. It wasn't just a simple case of lust; she'd been infatuated before, and this was different. He was a distraction, and he was undoing the control she'd worked so hard to maintain. Maia didn't like it. Except . . . no, she couldn't let herself dwell on it.

"So, how was your day?" Greg's attempt at sounding chipper wasn't completely lost on her, but she welcomed the change in subject.

"Um, weird." Maia proceeded to tell them about the injured dog, Hayley's strange behavior, and the even more disturbing behavior of the wildlife in between bites of delicious dinner.

Once they had finished, and their dinner plates were scraped clean, they passed around Beth's homemade Italian cream cake for dessert. If her mother had found time to make the complicated recipe, then things really must be good. Maia happily sliced off a generous helping.

"So, what was wrong with Hayley?" Beth asked. "She's always been so sweet when she's here."

"I don't know, Mom. Quite honestly, I don't. I mean, we haven't been friends for all that long . . ." Maia paused, thinking back to when the tall Brazilian had begun working at the park. "Maybe a month or so?"

Beth shook her head. "I really like her. She's full of spunk. Reminds me of myself when I was your age."

Maia bit her tongue over the snarky comment that threatened to edge its way out. Beth had always wanted her to be more assertive, more lively—a natural-born leader, master-of-the-universe type. She didn't mean to be so boring, but she'd also never truly felt like she could match up to Beth's daring personality. All she had were sarcastic retorts, the kind that stoked the wrong kinds of fires, and tonight, she just wanted peace.

"What's this about the animals acting psycho?" Greg shoved a large piece of soggy cake into his mouth. He had joined her bandwagon for inhaling large pieces of sweet food, or maybe, she was on his.

Maia shrugged around her own mouthful. "Dunno. The guy who owned the husky said it usually happens before a natural disaster. He said I needed to get you guys to safety."

Skepticism pinched the edges of Greg's dark green eyes as he peered over the black wire frame of his glasses. He opened his mouth, but whether it was to speak or to shove another piece of cake into it, Maia wasn't sure. He simply froze.

"Dad?" Maia asked. "Are you okay? Dad?"

This time, unlike Mac, Greg was really and truly frozen. No amount of snapping, waving, or even poking would return him to life. Beth, too, was frozen, wineglass halfway to her lips.

"Oh shit, oh shit, oh shit . . ." Maia ran her fingers through her hair, ignoring the mess she surely created in the process. Was this it? Was this the moment she truly went insane?

"Get out . . . now. . . . You must . . . leave. . . . Get . . ."

"Hello?" Maia looked around, panicked. The tension of the morning returned to her shoulders, and her mouth turned dry once more. Shaking her head, she closed her eyes and concentrated on what she thought she was hearing. Maybe it was just her imagination.

Fear caused goose bumps to erupt across the bare skin of her arms. She listened to the light whirring of the living room fan, its beaded chains clacking faintly. Maia took a deep breath, trying to clear her mind and slow her heart rate. The one advantage of Beth's recent new-age kick was that all the meditation sessions she had roped the family into had taught Maia how to better control her own mind. She matched the pace of her breathing with the slight breeze playing through the kitchen curtains by the open window. She focused on the whir of the small fan by her parents' bed, on the sound of Greg's humidifier sucking, cleaning, and expelling pollutants from the air, but still, underneath it all, the voice continued. Every time the air moved, the warning caressed her ears. Her heart stumbled in its attempt to find peace, and her fragile control slipped.

"Who's there? Show yourself!"

When there was no answer, she raced from room to room, searching. It wasn't until she returned to the kitchen, where the warning was the loudest, that the severity of the situation hit her: she was alone, and this, whatever it was, was very real. She tugged on the window's sash to close it, but just as she did, Nikki, the family cat, shot through the window with raised hairs and a howling screech.

"Nikki? You crazy-ass, you nearly gave me a heart attack!" Maia pulled the sash the rest of the way down. The moment it connected with the sill, the whispering stopped and her parents returned to life. Nikki weaved her chubby, orange tabby body around Beth's legs, howling.

"Goodness, Nikki. What's gotten into you?" Beth picked up the agitated feline and began cooing, soothing her. Maia smothered a gulp before plunking back down into the seat she'd vacated.

"Maia, are you okay? What were you doing?"

"Uh." She searched for words. "Letting the cat in?"

Neither of her parents seemed to register the fact that they had both been frozen for more than five minutes. She watched them warily as she collected the dirty dishes, stacking one sticky plate atop another. The clatter of silverware on porcelain was somehow alarmingly loud, and Maia cringed.

"Oh, I'll take care of that." Beth handed the fussy cat to her husband before standing and bringing the stacked dishes to the sink. "Do you mind taking Ms. Tomlin her casserole dish? Tell her the good news, and that we said 'thank you.'"

Grateful for the mundane task, Maia nodded and gathered the dish from the drying rack next to the sink. Ms. Tomlin was one of many neighbors on the street who regularly brought them meals. She didn't know what to make of the voice she'd heard in the wind, but as Maia set out for the woman's house, she was determined to return home with a tactic to get her parents out. A gnawing ache in the pit of her stomach screamed that, as weird as this day had been, something truly bad was surely going to happen. And soon.

By the time Ms. Tomlin's house came into view, she'd abandoned three half-baked plans and was working on a fourth that showed promise. Her steps quickened in excitement, and she felt the first genuine smile of the day beginning to take over.

Without warning, the earth shook violently, knocking Maia off her feet and onto her backside. As she scrambled to get up, the trembling ground turned soft beneath her feet, the concrete shifting like sand. Across the street, a crack burst through a neighbor's lawn with disturbing swiftness, ripping through their driveway and swallowing their beige family van and two toy trikes. The trikes' bells tinkled joyfully as they fell, the concrete above grumbling and popping as the crack continued to spread. The utter destruction of childhood memories caused a shiver to run down Maia's spine, immobilizing her with horror. She watched as the hungry break traveled down the street, engulfing more suburban life before it was joined by other rips, intersecting and running parallel.

The sound was deafening as the earth buckled and heaved, screaming under the birth pains of a tectonic shift. Houses were torn asunder all around her, and as her feet began to sink into the ground, her terrified mind locked onto one image only—her parents.

Casserole dish forgotten, Maia attempted to run, looking for any flat surface she could press her feet against. Survival instincts took over as she scrabbled, tripped, and stumbled her way mindlessly home. She was still half a block away when a large tree split from its roots and fell across her path. Leaves exploded from its branches as it hit the ground, swirling through the gusting wind. On the other side of the churning haze of green and brown, Maia caught the haunting glimpse of her house folding in on itself.

Chunks of brick and splinters of green shutter launched through the air as the cottage was swallowed by a large sink-hole, just another victim of the ripped earth. Maia stumbled over the debris in her path, her hands scraping as they met the detritus below, but she couldn't tell what she was touching, and she pressed her eyes together tightly as she gasped through her sobs. The image of her house collapsing and the sound of the screams coming from inside burned into her frontal lobe. Pushing herself to her feet and wiping at her running nose, she half crawled, half lunged forward, scrabbling across any-thing her fingers touched as her neighborhood continued to break around her. She had to get inside. They needed her. She had to—

The air left her lungs with a loud *swoosh* as something crashed into her back, and her world blinked into darkness.

5

A SHRILL RINGING in Maia's ears pulled her from the cave of her subconscious, where she had been happily drifting in the dark. There was nothing to return to—even in oblivion, she was aware of that much—and she didn't have any intention of leaving the coziness of her solitude. It was peaceful there, albeit too quiet. The ringing in her ears gradually grew louder, though, and feeling slowly washed over her body. She became aware of her chest rising and falling with breath, and her pulse had decided to gather force and perform a march through the fingers of her right hand. Before long, the pulsing became a throbbing, accompanied by a dull ache. Why did her hand hurt so much?

Maia tried to wiggle the offending fingers, but they were bound together. Frightened, she struggled with heavy lids and blurry vision, and after blinking a few cleansing tears away, she noticed that her hand was wrapped in gauze and bandages. Still lying under suffocating lethargy, Maia coaxed her muscles to respond. She lifted her arms, only to realize that both of them were covered in scratches and cuts, their edges poking out from beneath even more bandages. Her gaze traveled over the wounds to the rest of herself, at least the part that wasn't covered by a thick down blanket. Her shirt was ripped, caked with dry mud and who knew what else. The ringing in her ears faded as she pressed her fingers to each lobe, but the noise had been replaced with the muffled sound of someone yelling at her, as if from the other side of a thick glass wall. Or so it seemed. The voice became clearer the more she listened, and finally, she heard her name.

"Maia?" Someone gently tugged at her lifted hand. "Are you ar'right?"

She recognized the voice and pressed her eyes shut, suppressing a groan. Not him. Not now. Tucking her elbows beneath her, Maia struggled to sit up, only to be forced back down by dizziness.

"What—" she croaked. Her mouth was dry. It itched, and when her attempts at clearing her throat produced nothing but a coughing fit, she quickly surrendered to her body's warning, wrapped in pain. A cup of water was thrust into her shaking fingers. They stilled at the touch of something cool, and the slap of the water against the glass woke the blood running in her veins—a reminder of one life-giving liquid to another. Taking several greedy gulps, Maia sputtered before taking a deep breath and trying to speak again.

The words halted on the tip of her tongue as her gaze fell upon the distracting allure of the face above her. She quickly dipped her head, focusing instead on the paisley pattern of the blanket covering her legs. She rubbed the fingers of her free hand across the plush fabric, taking comfort in its softness. The texture reminded her of the velvety ears of the puppy she'd once begged her parents for, back before her father had fallen sick. She dug her teeth into her tongue, producing a quick burst of sharp pain, reminding herself that she needed to focus.

"What are you doing here, Blake?" she finally choked out. "What happened?"

He chuckled. Maia squinted up at him, trying to understand the wry look on his face.

"You said my name," he said. Affectionate wonder colored his tone.

"Uh, yeah?" Wondering if he, too, had hit his head, Maia pulled away to take in her surroundings. She was lying on a full-sized bed, in what looked like a cabin with only one room. Framed vintage woodland scenes hung on the light brown, timber walls; a wood stove in the corner kept the tiny room warm; and a small, tattered couch with a faded checker pattern of blue and red was shoved against the wall. In front of that was a rough, handmade coffee table that would have sold for an obscene amount of money in one of the hipster design stores in downtown Portland. Maia closed her eyes again. Portland. Home. Her home. Destroyed. The thought brought a surge of painful remembering, making the cabin's nooks and crannies nothing but a blur. On a normal day, Maia might have spent hours hounding Blake about where everything had come from, but this wasn't a normal day.

Squeezing the gritty lids of her eyes more tightly, she curled forward around her pain, as if she could hold it safe inside the confines of her torso. Forward, and into the arms of the one person she desperately wanted to avoid in this moment. Her forehead met Blake's strangely comfortable shoulder as his arms wound around her in a protective embrace. It felt nice. The usual skin-crawling irritation of being touched was absent. *Guys have held you like this before, you know*, her conscience whispered. *And you hated it.*

Not like this, she whispered back. As much as she wanted to lose herself in the surprising comfort of his arms, she knew it wouldn't erase the pain slicing at her heart, begging her to ask the question. Mustering her courage, she softly asked, "Where are my parents?"

Blake sucked in a deep breath, as though bracing for impact, and it was all she needed to hear. She already knew the answer. Had known it even before she woke up. Her parents were gone. She shuddered as the cold wave of loss washed through her veins, leaving only bereft numbness in its wake. Blake shifted nervously against her, his arms tightening briefly, before he finally said, "Nearly everything west of the Cascades, and part of northern California, was wiped out." He paused for a few beats, waiting for her to respond, but only silence answered. With obvious trepidation, he continued, "Scientists have been worried about the subduction of the plates in the Cascadia Fault for years."

"That's what Mac meant," she said. She wasn't even sure how the words left her mouth. Her head, still resting against Blake, swayed in place under the gentle force of his nod.

"Yeah-nah, that's what he meant." His voice was gentle. "I tried to warn you. Several times." He cleared his throat nervously, and Maia felt him tense as she lifted her head, meeting his worried eyes. The concern that tightened their corners was still there, and she remembered from her dreams how his face looked when it was relaxed and smiling. She shouldn't care about that right now, but . . .

His eyes searched her face before finally resting on her lips. He chewed on his own for a moment before launching himself off the bed. "Would you like some tea?"

Without waiting for her response, he began bustling about the tiny kitchenette.

"Do I have a choice?" Maia watched his smooth and sure movements. He knew where everything was, grabbing and handling things on instinct, at times without even looking. Did the cabin belong to him, then?

"Well, I was going to make some for myself, regardless." He shrugged. Maia smiled tightly. She couldn't understand why. She knew she should be crying; she should be devastated. Her family was dead. The home she was born in, had grown up in, was gone. She was in a remote cabin located God-knew-where, with a man who shouldn't even exist, but did. None of it made sense. None of it felt real. A frown creased her features as she placed two fingers on her chest, pressing and hoping to feel her heart, or at least its beat. It was still there, wasn't it?

She shook her head. "I know I should be a sobbing mess right now, but . . . I feel so numb. I don't—"

"You're in shock. It'll come."

Maia sighed, nodding her thanks as he handed her a chipped blue mug. She breathed in as the steam rose around her, caressing her face. Lavender, chamomile, rose, a hint of vanilla. Her insides melted at the aroma.

"I'm not looking forward to dealing with it, then," she said. "The falling apart part, I mean. I feel . . ." She flicked a glance at him, assessing his worthiness of witnessing her vulnerability. "I don't know. I just feel so . . . so old."

"You barely look a day over seventeen." Blake's quietly teasing gaze never left her as he pulled up a leather wingback chair that looked more like it belonged in a library than the tiny cabin.

She shrugged, taking a sip of the tea and burning herself. "You said you tried to warn me. Several times. What do you mean?"

Outside, the sun glowed orange over the tops of pine trees. Blake's eyes flicked nervously to the fading light, then settled on her injured hand. "It's nearly six. You hungry for dinner?"

Maia pressed her lips together, trying to withhold her agitation. Another dodged question. "How do you know it's nearly six? There's—" She made a quick assessment of the cabin, confirming her next words. "There's no clock in here. In fact, there's nothing electronic in here at all, and you're not wearing a watch." Her heart faltered in its rhythm. Ah, there it was. The thing that had been dancing around the edges of her intuition. This wasn't an ordinary, remote cabin, and she was suddenly certain Blake had had something to do with her very strange morning. Or was it yesterday morning? He knew something. Hell, he probably knew everything.

As if he could read her thoughts, he twisted his lips to the side, contemplating what he was going to say before raising a hand in surrender. "Ar'right, I'll tell you what I can." He took a large gulp of his tea and, with a tense jaw, chewed on his next words before finally spitting them out.

"You know how time stood still in your kitchen last night, and the wind delivered a message?"

Maia narrowed her eyes. *How'd he know that?*

Blake soldiered on. "Righto, and yesterday, remember how the animals were trying to find shelter with you? How 'bout plants? Do they now flourish under your touch? Well, electricity doesn't quite work right when you're near, either."

By the time his last words left his lips, Maia's breath was so short she was in full-blown panic mode. Gasping, she clutched at the blankets. Her mug tumbled from her grasp, only to be caught by Blake's deft movement. He placed both mugs on the coffee table before coming to her side. He rubbed the space between Maia's shoulder blades, then down her arms, coaxing her to breathe.

"Don't touch me! Please—" She shook her head, shrinking from his touch like an abused animal, struggling with the conflicting desire to simultaneously want him nowhere near her, yet needing to keep him close, to engulf herself in the comfort he offered. "I can't . . ."

He pulled away, but Maia suddenly felt cold, as though he had taken all of the room's warmth with him. This wouldn't do. Neuroses be damned. She was drowning, and she couldn't face the rising tide of emotion alone. She grabbed the collar of his gray polo and pulled him back onto the bed next to her. He hesitated, but she buried her face in his chest, clinging to him like he was the last piece of driftwood in a raging sea. Slowly, gently, he put his arms around her, and she let the storm of emotion take her.

A torrent of tears shook her as her reawakened heart began to shatter in earnest. *They're gone, all of them. Everything.* She really was an island of one, now.

By the time her sobs finally subsided into hiccups, the cabin was completely dark. A pile of wadded tissues littered the bed next to her, and she felt empty. She had never cried so much, or so hard, in her life. She wasn't even sure how her body still had the energy to breathe, to keep living.

Blake tucked a wayward curl behind her ear. "Can I get you anything? More tea, perhaps? I think yours has gone cold, but I can make more."

Maia didn't have the energy to answer, or even to shake her head. With her cheek resting on his tear-drenched shirt, her nose pressed into his clavicle, she gave in to his kindness and breathed him in. He smelled like the first day of spring. Like fresh, new light. Her eyes fluttered closed and she drifted, succumbing to the darkness once more.

MAIA WOKE TO the sound of loud purring and the wet kisses of a kitty nose sniffing her cheek. Too exhausted to do more than open her eyes, she was startled to find Nikki licking the bridge of her nose with a sandpaper tongue. She smiled at the cat's tenderness and, warmed by the familiarity of her family's pet, moved her fingers to scratch at the soft belly within reach. Closing her eyes once more, she held on to the image her mind conjured. She was in her bed, in her room at home. This was just another morning. The sun would soon be cresting the jagged peak of Mt. Hood, setting the snow-drenched cap ablaze just outside her window. Nikki was waking Maia up with the bath she clearly needed before snuggling against her chest and melting into a warm mass of fur and soft snores.

Only Maia wasn't at home, and the cabin was cloaked in twilight rather than the soft grays of dawn. The glow of candles cast shadowy caricatures across the wall she faced, and she was about to turn over and thank Blake for his kindness when the door to the cabin opened. She froze in place as a cold gust of air ushered in a new voice.

"Hey, man."

Behind her, the couch creaked. "Leo."

Leo? Maia's brows furrowed over this newest puzzle. *Leo, as in Blake's dog, Leo?* It wasn't a very common name. Nikki seemed unperturbed by the latest development and began to groom Maia's eyebrows now that they'd formed a line across her brow. Maia swatted at her softly, trying not to give away the fact that she was awake.

"So, did you tell her?"

"Well . . ." Blake drew out his answer. "That mountain of tissues is the result of me barely scratching the surface."

"Fail." The newcomer snickered. "I brought grub, by the way." There was the sound of something landing on the coffee table, and then the soft rustling of plastic and paper.

"Excellent, mate. Smells delicious. . . . What?"

The leather chair next to the bed squeaked under the weight of its new occupant. "How far'd you get on dropping the whole Mother-Earth-is-a-celestial-being-tryin'-to-kill-ya bombshell?"

Maia pressed her eyes closed and drew in a steadying breath, hoping to halt the adrenaline rushing toward her heart. She had to stay calm. A meltdown had already cost her answers once today. He, whoever he was, was talking about her; it was nonsense, of course, but he was still talking about her.

Blake cleared his throat. She wasn't sure if he was trying to hide a scoff, or if was meant to dislodge discomfort at the topic choice. "Sure, yeah, and then I'll just tell her, 'No big deal. You're just a casualty of war. A replacement, if she doesn't get to you first.' That's going to go over real well."

Fabric rustled across a shrugged shoulder, and a boot scraped against the edge of the coffee table.

"You could always start with the bit about how she's not really human. They always love that one." The newcomer chuckled roughly. "I bet you don't even know which memories have surfaced yet. Do ya?"

"None of me." Bitterness coated Blake's voice.

"She's gonna have kittens when she finds out the truth. What we are. Who she could be. You should have told her when we saw her at the park."

Maia bit her lip, trying to keep still. Her flight instincts had sent her body into survival mode, and she wanted nothing more than to jump up and demand answers. Her muscles tensed with the effort of exerting patience. This was more than she'd gotten out of Blake on her own, yes, but she didn't like getting the truth this way. And of course, none of it made any sense at all. Her brain shifted into full protection mode, denying everything with rationalization. Starting with the fact that there was no way Leo the dog could be Leo the human. That was insane.

Unfortunately, no matter how much logic she hid behind, her subconscious refused to remain silent. It reminded her, ever so gently, of everything she had seen, and intuition settled like a heavy stone in the pit of her stomach. There was simply too much that had happened, too many unexplainable occurrences, for her to ignore the possibility that denial could mean her death. Every new insight tugged at a veil of doubt and lies within her that she never knew existed, and a hunger to know more was awakening.

Blake grunted. "I didn't tell Maia anything at the park because Heidi was there."

"Naw, man, no way. I would've known if she was there. I can—"

"Yes, I know. You can literally sniff her out. Look, I don't have any proof. It was just a feeling, ar'right? I can't explain it." Blake cleared his throat again, and Maia heard his fingers scratch at his short beard. "It was just a feeling. Not as strong as usual. It felt off, somehow, but . . . yeah-nah, she was there."

"Well, I don't envy you, man. Fortunately, Maia's been listening to this entire conversation. So at least a tick of your work's done, now."

With that, Maia felt two pairs of eyes bore into her back. She rolled over and glanced at Blake's sheepish face.

"Busted," proclaimed the newcomer.

"I'll say." She eased herself up onto her elbows, and Nikki hopped over into the lap of the long-legged, copper-skinned young man in the chair. His dark eyes twinkled with mischief, offsetting the exotic, sharp angles of his broad cheekbones and the straight black hair that spilled down his shoulders and halfway down his arms in an inky curtain. He beamed at Maia while scratching the cat's upturned chin, and Maia saw teeth that were blindingly white, with canines too long to be human.

Maia gulped. His comment about her being non-human still rang in her ears, and she was now pretty sure he hadn't been lying. He clearly wasn't. *Great. Just great.* She couldn't believe she was even entertaining these thoughts. *Not human,* she inwardly mocked. *Just because he has weird teeth?* Eyebrow raised at Blake's silence, she glared. "Well? I think you owe me an explanation."

He sighed and ran his fingers through his long hair, then rubbed his hands together, clasping and unclasping them, before muttering, "I don't really know where to begin—"

"What did he mean about me not being *fully* human?" Maia demanded. It was only one of many questions now swirling through her head, but it was as good a place to start as any.

"See? Told ya." Leo sniggered.

Maia ignored him, plowing on to the next question like a troll in the girl's bathroom.

"Who's Heidi? How'd you know about, about—" She shoved her mounting hysterics down with a large swallow. "You better start talking. Now."

"Fine—"

A howl rang out in the distance and Maia jumped, gathering the blankets tighter around her shoulders.

Leo unfolded his long frame from his seat, letting out a short laugh at the cat's pathetic attempts to hang on before placing Nikki gingerly on the floor. "That'd be for me. Don't take it too easy on him, Maia. He can handle it." He winked and barked another chuckle. As he left, Nikki was hot on his heels, her striped tabby tail flicking in a saucy prance. Leo waited until the cat had sauntered through the door behind him before closing it with another wink. One moment, Leo's head could be seen out the door's long oval window, his silhouette illuminated by torches lining the path; the next, he'd disappeared. Another howl answered the chorus ringing through the forest before disturbed gravel crunched and scattered beneath padded feet and claws.

Choosing to ignore the implications of Leo's exit, Maia narrowed her eyes and turned back to Blake. "Talk."

He squirmed under her gaze. "*I hate this part.*" His words whispered through her mind, but his lips had yet to move. Maia blinked, but before she could add another question to the list, he said, "I'll try to make this as brief as possible. I have a feeling we don't have much time." His worried eyes flickered to the path Leo had disappeared down.

"We—Leo, you, me—are *praeses*, guardians of creation. We're made of a celestial energy that creates, renews, and transforms; the same celestial energy that created Earth, and every solar system, every galaxy and stretch of the universe. We were formed for the task of protecting and maintaining every planet affected by suns and moons, every planet that hosts plant and animal life. In the case of Earth, we ensure that she continues to revolve around the sun, that her moon trains the waves and guides the harvests, that her entire ecosystem survives."

"So, what, you're aliens?" Maia wasn't sure how she found her voice, but she knew that participating and keeping an open mind was the only way to make sense of this. It sounded crazy, and yet a small flame deep within her gut flickered in excitement. As absurd as Blake's words were, they *felt* right. Deep in her bones, she knew there was truth in his explanation. Even the usual cynicism that laced her inner thoughts thanks to the many fire-and-brimstone sermons of her evangelical grandparents had faded into a whisper.

"It's not like that. We're made from the same material used in human souls, but our purpose is to guard and protect."

"Like angels?"

He shook his head, smothering another secretive smile. Those damn smirks were starting to grate on Maia's nerves. "Yeah-nah. No angels or demons, although you will find much of our world buried in the mythology and religion of humans. We're made of a celestial energy that creates, but in order for it to exist, it has to have its opposing—or astral—energy, which means there are some *praeses* who contain only the energy to destroy. It is up to us, the guardians of creation, to maintain the balance between the two. Most demon and devil mythology stems from the actions of astral *praeses*."

"The Yin and Yang concept I can understand. But *praeses*?"

Blake nodded, relaxing at her seeming acceptance of his explanation. "It's Latin, which is the closest earthly language to what the universe uses. You could just as easily call us guardians, or spirits, or souls, I suppose, but . . ." He gave her a look filled with longing, then, as if he waited for her to puzzle out a complex math problem he knew she could solve on her own.

Maia frowned. "But you and I—why do we look human?"

"Before we are chosen as guardians of a system, we must live within it, to better understand it. Therefore, we must take human form. As you can see, once chosen, we"—he gestured vaguely to his figure—"we retain the vessel, frozen and unchanging."

Maia scoffed, but was secretly applauding everything he had told her. If only Nanna and Pops had been around to hear this. "I think my parents would beg to differ on the not-being-human bit, but you're saying you're immortal. Like a vampire?"

Blake avoided her eyes, looking at his shoes as he rolled awkward tension from his shoulders. "We can die. It's just—"

The cabin walls shook as the door burst open. Even though Blake had said they weren't angels, Maia couldn't help but feel Leo looked like an avenging one, his athletic frame limned in the torchlight from outside as he stood in the doorway.

"Time's up, lovebirds," Leo said. "Reed and Poppy need us."

Cutting off Maia's sputtering protest, Blake uttered a few curse words as he rubbed his hand over his chin and mouth in agitation. "Where? What's happened now?"

"New Zealand." Leo shifted his weight between his feet, his muscles clearly twitching with the need to move. To fight. "Looks like Heidi's struck a national park. Dude, whatever disease she's inflicted, it's spreading fast."

Blake nodded quickly as he stood. He moved about the cabin, grabbing books and clothing scattered all around the tiny space, shoving them into a small backpack. "You go on ahead. We'll catch up."

The air around Leo's form sparked with electricity, and Maia gasped. Where once a man in his mid-twenties had stood, a gray and white speckle-chested falcon now preened its feathers. Its keen, dark eyes blinked at her, and she could have sworn it was attempting a laugh at her expense before it set off into the night.

"What was *that*?"

"We didn't make it to that part, sorry, but Leo's a Corocottas."

"A what?"

"He has dominion over all the animals of Earth. He ensures that they each maintain the circle of life for their species."

"Of course. How silly of me."

With a tolerant smile at her wry tone, Blake zipped up the bag and thrust it at her. "Look, I'm sorry I don't have enough time to explain, but here." He shoved a small notebook into the front pocket of the backpack. "I wrote down as much as I could while you slept. I—" He shrugged, slightly embarrassed. "I'm sorry we couldn't . . ." His jaw clenched and his throat worked as he swallowed the rest of his sentence. His eyes pleaded with her to understand before he ducked his head to focus on straightening the straps of the backpack, yet again.

The muscles around Maia's heart tightened. She wasn't done getting her answers. Anxiety grew to impatience, and her fingers twitched around the strap of the backpack as he handed it over. She kicked the covers aside and slung the bag's strap over one shoulder as she stood. "Okay. But what's going on here? I don't understand."

Careful not to hurt her injured hand, Blake gathered her into his arms, tucking her snugly against his chest. Ear pressed to his sternum, the rhythm of his heart tapped a staccato of calm through her veins, and Maia sighed in relief. Pushing aside the concerns her conscience presented, she let her body melt into the undeniable comfort of his embrace.

When he spoke, his soothing tenor reverberated through her. "Since the sun's gone down, I can only take you so far. Just hold on tight, and keep your eyes closed, okay?"

Maia frowned, her retort muffled as her face was once again buried in his chest. His embrace tightened. The intoxicating scents of summer and light quickly enveloped her, washing her in warm waves. She felt Blake's lips brush against her ear, sending conflicting shivers down her spine as he whispered, "I'm a Sideralis, keeper of the sun. It's all in my notes, and everything you need is in that bag. You'll be safe from her, I promise."

Struggling against his strong arms, Maia finally managed to look up, hoping to lose herself in the deep waters of those always-concerned eyes. Instead, she found herself staring into the night sky. Bright, fluorescent lights obscured the blanket of stars normally splashed against the dark abyss, and Maia stumbled, unsupported, as her head swam. A sign for the Missoula International Airport swung into view, and as she struggled for comprehension, a new voice broke through her muddled thoughts.

"Miss, are you all right?"

A strong hand gripped her elbow, steadying her, as a middle-aged man in a sky captain's uniform looked her over. His kind brown eyes crinkled at the edges, just like her father's used to, and as she batted at the tears streaming down her cheeks, she wondered how crazy she looked.

Was she even wearing shoes? She peered down at her favorite sneakers. *How?* So many questions tangled and fought for dominance in her head. She still wasn't sure she believed any of what Blake had told her, not truly. But she couldn't deny that a part of her didn't exactly care, either. Maybe she was crazy. Maybe she had lost it and this was all just one big delusion. The only way to know was to follow it through to the end. Shaking her head, she noticed her passport and a one-way ticket to New Zealand crushed in her right hand.

"I'm fine. Honest." She held up the documents and took a few steps back to show she was steady once more. Sucking in a deep breath, she paused, holding it in as the realization of what she was about to do overcame her senses, prickling her skin with warning. If she got on that plane, she was diving into the deep end of whatever had obliterated her life. There was no going back. And if that was the only way she could get the answers she wanted, answers to whatever it was that was happening to her, then into the deep end she would go.

I can only control me. I am an island of one.

She let out the breath. "Where do I check in?"

7

BY THE TIME the plane landed, Maia's legs felt like brittle pretzel sticks encased in Jell-O, and she found herself flopping back into her chair after trying to stand. She had never taken such a long trip in her life, and though no one had approached her, she couldn't help but notice the intense looks some of her fellow passengers gave her during the flight. She wondered if they were part of Blake's "protection." Or maybe she was just paranoid now, as well as delusional. Yeah, that made more sense, and sense was what she needed a steady dose of.

Passengers stood and began to disembark as Maia stretched her head from side to side, pulling at the tense muscles in her neck. She rolled her shoulders back a few times and swallowed against the type of queasiness only gotten from skipping several time zones, little sleep, and breathing recirculated air. She was dreadfully exhausted, but at least it numbed her against the devastating emotions lurking in the deepest recesses of her heart. They were likely waiting for the most inopportune moment to attack, though, like the next time she pulled instead of pushed against a door, or accidentally walked into the men's restroom.

Maia shook her head at the absurdities that popped into her mind as she watched her fellow passengers stumble off the plane. Normally, she'd be one of the eager ones, rushing off as soon as possible, but as she dug her nails into her armrest, she felt the sudden grip of fear. It was the anxious kind. The kind that came up with the best excuses to skip out on life for a day. The kind that said that the covers and soft pillows on one's bed held all the answers to questions that hadn't been asked. Maia wasn't one to give in to petty justifications so easily, but getting off the plane meant shooting a flare and announcing her entrance into a fight she wasn't prepared for, and wasn't yet sure she believed in. She was entering the game at half-time and didn't know anything about her opponent, and even less about her own team.

Blake's notes had provided plenty of surreal entertainment during the flight, but not a lot of helpful information. At least the Greek mythology and Sunday school lessons that had fascinated her as a child suddenly made sense. Maia had never bought into the austere One True God her grandparents had all but beaten into her little heart. Even before her father's diagnosis had forced her to come to terms with her own mortality, she'd questioned. It wasn't the concept of an all-powerful God letting bad things happen to good people that bothered her—news headlines had convinced her that "good" people were the biggest myth of all—she just didn't think the creator of the universe was as concerned with its inhabitants as they all hoped. "Pride goeth . . ." was right.

While she waited for the passengers around her to filter their way toward the door, she pulled the backpack Blake had given her out from under the forward seat, settling it on her lap so she could use her uninjured hand to put away the notebook currently stashed in the seat's pocket. The notebook had covered the various types of *praeses*, which galaxies they were assigned to, and their multitude of roles. There was no indication of where the celestial energy that had created them came from, but it was apparently the key to giving the *praeses* their elemental power and authority. It was also clear by Blake's careful, yet vague choice of words that the topic of its origination was verboten. He only ever referred to it as the "Source," depicted by a simple sigil of a triangle with four lines slicing through its middle. This Source, whatever it was, had created not just the *praeses*, but all life, and humans, according to Blake, were nothing more than the lab rats of the cosmos, created for study. And if these *praeses* were masquerading as humans in order to test evolutionary theories, as Blake proposed, it was safe to assume they didn't always play by the same rules humanity did and had occasionally showcased extraordinary abilities, giving rise to the concepts that made fantasy creatures in fiction so rich and fascinating. Maia rolled her eyes as she pulled the notebook free from the seat pocket. It all suited a *Doctor Who* episode better than it did reality.

"What have I gotten myself into?" she muttered under her breath as she flipped through the book of hastily scrawled notes.

Blake had talked about each of the various *praeses* at length, from the harvesters of celestial energy, or "soul matter," known as the *Eros*, to the *Talis* warriors who were akin to guardian angels for the *praeses*, to the *Emortuus*, the astral equivalent, the Yin to the *praeses'* Yang. He'd included symbols, phrases of a strange language, and charts in the margins that resembled family trees, until Maia had begun to wonder just how long he'd been preparing this for her.

The last entry was Blake's theory about the current Terra guardian, whom they knew as Heidi but who the humans referred to as Mother Earth. He hypothesized that she was killing her replacements through staged natural disasters, though he admitted that her motivation was entirely unclear.

He also thought Maia was one her replacements.

After shuddering through the implications of that possibility, Maia had spent the next hour trying to understand the concept of "re-invoking," which she had decided sounded a lot like reincarnation, but with more control. Much like its sister concept, re-invoking had its downfall. Each new body meant a total memory wipe. Maia had paused at that. If she truly was one of these . . . well, praeses . . . things, it would explain why she mentally knew nothing of their world, while her instincts insisted that she did.

Ultimately, though, her only accomplishment had been adding to the questions swirling in her head.

With Blake's notes ping-ponging through her thoughts, she shoved the maddening journal into the backpack's front pocket, only to find another book blocking its path—a book she hadn't noticed before. She'd rifled through the bag's main compartment when she first boarded, but had somehow skipped a thorough perusal of the front. As the last of the plane's passengers trailed down the row toward the exit, she hurriedly pulled the new book free, stuffed the notebook inside, and zipped the backpack closed. Peeling herself out of her seat in a jet-lagged stupor, she stood and made her way down the aisle.

Once free of the plane, she glanced down at the book in her hand. It was a guidebook on New Zealand, and had papers tucked into its sleeve, fanning out from its cover. Tugging a slip out, Maia discovered directions and reservations to a hotel in Te Anau where she'd apparently have a room waiting. Perfect.

She stumbled through the airport, with its bright and crisp modern design, a marriage of wood ceiling beams held by steel braces, and managed to hop into the first cab she could hail. Distracted by the wanderlust that only a foreign city could ignite, she made a half-hearted promise to herself that, once settled at the hotel, she would attempt to finish the book she had found at the very bottom of the bag. Its cracked leather and linen pages were wrapped in a velvet cloth, and Maia wasn't sure at first if she should even risk touching it without gloves. The author was unknown, but every page was saturated with breathtaking poems, each one clinging to Maia's soul with a depth she had never known, but had always craved. The writer had clearly been captivated by a woman, and with each sonnet, his regard and admiration had turned into an unheard of love. Maia had never seen anything like it; no romantic movie, no love song, no poem could compare.

As the bright fall colors of New Zealand's countryside flashed by her window, she daydreamed, a new ache blooming in an unexplored corner of her heart. Was it really possible to love someone that deeply?

After Maia checked in to the small hotel and had gorged herself on her last two packets of airline peanuts, she took what was meant to be a quick shower. But as she stood under the warm water, slowly letting it turn cold, she let her exhausted mind wander. She stared at the clear rivulets skimming over her fair skin, running across her freckled shoulders and down her arms, dripping off the tips of her fingers like a tiny rain shower. Images of billowing black clouds swirled through her mind, and a strange sort of energy seemed to pulse through her veins in answer.

In a searing hot flash, all five senses sharpened, and she felt as if she could see the constant evolution of every molecule around her. Her heart dropped to her stomach as nervous fear surged up to drown her. Energy clung to her skin, feeding off her before instantaneously returning to her at a cellular level. She was acutely aware of every cell in her body, every nerve and synapse. She could hear the rush of blood, the pump and churn of organs, felt the steady growth of her skin, her hair, her nails, relished the flow of air through her nostrils, the way it slipped down her trachea and into her lungs. She shuddered in wonder as a swirling wave of energy coalesced and churned in her lungs with a faint ache, the gentle pain echoing the squeeze of her diaphragm as it pushed the now toxic air, bitter as it flowed over her tongue, back out again.

Confusion settled over her in a fog, pierced only by the clarity of these new sensations. It was as if she had been removed from her body and slapped awake on a spiritual level. She was one with the air that pressed against her, with the water that streamed down her back, with the ground that reached up toward her feet, disregarding the hotel's layers of concrete and steel. Maia pressed her hands between her breasts, one on top of the other, and felt her heart thrumming with more than just her own life. Instead of one pulse, there were two. Dizzying excitement awoke in her veins, buzzing through her nerves, swirling through her stomach, settling with an insistent and sensuous heat between her thighs. Mother Earth, indeed. Maia closed her eyes and lifted her face to the spray of water above her. Many women looked forward to the creation of life in the womb, but Maia had never given it much thought. How could anyone think of future life when so much death surrounded them?

The energy pulsed in answer again, and though the hot water had somehow returned to her shower, she shivered. Her mind filled with more than storms and rain as the process of creation unfolded behind her closed lids. Light sliced through unfathomable darkness. Water boiled forward, obscuring, shaping, and forming masses of land. Stars expanded and shrank like scattered diamonds across a black sky, illuminating a velvety blue palette. Maia's legs softened. She swayed under the dizzying burden of the images as they pressed and clamored their way into her mind. Plants and animals, both known and unknown, overwhelmed her senses. She smelled them, heard their cries, even tasted their flesh. It was too much. Her stomach heaved and her legs buckled.

Maia's knees met the floor of the ceramic tub, jolting her awake. Her teeth chattered as she knelt under the once more cold water, and a distant thought occurred to her as she turned the knob, cutting off the steady stream of water: was it she who had turned the water hot before?

With shaking fingers, she reached for a towel and hastily wrapped it around her body as she stumbled through the steam-filled room. The humidity of the tiny bathroom was suffocating, and she wrenched open the door, took the five necessary steps to her bed, and collapsed.

Exhausted, she lay with her face buried deep in the fluffy pillows. The mattress was surprisingly soft, and steam from the bathroom mingled with the dusty scent of the room's heater. Even with wet hair and a soggy bath towel wrapped around her body, Maia was comfortable. Comfortable, but not relaxed.

She knew better than to chalk what had happened up to another hallucination. She felt jumpy, and her skin crawled as adrenaline pumped through her veins, urging her to run, to fight, to create and destroy. Her chest tightened with the familiar signals of an impending anxiety attack, and she looked for different points of interest in the room, counting ten slow breaths as she focused on each. Her anxiety had begun when she was a child, a physical manifestation of the emotional trauma of spending summers with her grandparents. They hadn't approved of how her parents handled the education of her soul and had insisted she spend summers at their house instead. Unfortunately, her parents had felt incumbent upon them, since they had bailed Maia's parents out of early marital debt a few times, and relented. Maia's yearly "*do not conform to the world*" lessons were met with obligation; theirs, but not hers. Her anxiety had grown and worsened with each passing summer, until she was introduced to meditation, thanks to her mother's desperate attempts to find something that could heal her father. The idea that thoughts had energy, even healing energy, had given her strength to fight the anxiety head-on. It was still her biggest demon, but she was making progress.

As she finished her breathing exercise, willing her muscles to soften and relax, she wished for a hot cup of lavender tea. That, she thought, would be divine.

Eventually, the ache near her heart subsided, and she rested her head to the side, rubbing her cheek against the soft cotton of the pillowcase. Looking for a distraction, she stared at the seventies wallpaper in the hotel room and attempted to unpack the events of the last forty-eight hours. Her heart had already had its say, so she skipped over the destruction of her home and parents. She had other family scattered around the nation, but she felt there wasn't any point in reaching out to them; they'd never really been close. In some families, a health crisis brought people closer together, but in others, it shoved them further apart. Sure, it was possible they were worried about her, but it was more likely they had assumed that she and her parents were dead and had already returned to their own lives.

As bitterness tarnished her mood and tightened her muscles once more, she took another set of deep breaths. She had to calm down. Blake's journal had raised more questions than it had answered, and that was only if it was all true. But— what if it *was* true? How could she deny what she had seen so far? She couldn't have cracked or even imagined such a level of delusion on her own. Could she?

Maia shook her head. No, she didn't believe she'd gone crazy. So, what then? Where did that leave her? She had no home and, as far as she was concerned, no family. A higher being was out there trying to kill her, a group of non-human guardians were masquerading as people, and a man she never thought she'd meet in real life believed she was the next Mother Earth. Maia had never been one to run from a fight, but she had a feeling that, if this was indeed real, this was going to be the biggest fight of her life, and as sleep finally overcame her, she realized only question really remained:

Would it be worth it?

8

NINE DREAMLESS HOURS later, Maia woke with bleary, sleep-crusted eyes, feeling like she'd been run over repeatedly by a bulldozer. She couldn't account for how sore her muscles were; they hadn't hurt this much yesterday. Procrastinating, she lay on her back, limbs stretched akimbo and covering as much of the full-sized bed as her tiny frame allowed. She stared at the pattern on the popcorn ceiling. When she squinted her eyes, she saw what looked like the outline of a rabbit, twitching its long ears and wiggling its button nose. She clamped her eyes shut and rubbed them fiercely. When she opened them again, she blinked and exhaled her confusion.

"Okay," she muttered. "I'm not going crazy. There's no bunny on that ceiling."

Maia slowly disentangled her limbs from the fluffy comforter and piles of pillows on the bed, continuing a muttered mantra of "no bunny" as her feet touched the floor.

Standing beside the bed, she stretched her tight muscles with a loud groan before scratching at her side with the languid grace of a zombie. As her nails grazed her skin, she froze under the realization that something was terribly wrong. She was wearing pajamas, not her typical birthday suit nightwear. These weren't just any pajamas, either. They were cotton-candy pink flannel. Maia shuddered. She abhorred pink. She clutched at the soft fabric nestled against her skin, verifying its reality before prowling over to her backpack, but it wasn't where she'd left it. She'd dumped it by the front door, but instead, its bulging form now rested on the room's single chair, beneath the window. Her shoes were neatly stacked on the floor beside it, but her clothes were gone. And there was a tray on the table next to it, loaded with her favorite breakfast.

A vicious growl ripped from her stomach, and despite the weirdness of the morning, she nearly leapt onto the platter. She hadn't realized how hungry she was, and though they were just simple blueberry pancakes drenched in maple syrup, they were the best pancakes she'd ever had, even better than her mother's. Her throat tightened at that thought, and a quickly swallowed bite of pancake lodged in her airway. She grabbed the carafe of orange juice and poured herself a glass, gulping it greedily until the lump was gone. She then finished the last savory bites of applewood smoked chicken sausage and stacked the plates in a pile, ignoring the strange desire to lick them to gleaming perfection.

Lifting the tray to place it out in the hallway by her door, Maia revealed an envelope that had been hidden beneath. It wasn't the typical lick-and-seal envelope she was accustomed to, however. She glanced around her room, as if whoever had orchestrated this strange morning was somehow lurking in the shadows the morning sun had not yet chased away. Setting the tray down again, she went to the window and drew back the thin curtain, peeking out the glass to the street below. Seeing the cars in the parking lot and driving on the nearby road convinced her that everyone—except her, perhaps—was still sane and normal. The hand-folded parchment envelope rested heavily in her hands, like an artifact from an archaic century. She glanced out the window again, wanting to make sure there were cars outside and not horses and carriages. Shaking her head at her fleeting moment of panic, Maia turned back to the envelope.

"Hellcats," she breathed, breaking open the wax seal of the letter. "I have been through some weird shit lately, but . . ." Her grew wide as she read the anonymous short message in flowing calligraphy. "I have a feeling things are only going to get way more messed up."

She shoved her new instructions for the day in her backpack before pulling out a set of familiar clothes. At least these belonged to her, though she really didn't want to know how Blake had gotten a hold of them before the earthquake struck. Her hands shook slightly, and her face grew pink as she pulled out a bra and clean underwear. She tried not to imagine the handsome Australian sifting through her underwear drawer, looking at her boring—and decidedly non-sexy—cotton panties and bras. She suddenly wished she had listened to Hayley when, on a recent shopping expedition, she'd nagged about buying something silky or with lace.

Of course, she reminded herself as she balanced awkwardly to pull on her jeans, it didn't really matter what Blake thought about her unmentionables. That was the first and last time he was ever going to see them. Just because he had taken—and done—more than a glancing peek at her skivvies in her dreams didn't mean he was entitled to the real version.

"Yes," she muttered. Then, in a more determined voice, she said, "He won't be getting any more than that. Perv." She stuffed her feet into a new pair of hiking boots she found at the bottom of the bag. "How dare he sift through my underwear drawer, anyway." Giving her laces an extra hard tug, she relished in the slight burn of the strings between her fingers. The mild pain was just enough to edge her frustration back.

She stomped into the bathroom, brushed her teeth, and then finished packing her bag before stepping out into the hallway. She cringed as she let the door slam behind her, realizing that she had no idea what time it was. Maia hoped she hadn't woken anyone. Her guilt was soon eased, however, as she was greeted by the bright sunlight when she stepped outside, its vibrant rays filtering through the tall trees that surrounded the hotel, hinting at late morning.

She was so busy staring at the hotel's unique gray-pitched roof—the bizarre architecture of the building had gone unnoticed in yesterday's sleep-deprived state—that with a short cry of surprise, she nearly collided with a plump little man. A sign with her name quickly scribbled across it carelessly dangled between his pinched fingers as he stood next to a van, *Fiordland National Park* emblazoned across its gleaming white side.

Maia awkwardly caught her balance on the hood of a nearby car as an apology tumbled from her lips. "I'm really sorry. I wasn't paying attention—"

Clearly uncomfortable at the sudden contact, the man leaned back slightly, blinking a few times before recovering with an easy smile and sharper accent than a typical Kiwi. "No problem, young lady. Uh . . . you wouldn't happen to be . . . ?" He pointed at the sign.

"Yeah, actually, I am."

"Good!" He tossed the sign into the back of the van with a relieved smile, then hoisted himself up into the driver's seat. "I felt like a ruddy lunatic holding that sign. Name's Davies." He jerked his thumb proudly at his sternum before waving her on. "Come on!"

Maia would normally have thought twice about getting into a van with a strange man in a foreign country, but there was something about him that settled her gut instinct. The same flame of excitement that Blake's words had awoken leaped in recognition of her chauffeur. She felt a strange kinship with him, like she knew him somehow, and with a shrug, she reached for the van's handle.

"So." She slammed the passenger door closed as she buckled her seatbelt, trying to sound casual instead of nervous, as she felt. "I was told to expect a 'conveyance' to the Milford Track. I guess that's you?" She curled her fingers into air quotes at the word "conveyance," smirking at the formal language. She'd nearly expected a pumpkin and glass slippers.

"Well, it's a bit more complicated than that." Davies slapped a pair of Oakley sunglasses against his round face and, disregarding his own seat belt, started the engine.

At his words, Maia's heart took a nosedive. Complicated? Had she been deceived? He didn't *look* like a serial killer. He was short, and soft around the middle, and she vaguely wondered if his laughter reached his belly. He wore khaki cargo pants, hiking boots, and a forest-green fleece vest over a white Fiordland National Park tee. His thinning brown hair, double chin, and easy smile reminded her of her eighth-grade science teacher; that man was kinder than Buddha himself. He wouldn't even slap a mosquito noshing on his arm in the middle of summer.

The tour guide fiddled with the car's stereo before settling on a random song and stealing a quick glance at her wary expression. "Oh, I'm sorry. I probably should've explained better." His full lips stretched into another jovial grin, revealing rows of crooked, slightly yellow teeth. Despite being a feature that would make any dentist cringe, its inviting warmth quickly melted her rising anxiety.

"The journey to the track is a tad complicated. That's all," he said. "It's about a twenty minute drive to Te Anau Downs, which is where we'll get on a boat. Then it's about an hour's ride across the lake to the beginning of the track. Here!" He shoved a glossy brochure into her hands. "This will explain it. Now, just sit and enjoy the sounds of Elbow!"

"'Elbow'?" Maia raised her brows, giving a faint chuckle at the odd name. She scanned the photos in the brochure; they were gorgeous, but they still didn't quite do justice to the real thing right outside her window.

"Yeah. The band, Elbow! Don't tell me you've never 'eard of them?"

Continuing to absorb the precise and educational verbiage on the brochure, Maia shook her head.

"Ah, yes, you're a Yank. You guys don't know good music till we let you borrow some of ours."

Maia glanced up at his teasing smirk before returning the expression as she closed the brochure. "So, this is a New Zealand band, then?"

His expression faltered, and he look slightly insulted. "Elbow? A New Zealand band?" He sputtered for a moment. "Goodness me, no! These blokes are from England! My home." His look of insult turned almost dreamy before he shook it off.

"Oh!" Maia grimaced at her blunder. "Will you excuse this ignorant Yank, then? I've never traveled outside of the States before."

Davies's dismay instantly dissolved into a snort. "Of course. You can't help where you come from. I'm only living 'ere for my wife, ya know."

"Right, well, my dad really liked Genesis . . . so . . ." Maia's throat tightened against a resurgence of the pain within her chest.

"Funny you should mention—" With that, Davies was off on a lengthy discourse of British music and its long-reaching influence. Maia tried to pay attention to him as she let the mellow voice coming from the speakers wash over her. The fall colors of the scenery outside her window melded together as the van trundled past a mixture of buildings and scenery that smeared into golds, reds, yellows, and even blues and whites of every shade imaginable. It wasn't long after they left the city that the colors began to separate into trees, mountains, lakes, and a very few, unobtrusively designed homes, the rare mom-and-pop business sprinkled in between. So far, New Zealand reminded her of the Pacific Northwest with its bright homage to the beauty and splendor of nature. Even the buildings were designed to be swallowed by nature's palette, and Maia found she had to look hard to realize they were even there.

The van slowed as they drew near the park's entrance, and without breaking his lecture, Davies threw the vehicle in park before quickly scampering out, flinging the van door shut behind him.

Maia grabbed her bag and hastily followed, slightly awed at Davies's ability to speak without pausing for breath. Even after she'd slammed her door shut, he did nothing more than wave her down the path to where the boats were already waiting.

A vast number of people milled around, packing and unpacking their gear, shouldering bags, and snapping pictures. She awkwardly returned the smiles and waves a few sent her way as she walked by. Despite the friendliness, though, Maia still felt alone, distinctly apart from them, as if trapped inside a little bubble of her own creation.

So enamored with the smiling faces and the breathtaking scenery was she that her woolgathering forced her to scurry in Davies's wake. His legs were short, but he was fast and moved at what felt like an inhuman pace.

Upon reaching the docks, he guided her to a small boat and helped her climb in before checking the dials and fluids to make sure the vehicle was ready for their journey. Thankfully, he ceased his lecture on the history of British music in favor of instructing her on how to untie the boat so they could pull away from the dock.

As Maia's fingers fumbled with the tight knots of the rope, Davies's once deft movements gradually turned frenetic and anxious. His swing from jovial to impatient was overwhelming, but even with the tension radiating from the small man, she couldn't help but pause occasionally to stare at the dreamlike landscape and breathe in the intoxicating scents only nature could provide. Maia's awed wonderment turned sour as Davies's silence curdled from awkward to grim. Soon, the engine rumbled to life, and the boat began to vibrate along the water, swaying beneath her planted feet and locked knees.

Maia flinched slightly at the way the purr of the motor disturbed the Zen of the imposing mountains surrounding the obsidian lake. "This place is stunning," she shouted over the engine's growl. It felt wrong to express such sentiments at that level of volume.

"What? Oh, yeah. You get used to it." Davies's buoyant tone had turned jaded.

Maia frowned. How could anyone get used to this? She fought a strange tremble of anger at his words, and gripped the boat's railing under the watercraft's increasing speed. "So, Davies, why are we the only ones in this boat? I mean, all of the other boats are full of people, and the brochure said you have to schedule your tour ahead of time in groups."

"Oh, right." Davies's raised voice barely cut through the roar of the engine and the scream of the wind in her ears. His tiny brown eyes shifted rapidly before he focused them on the water, and his grip on the steering wheel went turned white. Maia waited, staring at him expectantly, but he only pushed the boat to go faster, until they were flying past all the others, chopping their way through the water. The force of the boat's sudden velocity threw her to its slippery floor. The roar of the wind and the crash of the boat slapping against the water drowned the sound of her curses as she slipped and slid her way into the nearest seat. Once tucked between the force of the wind and the boat's starboard side, Maia pulled up the hood of her jacket and hunkered down in the low seat, burying her numb hands deep inside her pockets.

She was positive that the trip took only about twenty-five minutes instead of the promised hour, but given that Davies's agitation had only continued to grow the closer they got to land, she decided not to press him for any more information. When they were finally close enough to the docks for her to get out, he pulled the boat to a stop and waited. He didn't ask her to tie up the boat. He didn't shut off the engine, either. Instead, he kept his death grip on the steering wheel and nodded to Maia's drenched backpack, where it now sat safely trapped between her clenched ankles.

"Remember that brochure I gave you?"

"Yeah, I've still got it." Maia patted the bag reassuringly before swinging it over her shoulder; she cringed when the wet mass *thunked* against her back.

"Good. On that brochure is a map of the trail. If you get out here and follow the crowd, you'll find your way."

Maia stared at his pinched face for a moment before disembarking, reveling in the fact that she actually landed on two feet and not on her backside, or in the water. The gunning of the boat's engine cut her small triumph short, and though she turned to give Davies a goodbye wave, the boat was already a speck in the distance.

Maia shook off the lingering strangeness of his behavior with a shrug.

After quickly consulting the map, she noticed the crowd of people making their way down the path in groups, a tour guide leading each. Maia picked the largest of the groups and tagged along, hoping to get lost in the sea of faces, and though she received a few curious glances, no one bothered her.

They had just passed over a footbridge when she felt a strange tugging sensation around her heart. Pausing in the middle of the trail, she clutched at her chest as her mind raced with possibilities. This wasn't an anxiety attack; she'd had enough of those to know. What, then? Was it a heart attack, a stroke, an aneurysm? She was too young for any of those, but dealing with her father's illness had made her morbidly curious about the various causes of death. She'd spent hours at her local library when her father was first diagnosed, pouring over medical books; it hadn't taken her long to feel as though she knew more than the doctors did.

When the pain didn't ease, Maia stumbled to a nearby log. She ripped the bottle of water she'd bought from one of the stands at the beginning of the trail from the side pocket of her backpack, tore off its lid, and sucked down large gulps as though it was the breath of life. Soon, she was sputtering and nearly bathing in it as water ran down her chin and onto her shirt.

An uncontrollable urge to move seized her, and a quick look around slammed her with the harsh reality that her group had left without her. She was alone on the trail. She stood and spent several futile minutes squeezing the water out of her dripping shirt. Completely soaked from the waist up, she zipped up her jacket to cover her mess.

The uncomfortable restless energy gave way to a new sensation, then; one that felt like someone was nudging her between her shoulder blades. It pushed her forward, not down the trail, but into the surrounding forest. Unsure of what was happening, Maia could nothing but obey.

9

MAIA DIDN'T KNOW how long she walked. It could have been one mile, or it could have been ten. She was in a daze, lost in a bright world of green, stumbling over moss-covered rocks and tree roots as the insistent but gentle nudging continued its pressure. It guided her through pain. If she veered off whatever course it had set for her, a burning sensation would sear its way through her muscles, tightening and cramping them like a buildup of too much lactic acid. The pain would only increase as she stepped—or, at times, crawled—in the wrong direction.

As the sun reached its zenith, Maia's stomach growled, breaking through the fog that dominated her mind. She stopped on shaking, wobbly legs, ignoring the obnoxious nudging in her back, and fell onto the nearest flat rock, slinging her bag to the forest floor. She lay sprawled awkwardly across the rock until her persistent stomach forced her to struggle into a sitting position. Her legs dangled over the rock's edge as she groped around near its base until she located her abandoned backpack. She dragged the bag into her lap, unzipped it, and dug around, searching for the bag of trail mix and banana she'd purchased with the water. Before long, she was taking large bites of the soft fruit, barely swallowing one sweet bite before taking another.

The slight rustle of the leaves around her quickly grew into an angry tremor, and before Maia could move, a sigh of frustration erupted beside her.

Letting out a muffled yelp, Maia twisted to look, but no one was visible until she returned her gaze to the fallen log in front of her. The banana stuck in her throat, and she nearly choked from the shock of finding a wiry Korean man sitting across from her, in a spot that had been unoccupied mere seconds ago. *Where'd he come from?* A few strands of silver hung at his temples, but his stoic face was unlined, making his age indiscernible. His dark blue jacket, black jeans, and dark green sneakers that tapped impatiently at the ground didn't help much, either. He ran his long fingers through his spiky black hair several times before leveling her with an annoyed glare, and she was struck by the conflicting realization that his look of aggression brought the sharp angles of his face into stunning relief. He was beautiful.

"Is it possible for you to eat and walk at the same time? We still have a long way to go."

The man's inhuman beauty quickly dissipated under his acerbic tone. Clearly she was keeping him from some important task. Maia sat back for a moment, dumbfounded and irked at the man's sudden appearance and attitude.

She chewed the last bite of her banana slowly, still staring at him, silently daring him into another outburst. With every passing second, his lips thinned further, and his eyes hardened with contempt. Realizing she didn't have a trash can available, Maia took her time stuffing the banana peel into the side pocket of her bag—the one that wasn't occupied by her almost-empty water bottle.

The man groaned again, pinching the bridge of his nose as if she was a student he had explained a very simple concept to, repeatedly. The tip of his nose had two small, subtle indents on either side; she wondered if they were permanent, thanks to repeated frustration in his life. "What are you doing?" he asked. "They said you knew about plants! Here, give it to me."

He held out his hand, palm up, and wiggled his fingers impatiently.

Maia placed the peel in his hand solemnly and waited to see what he would do. One dark eyebrow shot up at an angle before he tossed the banana peel over his shoulder and into the brush.

"Now," he said, pulling himself up to a full height that wasn't much more than her five-foot, four-inch frame. His tone dripped with condescension. "Ready?" Without waiting for her to answer, he spun on his heel and marched further into the forest. The insistent nudge between her shoulder blades urged her to follow, and she scrambled to keep up. Maia huffed as she finally made it shoulder-to-shoulder with him, panting against his fast pace.

Noticing that the nudging pain was no longer massaging her shoulders, she pierced him with a dark look, which he studiously ignored. "Is it safe to assume," she said, slowly biting out her words, "that you were quite literally the pain in my neck a few moments ago?" Carefully, she sidestepped a large, ankle-turning rock.

Rolling one shoulder in a careless shrug, the man answered with indifference. "You know what they say about assuming."

Maia rolled her eyes. The only reason she was following this man, who was clearly a sociopath, was because that insistent, nudging energy told her to. He radiated the same warm, powerful energy she was beginning to recognize, though. Blake, Leo, and, to a lesser extent, Davies had all shared it. The energy pulled on her intuition like a compass pointing north. She just hoped he was one of the other guardians that Blake had mentioned in his notes, rather than a serial killer taking her deeper into the New Zealand forest.

"Yeah, yeah, yeah," she replied. "Very funny. I get it. It makes an ass out of you and me."

He shot her a quick side-glare and continued picking his way carefully through the forest, trailing his hand over every piece of decaying and sick plant life within his reach. The deeper they traveled into the vegetation, the more they saw the ravages of the forest's infection. "Please do not lump your disposition with mine," the man finally answered. "Assuming is the mother of all fuck ups. I was merely guiding you."

"More like cattle prodding."

"As you wish," he replied. His hand caressed the outer edges of a tree's infected bruise. Concern softened his strict features as the bruise healed at his touch, but almost immediately, another replaced it.

The forest must have once been verdant with life, but Maia realized she was now surrounded with decay and death. What little green was left was covered in grayish spots of oozing sludge that steamed as it poured from holes in the trunks of trees and bushes. Dark brown patches of wilting vines and leaves covered rocks and boulders, and brooks and streams were the color of old blood as dead critters littered their rocky banks or floated in their sludge. The air itself was like acid; it stung Maia's nose worse than her mother's fertilizer ever had. They hadn't walked more than a mile before Maia could no longer control the pitching of her stomach. Gripping her knees, she curled forward as dry heaves bowed her body and she lost an entire day's worth of meals. This forest was suffering, and the effects wore on her.

"What is all of this?" Maia asked when she could finally compose herself. Now that her stomach was empty, she could talk. The man brushed his fingers over yet another dying fern as she pressed him for information. "What's making them so sick?"

He let out a shuddering breath. "I honestly don't know. I have an inkling who's behind it, but it's never been this bad before." He shook his head, rubbing a finger behind his ear as he paused, looking deeper into the forest. His eyes narrowed. "All I want to do right now is heal each and every one of them." He pressed his lips together, visibly gathering his resolve. "However, it's imperative that I get you to the meeting with Blake and Poppy." He said it as if he were trying to convince himself that delivering her was more important, but even Maia wasn't convinced.

Seeing the struggle in the tense lines of his body, Maia placed a gentle hand on his shoulder, turning him toward her. "Let me help." She placed her other hand on a nearby tree, and the effect was immediate.

The degenerating sickness melted away from the tree's bark and leaves, but it didn't stop there. The healing spread from that tree to another, to any and every other plant it touched; it was like an electric current being conducted through the roots and extended branches, washing over the forest in a visible wave of health. What she had seen in her mother's garden was child's play compared to the explosion of life before her.

The man sucked in a sharp breath, his eyes widening in disbelief. Realizing she was touching the shoulder of someone she hardly knew, Maia snatched her hand back, only to watch the healing reverse itself until all that remained was the tree she was touching.

"Stop!" He quickly grabbed her hand. Lacing his fingers with hers, he tugged her forward frantically. "Will you share your power with me? Please?" His voice was breathless with desperation, his eyes bright with an inciting gleam, and Maia felt a slight buzzing sensation where their skin touched.

Confused at his question, she stuttered when she answered. "Um, y-yes?"

"Here, spread your hands out and touch everything we pass. I think it'll speed up the process."

She obeyed, happy to see the forest healing as they marched on, but even happier to see the bright smile that spread across the man's handsome, angled features. Gone was the frustration and impatience, leaving only relief in its wake. Maia was once more taken aback by the lack of irritation she felt at the touch of his skin against hers. The feeling wasn't one of peace and comfort, like Blake gave, but it still felt right—somehow.

As he tugged her into the open space of a large clearing, her momentary buzz of happiness was immediately squashed by the angry sound of someone clearing their throat.

10

A SCOWLING BLAKE, arms crossed and body rigid, stood in a clearing whose brown grass crunched like chips under their feet. A misty, wraith-like figure hovered next to him.

"What?" Maia asked, staring back and forth between her guide, Blake, and their ghostly friend. As the figure drifted closer to examine her in return, Maia realized it looked like a young girl in Victorian-era lace pajamas.

When the figure opened her mouth, a sepulchral voice emerged:

"Quite oft
What we see
'tis but a mirage

*to what our heart's faulty
truth may be.*"

Maia smiled as the mystery of the poetry book in her bag fell into place. "I recognize those words! But what does it mean?"

Blake swallowed thickly and took a few steps forward. He gave the floating figure an accusing glare, but before he could answer, Maia's new companion slid his hand out of her grasp. "I think Poppy means that Blake is reading too much into things," he said.

With an injured huff at the sudden abandonment, Maia glanced down at her empty palm. "I don't see why it matters."

The man smirked before walking over to a nearby tree to examine its renewed health. He jerked his thumb in her direction. "She's got a lot to learn, this one."

"Yeah-nah. What all did you tell her, Reed?" Blake had finally recovered his voice, but Maia could still feel an angry hum of energy pulsing from his golden skin.

Reed shrugged, completely absorbed in the tree he was examining. "Nothing. We figured out she's already strong enough to share powers. That's all."

"Stars, already?" The familiar voice behind Maia made her jump.

Pointing at Leo's muscular form as he circled the group, she asked, "Does he always do that?"

Blake sighed, rubbing his temples. "Unfortunately, yes. Most Corocottas do. I'd like to say you get used to it, but . . ."

The reminder of Leo's species drew Maia's thoughts to Blake's notes on the various *praeses*.

"Right. The Corocottas." She nodded before turning to Reed. "And you are?"

Reed's answer was cut short by Leo's loud guffaw. "You mean to tell me, brother, that you dragged this poor girl through the woods without an introduction?" The Corocottas snorted in amusement, disregarding the withering look hoisted his way by Reed who, in turn, was ignoring a heated stare of accusation from Blake

"As the heavens collide, man!" Leo grinned as he turned toward Maia. "I wonder how you've lasted this long, chica, wandering off with a stranger like that."

Maia felt her cheeks burn.

"Leo," Blake growled in warning, and the Corocottas threw up his hands, surrendering with a nervous chuckle. His glance at Maia turned curious, and his head tilted with double-jointed ease as he assessed her with predatory quickness.

Maia regarded Leo's swift change in demeanor for a moment before she turned to Blake. "As much as I love reading the insane scribblings of a random Australian dude, and appreciate the exciting, free trip to a dying forest, I need answers. Start making sense, guys, or I walk."

Never mind that she had no idea how she'd get back, with only her passport and no money, but right now, she didn't care. She'd figure it out. If it wasn't for the humming celestial energy emanating from all three of them, calling to her in a siren's song, she wouldn't have followed in the first place.

Unfortunately, none of that soothed her anger at being embarrassed.

"Reed is a Nepenthes," Blake answered as he shoved his hands casually into his pockets. "His kind guard and maintain any and all plant life. Leo, as you hopefully remember, has the same role for animals, and Poppy"—he motioned at the transparent figure playing over their heads in the slipstream of a gentle breeze—"is an Ariel. She controls the air elements and thus weather, while I maintain the sun, along with any natural sources of light."

"Except for the moon." Reed's response was laced with a sense of pride and protection that Maia didn't quite understand. Was the moon somehow connected to plants?

"Except for the moon," Blake repeated, with an apologetic nod.

Maia rolled her eyes at the drama unfolding before her. "Shiny. So, what's the big deal about power-sharing?"

Reed finished his examination of the newly healed tree and rejoined the group. "It means Heidi is getting weaker."

"I see." Maia looked at the faces staring back at her, all of them serious, as she struggled to remember the details of Blake's notes. She was glad his bullshit sounded more like a B-grade sci-fi flick than something that could actually be true; its entertainment value made it easier to remember. *Yes, but,* the little voice inside reminded her, *think on what you've seen and been able to do so far. Can you really say that it's not true?* Maia mentally swatted the voice away. "Right, Heidi. The Terra guardian. Isn't that a good thing, that she's getting weaker?"

"Well . . ." Leo rubbed nervously at a small, raised scar across his square chin, and Maia saw his mask of confidence slip slightly. For the first time, she noticed how completely human he looked.

> *"From her breast she utters a lonely sigh*
> *the gust from which rips islands asunder*
> *and thunderheads crack across the night sky*
> *calling the waves to pull it all under.*
> *For centuries her whims sculpt the horizon*
> *Her teardrops swell the rivers of the lands*
> *drowning deserts until the next tide is in*
> *'tis all just clay in her careless cold hands."*

"You took the words right outta my mouth, little lady." Leo threw the wraith a grateful glance. Poppy curtsied with a coy giggle and began to trail him, skipping in his circling path.

Maia looked between each member of the group. "Yeah, still don't know what that means."

"As of now, it doesn't mean much," Blake said, taking a lazy seat on a flat slab of granite. He patted the spot next to him and Maia took a step forward, thinking he wanted her to join him until Reed cut her off, plopping down next to Blake instead. He then proceeded to pull off one of his sneakers, making an elegant show of dumping out pebbles.

Maia stood where she was, awkwardly fiddling with the zipper of her jacket, not really sure where she belonged.

"That we know of," Reed muttered, ignoring Blake's angry side-glare.

"What's that supposed to mean?" She chewed on the sudden smirk lifting the corners of her lips as Blake resorted to physically shoving Reed down to the far end of the boulder. Giving Maia an apologetic glance, he patted the seat next to him once more.

Leo's voice emerged from the muzzle of the gray wolf he'd transformed into. "What it means," he panted in a strange, slurring growl as he played a very hard game of tag with Poppy, "is that the transfer of guardianship has begun." He nipped playfully at Poppy's dress.

"*Generations of man witness her wrath*
She sweeps away souls with nary a tear
Nations fall to a fury Hell not hath
This power she wields, it has no peer."

Maia dropped her backpack before the stone slab and moved to settle between Blake and Reed. But she misjudged the depth of the granite ledge and toppled off the back instead.

Rubbing her sore backside as she stood, Maia brushed the leaves off her clothes and felt the heat of embarrassment creep into her cheeks at the many sets of concerned eyes trained upon her.

"What?" Maia chuckled, hoping to make light of her fumble. Clearing her throat with a shake of her head, she said, "So, let me get this straight. The more access I'm given to my own celestial power, the less Heidi has? And that's part of the transfer process, from one *praeses* to another?"

Blake blinked at her, seemingly surprised at her comprehension, but Reed shrugged, unimpressed. Maia inwardly breathed a sigh of relief that her tumble was so easily forgotten and circled around to retake her place beside Blake.

"The question is, how?" Reed asked. "We've never had two *praeses* of the same role active on a system before."

"I've been running through several theories," Blake said as Maia sat between them. "I even went through the records we have. We know that all praeses have both astral and celestial energy bound within them, and that until they are chosen, they don't have access to either form's power. So there's a possibility that, for every replacement Heidi takes out . . ." He spread his hands, leaving the statement dangling in the air, just outside of Maia's understanding.

"She loses power to Maia?" Reed asked, filling in the missing piece. He dug his fingers into the earth next to him. Tiny streams of electricity could be seen pulsing through the dry dirt, shooting toward the nearest dying foliage.

Maia struggled to keep up with the concepts they threw around so freely. She remembered seeing the terms in Blake's notes, but there had been so many that they'd started to blur together in her exhausted, jet-lagged state. She knew that a "system," as Reed called it, was the realm, dimension, or planet a *praeses* was assigned to, and that Earth was considered the Gaea system—now she knew where that term had come from, at least—but she didn't remember anything about celestial records. Unless they were part of the section she'd glossed over about soul palaces and the complicated politics of the "Council" whose every word was binding universal law the moment it was spoken.

Blake shrugged. "The Council's records indicate that one purpose of having several replacement *praeses* is to provide balance between the conflicting astral and celestial energies. If Heidi's picking them off and destroying more than she's creating, thereby disrupting that balance, then she'll grow weak as the celestial Terra energy seeks to balance itself. Our replacements are the pillars that stabilize us and the system. No *praeses* can survive without this balance. There is too much power. It's never been done."

> *"Until one turning her focus askew*
> *from the razor's edge of Balance she holds*
> *searching the forest lush with ash and yew*
> *a pit of despair within her unfolds*
>
> *She feels her flaw, her duties forgotten*
> *what once was Wisdom has turned to sour*
> *Tainted with Pride, her Honor is rotten*
> *through her fingers falls unraveling power."*

Leo's predatory growl made the tiny hairs on the back of Maia's neck stand on end, but strangely not from fear. She had an overwhelming desire to bare her teeth at the guardian and growl back, but she swallowed it as Leo's now human form nodded to the twirling wraith, acknowledging her insight. His shifts happened in the blink of an eye, and so often that Maia was never sure what to expect from him.

"We all know what an imbalance does to a *praeses*," Leo said. "She'll be just like—"

Blake shot the Corocottas a warning glare that instantly silenced him. "We can't assume anything."

Barely glancing up from his work healing the forest's vegetation, Reed shook his head. "Don't be foolish. It's better to assume the worst and be prepared for anything."

"Great, so now we're operating on assumptions?" Maia broke in. "Remind us again what that means, Reed?"

Without looking up, Reed replied. "*You're* the pain in the neck."

Fascinated by the light show emanating from Reed's fingers, Maia stood and moved to his side, dropping her gaze away from Blake's protective glare as she eagerly dug the tips of her fingers into the dirt as well. Her fingertips tingled with the Earth's pulse, and the soil's inhabitants bumped softly against the curves of her fingers. It wasn't as creepy or as gross as she would have thought a week ago. Now, it was no different than scratching behind a puppy's ears, the innocent desire for acceptance. There was so much life to nurture and protect, and it called to her.

Reed tilted his head in her direction and gently whispered, "Take a deep breath, slow your heart and your breathing, and then concentrate. Feel that tingling in your gut? That's celestial energy, the energy of creation. Just let go. Don't try to hold it in, release it the way you would one of those breaths."

With every exhale, Maia tried to relax further, thankful for her mother's meditation lessons and the hours she had spent on the floor of their living room "clearing her thoughts." A few more moments passed, but nothing happened. Then a snap and spark erupted from her fingers. Maia gasped and pulled her hand from the earth, but the energy continued to pulse from her palms, soaking into the ground beneath her and continuing its healing trail.

"What about this Council you mentioned?" Maia asked without looking up. "Can't they help?"

Leo barked out a short laugh and kicked at the ground, shuffling his boots as he cleared his throat around what she expected was an unfavorable retort.

Blake answered instead, weariness lacing his tone. "No one knows who the Council is. It's believed that they're former *praeses*, but they keep their identities hidden, even from one another. If they haven't stepped in yet, we can trust that they won't."

Maia groaned in frustration and turned back to Blake, locking her gaze with his. "But if there are supposedly thousands of you—and, wow, I can't believe I'm actually about to say this—if there are supposedly thousands of you scattered across the universe, can't *someone* help?"

Leo plopped down on the freshly healed, vibrant grass with a quick fold of his long legs. Soon, he was staring up at the pale blue sky, his head in Poppy's lap. Her translucent form made his head look as though it were floating, creating an odd tableau. He scoffed at Maia. "Stars, you like your cynicism strong. What's wrong, if you can't see something through the lens of your camera, it doesn't exist?"

The heat of embarrassment flushed Maia's cheeks. This time, Blake's warning was just a pulse of warm energy that caused Leo to flinch as if he'd received a static shock. Blake squeezed Maia's shoulder in quick reassurance. She jumped slightly; she hadn't seen him come up beside her. "I know you have questions, and we'll get to them, but right now, we need a plan."

Maia conceded with a reluctant nod as her thoughts strayed to her beloved cameras; they had surely been destroyed with everything else. Life was abrupt and unyielding in its turbulence, and photography was the only way she could pause time, trap a moment, however ephemeral. She even missed the tiny camera on her phone.

The conversation continued around her, with more theories and terminology Blake's notes hadn't mentioned. She wasn't sure whether to be comforted or terrified that they seemed to know only a fraction more than herself, and were equally unprepared for whatever was headed their way. She decided to settle on the queasy aftertaste of both. Soon enough, she was completely lost to their conversation, and all she could think about was the dying forest around her. Its sorrow and pain tugged at the pit of her stomach, and she could feel its sickness as if it was her own. Maia swallowed the nausea-induced saliva in her mouth and nodded through the exhale of a deep breath. Her throat ached in raw sorrow as she fought to keep tears at bay.

"Maia." Blake's voice was gentle as he called her back to the moment. She felt the burn of embarrassment in her cheeks as she realized they were all looking at her. Was she that transparent? "We know you've been through a lot, but we need to make sure you're in this fully before we reveal more."

Maia's laugh came out dry and slightly strangled; it made her sound like a deranged chain-smoker, but she didn't care. "I can handle it, okay? As psychotic as all of this is, it's better than sitting around trying to figure out how to grieve for my parents. I'd either be in a bar right now, or holding hands in a group singing 'Kumbaya,' or something. Trust me, this is my best option. I need a purpose, a mission . . . something." Her voice began to shake under the weight of her grief and anger. She sucked a stuttered breath through her teeth as her lips trembled. "If that bitch Heidi had anything to do with my parents' death, I want to take her down. I'm in. Trust me."

Her outburst was met with determined silence. Leo suddenly appeared very interested in the small herd of deer nosing around the edge of the recovered glade, and Poppy had somehow discovered a fascinating new piece of lace on the sleeve of her dress. Reed ignored her completely, seemingly intent upon his task of healing, and Blake could hardly meet her eyes. He chewed on his bottom lip, but as he quietly stepped closer, the glance he stole showed that he understood her pain, more than he wanted to admit. Maia felt as if she could drown in the energy pulsing from him. It was warm and strong, yet she knew that too much of its power could burn.

Finally, Blake nodded. "Understood." He turned from her then, abruptly, and began to pace. "Look, we've wasted enough time. Our main purpose in coming here was to contain the damage to this forest, and for Maia to meet Reed and Poppy."

Maia crouched, placing her hand on the soil next to her, and felt the gentle, happy rhythm emanating from the ground. The beat matched the same healthy rhythm she'd felt in the hotel's shower, and relief flowed through her, relaxing the muscles along her spine that had been tightened by stress. She smiled. She still couldn't come to terms with the story her new companions were feeding her . . . not yet, but she couldn't deny that this was the first feeling of happiness and control she'd experienced in what was too long to remember. As unbelievable as it was, she had just healed something on the brink of death. It was alive now, because she had been able to do something.

Blake paused in his steps. "Our next step is to try to talk to Lana, see if she'll help us."

Maia recognized the name from Blake's notes. "Lana . . . the guardian of water, right? The Nymph?"

At the mention of her name, Leo tensed, a strange kind of focus taking hold of him. He stood, his movements even more restless, and Maia thought she could hear the undercurrent of a canine whine echoing on each breath. The air shimmered around him, mimicking his agitation. "You know how Lana is," he said nervously, as if he wanted to brush all mention of her away from the conversation. "Her will flows and changes as quickly as the water she controls. Normally, I'd say we don't stand a chance at convincing her, but—" He stopped suddenly. His eyes shifted around, like he was looking for something, before narrowing. "I think that's about to change."

"Why?" Blake asked. "What's going on?"

Leo's form shifted like a mirage, his body phasing through several different animals—each of them predatory, Maia noticed. His head shook from side to side, as if he strained to hear something very far away.

"Leo, focus! What's going on?"

Finally, he settled on the form of a sleek black panther, his tail flicking like a whip as he stretched his jaws wide in a toothy yawn, an obvious display of power.

"She needs our help," he purred. His pink tongue slid over sharp canines. "In the Bering Sea. There's a village . . ." His large black head tilted, and his right ear twitched, listening. "Little Diomede. She's trying to keep it from being devoured by the ocean."

"Wait, how'd he—?"

Maia's puzzlement was cut short when she saw comprehension dawn on Blake's face, tension tightening the muscles of his shoulders. "Stars above and below," he breathed.

"What?" Maia asked. The mounting aggressive energy emanating from him and Leo made her skin crawl. The air around Reed vibrated green for a moment before he vanished completely, leaving several sparking piles of moss and leaves in his wake. "Uh, guys, am I missing something here?"

"Poppy, do you think you can take Maia this time?" Blake asked, ignoring Maia and turning to the Ariel. "We can't rely on human transportation right now. Maybe not ever, not if her energy is getting stronger." He turned slightly to Maia, explaining before she had a chance to ask. "The more you tap into your celestial power, the more it will disrupt any electricity you encounter."

Remembering the clocks and outlets at her house, Maia nodded. Poppy curtsied gracefully, but even she couldn't hide a nervous smile as she said:

"Whipping whirls of Western Wind rip through the mountain valley,

soaring over sandy shores until the stormheads sally.
Bricks are built to block its blow, tearing through the alley.
Yet courageous crews will on every coastline rally
To enslave it to the canvas of every ship and galley."

A strong wind blew through the clearing in answer to Poppy's raised arms. Leo narrowed his yellow cat eyes at Blake and stretched out his front paws, claws extending and clutching the soft earth beneath him.

"The West Wind? Do you really think that's the safest option right now?" he growled.

Blake nodded as he stepped forward, Maia's abandoned backpack in his hand. It bulged strangely. He pulled out a heavier coat than the one she had on, a scarf, a hat, and finally gloves, handing each to Maia as she watched in awe. *How?* she wondered as she put them on.

"I trust Poppy," he said. "She knows what she's doing. It may be one of the more erratic winds, but it's also the fastest and strongest during this time of year. She'll be fine, won't you, *mia regina?*"

Blake's warm grin and teasing tone had returned, comforting Maia as she slung the bag he handed her over her shoulder.

"Oh, so we're butchering my name now? Fun." Maia frowned despite the warmth his touch produced in her veins. Blake only answered with a vague smirk as she wrestled with his distractions.

They didn't have time for questions, and he knew she had plenty.

Despite the strong wind howling around her, she forced herself to focus on the mischief dancing through Blake's eyes as a thick cloud enveloped her and the howling became a distant sound. She never noticed if, or when, her feet left the ground, and she didn't feel as though she was moving. All she could see was the changing light outside the cloud as she soared higher, where the cooler air attempted to sneak its way into any crack between her warm layers it could find.

Pulling the hat low over her ears and tucking the scarf tighter around her neck, she stood, bracing herself for an unforeseeable landing.

11

SELENE SHIVERED AS she stepped into the glass court-yard of the Earth's Core, where Heidi was accustomed to conducting her business. Her silver hair rippled down the back of a white dress that shimmered against her curvy frame, the fabric blinking with the light of the brightest stars.

She paused and looked around the empty space; despite being Heidi's most loyal subject and friend, Selene still had no idea where the Terra *praeses* actually lived. She had a feeling that it wasn't much different from this place that radiated so much power, though. Jagged, clear spikes protruded from the ground, and though they looked to be made of glass, they held a symbiotic intelligence inside them, their power culled from the depths of the Earth, mixing with astral and celestial energy. This was the Earth's life force, its heart. The Luna guardian often wondered if those crystals knew every thought she had. Smoke filled each, undulating and shifting, its hue fading in and out of every color imaginable, pulsing with life. Except recently, the vibrantly fresh colors of life had slowly become unbalanced. Putrid, dark colors of decay and rot consumed their once glittering brilliancy. She'd never seen an imbalance like it. Something was very wrong, and it was something she couldn't account for. Unease and doubt tightened around Selene's heart, and she tried to swallow the control threatening to escape in choking hysterics. Heidi still hadn't arrived, but she must have been close; the crystalline structures were growing agitated, quivering in excitement.

Selene stood impatiently in the center of the room, near a stone podium, trying to take in every detail at once as her pale fingers traced the lace pattern of her dress against her thighs. The repeated motion soothed her nerves. The stone in front of her looked like nothing more than a plain, unassuming column, resembling what one would find at the Parthenon in Greece, old and crumbly. But once Heidi arrived, it would hold an immense concentration of power—*her* power.

Selene shuddered once more and swallowed the sick feeling rising from her stomach. She knew Heidi planned to do something huge and spectacular, but the glint in her eyes when she'd spoken of it last was dark, a look that Selene had never seen in Heidi before—one that she now feared. She turned abruptly to stare across the podium at what she deemed was the source of all this tragic mischief. She'd always liked the expression "if looks could kill," and she wished she had the power to destroy with a glance. If she did, she would have reduced at least one of the two chairs before her to ash.

As she studied them, Selene twisted and untwisted the edges of her long bell sleeves around her wrists, releasing her anxiety. They weren't just chairs, but with so much fear and anger jolting through her heart, she couldn't bear to think of them by their proper term.

Thrones.

That's what they were, though their intended occupants never sat in them together like they were supposed to. The one on the right was made from a bright yellow metal—not gold, but something rare that humans would never discover because it was derived from the core of the sun. Etched into the shining metal were geometric, art deco-like shapes that shimmered in veins of bright oranges and reds. The throne burned, glowing from the inside out.

Selene squeezed her eyes shut as the power of the sun's light pounded behind her skull. She much preferred the coolness of her moon.

With a raised hand, she shielded her face from the Sideralis's throne as she studied the one next to it. It was slightly more macabre in look, made from the long bones of prehistoric birds, their feathers and the fur of other long deceased animals interwoven with equally extinct plants to create a cover of grotesquely exquisite beauty.

Selene knew very little about the decision to exterminate the dinosaurs, but apparently it had caused a big enough rift in the team that the plant and animal *praeses* of the time were replaced shortly thereafter.

She was still standing frozen by the podium, staring at the throne, sifting through the various pieces of gossip she knew about that time, when she heard the sharp snap of impatient fingers. Acting on instinct, she flung herself to the ground, prostrate, and listened to the approaching clack of stiletto heels against the glassy floor.

The noise stopped. Something soft brushed her cheek, and she breathed in the heady scent of the fur-lined robe tickling her nose. She heard another snap. Peering up through her silver hair, she saw a hand above her motioning for her to rise, while the pointy toes of a white, leather-covered shoe tapped dangerously near her fingertips. Selene brushed her lips against the leather of the shoes and rose on quivering legs that never showed though the fluid and practiced motion. She adored Heidi, irrevocably and undeniably, but she was never sure what kind of mood the Terra guardian was in at any given time. She was more temperamental than Lana's water, or one of Poppy's storms.

Selene glanced quickly at the round, almost girlish features of the Terra guardian before averting her eyes in respect, settling her gaze instead on the thrones across the room.

Heidi said nothing as she flicked a long strand of light auburn hair over her shoulder. Selene strained her ears as the strands whispered and rustled over a dress made of dinosaur skin, but that sound wasn't what she listened for. Heidi refused to let her look, but Selene knew that a prick of Heidi's finger, a drop of blood on the unassuming column, delivered a physical manifestation of Heidi's celestial power, bound with the destructive flesh and blood of the human vessel that all *praeses* were required to maintain as their outer form. The small ritual brought forth an active replica of the globe, measuring three feet in diameter, and from that replica, Heidi could control or change the territory managed by the other Gaea *praeses* on a much larger scale.

As soon as Selene heard the gentle *slap* of the blood drop hitting the bottom of the column, she felt a rush of energy pulse through the room. She looked up, finally, at the Terra guardian, who had a cruel, childish smirk on her face as she shooed Selene forward. "Walk," she said. "Go on. I know you want to." Her smoky voice didn't quite match her looks, but it certainly made obeying orders a compulsion.

Of course, Selene didn't need any compulsion. She would always obey Heidi, just like Lana would always obey Selene's gravity. It was physics. Almost involuntarily, her body began to glide forward, as though the globe had somehow tied an invisible rope around her waist and used it to pull her in a circle, itself at its center. The first time it happened, Selene had giggled at the silliness of it all, the way she had circled the Earth in the same manner as her element. Plus, it tickled. But the fun had ended when that first meeting dragged on for over twenty hours, and Selene hadn't been allowed to stop as long as the globe was up. The tickling had soon become an annoying, scratching sensation, which quickly made her weary of her situation.

Now, she dreaded the entire process.

"Tell me, Selene, dear." Heidi spun the globe slowly with her fingertips, stopping it every few moments to stare at a particular spot on the surface before moving on. "What news do you have for me?" Her tone was condescending no matter who she talked to, but Selene couldn't help taking it personally.

"Well, I spoke with Leo, and—" She paused and gritted her teeth as she passed the opposite side of the globe. It didn't matter that Heidi could hear her no matter where she was in the room, she still insisted Selene make eye contact when she spoke. When she reemerged around the curve, she continued. "And . . . he didn't say anything of importance."

"Didn't he? Are you sure?" Heidi stopped the globe and stared at the Western Hemisphere, puffing out her round cheeks in steady concentration. Selene took the time she had around the next curve of the globe to think about her answer.

When she neared Heidi again, the crease in the Terra guardian's chin, below her frown, was a good indication that Selene's next words would not be easily received.

"Yes, I'm sure," Selene replied. "Other than teasing me like usual, he had nothing important to say."

Heidi sighed delicately. "You know, Selene, I must say I am very disappointed in you."

Selene's chest tightened.

"For a woman, your powers of manipulation over men are nonexistent. I think you may be losing your touch. You couldn't get anything out of Reed or your brother in the last week, yet a little birdy told me plenty in the last hour."

This time, when she passed, Selene kept her gray eyes to the ground, avoiding the gloat in Heidi's hazel ones.

"Honestly, girl, I don't know how you live with yourself."

Selene's heart thudded madly against her chest. Heidi had the look of someone who enjoyed shredding the wings off butterflies, and she was known for her cruel punishments. Selene didn't want to think about what her latest infraction would cost her. Throwing her shoulders back as she walked around the opposite side of the globe made her feel strong in the moment, but the feeling quickly faded as she crossed Heidi's path again. The room began to hum with a new, stronger energy. Selene had felt it before over the centuries, but only in small increments. Now it was stronger, much stronger, and before she was out of Heidi's reach, the Terra guardian reached out and caught a tight fistful of Selene's silver hair, the bright locks standing in stark contrast against Heidi's dark skin. She jerked the Luna guardian back against the motion that pulled her forward, and Selene's knees almost buckled under the surge of power—her own power—fleeing her body. She swayed with weakness, even as she heard Heidi's impatient command: "Don't go fainting on me now, you weak little princess."

Anger and embarrassment could be a powerful source of energy, and fueled by the insult, it achieved the desired effect. Selene kept herself standing, but she gasped and twisted her body around, attempting to glare at Heidi—her only form of rebuttal.

Instead, what Selene saw gave her a glimpse into what Heidi was really doing, and her eyes widened in horror.

Heidi was channeling Selene's gravitational powers to control water, *Lana's* water, and from the swirling motion she made with her free hand over the Bering Sea, Selene knew that she was kicking up quite the storm. The waves fought back against her as they attempted to keep the rough seas from drowning a tiny island in their midst.

The waves were failing.

Keeping one hand in the Luna guardian's hair and the other over the water, Heidi turned her eyes on Selene. Her pink, tiny lips pulled into a cruel grin, and she flashed a row of tiny white teeth. She knew her battle was almost won.

Helpless, Selene watched a series of waves wash over the island, one by one, effectively burying it in the sea. As the land disappeared from view, Heidi dropped the hand she'd had hovering over the waters and twisted the other.

Selene cried out as strands of her hair were ripped from their roots, and Heidi yanked again, slinging Selene to the slick stones below. She slid across the floor, finally stopping at the other end of the room, where she curled in on herself in a tiny ball. The *clack* of Heidi's heels drew near, and the muscles in Selene's body tensed like a swarm of angry bees. Heidi's leather shoes stopped next to her right shoulder, and despite the powerful humming energy she felt being lowered into the ground next to her, Selene didn't dare move. Not even when a surprisingly gentle touch caressed her long hair.

"I'm going to tell you what I found out, Selene, and then you'll understand what's been done."

Selene struggled to rein in a shiver that wracked her body as Heidi's soft voice grated on her already frightened nerves. The Terra guardian shushed Selene, as though she was comforting a small child.

"The boys have found my replacement. They seek to aid her in destroying me and taking my throne. But don't worry." Heidi rubbed a hand across Selene's shaking shoulders. "They will never succeed, especially now that I have destroyed the island of Little Diomede. Their only hope for success resided there, and it is now buried deep within the ocean."

Selene gulped her next breaths in a vain attempt to steady her thrashing heart. Despite Heidi's attempts to calm her, her suspicion rose. Heidi never told Selene anything of significance; she preferred her team to remain in the dark.

"Wh-why are you telling me this?" Selene tilted her head to the side to look up into Heidi's calculating features.

"Because you are going to deliver a message to them for me." Heidi beckoned Selene forward. As the trembling girl raised her torso up off her curled up legs, Heidi enveloped her in a tender hug. Pressing Selene's delicate face to the bare skin peeking out above her low neckline, Heidi rested her round chin on the young *praeses's* silver head.

They exchanged no words, but as Heidi ran her fingers through Selene's hair and across her temple, the hum of her strange new energy, tinged with bitterness and hatred, made the message loud and clear.

12

A SLIGHT JARRING sensation reverberating through her legs was Maia's first hint that the ground beneath her feet was now solid. The landing wasn't as rough as she'd feared, thankfully, and the journey hadn't actually been all that unpleasant. She felt, oddly, as though she'd only spent a few minutes within Poppy's little bubble. Unfortunately, the relative ease of travel didn't prepare her for what happened next.

The sound raging outside the bubble wasn't one she had ever heard before, not even when the earthquake had hit her home. She couldn't tell if the screams belonged to the wind or people, or maybe it was both. The sound of buildings being torn apart was one she wished she didn't recognize. Another fierce, crashing noise she couldn't place was followed by angry shouts, but it wasn't until the cloud lifted that the chaos erupting outside her little bubble hit her like a freight train.

Maia stumbled, and the wind stabbed her face with icy nails, ripping at her skin. Hoping to hold off the numbing pressure, she squeezed her eyes shut and covered them with her hands. A steady hand gripped her elbow before she hit the ground and something solid crushed against her.

Her hands were trapped for a moment, until she wiggled them free and realized that her face was plastered against a familiar blue shirt, and that the wall she'd hit was very warm and chiseled. She rubbed her cheek against the soft flannel fabric, lost in the moment as she listened to the happy humming noise that emanated from Blake's chest as his strong arms wrapped around her. She was warm there, and she didn't want to move, but the happy hum shifted into something worried, agitated. She lifted her head.

Her view was the underside of Blake's chin, and it was moving quickly as he spoke. Maia gave herself a mental shake and pulled back, stepping away from the shelter of Blake's arms and the warm energy his body had given her. He didn't resist her movement, and she was grateful, but it wasn't until she'd put a few steps between them that she was able to concentrate on what was happening around them.

They were standing next to the algae-covered boulders of a jagged jetty, a tiny crop of buildings behind them. The place was the epitome of remote, and couldn't have consisted of more than twenty buildings. Poles stuck into the ground at odd angles, and the ramshackle buildings of the community were pieced together in a rough but efficient manner. A few of the homes jutted out from the mountain that comprised nearly the entire tiny island, but most of the small dwellings were raised on stilts. The entire village groaned and shuddered under the violence of the wind that agitated the sea around them. Grabbing hold of a nearby pole sunken into the grass at a slant, Maia strained her ears, willing the voices to become clear despite the destruction surrounding them.

"Lana, what's happening?"

Blake stood behind a slender Haitian girl whose short brown curls bounced wildly in the wind. Her colorful sundress appeared out of place, whipping around her calves as her feet dug deep into the sand, and every line of her body was held taut with the fluid elegance of a dancer, her long arms raised before the raging sea. Her energy and movement alone made it very clear that if Lana had ever been human, it had been a very long time ago.

The Nymph peered over her shoulder, her golden eyes puckered in anxiety as she looked first at Blake, then at Reed and Leo as they stepped into place beside him. She turned her face back to the invisible wall she held up against the sea, and her shoulders slumped as the pressure became too much for her. Her body swayed with an uncertain rhythm, as if the push and pull of the tide called to her; her skin shifted with barely noticeable ripples.

"*Merde*, I don't know!" she shouted over the melee. "The Bering is usually difficult this time of the year, but I don't understand what's gotten into her. It's as though she's trying to devour the island!"

Blake clenched his jaw, and Reed gave a suggestive glance over his shoulder at Maia, still huddled by the pole. Placing a hand on the older man's shoulder, Blake gave Reed a shake of his head before returning his attention to Lana, who still struggled under the weight of the sea.

"What can we do to help, babe?" Leo asked. He'd finally stopped his agitated shifting, slipping into and out of different animals, long enough to speak.

"*Amour*, I don't know. It seems—" The Nymph hesitated, and then groaned as her feet sank deeper in the sand.

Poppy appeared on Lana's right and placed one hand over the girl's extended one, raising her other. For the moment, it seemed to give Lana relief. The waves began to slowly ebb, but somehow, Maia had a feeling they were just regrouping.

"*Mon dieu*," Lana panted. "Gather the village at the meeting hall. It leads into the center of the island, via tunnels. Poppy and I can only hold this wall for another twenty minutes. Maybe."

She looked to Poppy for confirmation and once the Ariel nodded, Blake turned to the others as they moved closer to Maia's hiding spot. The pole was becoming increasingly wet and slippery thanks to the ocean spray, and although she'd accumulated several scratches on her face from flying debris, she was determined not to loosen her hold. Who knew if she wouldn't simply fly away?

The men stopped in front of her, and with a start, she realized that none of them were bundled up like she was. Even though the wind whipped their hair and clothes, they looked neither cold, nor wet, despite the constant spray of the angry ocean. Maia's head spun with this new mystery as Reed's agitated voice broke through the howl of the storm.

"Blake, you know Maia could stop this. We all could, if we share the burden."

Blake shook his head. "Now's not the time, mate. We need to find out what Heidi knows first. I won't risk it."

Reed's only response was a dissatisfied grunt as he turned to stare morosely at the island's scant vegetation. Maia looked to Leo, but his eyes were glued to Lana as he wore a trail in the sand with his pacing. His protective growls grew more frustrated with every second.

Blake grabbed both men by the shoulder, until they finally made eye contact. "Look, the villagers know about the tunnels. A lot of them are already making their way there, so let's just help them get to safety, ar'right?"

Immediately, Leo nodded and set off, pausing only to lift his nose in the air, searching for signs of stranded villagers. It seemed he was every bit an animal even in human form.

Reed shrugged a disdainful shoulder and sauntered off at a leisurely pace. He didn't even pause when Blake reminded him to rescue the people and not the plants, just gave him the middle finger and walked away.

Blake chuckled when Reed's angry form broke into a run as he dashed into a nearby home. Turning to Maia, he grabbed one of her gloved hands and, with much coaxing, loosened her iron grip on the pole.

"It's going to be ar'right, *mia regina*. No one's going to hurt you while I'm around." Despite the anger that welled up at his comment and his self-satisfied smirk, Maia felt like a frozen Popsicle, and she was certain that if she moved, her bones would shatter. When Blake wrapped her in his arms, though, he warmed her enough to help her spit out a retort.

"Fuck up my name one more time, and I'll—"

"You'll what?" His husky laugh reverberated in her ear, causing the blood in her veins to boil in places she'd forgotten existed. He slid his fingers between the edges of her gloves and sleeves, and his touch on her bare wrist warmed her instantly to the core, like a cup of hot cocoa on a snowy day. His lips brushed her ear and she nearly lost his next words in the howl of the wind that whipped at the ends of her scarf. "It means, 'My Queen.'"

Thanks to the inebriated haze slowly working its way to her brain, he finally managed to pull her close. She was saved from attempting a witty comeback by the loud, crunching sound the pole made as it was flung into the storm.

Blake's joking manner subsided as he pulled Maia down the rubble-strewn streets.

Good God, she thought, *is this going to be a constant in our relationship? Wading through natural disaster and devastation?*

She nearly rolled her eyes at herself for already thinking the word "relationship" in terms of she and Blake, but Leo suddenly came sprinting forward to meet them. Skidding to a graceful stop, he fell into step beside them as Blake tugged Maia toward the safety of the meeting hall.

"Blake, the school's turned into a Death Star garbage compactor around those kids. And I ain't no R2-D2, man."

Blake looked between Leo and Maia, one each on either side of him, torn guilt straining his handsome features. He looked down a side street to the largest building in the town, holding up surprisingly well in the storm, and then behind him to the waves that were already beginning to crash to shore. Lana and Poppy had lost their battle, and it was clear that there was little time left.

Maia made his decision for him. "Blake." She grabbed his face with both hands and forced him to look at her. "Go. You need to go. I'm more than capable of making it on my own." She nodded toward the building. The sign marking it as the town hall and community center ripped away from where it was nailed near the building's entrance and flailed wildly over their heads, barely missing Leo's shoulder. Maia grabbed a wide-eyed Blake by the shoulders and shoved him in Leo's direction before she took off in a sprint toward the building, dodging flying debris and ignoring Blake's pleas for her to return.

She sprinted on, not looking back, and when she could no longer hear him, she hoped that it meant he'd gone to the school with Leo. She continued down the street as fast as she could, fighting the wind that pushed her sideways and cutting between buildings or beneath the risers to avoid large pieces of the village hurtling through the air.

She was only a few buildings away when the strong wind pushed her under the risers of a sturdy stone, solid-framed building that must have comprised the town's only office space. As she huddled against a post, steeling herself, she realized how cold she was without Blake. Tucking her scarf around her neck and fluffing the folds to make it bigger, she felt her ears prick up. Confused, she placed a hand over each lobe to make sure she hadn't grown the ears of a rabbit, and heard a new sound—crying. It was too faint for a normal human to hear beneath the storm's noise, but Maia wasn't sure how much of her humanness she had left. Every time the Earth's pleas, strength, and energy sizzled through her veins, she felt . . . well, she felt otherworldly. But now wasn't the time to define whether or not her humanity remained. Someone, or something, needed her. The noise came from deep within the sturdy stone and plank building above her. She twisted around, searching for the source of the sound, but found none.

Maybe she had been hearing things after all? Maia turned to look out into the street again; she was so close, maybe a hundred feet from the meeting hall. Close enough to see a few more crouching figures charging through its doors and into safety, and she hoped that if she ran fast enough, the clear path before her would remain that way.

Before she'd even lifted one foot off the ground, though, the cry came again. Louder this time, and sharper. She didn't know how she knew, but her emerging instincts told her that the cry had come from one of the back rooms.

Without thinking, she clamored up the building's decaying wood steps, rushed through the building's front room and down its single hall, sloshing through the water that was quickly pouring in and soaking the bottom of her pants. The crying grew louder as Maia drew closer to the door at the end. It sounded like a small child pleading, but she couldn't understand the words. Anxiety gripped her. She hoped a language barrier wouldn't prevent her from helping these people.

Her last step toward the door nearly had her face-planted against its plywood frame as she lunged forward. It took her a moment to realize that the misstep had been caused by her boot catching under something. She looked down, squinting in the low lighting as she tried to wiggle free, but the foaming black water was already creeping up her ankles, obscuring her vision. Maia groped blindly in the icy liquid, its white foam like bubbles in a bath, but her gloves were too thick for her to make out whatever was holding her down; she ripped them off and plunged her hands into the water, grasping for the object. The arctic sea water numbed her fingers before she could figure out what had caught her. Her fingers were red with freezing cold when she pulled them out of the water and shoved them deep into her pockets, her gloves nowhere to be seen. No matter how much she wiggled and strained her foot, it wasn't going anywhere, and the cries behind the door turned to muffled sobs as the rising water reached her waist.

Panicking, Maia slammed her numb hands against the door, screaming for help. She grabbed the brass doorknob and twisted it feverishly, hoping for an answer from whoever was on the other side.

The water lapped at her chest and she couldn't feel her lower body, but the door finally cracked under her fists. At first, she thought it was the pressure of the water swirling around her. Then she realized it was *her*. Despite the dents she'd made with her fists, the door still held strong.

The water reached her neck, and the only thing she could feel was the thud of her heart, frantically attempting to circulate blood to frozen limbs.

She shut her eyes and took several deep breaths as the frigid water licked her chin. *I'm not going to die freezing my ass off!* Her screams turned to gasps as her lungs refused to work. She was immobile, trapped, freezing—drowning. It was sudden and strange, but images of the ancient and crumbling temples of Asia, the cathedrals of Europe, the vast horizons of countless countrysides flashed through her mind. She desperately missed the weight of her camera's strap across the back of her neck. She had always wanted to travel, to capture every beautiful and wondrous sight with her lens. Just not like this. She thought of her father, tried to adopt his positive mentality, to choose the last thing she would see instead of a warped door and icy water.

The water was just under her nostrils now. She was certain she only had a few seconds left to breathe. She knew she could tilt her head up, could try to hold on for a little longer, but she quickly gave that up. It was pointless. She was miserable and wanted it to be over. So she let it.

Water flooded her mouth as she opened it wide and succumbed.

13

THE LAST IMAGE that flashed into her mind as darkness crept over her consciousness was an unexpected one: a face with sparkling blue eyes flecked with silver, framed in dirty-blond hair, wearing a mischievous grin. The grin puckered dramatically, the nostrils flared like the gills of a fish, and the eyes crossed under wiggling eyebrows.

A laugh gurgled in her throat; deeper down, something warm began to grow again, almost as if Blake was standing right next to her, touching every part of her skin. If hope could be felt by touch, she was sure it would have matched the velvety soft feeling warming every stressed muscle and tendon, straight down to her bones. She went from pleasantly warm to burning as the pins and needles of circulation began to wake her appendages, and she thrashed wildly, unable to notice the way her arms had been freed, or that they were suddenly dry. Maia coughed and looked down, blinking and rubbing her eyes in confusion. The water was receding . . . but how? She stared at the soaked carpet; her boot was wedged into the small hole of a decorative cabinet, soggy papers spilling out over open drawers.

Maia looked behind her, bewildered. Had Blake managed to find her?

But no one was there. Just her.

The water retreated to the end of the hall where, in the front room, it reached nearly to the ceiling. It was as though a glass wall held the water back, even as it strained and coiled with pressure.

Crouching into a squat, Maia slid her hands beneath the cabinet and lifted it with surprising ease. It was lighter than it should have been—lighter than a marshmallow, even—and she tossed it to the side.

Captivated and confused by the lack of moisture on her warm hands, Maia reached again for the brass doorknob. It resisted her when she first twisted it, metal screeching against metal, but with another yank, it broke off in her hand. She pushed the door open and dashed into the room.

A woman lay unconscious on the floor, a large gash on her head dripping blood that pooled and mixed with the inch of water on the ground. Two small children huddled by her side. The oldest couldn't have been more than eight, and he rose quickly at Maia's loud entrance, his tear-streaked face defiant as he pushed his little sister behind his back. He muttered a command to her in the foreign language Maia had heard in their cries.

Maia took a step forward, but the boy backed up, nearly causing his sister to stumble over the woman's legs. The little girl screamed and pointed at something behind Maia. She twisted around and saw the wall of water looming closer, furious at being held at bay.

Instinct alone made Maia throw up an arm, mimicking the way Lana had reacted to the ocean outside. The water stopped in its tracks, but the force of holding it back pressed against her arm as though she pushed open a heavy door. Her muscles strained; she braced her feet against the floor, but she wasn't sure how long she could hold it.

As her arm weakened from the effort, she turned toward the children again. "Can you speak English?"

The little boy nodded. His sister's dark head peeked out over his thin shoulder.

"Good. My name is Maia, and there's a really bad storm outside. I need to get you to safety, okay?"

The little boy shook his head and pointed to the woman on the floor.

Maia took another hesitant step forward and heard the water follow, splashing and churning in frustration. "Is this your mother?"

The boy shuddered, his clothes dripping wet, and shook his head.

Maia reached behind her and closed the door before rushing to the woman's side, kneeling and checking for a pulse; she had none. The water outside slammed against the door, pouring in through the cracks, but it stopped three feet away from where she crouched. It formed a circle around her, nearly ten feet in diameter, and though it filled the room quickly, she and the children standing next to her remained untouched.

Maia held out her hand to the little boy. "What's your name?"

His eyes flicked to the woman on the ground nervously as the water built around them, and he slowly took in the dry circle he and his sister stood in. Putting a protective arm around his sister, he placed his hand in Maia's warm one, grasping it firmly. "Aleksei," he said. Then he nodded to the little girl clutching his waist. "Innya."

Maia shook his hand. "It's very nice to meet you, Aleksei and Innya." She gave them each her most comforting smile, and before she could encourage them to follow her to safety, the little girl twisted away from her brother's grip. She threw her tiny arms around Maia's neck and peppered her cheeks with kisses. Maia squeezed the little girl back and looked into her smiling face as the child babbled in an unknown language, then looked to Aleksei. Worry tightened his young brow.

Placing Innya on her hip, Maia stood and tugged Aleksei along by the hand. Their circle of dryness moved with them, keeping the swirling waters at bay as they hopped over fallen furniture, their shoes squishing in the wet carpet. Maia kicked the door open and guided the children through the strange hallway formed of walled water.

"What's she singing?" Maia asked Aleksei. Innya had begun to clap her hands, and she bounced excitedly to a little song that chirped out of her like she was an excited nightingale. Aleksei shrugged his shoulders with the mature indifference of an adult.

"Baby songs," he mumbled. Concern continued to crease his small features, though, and he soon tapped his sister's leg, begging her to hush. Innya responded by nodding and humming instead.

Maia didn't hesitate when they reached the doorway leading to the street. Regardless of the raging ocean before her, she was certain that the warm bubble she'd created would protect them until they reached the town hall.

One step forward, however, and she realized she was wrong. Though the water continued to be held mostly at bay, it splashed around their ankles and thighs when she threw open the door, soaking them in seconds. Maia felt the heat retreat from her body as the goose bumps returned. She closed her eyes for a moment and took a deep breath. Remembering Reed's instructions from the forest, she tried focusing on the energy within. Clearing her mind, she turned inward, feeling the heat of creation on the edges of her senses, receding quickly amongst the noise. Here, the storm was too strong; there were too many angry elements to control.

Looking around frantically, she exhaled, trying to release the anxiety-laden air that constricted her lungs and made it impossible to breathe. Then she saw their salvation, a tiny boat that came bobbing within reach. Placing Innya on the floor of the room behind her, she turned to face the storm and grabbed the approaching skiff, holding on to a long rope attached to its prow. Tying one end to the railing of the stairs next to the door and hoping that her clumsy knot would suffice, she grabbed the siblings one at a time and placed them on the floor of the boat.

She peered into the vessel, her hope falling again when she saw no oars. They had to move, though. Maia peered at the raging waters; could she swim it? She rolled her shoulders back, massaging and stretching muscles she hadn't deployed in that fashion in years. She was grateful for childhood swimming lessons, but whether or not she was strong enough to fight the current and pull the boat, she wasn't sure. She bit her bottom lip; it didn't matter, though. She'd have to at least try. She untied the rope from the railing and tied it securely around her waist instead.

"Hold on to your sister," she yelled to the boy. "I'm gonna have to swim!"

Aleksei nodded, and he wrapped his arms tightly around the little girl as Maia dove into the icy water.

The heat inside her body was still there, but under the water, it rapidly grew weaker. It took all of Maia's inner strength to hold on to the energy while her arms sliced through the cold water. It wouldn't do the children any good if she froze to death; that thought alone spurred her onward.

Her arms and legs grew heavier the longer she swam. Slowly, they began to numb again. She pushed forward, attempting a glance over her shoulder to make sure the children were still safe. Saltwater burned her eyes, blurring her vision. It clogged her nostrils and throat with each turn of her head. She narrowly missed being hit with a piece of flying, floating debris as she coughed and sputtered. Still, when she looked back, she managed to make out the two small figures in the boat—huddled, wet, and cold. But safe. They were safe.

Finally, she reached the town hall. The front doors were already completely drowned in water, so she grabbed a piece of floating debris to smash a window that let into what looked like a small office. Holding the boat as steady as she could, she found purchase on a narrow ledge with her feet and bashed through the window. She gripped the window frame, muscles straining, as Aleksei helped his sister over the broken glass and into the room. Inside, worried voices and a crowd of hands swarmed the window, pulling the children through to safety.

Maia had just caught the sight of two familiar, worried faces when a deafening crack above her diverted her attention.

She looked up, and barely had enough time to raise her arm before a part of the easement above came crashing down in a flurry of splintered wood, slamming into her temple. Spots exploded behind her eyes, and her vision was snuffed out once more.

14

MAIA FELT COOLNESS on her cheeks. The rest of her body was quite warm and comfortable, but a fresh breeze ruffled through her hair, tickling her scalp. Was she outside, or stuck under an air conditioning vent? Her forehead bunched up in confusion. Her eyes felt glued shut, but she could smell fresh earth all around her as the breeze laughed and played. She reveled in its voice.

For a moment, Maia felt important in the breeze's attention, and she smiled pleasantly before another thought skipped through her mind: none of this added up. Something wasn't right.

Opening her eyes, she noticed Poppy twirling over her head, dancing with an invisible partner, singing a bawdy Celtic song that Maia was sure would make her blush if she could understand the words. Poppy's dancing was suggestive enough.

Her head throbbed and she let out a slight groan as she stretched, splaying her fingers across her stomach, feeling their strength. Focusing on them was a welcome distraction, but it was short lived as, next to her, the bed shifted suddenly. Letting out a yelp, she nearly tumbled to the floor before a strong arm wrapped around her waist and placed her back against the sunken feather pillow.

"Didn't mean to frighten you."

Maia looked up into a pair of very worried blue eyes, and the bed shifted again as Blake stood, stuffing his hands in his pockets, his accent growing thicker with his concern. "There really is no other place to sit in here." He motioned to the cramped room, spreading his arms wide. His hands touched the opposing walls, which were unfinished and colored by a mixture of dark gray and black, with streaks of glittering white sprawling out in various directions. They looked wet to the touch, but when she swiped at the wall with a finger, it was completely dry.

"Oh." Maia looked down then, mortified to see that she was wearing a different set of clothes. She felt like a prude, Victorian debutante as she pulled the covers up to her neck, and her squeaked, "It's okay," was quickly bulldozed by a more important question. "Who changed my clothes?" She looked at Blake as she squirmed down further into the flannel quilt and willed her face to stop burning.

Blake cleared his throat and looked away. "Lana did, with some of the tribe's female healers. It, uh, was necessary to keep you from getting hypothermia. You were pretty wet."

His voice cracked on the last word as he turned his attention to the poem Poppy was reciting now that her song was over.

"Huh." Maia lifted her head from under the covers to ask the next most important question. "Where are we? Are the children all right?"

Blake met her eyes once more, wearing an unreadable expression. His t-shirt was gone, replaced with a dark gray cardigan and dark, inky jeans. Maia wondered where he got all his nice clothes from—frivolous thoughts helped keep her from drowning in the depths of his gaze—when they were stuck in the middle of nowhere. A flooded middle of nowhere at that.

"Aleksei and Innya? They're fine. They're with some relatives of theirs. They'll be glad to see you're well, though. We've had a bit of a hard time keeping them away." He smiled and shook his tousled head, ducking it low as he concentrated on his shoe scuffing the floor. "Innya seemed to think you needed to be kissed awake like some sleeping princess."

"Oh." Maia wasn't sure what to say, but she was glad his eyes weren't witnessing the blush that spread across her cheeks like wildfire.

Blake waved a hand idly in the air, indicating the room. "The town's community hall doubles as their tribal meeting place. It's set into the mountain, and there are tunnels that run throughout, leading to Russia. The entrance has now been sealed, as the island is submerged."

A soft knock sounded on the stone doorframe of the tiny room, and Lana poked her head in. "She awake?"

Blake nodded and she strode in, her corkscrew curls bouncing with every step. "*Bonjour.*" She extended a dainty brown hand. "I don't think we got a chance to officially meet. I'm Lana."

Maia grasped the cool hand and shook it, feeling nervous as she remembered that this woman had seen her naked. Judging by the Beyonce-like curves that filled out her maroon, V-neck sweater and black skinny jeans capped in little black booties, Maia was sure Lana had zero body confidence issues.

"It's nice to meet you, too. I, uh, guess you know who I am?"

"*Mais oui.*" Lana's laugh was like the pleasant sound of a gurgling brook. "Everyone does. Speaking of which, now that you've woken, the tribe has called the ceremony into session."

The irritated pulse of Blake's energy was palpable as he turned a stony expression on Lana. "No. Tell them they're going to have to wait. Maia isn't well enough. She still needs to rest."

Maia opened her mouth to protest, but was interrupted by Poppy, who had ended her latest song and dance and sat primly in the doorway, hovering in an invisible chair.

"'*Mine little hill is all the world!' spake he,*
until mankind stepped beyond the treeline.
'*Mine little tribe is most mighty' spake he,*
'*til emerged the armies of Byzantine.*
'*Mine island's alone in all the sea!' spake he,*
Until fleets with cannon cut through the waves.
'*This nation of mine is most prime!' spake he.*
'*til standing beside Plato he fled the Caves.*
'*This Creed of mine is most righteous!' spake he.*
Even now he awaits the Lord's Salvation.
'*Around mine Earth revolves the Sun!' spake he.*
And coerced Galileo's recantation.
Whatever may be that Man has decreed,
look not at his words but unto his deed."

As she ended her poem, she stuck out her tongue and blew a raspberry at Blake.

Lana threw her head back with a throaty laugh. "That's my girl!"

In the face of Blake's glare, she wiped her eyes of amused tears. "Sorry, cher, but you had it coming! Stop being a control freak. It's time for Maia to face the music. She needs answers . . . we all do."

Poppy nodded her agreement and twirled out the door, while Lana looked back and forth between Blake and Maia for a moment, her full lips pursed in a smirk. "I'll see you in the great hall in five." She spun on her heel and followed Poppy, calling over her shoulder, "Don't make me come back and drag you out there!"

Blake snorted and rolled his eyes before realizing that Maia was already slipping her feet into a fresh pair of boots. Thankfully, Blake's ability to conjure decent clothes seemed to extend to her, too. The white sweater she'd found at the foot of the bed wrapped her in its touch and had a wide enough neck to allow it to fall slightly off one shoulder, and the skinny jeans fit her like a second skin. She hated to admit it in a time like this, but the boots she was carefully pulling on—comfy black knee-highs with buckles crossing the calf—were the same ones she'd lusted after in a Portland store window for months. She'd never have been able to afford them, not when her entire paycheck had gone to helping her parents pay for her father's treatment.

"Whoa, slow down, *mia regina*!" Blake reached out to steady her as she stood on shaky feet. She ripped her elbow from his grip as she stomped by him and out the door. A wave of irritation shivered across her skin. She couldn't let him know how she felt about him. She still hadn't decided what those feelings were, even, or how to label them.

"For the last time, my name is Maia, and I *don't* need a knight in shining armor." She slammed her feet extra hard on the stone floor to prove her point, despite needing to hold on to the cave's slick wall for balance.

"Fine, fine. I get it, but at least let me show you the right direction." Blake pasted on one of his dazzling smiles, but it didn't hide the hurt on the rest of his face. Regardless, it still melted her insides, and she hated that it did. Using her anger to steady the buzzing in her brain, she powered forward, following his direction.

They didn't have very far to go before they walked through a large arch that opened into a wide room. Inside, there were about thirty men and women waiting. Some were huddled together on wooden benches, deep in conversation. Others had formed a group at the front of the room, talking to a man wearing what Maia assumed was the traditional dress of the tribe. Her presence went unnoticed, and the room's tension continued to crackle and strain as she followed the wide path between the rows of benches to where the man stood.

The room stilled as everyone's gaze rested on Maia and Blake, and even in the silence, there was a strange hum of energy vibrating throughout, punctuated by the ominous drip of water falling from the stalactites encircling the space.

The crowd surrounding the tribe's chief parted, staring unabashedly at Maia and Blake as they came to a halt before the old man.

When she looked into the kind face of the chief, Maia's face fell slack in awe. His long hair peeked out from his head-dress, completely white in color, but his face was unlined.

The only mark of age his face bore was the wisdom in his nearly black eyes.

He bowed deeply before Blake, then again before Maia. Blake returned the motion, and Maia mirrored their movements, glad no one could see the sweat forming tiny pools in her palms and beading across her brow, in spite of the room's damp chill. The chief motioned to a pair of chairs behind him. Maia noticed with a start that they looked suspiciously like thrones, carved out of the cave's stone and set into the rock. Blake easily folded his tall figure into the one on the left, without hesitation, and motioned for her to sit next to him. A reverent solemnity laced the tension in the room, causing Maia to lower herself as gracefully as she could. Her knees had other plans, however, wobbling in nervousness, and she plopped rather than sat. She could feel in her bones that, whatever was about to commence, it was sacred.

Facing the township now scattered about the room, the chief stood next to a large fragment of jagged rock, covered in the same kinds of symbols and glyphs Maia had seen in Blake's notes. She rubbed her right hand on her armrest and was surprised to notice that one of the symbols had been carved into the stone under her fingertips; it resembled a trifecta, but with four extra loops. She ran her fingers along the symbol's smooth edges, and the rhythmic pattern of her moving fingers relaxed her until her muscles felt as though they'd dissolved into liquid. It wasn't long before she could no longer hear the chief's steady voice as he addressed the room, could no longer see the sweeping gestures he sent in Blake and Maia's direction. It was as though her eyelids were made of a soft silk, sliding down from her brow. She felt strange, and soon, she had lost all feeling entirely.

Her world didn't darken, though. Instead, the room before her disappeared in an amber haze of soft light, until Maia found herself in the most beautiful garden she'd ever seen. Nothing could compare to the vibrant colors that arrested her eyes, not even the Photoshopped pictures from the gardening magazines and books that had littered the coffee table at home. Flora carpeted the ground in velvety soft leaves and silky petals, and trees of every size and canopy covered the sky above her, revealing only trace amounts of blue and blinding sun peeking through. Maia couldn't name or even recognize the plants she saw, but they awoke all of her senses, as if she could feel the very essence of each color, a concentrated jolt of the creation energy she had felt before. The myriad of plants whispered, as if each had their own personality and words to say.

She didn't notice when she began moving, but suddenly, she was floating, making her way between the vibrant foliage, listening to the chatter. She felt as if she could understand them, not their words, but their needs and wants, the way a mother understands each of her child's different cries.

Maia walked through a series of unmarked paths and eventually entered a tiny clearing with a babbling brook running through the center. At its side, its neck bent delicately to get a cool drink, was an elegant creature, its body like that of a deer, but with a thick black stripe that dashed across its side and antlers that twisted gracefully, like a dancer's body. Instinct begged her not to approach the wild animal, but as it lifted its head slowly, piercing her with large, intelligent eyes, Maia couldn't help but draw closer. Soon, she was near enough to see each droplet of water escape its soft chin.

"Maia Thompson," it said. Its voice echoed with ancient wisdom, but was unlike any voice Maia had ever heard.

She wasn't quite sure where her body was, so Maia was surprised to hear her voice reply, "Yes?"

The creature blinked slowly in response. Walking on thin, nimble legs, it led her to the shade of a nearby tree that Maia was sure had never existed in the lifetime of humans; it dispensed small, fluffy lavender flowers into the light breeze like a colorful snowfall. The creature sat, then waited until Maia had joined it before continuing.

"Maia, you have been chosen as the next Terra *praeses* of Earth. Are you ready to accept this role?"

She hesitated, a strange disappointment settling on her shoulders. She'd thought for sure that this would entail some sort of ceremony and solid oath.

"It will, on both accounts," the creature said, answering her confused thoughts. "Whether you choose this path or not."

Maia wanted to feel peeved at the intrusion, but she wasn't. There was an odd sense of attachment to this creature, and suddenly, she couldn't bear to disappoint it. "Do I get a chance to think about it? I mean"—she attempted to wade through the anxiety tightening like a steel trap around her chest— "couldn't I know more about it first?"

"I see that you are afraid. This is good," the creature replied, slowly nodding.

Maia felt her silky eyelids slide down in blinking confusion. Strange, to feel a reflex so acutely.

"Ask me what you will," the creature said. It gained a keen tilt to its head, and its round eyes roamed over her face, making her feel vulnerable, as if it knew all of her secrets.

Before fear could suffocate Maia in its grip, she became aware of her body. She felt the tickle of the grass beneath her bare legs and, looking down, saw her folded knees peeking out from the hem of a light yellow eyelet dress. Taking a deep breath, she gathered her thoughts and began with the easiest, least obvious question she could think of.

"Who are you, and where are we?"

The creature's mouth tilted at the edges in what Maia hoped was a smile. "I am a gazelle, and my name is not important right now. However, we are in a safe place, built by your soul's consciousness, and it is my job to guide you as you make your decision."

"Don't you mean subconscious?"

"I am not mean. I am reason."

Maia rolled her eyes at his vague answer before swallowing thickly under his disapproving glare. It wasn't exactly the kind of answer she'd wanted, but there were more important questions to dwell on.

"Fine. Whatever. Can you at least tell me what, exactly, I'm expected to do?"

"Your path to accepting this role is unclear at this time. You must decide your course of action."

The answer irritated her, but only slightly. It was vague and annoying, yes, but it also gave her hope: she could still make her own choice.

"What can I do to stop Heidi from destroying the world in search of me?"

"You are almost at the right question, but not quite," the gazelle said. "But since we are low on time, I will answer the correct one: you are the only one who remains to restore Heidi's balance, but first, you must find your own balance of energy by choosing which energy to take. No one can tell you how to accomplish this. You must use the resources given to you. A general is useless without his most loyal soldiers."

The gazelle's answer only confused her further. "I don't understand. Is there a choice between having celestial and astral energy?"

"There is always a choice. A *praeses* is not exclusively a guardian of this planet, nor do they all consist of one energy over another. Each has both, some more than most. You must choose: will you create, or will you destroy? Or will you straddle the river, a foot upon both banks?"

Maia avoided the gazelle's eyes as it spoke. She stuck her pinky through one of the larger eyelets of the dress as she let its words sink in. "That sounds . . . complicated."

The gazelle smiled. "Spoken like a true *praeses*."

She smiled finally. "You know, for a guide, you really aren't very helpful."

It nodded. "You wish me to give you answers to an uncertain future. That is not my job. You will have to suffer the consequences of your chosen actions, good or bad, like everyone else."

"Hmph," Maia snorted, stretching her legs out before her and wiggling her toes.

"You have not asked me about your *fulcrum*. Do you not care to acknowledge him?" The gazelle's tone was one of modest surprise.

Maia quirked a quizzical brow. "*Fulcrum?*"

The gazelle nodded sagely, the tips of its horns coming dangerously close to Maia's eyes. She dodged her head to the side. "Indeed. At your galaxy's birth, the deaths of the first stars created a unique black hole. The souls of the praeses were pulled from the depths of this black hole, from its anima. This anima was then split, creating astrums and, if the stars died close enough together and their black masses combined, the twins known as novae. Every praeses must have an equal, an astrum to align and balance their gifts and powers. No astrum will ever be whole without the other, its fulcrum. Your soul is no different. Creation does not build without chaos; chaos does not destroy without creation. Power is born of weakness, and weakness of power. It is what you are and what he is. I believe you humans have a term . . ."

The gazelle tilted its head in puzzlement as Maia tried to remember if she'd seen anything about this in Blake's notebook. "No, the term 'soul mate' no longer fits, but it comes close."

Maia chewed on her lip as the pieces of the explanation clicked into place, her head bobbing slightly as realization sank in.

"Balance." She breathed a heavy sigh at the weight of the idea. She had always been taught to value independence. That it was better to only need herself; that true happiness came from within. The idea that she needed the help of another, in any capacity, rankled against that foundation. She looked up into the tree's branches. The shedding blossoms brushed against her face, soft as feathers. "Even so, soul mates are a fantasy. You can't expect me to believe there is only one person out there for each of us?"

A few moments of silence passed. Startled at the quiet, Maia looked around for the gazelle, thinking perhaps it had left. Instead, she found that its small body was still curled up next to her, an eon of patience in its large eyes. Maia frowned, unsure of what to say.

It shook its head finally, its twisted horns swaying as if it was laughing. "Humanity has blinded you into seeing walls and chains where there are none. You doubt what could be. Even after all you've witnessed." Its voice hardened. "You will not win this war without it. You have a duty now, child."

"I didn't ask for any of this." Maia wasn't sure where her anger had come from, but it erupted in her chest like a volcano. "My home's been destroyed, my parents are dead, my *life's* been turned into a Z-rated sci-fi flick." Her chest rose and fell with the wave of her words, and she welcomed the pain of the soil and stone cutting into her palms as her fingers dug into the earth beneath her. "I don't have to believe in anything. Ignorance is bliss, isn't it?"

Her skin flashed hot, then cold, and she shivered against the premonition in her gut. Her life had been mediocre—miserable, at best—and she knew it. Guilt tumbled through her, making her nauseous, and her head swam with shame. How could she say that about everything her family had given her? Her parents and home were gone, and in some sick, sad way, she was relieved? She was horrible. Suddenly, she was eager to believe she wasn't human. Maybe that could explain why she was glad that it was all finally gone. She didn't have to waste her life away on the precipice of not knowing, uncertain whether or not the next day would bring joy or the despair of death. It was over.

"If you are quite finished, Maia?" The gazelle sighed as Maia's fists slowly unclenched and she relaxed. "Good. I suggest you find your *astrum* quickly, for he is an important part of this equation."

A mischievous golden face flashed through Maia's mind as the gazelle spoke, and she opened her eyes quickly before the mirth of the blue eyes in her thoughts could produce another giggle from her. It annoyed her, the way his image could appear at any time, how not even the serenity of this place could erase it. She was going to need to sort through her mixed feelings of animosity and unreasonable desire, and soon. She needed to focus. If this was truly war, she didn't have time for flirtation, or any of this *astrum*, soul mate nonsense. Her heart had been torn asunder one too many times. Now, it belonged to her alone.

Maia glared at the gazelle, who replied with a lazy blink. She had more questions now than ever. Blake's notes hadn't mentioned these *astrum* or *novae*, and she had a feeling that the gazelle's explanation had only scratched the surface.

"Fine," Maia lied. "I'll work on it."

"See that you do." The gazelle raised itself languidly from its position and began trotting away. As it bound over the tiny brook in a single graceful leap, it turned back to Maia, who watched it, astonished and confused at its sudden exit.

"Our time is up, Maia Thompson, but here is a hint: the answer to the next question is, 'Yes.'"

With that, and a flick of its black tail, it turned around and disappeared into the thick brush.

The amber haze clouded Maia's vision again, and as the exotic garden faded away, the cavern room and its ongoing meeting swirled into focus.

Maia wasn't sure what she'd missed, and she touched her chin on the pretense of scratching an itch to make sure she wasn't drooling. She stole a sideways glance at Blake, who smiled at her. There was a slight squeeze of her left hand, and she realized his fingers were clasped around hers and that his gentle energy was pulsing through her veins, making her more alert. She offered him a weak smile in return and gently tugged her hand free. He frowned at the action, which she purposefully ignored. As Maia rubbed her palms together, checking for perspiration, the chief turned to face them. The rest of the room's occupants rose to their feet and joined him.

"Maia Thompson." The chief's voice echoed against the walls like a pealing bell. Leo, Poppy, Reed, and Lana stood behind him, looking at her as though she held the key to something precious.

"Here." She was shocked at the strength of her voice, despite the nervous flutter of her heart, beating like frantic wings, creating a pulse she felt against the lining of her stomach.

"Will you accept the responsibility placed before you?"

Her mouth gaped in uncertainty, opening and closing like a fish gasping for air. Was this the question she was supposed to say "yes" to? She wasn't even sure what she was agreeing to.

Swallowing thickly and feeling the pressure of the expectant glances in the room, Maia took a deep breath. "Yes."

A sigh of relief rippled through the room's occupants. The energy emanating from it caressed her face and enveloped her like a warm hug.

The chief smiled warmly. Holding out his hand, he directed her to the ancient stone next to him as she moved forward.

"Maia, please place your hands on the stone." He nodded to the rest of the guardians, who joined her and crowded around the stone, shoulders bumping softly.

Maia wrapped her hands around the tip of the jagged rock, where the chief had indicated. Blake stood on the other side and wrapped his hands around hers, intertwining their fingers. On her left, Poppy wrapped both of her soft hands around Maia's left forearm; Lana repeated the same movement on Maia's right. On either side of Blake, Reed and Leo each pressed their hands to Maia and Blake's intertwined fingers, until finally, Maia felt the pulsing energy of every guardian pouring through her skin. The round stone beneath their hands pulsed and glowed with the various shades of nature as a new myriad of tingling energy and adrenaline-fueled strength surged and prickled through Maia's veins, strengthening her bones and muscles in a way she never thought possible. She felt the fibers of her muscles expand, the alveoli in her lungs bloomed like fresh buds in spring, and her bones, themselves, seemed to gain density.

"Brothers and sisters," announced the chief, "you bear witness today to the binding of these five souls to our Mother Earth upon this Core crystal. We have been entrusted with the knowledge of this vessel of celestial energy and placed as protectors of its location. As such, we are proprietors of not only this symbol of creation, but also the power it holds within."

Heat prickled across Maia's skin, followed by a cool breeze. She felt water rushing through her veins and pounding in her ears, and a primal instinct known only to animals quickened her heart. Finally, much like the ivy seen slithering down the trunks of trees, her hair began to grow, thick locks curling and tumbling over her shoulders, cascading down her back. She shivered in surprise as the physical exertion of these changes caused beads of sweat to erupt along her hairline and upper lip.

The chief turned from the crowd as they murmured their acquiescence, bearing witness to the ceremony before them. His dark eyes searched the face of each *praeses* around the stone and, finding what he was looking for, he uttered the binding words.

"Maia Thompson, you are now bound to these souls as they are bound to you. Their energy flows through every fiber of your being, but be warned—full use of their energy is forbidden without their express permission. Do you accept their sacrifice?"

Maia cast a frightened look at each of the faces before her, weighted with the guilt of such a burden. To her surprise, each one, even the reluctant Reed, assured her with a nod or smile what her answer should be.

"Yes."

15

THE CEREMONY CONCLUDED with a last spark of
light from the stone, and the cavern erupted in happy chaos.
Awestruck, Maia stood by, her tingling hands falling limp to
her sides as the entire village swarmed into the cavern. People
were embracing, laughing, crying, singing; delicious-smelling
food was brought in and the benches were shoved to the side
to make room for pop-up tables. Music began to play in the
corner, the sound growing louder as more musicians pulled
up chairs and joined in mid-harmony. It was surreal, even
before Maia realized that she had a long line in front of her,
made up of the townsfolk who were bringing their children
to shake her hands and give her hugs; she was thrilled to see

Aleksei and Innya in the hands of a kind young couple who could have easily been their older siblings, though.

Maia kneeled to wrap her arms around the excited toddler whose arms were stretched to the sky, waving with the excited request for attention. Innya immediately jumped into Maia's outstretched arms and wouldn't let go as she stood to ruffle Aleksei's black hair, and shake hands with their new family. Maia wanted to ask the young couple their names, but before she had a chance, they were jostled to the side, Innya reluctantly pried from Maia's waist as the jubilant crowd of well-wishers waited impatiently for their turn.

Through it all, overwhelming anxiety hovered at the edge of her emotions, threatening to bleed through as she stared, exhausted, down the never-ending line. When a cool hand gripped her arm and started pulling her away, relief flooded through her.

"All right, everyone, Miss Thompson needs to eat, too. She's not invincible yet!"

The crowd laughed with good nature as Lana led Maia to a table already occupied by the rest of the Gaea *praeses*, who were busy digging into their own steaming plates of food.

"Wow," Maia said. She sat next to Blake, in the only seat left open. "I didn't think you guys ate."

"Well," Leo answered around a mouthful of ribs. He had one arm slung around Lana's shoulders, and he ran a tender thumb across her collarbone. Maia shivered at the intimacy that radiated between them and wondered idly if they were these so-called *astrum* things. "Technically, we don't have to."

"Yeah," Reed piped up, his own plate towering with a colorful, leafy salad. "But good food is a terrible thing to waste."

He threw Maia a wink and a teasing smile before stuffing a large bite into his mouth.

Maia didn't know what to make of his change in attitude toward her, but before she could ponder it, a burst of jealous energy brushed against her senses and she quickly forgot about both Reed and her growling stomach.

"All right, that's it." Shoving her plastic chair back so hard it toppled over, she grabbed Blake by the collar, pulling him up with more strength than she thought she had. "We need to talk."

Trying to ignore the fact that her tug on his collar had almost ripped the sweater right off his toned body—and had exposed a sliver of the golden stomach underneath—Maia did an about-face and stormed off toward the closest tunnel. She only half hoped that he would take the hint and follow.

She was less than two steps away when she felt him matching her stride. It was indescribable, how intimate his very presence felt, even without a word or touch. Before Blake, she'd never been so keenly aware of someone's presence in her life, and it caused goose bumps to skitter across her shoulders.

The tunnel she'd chosen was close to the kitchens, which meant every person she passed was too laden with food trays and utensils to do more than give her a bright smile and a thankful nod. Maia was grateful for that; she wanted to get this over with, for better or worse. Rip the Band-Aid.

Crossing her arms tight around her chest and hunching her shoulders to contain the nervous butterflies fluttering around her ribcage, she stepped into the first doorway she could find. Realizing too late that she'd stepped into the pantry, she turned around to leave, but instead bumped right into the lanky Aussie dogging her every step.

Grunting in frustration and swallowing her nerves, she pushed against his solid barrel of a chest. "Not here," she grumbled. She shoved by him and continued down the tunnel, past the battery-run floodlights fastened to the walkway every few feet. The industrial glow of the fluorescent bulbs bothered her; their sterile brightness intruded upon the beauty of the cavern walls.

The next door she came to led into a small room that looked like it might have been someone's bedroom and office, judging by the old army cot shoved between the wall and the modern-style desk that looked like it had come straight out of an IKEA catalog. Hoping Blake wouldn't get the wrong idea about the bed, she chose to stand in front of the only remaining wall, situated next to the door. Unfortunately, that wall was already occupied by an overflowing bookshelf. By the time Blake entered, shutting the door behind him, it was nearly impossible for them to face each other without touching.

Maia folded her arms across her chest again, attempting to keep even the fabric of her sweater from touching him. The close confines of the room made her stomach flip. If he was anything like her ex—she glanced nervously at the door, trying to remember every self-defense move she had learned and wondering if she could remember the way back to the party. Attempting to regain control of her tumultuous nerves, she leaned back against the bookshelf, testing her weight against it as Blake faced her, his teasing eyes continually flicking to the cot and back to her.

"So." He stuffed his hands into the pockets of his jeans, and Maia gulped as she watched his sweater bunch and strain against his muscular shoulders. Chastising herself at the strange yearning tugging its way through her heart, she gave herself a good shake. She should be scared, shouldn't she?

"What is your problem?" She demanded, and watched with slight satisfaction as the adorable smirk he often wore quickly faltered at her tone. But that same satisfaction soon became tinged with a nagging guilt. Blake had never given her any reason to conflate him with her ex, had never given any indication that he would ever hurt her. Yet her instincts continued to battle between pulling him close and running far, far away. She just didn't know anymore which emotion was true.

"Ah . . . I'm not sure what you mean?"

Frustrated, Maia ran her hand through her hair—now much longer than she was used to wearing it—and her fingers caught at the nape of her neck in a thick tangle she had to shake free. Her cheeks were tinged with heat by the time she was done, but she was unaware of how much more alluring her anger-infused embarrassment made her to him.

"Every time someone of the opposite sex speaks to me, touches me, or even looks at me, you get all possessive and jealous. You do this bizarre . . . I don't know, humming thing. It's freaking me out. What is that?"

His eyebrows bunched over his confused cerulean eyes as he took a step forward, frowning slightly. Maia's breath hitched at his even closer proximity. "I'm sorry." His voice was almost a whisper, his breath a warm caress. "I thought . . ." He seemed to be struggling for words, but all Maia could think about was how close he was. He smelled like freshly baked snickerdoodles, and . . . are those freckles under his eyelashes? She knew girls who would kill for long lashes like those. "Didn't you—don't you—feel it, too?"

Maia had to pinch herself to focus on the fact that his thin, precisely defined lips were her asking a question—and where only a hair's breadth away from her own. The room spun.

Maia struggled to concentrate, grasping at the questions dancing through her thoughts. What did feel when she was around him? Her only answer was, irritated, frustrated, but then . . . she wasn't ready to put a name to the other emotions fighting their way through her childish insecurities. A thesaurus would be needed for that task. But there were those dreams, too. She'd seen him before. It was like he'd always been there, but—no. She closed her eyes against the clamoring questions racing around her mind, inciting her nerves into a riot. That was crazy.

"F-feel what?" she managed to choke out as she searched for something, anything, else to look at besides him.

He sighed softly, and the smell of the first breeze of summer caressed her face as he stepped back. A big part of her wanted to pull him back into the empty space before her, but she squeezed her arms tighter around herself and pinched her arms once more to stay focused.

"I'm sorry. It's just—" He had removed his hands from his pockets, and now busied himself with locking his fingers together, twisting them back and forth. Maia wanted to kiss him. The images of her dreams returned stronger than ever, and her lips nearly burned with the memory. She had only seen glimpses of ease and lightheartedness in the brief time she'd known him—and that was when it hit her. The only times he'd looked relaxed and even remotely happy were when he was looking at her, teasing her. She had taken it for a nuisance, but the very thought that it could be something more melted her insides like butter. Her heart thudded wildly in her chest and her breath came out an uncertain shiver. *Good God, what is this man doing to me?*

Several heart-wrenching emotions warred across his handsome features before he took a deep breath, steeling himself for something. Gripping the desk behind him for support, Blake looked at her imploringly. "Do you remember when you woke up at the cabin?"

Maia's eyes widened at the question as a long-forgotten emotion swept through her. "Yes," she said. Her shoulders slumped under a grief she still didn't know how to deal with. From the look on his face, Blake hated bringing up such a fragile memory, however important. Still, Maia averted her eyes.

"Remember the first time you said my name?"

"Yeah." She relaxed a bit as she realized the conversation wasn't going to dwell on her pain, and the corners of her lips tweaked up slightly. "You seemed oddly shocked at me saying it. What's wrong, never had someone say your name before?"

His eyes brightened, his spirits lifting at her teasing tone. When he spoke, though, he sounded as if he was still proceeding with caution. "Well, it wasn't just anyone saying my name." He raised his brows and leaned forward, as if he expected some kind of "eureka" moment from her.

Maia let out a trembling breath before shaking her head again. Blake's eyes roved over her face, memorizing her every response. She lifted her eyes to meet his once more.

"I'm afraid I still don't get what's going on here. I said your name, who cares? I just want an answer. I want to know why you're acting like a jealous boyfriend all the time. I mean, we hardly know each other and aren't exactly—"

Maia's rush of words were drowned out by the press of velvety soft lips against her own, moving as if in desperation for her to remember something . . . anything.

Her body felt like it had warm syrup running through her veins. Strong hands pressed against her cheeks before gently running through her hair, up and down her spine, and finally, firmly, gripping her hips, pulling her closer. He kissed her as if his next breath depended upon the taste of her.

Something inside her broke. Whatever wall she had constructed to guard her reality from those dreams came crashing down the minute his fingers found the bare patch of skin between her sweater and the waistband of her jeans, the instant his lips urged hers to surrender, and she did, gladly, white flag and all. Suddenly, she was exhausted from fighting a battle she knew didn't belong between them. No one had ever touched her with such tenderness—or passion, for that matter. The overexcited, puppy-style kisses of former boyfriends were nothing compared to the kisses of a confident man. She groaned and eagerly wrapped her arms around Blake's neck, melting and molding to his strong frame.

Suddenly, she remembered. She wasn't sure what it was, exactly, because the swirl of images flashing through her mind made no sense, interspersing with her too-real dreams as lightning flashed behind her lids. Emotions that she'd never experienced before, that she was sure belonged to her but had been lost, were finally being recovered, and all the confusion, the doubt, the fear, all of it vanished. She gasped in the heady sensation of suddenly being complete, of a deep hunger being sated, of possessing a happiness she never knew existed, as tears streamed down her cheeks. She felt at home. It didn't have the traditional four walls, roof, garden, or an address, though. No, this was different. Her soul breathed a sigh of relief, like a tired blue jay lost in a storm, finally coming home to rest.

Blake gently kissed each of her closed eyes, and her trail of tears were replaced by the fire his lips left as they traveled down her cheek to her neck. The hungry lips continued to sear a path down to the edge of her collarbone, peeking out from the neckline of her shirt. Maia ran her fingers through his curls as he buried his face in her neck, leaving soft kisses, and growled, "You don't know how hard it's been. I saw what he did to you." He tenderly kissed a raised scar on her shoulder where her abusive ex had once broken a bottle; he had been aiming for her head. The skin tingled under the heat of Blake's tongue. His kisses moved to the space between her breasts and hovered at her heart. He breathed, "I know what they've done to you here." She knew he was referring to the emotional manipulation of her grandparents—like carrions ripping at the tender flesh of the trusting innocent. He gripped her tighter, burying his face in her neck, voice shaking. "I should have done something. I could have . . . ."

She pulled his face back up to hers after giving him a tight squeeze. She wanted to look into his eyes again. Now, they brimmed with his own tears, but for once, they were relaxed and not struggling with the weight of concern.

"I don't know how crazy this is going sound, but—I've been dreaming about your face," she said.

He raised a doubtful eyebrow, followed by his signature smirk.

"Well," she conceded, running the tips of her fingers around the glorious contours of his jawline. He sighed softly in relief, as if the tension that had been squeezing his heart had finally shattered and fallen away. "Okay, more than your face." Maia pressed her lips to his softly, inhaling him as completely as she could. "You've been there for as long as I can remember. And it was enough. You don't know how much your presence, even in those dreams, helped."

Blake smiled, relief touching his eyes, mingling with the tears there. The sight warmed Maia, reaching to the last frozen tundra of her stubborn defense. "You received my message, then. I wanted to do so much more, but I wasn't allowed to interfere. Your experiences have shaped you, Maia, into the woman you are meant to be. To prepare you for this power, this role." He tilted her chin up with gentle hands and kissed her with a heat that only the sun could possess. It ended too soon, and Maia let out a slight sigh of loss.

"But why don't I remember you? I remember—somehow—feelings for you, but . . ." Maia frowned in confusion.

Blake picked up her thought. "Remember, in the notebook, how I mentioned that when we take a human form, we can either re-invoke into new lives or continue as if immortal?" She nodded, and he continued. "Good. You chose the former when I became Sideralis. We were supposed to be chosen together, but . . ."

Now it was Blake's turn to be at a loss. Moments ago, Maia would have reveled in his confusion, thinking it served him right. Except, now it didn't do either of them any good.

"I take it that's not supposed to happen?" She traced the outline of his shoulders in soft swirling motions and his tension eased.

"No, but we aren't the first to be separated during our tenure. There have been others—"

"Who?"

His smile was gentle as he continued. "Their story belongs to them, and our story is a long one. As much as I would love to rehash our history right now, I'm afraid we better head back. I guarantee you that people are going to come looking for us soon, and they probably wouldn't appreciate us fraternizing in the chief's quarters." He gave her a wicked wink as Maia stifled her giggles with more of his kisses. This time, she was the one who let her eyes wander to the cot.

As if reading her mind once more, Blake groaned. "Don't tempt me, woman. Believe me, I've waited long enough for you. We're gonna need more than a measly cot."

Maia sighed, her voice husky with promise. "I know."

16

"*ALORS!* I SEE you've kissed and made up!" Lana laughed as Maia and Blake returned to the table hand in hand.

"Indeed," remarked Reed as he pushed a breadstick around the edge of his now empty soup bowl, sopping up the dregs of his stew. "Literally!"

Maia felt the blood rush straight to her hairline, and she tried to hide her embarrassment in the large sandwich she'd snagged on the way back in.

She snuck glances at Blake, conversing now with Leo, every few minutes, and each time, the muscles in her chest—normally on a mission to strangle her heart and lungs in the name of anxiety—relaxed as his animated gestures struck a chord of familiarity. All of this vague emotional recollection was going to take some getting used to, at least until she and Blake could find time to catch up more fully. She wasn't sure how much he'd be able to fill in for her. She was only assuming that he hadn't re-invoked, but he had never said so explicitly. Her thoughts now stewed on new possibilities, wonders, and curiosities. Maia sighed a little, yet couldn't help the smile that followed, knowing that the memories would be pleasant. They had to be. And at least she'd finally have some answers.

Looking to Blake again, Maia noticed that the stressful tilt to his shoulders was gone, and he seemed much happier now that they had talked. Her woolgathering must have been obvious, because Lana disentangled herself from the Corocottas like the tide slipping from the shore, leaving behind an understood promise to return with a lingering kiss. The Nymph poured herself into the chair across from Maia, a playful grin tugging at the edges of her full lips.

"So," she drawled, her hazel eyes alight with mischief. "Blake filled me in on what he's told you about our world. But I'm curious, how much of your past *did* his kisses unlock?"

Maia fought to keep another goofy grin from spreading across her features, but it won, and she bit her lower lip. "Good question," she replied. "I don't know how much I'll be able to handle remembering. Apparently, I re-invoked. I keep having these strange, waking dreams that flash through my mind, but they don't make sense. I remember emotions, mostly. I still don't quite understand everything that's going on, but I remember how I felt about him, and I know that we're—I can't believe I'm saying this—supposed to *be* together. That much I'm sure of." She hastily popped a potato chip in her mouth and followed it with a large gulp of water to prevent herself from blabbering further. Lana's head tilted slightly in puzzlement, and Maia suddenly worried that what she'd said was strange. Did she say too much?

Lana finally put her out of her misery, though, while simultaneously adding to her overall confusion with her next words. "I've never heard of anyone having their memories return in dreams. Then again, I haven't known that many Terras." She shrugged with a gentle smile. She tapped her forehead with a finger before continuing. "At least that I can remember. Maybe it's a Terra thing. Once you officially take over as a Gaea *praeses*, you'll have a lot more access to your memories, but the human form we are required to maintain still restricts a lot of that." She leaned forward with a conspiratorial whisper, punctuated by a wink. "I think they don't want us getting too distracted."

"Distracted, hmmm?" Leo had turned his attention to them as Blake fell into conversation with Reed and Poppy, answering their questions. His hands gripped the curves of Lana's waist as he pulled her toward him, nuzzling her neck just below her earlobe with a playful nip. Lana melted into his embrace with a suggestive wiggle, angling her head toward his. Leaning in, she brushed her lips lightly against his before hovering there. "Can I get you something else to eat, my love?"

Maia wasn't sure whether to gag or be jealous. She glanced at Blake, who returned her look with a smirk and wiggling eyebrows. Maia's attention was once more diverted to the canoodling couple as Lana burst into a fit of giggles, hovering just out of Leo's reach, her hand on his chest restraining him from stealing a kiss.

"Damn, woman . . . you're really gonna tempt me like that?"

Lana's mirth swirled gently amidst the din of the great cavern hall. "What can I say? I'll lose my woman card if I don't manipulate you with food and sex."

Leo's booming laugh shook the table before fading into the contented purr of a lion.

Maia cleared her throat. As fun as this Lifetime Special was, she wasn't done getting her answers.

Leo turned his calculating gaze to her. "I've interrupted your man-bashing, haven't I, ladies?" He smiled again, showing sharp teeth, as Maia protested with a shake of her head. "Let me guess, little lady. I bet you believe 'soul mates'" —he made air quotes with his fingers— "is nothing more than Hollywood propaganda regulated to rom-coms and Mommy porn?"

Maia's mouth went dry. Had the ritual binding her to them meant that they could now read her mind? *Oh, God.* But before she could loosen her tongue from fear's vice grip, Lana patted her hand with a wink.

"Don't worry, *chére*, the answers will come. Besides, Leo was the only one of us sappy enough to actually believe the *astrum* story when he first heard it." A mischievous grin spread across her features. "I bet you can guess who took the longest to convince."

Answering Lana's warm smile with one of her own, Maia glanced at the usually ornery Nepenthes guardian sitting at the other end of the table. Her notice of him was well-timed, because Reed's eyes widened in pain and he clutched at his head with rigid fingers, squeezing his temples between sharp breaths. Something was wrong, and horror crashed through her as she watched Reed clench his jaw so hard she wondered if the bone would break under the strain.

"Reed?" Maia jumped up, but Blake put a gentle hand on her arm to stop her just as Reed slumped forward in his chair, resting his head in his hands. "What's going on?" Maia asked. Her whispers were frantic as Blake gave her hand a warm squeeze. "Is he okay?"

"*Everything is fine.*"

She jumped when the voice skipped softly through her mind—except it wasn't just in her thoughts. The voice reverberated deeply, down to the very marrow of her bones.

"What was that?" she asked, looking around for the speaker. Her question perished, unanswered, as the others were turned from her, gathering around Reed. Seconds stretched before he finally lifted his face. His lightly tanned skin was drained of all color, and a slight sheen ran across his forehead.

"That," he said, seeming to choke on his words, "was Selene. She has a message for us. We're to meet her tomorrow night, at the falls."

"But how are we going to get there?" Maia's concern evolved into a tidal wave of questions. "Isn't this island completely submerged? And how did you know that was Selene?"

Reed pinched the bridge of his nose and shook his head slowly, taking deep breaths as Lana jumped in, frowning in worry.

"Reed and Selene are *astrum*." Lana paused, drawing in a ragged breath, her eyes flickering to Blake as Leo placed a comforting arm around her shoulders, rubbing at the goose bumps that had emerged along her skin. "*Astrum* can communicate internally, soul to soul, at any distance. But—*mon dieu.*" Lana's curls quivered as a shiver ran through her. "Selene has placed a wall between herself and Reed. It makes any communication between them very hard, and"—she flickered a worried glance at her friend— "extremely painful."

Maia's lips remained frozen in a silent *O* as Reed continued to rub his brow, shivering each time he exhaled.

"Perhaps I can be of assistance?"

Everyone turned to find the chief standing at the head of the table, Poppy floating behind him. Maia had been so worried about Reed that she hadn't even noticed the Ariel leave the table.

The chief still wore the traditional robes of his tribe, but he had removed the large headdress, and he stood with his hands clasped before him, gazing with wise eyes at the cluster of *praeses*. Staring at his kind face, Maia remembered the gazelle from her vision and wondered if it was possible that the chief and the gazelle were one and the same.

"I realize we have not had much time to discuss the events at hand," he said. Despite having hearing that was better than perfect, they all leaned forward, anxious for his next words. "However, there is much about this island and our tribe you do not know. We were placed here by Earth's first *praeses* as keepers of their legends, and as a safe haven in times of war. And I am afraid that you are, indeed, now at war, a war of the chosen. For you have all been chosen as guardians and protectors of our Gaea, this Earth, and it is your duty to protect it against the forces who wish to destroy it."

Maia looked around the table at the serious, determined faces of her new friends. For the first time, the task set before her was beginning to sink in. This wasn't just some fairy tale she could hope to wake up from. This was real, with real consequences.

Lana straightened. "Monsieur, we need to get off this island to meet with one of the other praeses, but we are lost beneath the ocean. We can leave, but Maia does not yet have the means to do so, and the people here . . ." She trailed off, not wanting to be the one to say what everyone else was thinking.

The chief gave her a gentle smile and a nod of his head. "Do not worry, Lana, *praeses* of the waters. This cave is old, and the guardians who helped create it also ensured that there were tunnels to run deep beneath the ocean that crossed into Russia. It will take four hours to walk by foot, and it leads directly into the village of Uelen, where I have a sister, Marissa, who will give you lodging. Here." He stretched out his hand, holding a large silver coin. "Give this to her, and she will know that I have sent you."

Blake accepted the coin, clasping the chief's hand in both of his, and bowed deeply. The chief returned the gesture, and Maia winced slightly at the proximity of their bowed heads.

The legs of a chair scraped loudly across the floor as Reed pushed it back, the tension in his posture tighter than a bowstring's.

"Thank you, sir." Reed's voice was full of relief as he turned to face the rest of the group. "We should get what we need and leave immediately."

Blake clasped a comforting hand on the Nepenthes's shoulder. "No, we'll leave first thing in the morning. It's late, and Maia still needs to rest."

For once, she wasn't irritated by Blake's protectiveness, or the fact that he was speaking for her. Having someone who cared enough to think of her comfort for once was kind of nice. Despite the urgency of their need to move, she gave herself a moment to revel in the luxuriousness of it.

Then she shoved her chair back and stood, placing a hand on Blake's arm. "Thank you Blake, but"—she looked at Reed's strained features and gave him a quick nod of understanding—"I already feel a lot better, stronger. I won't hold you guys up. Just let me pack some food and see if I can borrow a jacket, and I'll be ready to go."

Blake opened his mouth to protest, but Maia turned away from him, toward the chief. "Is there a coat and backpack I can borrow? My belongings were lost in the storm."

The chief smiled and nodded before addressing the crowd of people that had begun to form around their table, anxious to hear of the *praeses'* plans.

"Maia." Blake's eyes were pleading, and tension had returned to his stance. "Please, you might be stronger, but this journey will be a long one. You can't travel the way we do yet, and until we leave the caves, we aren't going to be able to help you much."

Rising onto her toes, Maia placed a swift kiss on his cheek. "I know, but don't worry. I'll be fine."

He started to argue, but was interrupted by Poppy's lyrical voice as she twirled and danced across the table.

"As grains dwindle through the glass of Cronus
lives arrive and depart in voids between
In those moments ephemeral it is our onus
to honor the constant that lives unseen.
Upon the Emerald Tablet thus inscribed
it read: 'Love is the foundation of all . . .'
The Wisdoms of Thoth teach us love inside
is a power untapped awaiting our call.
Legacies of the viridian sage
Hermetic writ: 'As without, so within.'
For reserves of strength, look not to your rage;
instead look to your Kith. Look to your Kin."

"See?" Leo joined in. "Nothin' to worry about. If Maia starts getting tired, we can loan her some energy and she'll be fine."

"You can do that?" Maia asked, her eyes wide.

"Yup," replied Leo. He shot her a wicked grin, avoiding the death glare Blake was shooting his way. "Remember, we're bound to one another, soul to soul. All of us."

"Right," she muttered. The weight of her new responsibility settled on her shoulders. "How could I forget?" She turned at the gentle nudging of someone behind her, and was greeted by a pale green jacket, a small backpack, and a large hug from one of the town's ladies. Maia hugged the little lady back and said, "Thank you." In return, she received an explosive lecture of some sort in the same native tongue that had been buzzing intermittently around the room all day. By the lady's stern voice and many hand motions, she was reminding her to zip her jacket all the way up, Maia soon got the idea, and the chief kindly steered the old lady away.

Her throat tightened at the motherly lecture, and Maia dashed away the tears running down her cheeks with the back of her hand before sniffing and violently stuffing her hands through the armholes of the jacket.

A careful hand grabbed the other side of the coat, holding it out for her, and she was grateful to not have to chase the other armhole in a tearful rage. Once she'd zipped up, Blake placed another scarf around her neck; she still couldn't figure out where he was getting all these things from, but she was determined to ask him soon. He pulled her close, sheltering her from the flurry of bodies around her as people began to clean up the festivities and their friends got ready to leave. Blake brushed a gentle kiss across her lips and whispered, "Don't worry, you will have time to grieve, I promise. Until then, I will hold it for you for safekeeping."

And then she understood why the grief of her parents' passing and the destruction of her home had not yet pulled her under. Maia had thought that she'd cried them away, and then, like the emotionally evolved person she had always hoped to be, she had let go in acceptance of her new reality. She'd thought that maybe she was too horrible to grieve their loss properly, had been ashamed to feel mostly relief.

In truth, it was only the shadow of grief that existed in her heart. The real emotions resided with Blake, and the time would soon come when she would have to deal with them fully.

But not now. Now, there was a war to fight. Shouldering their backpacks, Maia and the rest of the guardians received a triumphant farewell as they turned to the darkness of the cavern's secret tunnels. It was time to find Selene.

17

THE TUNNELS WERE not lit, but the light of Poppy's form as she drifted ahead was enough to guide their way. The path was wide enough for only two people to walk next to each other, and the cave's walls were so monotonous that, normally, Maia would have been quite depressed at the lack of scenery to occupy herself with. This time, however, she had too many questions to ask to pay attention to much of anything else.

Poppy twirled and sang as she floated along in her usual style, followed by a hurried Reed, who had to be reminded several times to slow down. Blake and Maia walked behind him, followed by Lana and Leo; the latter pair had their heads tilted together, their dark and copper hair interlocking as they whispered between kisses and laughed softly with each other.

Maia stole a couple of glances at them, whenever one or the other released a peal of laughter at some inside joke. "Are they *astrum*, too?"

Blake looked at Leo and Lana over his shoulder before meeting Maia's eyes with a smile. "Indeed. They haven't seen each other in a few weeks, though, so despite always having the ability to talk to one another, they still find plenty to catch up on in person."

"Okay, so, what about Poppy and Reed?" Maia said, watching the Ariel's twirling form at the head of the group. "Are they also *astrum*?"

"Stars, no." Leo barked out a quick laugh and poked her in the back.

Maia shrugged as a shiver of irritation radiated down her spine and embarrassment heated her cheeks.

"Come on, Leo, you know how these things are. She didn't know," Lana said, giving the Corocottas a knowing look. She raised her eyebrows as she patted him on the ass, eliciting a wolfish grin in reply. "Besides, all she knows is what humans refer to as love, and how limiting that feeling is."

"So, you never explained about Poppy," Maia interjected, changing the subject before Leo and Lana's flirting could derail her quest for answers. "Why does she only speak in poems?"

Lana nodded, appearing relieved at the opportunity to shake the otherwise solemn mood hanging over the group. "Well, as the Tempest *praeses*, she's an air spirit, an Ariel. It's extremely difficult to maintain a human form and have a connection to the elements of air. She also hasn't been in contact with her *astrum* for a very long time, and we think that may have made her condition worse. She chooses to speak in only poetry, but we aren't sure why. We think that perhaps he was a poet the last time she saw him."

"Hmm." Maia fingered the tip of a thick strand of her hair; she'd forgotten how much she enjoyed having it so long. Lana's word's allowed tidbits of the facts she had been picking up to finally fall into place, like the obnoxious little puzzle pieces they were. She remembered Blake's comment about other *astrum* being separated and it being their stories to tell. Feeling uncomfortable with the idea of missing something more, she hurried on. "That's another thing I don't understand. How do the *astrum* get separated in the first place? I mean, how did we"—she pointed to Blake and herself—"get separated, and why did I not know it was him when I saw him?"

Blake shook his tawny curls, appearing helpless as he shrugged. "We aren't completely sure. Other than the human mind not being able to contain the memories of our past lives, your experience shouldn't be what it currently is. You and I were supposed to become human at the same time. That way, no matter how many times we cycle through the human experience or maintain the same vessel, we could always find each other."

"So, what happened?" Maia zipped her jacket up higher, tucking her chin beneath the collar. Wherever they were, it was getting colder the further they walked. Blake grabbed her cool hand in his warm one, and she instantly felt a surge of heat crackle through her veins.

"That's what we haven't been able to figure out. For some reason, I was chosen as the next Sideralis guardian, but you remained human, re-invoking and losing your memories. We got separated, and I've had to keep my distance."

"You have?" Maia whispered, looking into his face as a millennium of sadness flashed across his features. Without premeditated thought, her fingers wrapped around the lapel of his coat, tugging until her numb lips met his. His breath quickened, the warmth thawing her lips. His energy seeped straight into her pores as he wrapped his arms around her, infusing her with his heat.

Loud whistling, followed by several excited innuendos, was thrown their way before Reed cleared his throat loudly. Blake and Maia parted quickly, faces red and sheepish, as Reed glared at them.

It only lasted a few seconds before he marched off again, growling. "Hurry up! You two can get all caught up later!"

Maia settled for holding Blake's hand as they followed, muttering. "He's intense."

Blake gave her hand a squeeze. "Being away can be hard, but having your mate block you?" He gave a low whistle. "I can't imagine that. It must be the worst."

Reed was at least five feet in front of them, but Maia knew he'd heard their hushed voices when his broad shoulders hunched, higher and higher until he wore them like earrings. She and Reed had never really hit it off, but she thought of how easygoing he'd been just hours before. And now?

She didn't want to hurt him more with their conversation, but there was still one more question Maia needed to know the answer to. Maybe now was the perfect time to attempt this soul-to-soul communication she'd heard them talk about.

She tried thinking the words to her question a few times, but when Blake didn't answer, she assumed it didn't work. She tried looking at him, but knew that was wrong because he hadn't been looking at her when he spoke to her before. She was certain now that both times she'd heard a disembodied voice in her head, it had been him. Besides, as Maia understood it, *astrum* didn't need to be near one another to communicate. She focused on her emotional memories of him instead—the way he made her feel, and the way she seemed to already know and understand everything about him. Even the way he sometimes chewed on the inside of his cheek when he was concentrating, or how he twisted his fingers together when he tried to rein in his temper. Forming the words deep in her heart, she released them the way one would a deep breath.

The result was instant. Blake turned to look at her, his eyes wide, before he smiled and answered her question the same way.

"You want to know why Selene is blocking Reed?" he asked.

"Yes."

"Heidi."

"I don't understand."

"Remember when you studied astronomy in school and they taught you that the Earth revolves around the sun?"

"Yes."

"What revolves around Earth?"

"Oh, I see. Selene is the moon guardian."

"Right." Blake shot her a proud grin, to which Maia rolled her eyes in answer. *"And by default, she spends a large amount of time with Heidi. The Luna and Terra guardians have traditionally always been close."*

"Then why is Heidi keeping Selene from Reed?"

"She isn't, not technically. She manipulates and uses Selene, preying on her instinctual draw for her own purposes. Whatever she's planning right now, she doesn't want us to know. We would if Reed and Selene were connected."

"Do you think Heidi is forcing Selene to block Reed?"

"*I doubt she's holding a gun to her head, so to speak. Like I said, Heidi can be very persuasive.*"

"Okay. So, then, let me ask another question: what's the traditional relationship between the Sideralis and Terra praeses, since the Earth revolves around the Sun?"

Blake gave an audible sigh and tightened his grip on her hand before answering. "*Traditionally, the Terra and Sideralis are astrum, but couples have been getting separated in the past twenty cycles or so. It's only recently come to light as the numbers have grown. It's normally a rarity.*"

"Has no one tried to find out why?"

"*Yeah-nah, the Council and its Talis warriors—the army that guards the chosen praeses—are conducting an ongoing investigation. Nothing has been announced, but I doubt it ever will be. Far be it for the Council to admit a mistake or weakness. It will most likely just be quietly resolved.*"

Blake sighed again before his next thoughts rushed through her. "*You know that there was nothing between Heidi and me, right? I was waiting for you.*"

Maia gave his words some thought as she searched them for truth. She hadn't really considered that a possibility before and, feeling confident in his intentions, she nodded, adding, "*I believe you. Sorry I kept you waiting.*"

That earned her a weak smile. "*I have to warn you, though. Heidi's astrum is also a Sideralis, but for some reason, she won't look for him. The only one who can find him is her—and the Council, of course—but she won't look for him or ask for help. She seems determined for me to take his place.*"

Maia stopped in her tracks. Leo and Lana almost walked into her from behind, their own silent conversation coming to a halt.

Her voice was sharp as it ricocheted off the tunnel's walls. "What?"

18

"WHAT'S WRONG?" LANA looked worriedly between Blake and Maia.

Maia shook her head, not sure if she wanted to share what Blake had just told her. "Nothing. Sorry." She placed a hand over her heart and felt the angry pulse coming from her core. Turning to Blake, she said, "I guess I know how you feel now."

"Ha!" Leo softly knocked her shoulder. "So you won't be getting all pissy when he starts getting possessive and jealous, eh?"

"Oh, I don't know about that." Maia started walking again before they lost their overexcited leaders. She bypassed Reed entirely and drew close to Poppy, listening to her song as the Ariel continued to dance and twirl her way down the tunnel.

"How time passes in this forsaken keep,
 Eons I've rattled these cold walls of stone
 A seeming Eternity absent sleep
 As I've haunted these tower halls alone.

 I remember still the warm aroma
 of the kitchens alight set to entertain
 but fires have died, absent persona
 bearing all the joy of an opened vein

 I remember still sounds of laughter 'n song
 as cheer and delight frolic'd through these halls
 Now all has been silent for far too long—
 creepers through mortar have corrupted these walls.

 I remember still the touch on my flesh
 as the love of another's sweet caress
 Now agony as memory unbidden comes fresh
 to reach into my soul, my pains coalesce."

Poppy stopped suddenly and stood, eye level with Maia, real tears flowing down her misty face.

"Oh, Poppy." The weight of the Ariel's sorrow pressed down on her. "I am so—" Before Maia knew what hit her, a suffocating darkness had enveloped her, and there was nothing. Absolutely nothing.

Oppressive silence pressed against her on all sides. Blackness met her eyes, and her arms and legs ignored her brain's commands to move. It was as if they were suddenly absent.

She wasn't even sure if her eyes were open; she couldn't feel her lids anymore.

Then, almost just as suddenly, Maia's senses snapped back into place with a sharp sting, as if she'd been slapped. Stars swam in her vision and her head felt light. The muscles in her calves ached and her fingers trembled as she steadied herself, her stomach lurching with nausea. She swallowed against the rising bile, blinking at the new scenery before her. At first, all she could make out was a squat row of bushes, surrounded at their bases by little white and pink flowers. Rubbing her tired eyes, Maia recognized the little landscaped plot, and when she lifted her gaze, she realized she was standing in front of the entrance to Legacy Emanuel Medical Center, in Portland. She spun around, taking in her surroundings a second time. How had she managed to go from a cave in the middle of the Bering Sea to Portland? This was Portland as she remembered it, too, quirky and beautiful, not the current one ravaged by the very nature it worshiped.

A familiar face came toward her.

"Mac?"

Though he was only a few feet away, he didn't look up from the paperwork he held in his hands, steadily reading and flipping pages back and forth as he walked purposefully through the parking lot, dodging cars and curbs as though he knew the placement of every one on instinct.

"Mac!" Maia yelled louder, still in denial that this painfully detailed scene wasn't real. She waved her arms above her head, repeating his name as he drew nearer. His face, creased with worry, remained bent over his papers as he stopped at the car parked next to the shrubs, fumbling for his keys. The keys fell from his pocket with a bell-like tinkle, but still his eyes remained on the paperwork, even as he knelt and patted the ground. Maia tried picking them up for him, but her fingers slipped right through the glinting metal, as though she were made of nothing but air.

She yelped and stumbled a few steps back. Mac found the keys, unlocked his car door, and climbed into the rusty black Golf TDI.

He lingered after he turned the car on, shuffling papers as the car's air conditioning dried the slick auburn curls that had been sticking to his forehead and blew them around his face like a fiery halo. Moments passed, Maia watching as a ghostly spectator, until Mac suddenly threw the papers to the passenger-side floorboard. He punched the steering wheel viciously—once, twice, then a few more times.

Maia jumped back at his rage. She'd known Mac her entire life—they'd even gone to high school together, though he'd graduated the same year she'd entered—but she had never seen him act out in anger before. He rubbed the stubble on his cheeks and chin roughly, then threw the old car in reverse, grinding the gears in his haste to pull away.

Dumbfounded, Maia stood helplessly as his car turned down North Vancouver Ave, growing smaller. When it disappeared from view, darkness pressed down on her a second time, and the scene changed.

She now stood in the trenches of a battle, and immediately gagged at the coppery smell of blood, the tanginess of sweat mingled with fear, and the stringent scent of earth, urine, vomit, and excrement. The horizon trembled in blinding light and the ground shook, dropping her into a sprawling heap in the mud. All around her, she heard the screams of artillery being fired, the shouts of orders being given, and the buzz of planes overhead. Dirt and gas swirled in the air, and the bodies around her fell. Covering her mouth with her hands, she shrank lower into the slimy mud, made as much from the soil as it was blood. She didn't even realize that she should have felt the cold, wet earth seeping into her clothes; she was too distracted by the alarming sight of a British flag riddled with bullet holes that came drifting down into the trench.

Movement caught in the corner of her eye. A young man with a medic patch on the arm of his murky brown uniform hurried toward her, dragging a medium-sized bag. He stopped two feet away and knelt to check the pulses of the men lying at her feet. He must have found someone still alive, because he began shouting frantically at one of the bodies crushed by a comrade who had landed on top of him in pieces. His words were drowned out by the noises of war, but he pushed the dead man off his patient and began checking the soldier for injuries. Maia wanted desperately to help, but she was forced to just watch, knowing, somehow, that anything she tried to do wouldn't work. She wasn't even sure if she could manage to unlock her joints and move toward him; they were stiff with fright, stressed by explosions and the constant *pop* of gunfire. Her senses were overwhelmed as the adrenaline of fight or flight overpowered her. The muscles in her shoulders and core tightened, and her legs begged her to move. Her fingers scrambled along the dirt, searching for a weapon. But just like when she'd tried to grab Mac's keys, her hands found no purchase. A thought whispered across her mind. *Even if I find a weapon, then what?* She'd never been in a fight before, not like this.

A dull ache of emptiness thumped through her rapidly beating heart as doubt fluttered through her stomach. Something within her, a sort of half-forgotten instinct, told her that might not be altogether true.

She pressed her hands over her ears as another deafening boom sounded directly above her, causing the trench behind her to cave in, spraying mud and debris in all directions. The medic looked up for a moment, and straight through Maia. His gaze turned worried, and he turned back to his patient, but something about his face startled Maia. It was familiar, but she couldn't quite see it through the mud and blood caking his features. She watched as he took a long strip of fabric out of his kit and bound the soldier's head. Removing his own helmet, he placed it on the wounded man, covering the makeshift bandage.

The medic raised his face again and shock rippled through her. The man pulled the wounded soldier to his feet and slung him over his shoulder in a fireman's carry. Without his helmet, the medic's face was framed by auburn curls, and the features—leaner and with sharper angles—were known to her.

But what is Mac doing here?

Maia wrenched herself from her hiding place to follow him, stopping short of a fresh pile of bodies that Mac had to climb over. How far could she actually follow him? An object in the curled fingers of a dead soldier caught her eye—a bolt-action rifle. It triggered a hazy memory of her grandfather showing her his collection of antique guns. Every time she'd gone to his house he would quiz her on them to make sure she was paying attention to his ramblings, and this gun in partic-ular was one she recognized from his tales about World War I.

She was an entire century in the past.

As soon as the information clicked, the earth around her shuddered violently, knocking her off her feet. This time, when the blackness came, she didn't fight it. She was thankful to leave this nightmare behind.

She opened her eyes to a cobblestone street, and a loud neighing sound followed by the clattering of hooves had her scrambling out of the road. If she was solid, she would have ended up seated in the lap of a young gentleman and his wife, enjoying a luncheon at an outdoor café. Maia turned in circles on the sidewalk, taking in the changed world. The blue sky was muted by the haze of smoke from countless chimneys coughing soot into the air; orange light glowed within the greasy panes of street lamps that lined the avenue; and the air smelled of horses and refuse. It was definitely the Victorian era, she noted, watching ladies stroll by in lace and bustles, arm-in-arm with men in top hats sporting canes as they deftly skirted loose cobblestones and gray puddles or piles of trash. In the distance, she saw the Eiffel Tower—she must have been in the turn of the century, then—and the French names on the buildings confirmed her location. She wasn't sure what she was doing here, but since she'd seen Mac in her last two visions, or whatever the hell they were, she figured she would stay where she was and wait for him again.

She wasn't disappointed. A few minutes later, a young man rushed around the corner, wearing the familiar shy smile she was always used to. His hair was still red, though extended in large sideburns befitting the fashion of the time, and his blue eyes twinkled mischievously as he sat down at the only open table near the busy bistro. He carefully unfolded the newspaper that was tucked under his arm, and after giving his order to the waiter, he immediately disappeared behind it. Knowing he couldn't see her, Maia walked around the table, intending to plop down next to him to watch until she was shuttled off to the next location. When she got to the other side of his newspaper, though, she realized that he wasn't reading at all. He was looking around at the sidewalk and its passersby every few moments, tugging at his cravat and occasionally fiddling with the brim of his top hat, resting on the seat next to him.

The waiter brought Mac his drink, and the former was thanked quickly before Mac returned to his study of the sidewalk and street. Maia watched the road with him, until another surprisingly familiar face came bouncing around the corner. Even though her corn silk hair was pulled away from her face and tucked tightly into a smart brown hat that brimmed with feathers and a large burgundy bow, the merry smile, twinkling eyes, and pert nose were unmistakable.

Maia shut her gaping mouth, her heart quickening as a grin swept across her face. Finally, she had an inkling of why she was here. Mac stood so abruptly he knocked his drink over, and he mopped up the stain on his trousers with his handkerchief while muttering curses to himself.

"Monsieur Roux?"

Mac's flushed face rose slowly as the pretty young lady stopped before him, biting her lower lip to hold back a giggle at his predicament. Maia took in the girl's austere brown and gray plaid dress, made lively with another burgundy sash at the waist and the soft waterfall of lace and silk between the dress's lapels. A quick glance at the crowd surrounding the young woman, and Maia could see that she was dressed in the height of fashion; three more women walked by wearing similar day dresses.

Mac's gaze hungrily swept over the young woman, lingering at the small patch of exposed skin between the dress's high collar and the bottom edge of her ear.

"Pop—uh, I'm sorry, Mademoiselle Bertrand." He bent over her hand in a quick bow and nodded to the matronly woman hovering at Poppy's elbow, boringly dressed in dark gray, without a hint of color. Her narrow brown eyes analyzed his every move. "Madame Lefèvre." Mac fixed his eyes respectfully on the plume in Poppy's hat as she struggled to contain her mirth. "How are you on this fine d-d-day?"

Poppy let out one of her giggles, even as she attempted to tamper her features into socially acceptable fashion.

"I was just on my way to your home—"

Madame Lefèvre harumphed at Poppy's inappropriate statement. Maia smiled, not at all surprised that Poppy was the type to rebel against the social decorum of her time.

"You were?" Mac's gentle face erupted into the biggest smile Maia had ever seen on him.

Poppy returned the happy gesture. "Yes. Papa was wanting to know if you would join us for supper tomorrow. He was in raptures over the poems you contributed to his anthology. Here." She thrust two small, folded letters into his hand. "He wanted me to leave this for you."

Mac looked down at the papers curiously. "But there are two letters here. He wants me to have both?"

Poppy dropped her eyes demurely, which Maia clearly saw for the farce it was. She focused on smoothing nonexistent wrinkles from the sash at her waist with kid-gloved hands before she finally answered, "Oh, yes, both are for you. So, will you come, then? Tomorrow night?"

Mac barely nodded before she exclaimed, "Excellent! Good day, Monsieur!"

With a flounce of her bustle, she was gone as quickly as she had arrived. Madame Lefèvre leveled a scowl at Mac before hurrying after her charge.

A stunned Mac sat, looking at both folded papers for a moment before he set one down and eagerly, with trembling fingers, opened the smallest one.

Maia looked over his shoulder at the single word printed in flowing letters on the page: *Yes.*

Mac let out a rushing breath that he seemed to have been holding for eternity, and stared, wide-eyed and elated, at the paper clutched between his tight fingers. He refolded the letter precisely, kissed it, and stuffed it not into his jacket, but into the folds of his shirt.

As Mac cracked the seal of the second letter, Maia felt the blackness wrap around her once more.

19

MAIA DIDN'T HAVE to wait long for the next scene to come her way, but this one was different. Her vision was black, but she could hear voices nearby, both frightened and angry. She couldn't make out what they were saying, though. The sound was muffled, as though under water. She strained to understand their words before realizing that she could feel her body again. She wiggled her toes and fingers first, felt the weight of blankets pressed against her body. Her head rested on a scratchy pillow, and the bedsheets smelled faintly of mold. As the voices became clearer, it was obvious that this was no new vision.

"Why is she calling for Mac?" Maia instantly recognized Blake's thick accent. "She hasn't mentioned him since we left Portland."

"Blake, *cher*, relax! Seriously, this is getting ridiculous—"

"I don't care!" He cut off Lana's attempt at calming him down. "I want to know what's happening! She's not waking up, and if Mac had a hand in this, somehow—"

"Yes, and have you also noticed the other name she's been rambling on about? There has to be a connection."

"Fine. Go get her and bring her here, then. She's been silent about this too long. I want answers!"

"Okay, okay! Don't get your panties in a twist, *ami*."

The Nymph left the room, the door shutting softly behind her. Maia opened her eyes, expecting to see a very angry Blake with unruly hair standing above her, but she was surprised, instead, to see another face swim into view. Many faces, in fact. It took her a moment to realize that she was looking at an old picture, a famous actor—whose name she couldn't recall—in his younger years, surrounded by more pictures of other famous actors and musicians, each with hearts drawn around their faces. She must have been in the old room of a teenager. Her gaze latched on to the ceiling, where glow-in-the-dark stick-on stars confirmed her theory. Finally, her eyes found the only face she was interested in, the exhausted lines of his features reflecting his frustration.

"Blake?" She was surprised that her voice sounded only slightly groggy, but otherwise normal.

"Hey." Blake smiled. He reached for her hand and drew comforting circles on the back of it with his thumb.

"I guess third time's the charm?" She waved at her prone body in yet another bed, feeling completely over this Sleeping Beauty phase she seemed caught in.

Blake smiled wryly. "Not sure. You collapsed in the cave after Poppy's song about her lost *astrum*. We did everything we could to revive you, but nothing worked." He let out a guilty sigh, running his fingers through his hair until the curls were springing out in every direction.

Maia's heart swelled, almost painfully, at his concern for her. How could her chest contain the heart of two so easily?

"I know what happened." Seeing a flicker of hope in Blake's eyes, she amended her statement. "Well, at least I think I do."

The door opened again and Lana, dressed in a dark blue cable-knit sweater and gray corduroy jeans, walked in, followed closely by an unusually somber Poppy.

"Poppy!" Maia pushed herself up on the bed, thankful that the room, with its chipped and cracked, childish furniture, didn't spin.

The Ariel floated before Maia with raw hope on her face, her hands clasped before her white nightgown.

Maia grinned. "Poppy, I think I found him, your *astrum*."

The young girl said nothing, but waited with wide eyes as Leo and Reed joined them in the small room. Leo stuffed himself into the bean bag chair while Reed lowered himself down into the folding chair situated in front of an outdated desktop.

Ignoring them, Maia continued. "Does he have reddish hair, blue eyes, and is about . . ." She trailed off, looking at the guys. "About Leo's height and build?" She pointed at the Corocottas, but he'd turned himself into a house cat and looked quite comfortable curled up in the middle of the soft chair.

Everyone followed Maia's pointing finger, and Blake uttered an exasperated, "*Leo!*"

The cat perked his head up in the lazy fashion of a typical feline and proceeded to lick his paw with an indifferent air.

"Could you please remain human for a moment, mate?" Blake growled.

Reed kicked the bean bag chair in agreement with the sentiment and glared at the cat as Leo gave his tail a good cleaning. Leo looked up at them mid-lick, and gave a feline shrug before turning back into a human. Maia smiled, amused at the exchange, but also wondering how long she'd been unconscious, because the moment Leo changed back into his human form, she noticed that he, too, had changed into fresh clothes.

"You guys are no fun," he grumbled. "Besides, this thing is too small and being a cat was the only way I could fit!" He punched the bag for emphasis. Lana rolled her eyes and plopped onto his lap.

"*Allez.*" She waved her hand. "My big butt and I can handle this." Looking none too put-out, Leo squeezed her midsection, resting his head on the pillows of her substantial chest with a smugly content expression as Lana wrapped her arms around his shoulders.

Maia turned back to Poppy, whose expression hadn't changed. "So, Poppy, about Leo's size?"

The Ariel nodded.

"And when you last saw him, he went by the name of Monsieur Roux?"

Poppy's uncertain pout stretched into a surprised grin, and she nodded so enthusiastically Maia feared her head would fall off. She touched the Tempest *praeses's* hand, surprised to find it was just solid enough for her to feel. It was as though she had placed her hand in front of an air vent, and she could feel the solid pressure of cool air pressing against her skin before it spread out into the surrounding atmosphere.

Maia's face broke out into a grin big enough to make the Cheshire Cat proud. "I know who he is, then!" She swung her legs out of the stack of blankets piled on top of her and launched herself at a stunned Poppy, wrapping her in an exuberant bear hug. She was so excited she could hardly make sense of her jumbled thoughts as she tried to decide where to begin, but finally, she pulled back enough to say, "His name is Mac, now, and oh, God, there is so much to tell you! Not only was he my boss, but I've lived next to him and his mother my entire life."

The room spun as Poppy twirled them around, and Maia laughed, just as giddy with her news. "Finally, something good is coming out of this madness. He's been lonely for so long. I could never quite explain it, but I could tell there was always something missing from him. We must find him right away—"

Poppy released Maia, floating back a few steps, tears streaming down her translucent face as her chest hitched on a sob.

"Poppy!" Maia clutched the sobbing girl's shoulders in alarm as Lana rushed to their side, putting her arms around the Ariel, as well. "Are you all right?"

Lana rubbed the young woman's back in soothing circles. "She'll be all right, *chére*. I think." She bit her lip in uncertainty.

"How did you do it?" Reed asked suddenly. Maia looked over at him, his face unreadable as he swiveled back and forth in the office chair. "No *praeses*, Gaea or otherwise, has ever been able to find someone else's *astrum* before."

"I, um . . ." She glanced nervously at the curious faces turned toward her. "I don't really know." She slumped down onto the bed again, her joy fading at this latest mystery. She traced the flower pattern on the bedspread with her finger to avoid the five pairs of eyes trained her way. "After Poppy's song ended, everything just went black, and then I saw Mac. It was strange. I saw him leaving the hospital, then I saw him in a battle—I think it was the First World War—and then I saw him in Paris. I saw him there with Poppy, and that's how I knew."

She took a chance and raised her eyes, attempting to avoid the whispers and knowing glances passing between the other *praeses*.

"Where are we, by the way?" she asked.

Blake sat down on the bed next to her and slid his arm around her shoulders. She nestled her head in the crook of his neck. "We're at the house of the chief's sister. This is her daughter's old room."

Reed stood. "Well, fantastic." He gave them a sarcastic thumbs-up before his fake smile dissolved into his typical scowl. "We now know she's strong enough to travel without our assistance, which would have been nice to know a few hours ago. We don't have all day to arrange travel from here to Niagara Falls."

"Niagara Falls? That's where we're meeting Selene?" Maia asked.

"Yes. Tonight, remember? So we better get a move on."

"Bruh—hakuna your tattas." Leo shifted into a sloth and draped himself over the bean bag chair, his long limbs stretched out, one hand groping lazily at Reed's legs as the Nepenthes moved to stand near the door. "We have plenty of time, man. It's still technically yesterday there."

Reed scowled at Leo as Lana, who was still trying to comfort a quietly sobbing Poppy, kicked the sloth's chair.

"No, we can't afford to wait, and I'm well aware of the time zone differences," Reed snapped. "But things happen, obstacles come up, and I don't want anything to prevent us from getting there on time. You should want the same, Leo. Selene's your *novae*. Show some concern. Besides"—he leveled a hard glance at Maia and Blake—"someone still has to teach the kid how to travel."

Maia felt the heat of her anger flush her skin, rising from her chest to her neck. "Why am I still a child to you? Just because I'm younger than you doesn't give you license to be an asshole. If we're all supposed to work together, then it's about time you showed a little decency."

Blake tightened his grip around her shoulders, but Reed only needed to take half a step in the tiny room before he was nearly nose-to-nose with Maia. "When you start showing up for yourself, then you can expect us to show up for you," he said. "Respect is earned, not demanded."

Maia opened her mouth to respond, but no words came out. Doubt, and a feeling of unworthiness, scratched at the edges of her already confused emotions. She felt as if she'd been dropped into the middle of the ocean since this all began, and told to find the shore on her own. It didn't matter that she was surrounded by stronger swimmers, she was alone. Reality weighed on her, and she felt her shoulders sag. She snapped her jaw closed, and Reed smirked knowingly at her hesitation. "Let that marinate for a bit. You aren't the only chosen one, you know." A green spark of energy and a thunderous *pop* was the only warning before he disappeared.

"Shit." Maia slumped, shaking from the confrontation, and ran clammy hands over the thighs of her jeans. "I fucked that up royally, didn't I? And here I thought he was starting to like me."

Blake's thumbs dug into the tense muscles of her shoulder blades, and he whispered, "He hasn't spoken to Selene in over a year, and the longer they're apart, the crankier he gets. Even at that, Reed has never been easy to tolerate. Don't worry, he'll come around." But despite his soothing voice acting as a balm to her agitated nerves, Reed's words continued to spin through her head, taking root in her self-image.

The silky Haitian cadences of Lana's voice broke through the tension. "You know," she said. Poppy's sobs had finally subsided, and the Ariel had curled up on Maia's pillow, sniffling. "We could just loan Maia some of our energy, since it's clear she already knows how to use it."

Poppy nodded as she reached a hand toward Maia's shoulder. Blake stopped her before they could touch, shaking his head. "Poppy, are you sure? You're upset right now. You need your strength."

When the Tempest nodded again, Blake gave her an encouraging smile. He released her hand, and the instant Poppy touched Maia's shoulder, she felt a sudden cold surge of energy jolt through her veins, waking her up and leaving her feeling as though she'd slept for a week straight.

"Damn," Maia breathed. Poppy removed her hand, looking slightly more transparent. "That's better than coffee."

Blake chuckled as Maia stood from the bed, stretching sore muscles.

"So," she said, placing her hands on her hips. "Who's going to teach me to, um, travel?"

20

AFTER AN ANXIOUS silence, Leo—human once more—
was the first to speak.

"Um, ha . . . we don't exactly know how Heidi traveled."

Maia tensed in panic before she attempted a more logical
route. "Okay, well, how you do guys travel?"

"We all travel according to the elements we govern," replied Blake. "For instance, I travel through the sun's rays."

"Really?" Maia said. "Even at night?"

Blake flashed her another heart-melting grin. "The sun is
always shining on the Earth, it just depends where."

"That pretty much goes for all of us, if you think about
it," answered Lana, cuddled up in Leo's lap again. "I travel

through water." A visible tremor radiated through the Nymph as the words passed her lips. Leo squeezed her tighter, placing a kiss on her cheek. "Leo can become any animal he chooses; Reed travels through the roots of plants and, in short bursts, through the oxygen they create; and Poppy—" Lana smiled as the Ariel began twirling again in what tiny space was left on the floor. "Well, you've already experienced her travel."

"But no one knows how Heidi does it?" Maia looked to each guardian for answers.

"Blazing fire burns across the terrain
alighting gently to claim its domain.
Celestial silver skims across the sea
introducing herself with swift decree.
Waves wash the world from coast to coast
to saturate soils playing at host.
They fade to mist then rain, changing its form
till it travels the realm as a thunderstorm.
They seep into the Earth to nourish the roots
beseeching flora to bestow their fruits.
Thus feeding the fauna that clamors and strides
together in colonies, herds, and prides
only to begin the cycle anew
as twilight dawns on morning dew."

Poppy curtsied to each of the *praeses* in turn before stopping in front of Maia, who received her lowest curtsy yet before the Ariel extended her pale hand.

Maia stood and reached out, grabbing Poppy's light palm tentatively. She wasn't quite sure what Poppy's newest poem meant, but she trusted her.

"Man, are you sure this is a good idea?" Leo asked, as he and Lana, their hands purposely groping and stroking intimate places, struggled to extract themselves from the squishy chair.

"Blake?" Lana looked at him, chewing on her lip in concern.

Blake stood stiffly beside Poppy and Maia as they hovered a few inches off the ground. Raking his hand through his messy, sun-kissed curls, he finally gave Lana a small smile before nodding. "Yeah-nah, she'll be fine. Poppy knows what she's doing." He stuffed his hands in his pockets once more. "If she says Maia is ready, then she's ready." He nodded his head again, as if to convince himself as much as the others. Feeling his uncertainty weighing on her, Maia looked down at him, but when she met his eyes, he said, "You've got this. I know you do."

"What, exactly, do I have, though?" Her head tapped the ceiling and she winced as tender spots blossomed in pain, and her eyebrows raised nearly to her hairline. She hadn't realized she and Poppy were rising. She found Blake again and swallowed her irritation at the hum of his protective nature, still roiling inside him. It was taking a lot of work for him to override that instinct.

"You have the ability to use all of our powers and travel any which way you choose," said Reed. Maia wobbled slightly in mid-air at his sudden reappearance. He leaned against the doorway, arms crossed and still glowering, but he shot her an apologetic smile, one that looked more akin to a painful grimace. Maia wasn't sure she entirely forgave him, but she returned his apology with a curt nod while Blake shot Reed a warning glare, which the Nepenthes returned with narrowed eyes. Poppy let go of Maia's hand, and after a terrified second of waiting for the fall, Maia realized that she was still floating in the air, unsupported.

She couldn't quite describe it, because it was nothing like the cloud she had traveled in under Poppy's protection before. They were indoors, so there was no wind to hold her up, but the minute Poppy had touched her hand, she'd felt the guardian's energy and power, from the warm air blowing from the vents, tugging at her skin like an impatient child, to the stagnant air content to just exist and circulate through their bodies, through the one plant sitting on the desk in the corner, and, finally, the pulse of energy that radiated from Poppy, herself, like a beacon of light in a deserted cave. That same energy, Maia realized, now came from her own core, pulsing outward in steam-like waves that resembled Poppy's ethereal form. Once Poppy had released Maia's hand, she was on her own, and every particle of air in the room came alive to support Maia's weight.

"Incredible," Maia breathed, the sudden, excruciating awareness of something she took for granted every day was exhilarating. "Okay, how do I get down?"

Blake tugged on her pant-leg, pulling Maia down until her feet touched the floor again. Once back on the ground, the air itself seemed to roll off of her in waves as Blake grabbed her forearms and pulled her close, sliding his hands under the long sleeves of her sweater. For a moment, Maia wasn't sure why he was holding her so awkwardly, until a warm energy pulsed through her, heating her insides completely.

"There, that should keep you warm while you travel." He placed a soft kiss on her lips, leaving an even deeper—and more pleasant—warmth behind.

Lana placed a cool brown hand on her shoulder, and Maia gasped as a rush of cold splashed over her like water.

She examined her clothes, expecting them to be soaked, but they were still completely dry. The Nymph giggled. "It's just extra energy, *chère*, and besides, it could come in handy if you decide to go for a swim."

Maia chuckled. "Thanks." She rubbed her hands over her arms a few times, and Blake's warm energy returned.

Another hand weighed on her shoulder and this time, the energy was a heady rush, like a shot of espresso to her heart. She felt physically stronger, as though she could run for miles without tiring.

"In case you fancy turning into a bird—"

"Or a cheetah?" Maia countered. "Because I think I could easily take one in a race right now."

"No worries. Just take a few deep breaths and try to regulate your heart. You'll be fine." The Corocottas thumped her on the back, knocking the air out of her, before returning to Lana's side and draping his arm casually around her shoulders.

"You say that like it's easy," Maia gasped. She placed a hand over her heart and took several deep breaths to calm the organ's hammering. She tried visualizing the muscles of her heart, covered in dark blue veins, connected by aortas that stemmed out to provide life to her body. She could see its spastic beat in her mind's eye, and she imagined it slowing into a steady rhythm, but when its pace didn't change, it was clear that it was reluctant to listen. Was this how Leo felt all the time? No wonder he was so hard to pin down in a single form.

She was so busy concentrating that she didn't notice the tense gestures and murmured whispers passing between the *praeses* until Reed suddenly grumbled, "Fine." Evidently giving in to the others' threats and cajoling, he stomped his way over to her, making each of his three steps count.

He slapped a hand on her back, and Maia's racing heart slowed as a new aura took over. A feeling almost like stretching came over her, but it wasn't like being pulled; it felt more like *growing*. She opened her eyes and held out her arms, wiggling her fingers, glancing down at her legs and rising up on her toes. She certainly felt taller, but when she looked up at Blake, she was disappointed to realize that she still came no higher than his nose.

Although, she was astonished that Reed had given her anything at all. When she looked at him, he was already shrugging his shoulders as he walked back to the tiny bedroom's door, wrenching it open. "It's just so you won't fall behind," he said gruffly. "I'm going to let Marissa know we're leaving."

Everyone else filed out into the narrow hallway behind him, leaving Blake and Maia behind.

Blake picked Maia's backpack up off the floor and handed it to her with a wink and a bow. "Fresh clothes for Her Royal Highness."

"How do you keep doing this?" Maia rummaged through the bag with barely suppressed excitement, pulling out the new clothes and stuffing them back in as she turned through everything. She even found a new toothbrush, toothpaste, and her favorite jasmine-scented body wash.

"There's only one store in Portland that carries this body wash," she said, dangling the bottle in front of his nose. "I know, because my coworker's mom owns that store. Family recipe."

His lips quirked up at the corners in a devilish smirk. "Secrets are what keeps relationships exciting, don't you think?"

Maia "hmphed" and zipped up the bag.

"There's a bathroom down the hall if you feel like freshening up." He pointed in the direction everyone else had walked off toward.

"I thought we were leaving right away?" The idea of taking a hot shower was gleefully appealing. Looking at the digital Hello Kitty clock by the bed, she realized it was one-thirty in the morning, and with everything that'd happened in the last few days—along with multiple time zone changes—she wasn't even sure when she'd bathed last. The moment Blake turned toward the door, she snuck a quick sniff at her underarms.

"Yeah-nah, we can wait. Trust me," he said. Maia glared at his back as her cheeks reddened in embarrassment. He paused in the hallway, opening the bathroom door for her, and explained. "Leo's going to want to eat. He's a curious animal who likes to try everybody's cooking."

"I hope you're right." Maia walked past him and turned on the tiny bathroom's heat lamp. "I just don't want to have to ward off Grumpy again."

"He won't be a problem, promise." Blake stood in the doorway, his lips twisted as if he held back a grin.

"What?"

"Just wondering if you need any help with those." He pointed to her clothes.

"Get out of here!" Laughing, she pushed the tall Aussie back into the hallway and slammed the door on his grinning face.

21

HEIDI PACED IN her throne room. The *click* of her claw-heeled stilettos reverberated off the walls, a rhythmic noise she always found comforting. Actually, any noise she could make was one she liked, especially when it made people look up and pay attention. If it made them stop what they were doing completely, or disrupted their day somehow, so much the better. She spun around to walk back the way she'd come, and her long dress swished in harmony to the sound of her heels on the stone floor.

She paused for a moment, and the room's crystal columns that followed her every movement slowed. At her command, they joined together to form a ten-foot mirror. The crystals were semi-intelligent, but she'd had to train them to form a solid sheet with no visible cracks, one that would show her best side at all times.

It'd taken time, but she'd done it. Patience had had nothing to do with it.

She let out a disgruntled sigh as she twisted back and forth, looking at her slim figure in the glass. Her dress was a deep black leather today, giving her auburn hair a darker hue and bringing out the subtle golden glow of her brown skin. It had a narrow V-neck that almost reached her belly button, and a collar that was accordion-pleated on one side and curved on the other, while the bodice ended in a peplum shape that rounded over her hips, and the skirt fell loosely to the floor with a long train that glittered with tiny chunks of polished, uncut gold. The gown's high slit showed off one of her long legs, and her white and black stilettos had been made from the clawed feet of an eagle. She adjusted the gold belt around her waist, tapping the hard metal with a long, pointed fingernail as she examined her features. She'd painted her lips a blood red color, lined her hazel eyes in black kohl, and smoothed her hair back into a high bun. She was perfect.

The question was, would she be perfect enough for *him*?

Self-doubt made her heart drop before it was once more buoyed with irritation. With a flick of her hand, the glass mirror shattered back into individual columns, and they spread out to the sides of the room again as Heidi made her way to the empty thrones that occupied the north wall. She ran her hands reverently along the geometric patterns of the Sideralis's throne, occasionally dipping a long nail into the fiery red-and-orange grooves. The energy they held warmed her to the bone in the way the Sideralis himself refused to.

The pain of desire clenched her heart and she sighed heavily as a tear escaped down her cheek before she could wipe it away.

"Ah, the heartbreak of unrequited love."

The silky voice in her ear made her jump. Heidi turned, expecting to see someone standing right next to her, but the tall figure leaning against the expansive room's far wall was the picture of ennuied grace.

"Now," he chuckled, "don't mind me. I don't want to ruin your special time." He shook out the cuffs of his sleeves and straightened his tailored suit, examining his silver cuff links with the air of someone completely engrossed in his task.

Heidi touched her face briefly and was relieved to find that it was dry before she squared her shoulders and leveled the man with her best icy glare.

But he continued adjusting his already perfect suit, flicking invisible dust off the lapels, shifting his pocket square until it tilted just so, wiggling the knot of his tie closer to his throat before he smoothed a pale hand down its front.

Finally, he looked up at her. "All done, my dear? Good." He materialized beside her, flashing a brilliant smile before disappearing again as she blinked. She could never get used to his startling movements. He never just casually moved across an expanse of space, or traveled from location to location the way a human, or even one of her fellow *praeses*, did. Sure, with a focus of will, they could latch on to the aura of their gifted element and transport themselves nearly any distance, but they didn't move like him. No one she'd ever met did. From one blink of the eye to the next, he was in a completely different place or position.

He circled the podium in the center of the room now, casually trailing his long fingers across its top, the movement made even more disturbing by the missing transitional motions of a step or raised hand.

Heidi's breath came up short as she watched him defile the outlet of one of her greatest powers. If he had been anyone else, she would have chopped off his entire arm for the infraction.

But he wasn't just anyone.

"I have not seen you in some time, my lord." Heidi gritted her teeth, wanting to get this meeting over with as soon as possible. This man gave her a strangely sick feeling. He was unnatural. There was no other word for it.

"Yes." His short dark hair glinted in the light of the extra stars Heidi had stolen from Selene to brighten the room during his visit. "I have been very busy as of late. You, not so much."

"Not so much?" Heidi scoffed, trying to keep her anger in check, and failing. "I just drowned Little Diomede. There's no way the other *praeses* are going to make it out alive, and—" He raised a disbelieving eyebrow, causing her to stumble as she finished, "Even if, by some miracle, they do survive, they won't last long."

"Oh, so you have a plan, then? Come." He smiled, revealing two rows of impeccably straight white teeth, and gestured for her answer with the wave of a hand. "Let's hear it."

"No." Heidi placed her hands on her hips, her red lips pressed into a thin line.

"*No.*" He scratched a manicured nail against the flat top of the podium. "Is that any way to talk to your savior? You didn't know what true power or knowledge was until I came along."

Heidi sneered. It didn't matter that what he said was true—she hated owing anyone. "I'm not telling you anything, not until yo—"

Air escaped her in a sudden rush and the words died on her tongue. She grabbed her throat, her lungs burning as she gasped, but there was nothing. No air. Her nails sliced into the skin of her neck as she fought to open her throat. A dizzy darkness settled in her vision and she dropped to her knees, looking up at the tall man, wheezing.

"Heidi, Heidi," the man sighed, clucking his tongue while he stroked his chin. His gaze was on the ceiling, taking in the extra stars twinkling above his head.

Heidi fell on her side, her body rigid and awash in burning fire that licked its way through her veins with a savage greed. Through it, his voice rang clearly in her ears.

"It doesn't matter if you don't want to tell me, because I already know. I *always* know. And you know what will happen to you if you do not fulfill your end of our bargain." There was laughter in his tone. "Deliver the *praeses* to me as a team, completely whole, and I will ensure your place among the greatest in the heavens. You have one week."

All at once, air rushed back into her lungs and her body came back to life. She scrambled to all fours, still clutching her throat, choking for breath.

She looked around the cavern, but he was gone. Certain of her solitude, Heidi slumped, her hands dropping to cling at her chest. "I don't understand," she muttered. "Why as a team? Why can't I just kill them?"

"Because," the voice whispered. Heidi scuttled backward until the ridges of one of the columns dug into her back. "A general *needs* his army."

22

"CHRIST, MAIA. NEED a bib?" Leo thumped her on the back, laughing at Maia's gaping gaze as the other *praeses* walked up the wooden observatory stairs leading to the falls. The park had closed hours ago, which meant no one was around to see five people and one ghost hopping over the safety railing, despite the tumbling water and its fierce spray inches away. They should have slipped off the wet rocks, and their skin should have been torn from their bodies by the force of the water's fall, but instead, they remained safe and dry with Poppy leading the way. The Ariel provided a shield of controlled air, while Blake brought up the rear, providing heat via his outstretched arms.

They had arrived the afternoon before, and Maia had astonished everyone with how much she'd slept. Apparently, the energy they'd loaned her hadn't lasted long, and it had left her body completely exhausted after it dissipated. They'd let her sleep, though, and when she realized that she'd done so without triggering the small alarm clock on the night table to short and explode, she'd felt a surge of guilt. Not once had she thought about Marissa's electronics, while the kind woman had fed and cooed at them. But they hadn't exploded, she realized, even with so many *praeses* in her home. The guilt of her negligence made Maia cringe, but when she'd broached the subject with Blake, she'd learned that the answer had to do with the interaction between *praeses*—specifically, their auras. A *praeses's* aura acted like a sort of energy conduit when enough *praeses* were around, keeping the energy cycling between themselves rather than creating a nuclear explosion.

It had been a fascinating conversation, and Maia wondered if she'd ever learn all there was to being a *praeses*.

Now, however, it was time to work, and it was with an uneasy certainty that Maia realized no human could ever have been so close to Niagara Falls without being pulled under. The steps of the *praeses* and their charge did not falter, but despite Poppy's protective shield of air, Lana winced uncharacteristically at the sight of the water. Leo positioned himself between his mate and the falls, distracting her with conversation and jokes, and a few passionate kisses thrown in for good measure.

"So, why here?" Maia called over the deafening noise, the falls thundering in her ears. "What's so special about this place?"

They neared a small crevice in the rock that allowed them to pass behind the falls, and Maia waited as they moved, single filed, along the passageway before coming upon a cave with one wall made entirely of cascading water; Maia could reach out and touch it if she felt daring enough.

Lana leaned close once they were inside the wide open space and whispered, "This is where Selene and Reed first met as Gaea *praeses*, where they first sealed their bond." Maia wasn't sure how she was able to hear Lana over the churning water that vibrated through the stones beneath their feet, but she suddenly felt very foolish for yelling.

"Bond?" Maia whispered back. "What's that?"

Lana looked around as each *praeses* took up a specific position around the room. "It's kind of like the marriage ceremony of humans, but much stronger. Once chosen as acting guardians for a system, *astrum* seal their bond to allow them access to their mate's soul, for communication and healing purposes. It's extremely powerful, and there is no 'till death do us part.'" Lana gently guided Maia to a spot directly across from Blake, who nodded at her with a wink. Reed stood to her right, Leo to her left, a perfect ten feet between each of them. Lana took her own place across from Leo, and Maia noted that Leo's expression was the most somber she had ever seen on him.

"Maia." Blake called her name, and when she turned toward him, she saw first that the silver flecks in his eyes were dancing merrily, then that his hands were extended to her, palms up. Unsure of what to expect, she followed his lead. Lately, she'd begun each new experience draped in cynicism, but every time, she'd emerged with a deeper understanding of herself and a supernatural awareness of the planet and its lifeforms she had always taken for granted. Her piqued curiosity was balancing on the delicate edge of knowledge's addictive blade.

She mirrored Blake's motion and he smiled, gesturing for her to turn her palms down. She did. They weren't physically touching, but a controlled stream of electricity crackled and hung delicately between them as their extended auras met.

The tips of her fingers prickled with energy, not painful but just slightly irritating. She pushed the sensation from her mind as she focused on Blake's confident gaze. A moment later, she felt the same prickling sensation in concentrated points on each shoulder, and between her shoulder blades. A quick glance around revealed that the same streams of energy she shared with Blake was now shared with Leo, Lana, and Reed, too. The only difference was that Lana and Leo each held one hand toward each other and one toward her. Reed had extended one hand toward her as well, and a small lump of pity formed in her throat as she noticed that his other hand was empty. Poppy walked in a slow circle around them, her fingers trailing on the damp walls of the circular cavern. Despite the emptiness where Selene's absence weighed heavily, Maia felt strangely at home, and she relaxed as she returned her gaze to Blake.

Their eyes locked again. The whiteness of the electricity sparking between them glowed orange and red, and memories floated through her mind like flickering channels. Real memories. *Her* memories.

Finally, there were scenes to go with the emotions she'd felt when she realized who Blake was. It took her a moment, but it became clear that the images were of past lives the two had shared. His face had never changed, just as Mac's hadn't in her visions of him and Poppy. They laughed, they cried, they fought. They were not perfect by any means, but they loved in every way both possible and impossible. More of the tumultuous emotions ravaged her senses. The adrenaline rush of thrill, the irrationality of jealousy, the stomach churning

anxiety of protective worry, and the completeness of uncondi-
tional, unquestionable love.

The ground beneath her feet began to shake, and Maia
would have fallen if not for the firm grip Blake had on her
hands and the steady look in his eyes. Just as suddenly as he
appeared at her side, there was silence. Not even the noise of
the falls could be heard.

Maia gasped and blinked a few times, and a strangled cry
from Reed drew her attention. She looked at him, and followed his gaze over her shoulder. She turned in Blake's arms,
and as she did, he put several feet of distance between them,
moving to stand near Leo. Before her bruised ego could register his actions, a bright figure appeared in the empty space
ten feet behind Reed.

The woman might have been in her late twenties when
she was human, but she clearly no longer held any mortal ties.
She was completely silver, from head to toe. Her skin was so
light it was milky, her hair dark gray, her eyes midnight black,
and her dress was layer upon sheer layer of fabric, glittering
with scattered diamonds that winked like the stars. The bell
sleeves of the dress reminded Maia of the pictures of Queen
Guinevere she'd seen in books, and she wondered from what
time or place this girl had come.

The woman stood completely still, her head tilted at a
haughty angle. Despite her unusual coloring, she was excep-
tionally gorgeous, and she must have known it.

Reed approached her slowly, as though she was a frightened animal that might run away. Her dark eyes studied him
carefully, and Maia knew they were having a conversation.
After a few moments of silence, the girl finally looked down
shamefully, as one charged with a heinous crime would. Her
shoulders slumped in defeat. When he was only a foot away,

she raised her hand to him; he returned the gesture. Her white-silver light joined with the green energy that emitted from his extended hand, twisting and curling together.

"Tell them." Reed's voice shook with anger. "Tell them what you know."

The woman threw her shoulders back and leveled each of them with a stern glare, saving her last look of hatred for Maia. "You are all in violation of the covenant."

Covenant? Maia had not yet heard of any covenant, and she wondered yet again if there would ever be an end to the things she didn't know about this new world.

"'Thou shalt not usurp the authority of another, by impediment or design,'" the woman quoted.

Great. Maia's shoulders tensed in irritation. *Things are getting fun now . . .*

"We are aware of the covenant." Blake's voice was strained with anger and impatience.

Lifting her head a little higher, in a way that made it possible for her to look down upon even the tallest men in the room, the woman replied, "Our Lady is gracious, and desires you all to come forward with the replacement."

"Tell them all of it, Selene," Reed growled.

Selene gasped at his tone and, for a moment, appeared uncertain. Maia wondered if Reed had ever spoken to her like that before. "If you fail to bring the replacement forward," she finally said, "you will each be punished."

"You mean we will be replaced?" Lana asked.

Selene shook her silvery head. "She said nothing about being replaced. Only punished."

The tension in the room was palpable. Leo turned to Blake for reassurance. "Can't you do something?"

Blake hung his head, digging the toe of his black boots into the stone floor. "You know I've tried." He looked squarely at Selene. "There is only one thing Heidi wants from me, and I'm not giving it to her."

"If you weren't such a stubborn ass about things, this wouldn't be happening!" Selene lunged forward, her anger balling her tiny white hands into fists. Reed dropped his hand, a look of anguish on his face as he grabbed her shoulders, holding her back. "Why are you so selfish?" Selene yelled at Blake. "You're never going to find her, you know. If you would just be with Heidi, this whole mess wouldn't even exist."

Maia's gaze flickered from one tense figure to the next. Her teeth worried at her lower lip. It was clear that neither Selene nor Heidi knew who Maia was, not entirely. She understood now why Blake had moved away so quickly, leaving her shuddering with cold. But she was getting sick of passively sitting on the sidelines, and despite the hard determination in the expressions of her fellow *praeses*, she pondered if she should speak up for herself.

As usual, though, Blake seemed to be perfectly tuned with her conflicted feelings; he stepped forward, blocking her from Selene's view.

"*Don't say anything.*" His words reverberated through her soul.

"*Why not?*"

"*If Heidi knew you were my* astrum, *any strategy we'd have for defeating her would be useless. She would strike without mercy. She'll destroy us and everyone on this planet.*"

"Blake." Selene's eyes turned wide and pleading. This wasn't the manipulation of a woman used to getting what she wanted; the terror in the Luna guardian's eyes was authentic. "Please, just talk to her. Tell her you love her and that you will be hers. Then all of this will end. We can go back to the way things were before."

Blake's shoulders hunched with the weight he carried, and Maia didn't have to see his face to know he was chewing the inside of his cheek, choosing his next words carefully.

"I'll try to reason with her, but—"

"Reasoning won't be enough!" The Luna guardian stomped her tiny foot. "You have to tell her, Blake. Heidi wants her head"—Selene pointed a shaking finger at Maia—"and she wants you by her side. She won't accept anything less!"

As Blake deliberated, the rest of them held their breath. Maia appreciated what the others were attempting to do for her, but as the tense energy in the cavern swelled, she felt it squeeze her lungs. She opened her mouth for a gasp of air, and was just as surprised as everyone else when her own words joined the fray.

"Blake?" Every gaze turned her way. "I think you should go to her. Tell her you love her, that you'll be hers."

"Maia, no!" Lana gasped as she stepped from Leo's side, coming to stand between Blake and Maia. "No, you can't do this! We need you! You're—"

"No one. I'm no one." The words were harder to say than she'd thought, but she choked them out and gave Lana a warning glance. Touching the Nymph tenderly on the arm, she stepped around her until she was standing next to Blake, facing Selene, careful to keep a chaste distance between herself and the Sideralis. The roaring sound of the falls behind them was muffled white noise in the alien stillness. The air was clearly alive in this holy place, and it pricked and nudged at Maia's skin. Wisps of heat and cold snaked through her hair, like the fingers of a lover, but with no more strength than a breath. Her ears pricked at the sound of water droplets gliding down the smooth cavern walls. Once again, the awareness of life consumed her, and instead of fighting it, or being frightened this time, she welcomed it. Her heart warmed with feelings of adoration, and she met Selene's heated gaze.

"Would you please give Heidi a message for me?"

Selene's shock was a look of wondrous disgust.

Maia plowed on. "Tell her that I have no desire to be the Terra guardian, and that I do not wish to take her place. Blake will agree to stand at her side, and I will agree to not pursue my role as a Gaea *praeses* if she will agree to not cause further unnecessary harm to Earth or to the others."

Selene shook her head. "That won't be—"

"No," Blake interrupted. "It will be enough. Heidi needs to understand that we will not bow to her every whim, and to learn a thing or two about compromise. Selene, I can't control what Heidi does with the other replacement *praeses* under her power, but you and I can control *her*, and it is our responsibility to do so."

"No." Selene shook her head again. "I have no control over her. You don't know what she's like. She's too strong!"

"Selene." Reed's voice was as soft as his touch as he slid his fingers down her arm and took her hands in his. Maia recognized the shudder that passed through Selene's body at her mate's touch, and the Luna guardian closed her eyes, her silvery eyelashes brushing her cheeks before she opened them to meet Reed's gaze. "Selene, I have faith in you. I've told you before, you're strong. You can do this, lovest. I know you can." He stepped closer to her, hesitating slightly. Reading her face for permission, he tenderly tilted her chin up as he placed a soft kiss on her lips.

The room waited solemnly for her reaction. With a tiny gasp, Selene wrapped her arms around Reed's neck, returning his gesture with a fierce passion that caused every trace of tension in the room to leak out into the falls.

They broke from their kiss, and Reed wiped away the tears running down Selene's silvery cheeks. She nodded, shaking and sniffling. "Fine. You've convinced me," she said. Her eyes shimmered through her tears as she faced the rest of them.

"I will return with Blake, and we'll . . ." She took a shuddering breath and braced herself. "We'll pretend this never happened. But be warned . . . since Heidi is the only one with knowledge of all our replacements, they are still hers to command. I believe she is using them as spies, and she may try to use them as weapons."

A hush fell over the cavern at her words, and the others exchanged worried glances before Reed twisted his fingers around hers and tugged her toward the entrance of the cave. "We will be careful, but before you go, will you walk with me for a bit? I've missed you."

Selene hesitated, throwing a wary glance in Blake's direction.

"Go on," Blake said. "I'll be there in about five minutes, I promise. You two need some time together."

Selene ducked her head with a small smile, and Reed threw Blake a grateful glance as they made their way out of the cave.

As soon as they were out of earshot, Blake rounded on Maia, a fierceness in his eyes that she'd never seen before.

"Are you crazy? Do you know what you just did?"

Unflustered, Maia shrugged and shot back. "Strategy. I pimped you out to buy us some time."

"Why?" Just as suddenly as it came on, Blake's frustration melted away into hurt and confusion. "Aren't you jealous?"

"Should I be?" Maia closed the gap separating them. She looked into his cobalt eyes and placed her hands on his hard chest before running them up to his shoulders and clasping them around his neck, her fingers rubbing the short hair at the base of his head. She said her next words with utmost certainty, without hesitation, surprising even herself with how much she meant them. "I love you more than love allows, and nothing can destroy that. You have never earned my mistrust."

Blake wrapped his arms around her and pulled her close, until his lips touched hers, and Maia thought her bones would melt in the heat he poured into her. A small piece of her heart crumbled as she realized the full force of what she'd done. She'd be apart from him, and she had no clue for how long or even if they had a plan that would make it worthwhile.

"*You know how to reach me.*" She pushed the thought through her core and into his, their hearts pulsing against each other as if having a conversation of their own.

"That's why I love you, *mia regina*," he murmured against her lips. He squeezed her tightly one last time, sending an overwhelming flood of energy into her body before releasing her quickly and turning to the others.

"If anything happens to her—"

"Yeah, yeah, you'll fry us to bits. Got it." Leo attempted a grin as he pulled Lana into a side embrace—for his own comfort, probably, as much as for hers. The Nymph wrapped her arm around his waist, her eyes fearful.

"Please be careful, Blake. Don't let her poison you."

"Don't worry," he said. "I've had plenty of time to grow immune." He shot a glance back at Maia, a flurry of unreadable emotions passing through his features as he stepped into the dark passageway and disappeared.

Maia's heart felt as if it'd been ripped in two.

Aside from the tumbling of the falls, the room was quiet again. A figure reappeared in the doorway and hope filled Maia's chest, but it withered quickly when she realized that it was just Reed. He had nothing to say, but he looked as lonely as Maia felt. He waved the group forward, and one-by-one, they followed him out.

Three halves, and one whole couple, remained.

23

HALF-EMPTY CONTAINERS of Chinese food littered the hotel room's dining table, but even after devouring their midnight snack, Maia and the other *praeses* were still arguing about the best way to carry out their next step.

It'd been hours since Blake left with Selene, and neither Maia nor Reed had been able to get much from their respective mates. Not for a lack of trying, though. They knew both were still alive, but while in Heidi's presence, neither of them could talk much. It didn't matter that Heidi seemed to be accepting their deal for now. The reminder of her access to replacements unknown meant that they were more exposed than they knew.

Leo sat on the couch, his feet propped on the messy coffee table as he flipped through TV channels with one hand. With the other, he stroked Lana's thick curls, her head nestled in his lap.

Reed sat next to the couch, on the edge of a large recliner, and after clearing away the containers that had migrated from the dining table to the coffee table, he'd pulled out the hotel stationary and begun to fold origami shapes. Maia watched him carefully from her own recliner, the seat stretched out until it almost felt like a proper bed. They were all exhausted, but nobody was willing to rest until they'd agreed upon a plan, and Poppy wanted to hear every bit about Mac she could get out of Maia. Switching between the two conversations, Maia jumped on the silence between the other *praeses* to try to convince them of her idea, that they should each train her in their elements so they could stage a battle against Heidi, and maybe even win.

"I'm telling you guys." She propped herself on one elbow as Leo finally settled on re-runs of a reality dancing show. "It's the only way."

"And I'm telling you, for the *last* time"—Reed looked at her as though she were a child arguing with her parent over staying up an hour past her bedtime—"no. We're going to do exactly what we said we were going to do. We are staying out of their business. Like we should."

"You mean, we're going to do nothing?" Maia asked incredulously.

"Maia, *chére*." Lana lifted her head from Leo's lap just far enough to look her square in the eyes. "Please, you told Heidi you were going to give up your status and that she could have Blake. She'll know if you try to use your powers to grow stronger, and then the deal's off."

"But, Lana . . ." Maia sighed as she attempted a new angle on the old argument. "I only said that I had no desire to be the Terra guardian, to replace her, which is technically true. I never promised that I wouldn't, nor did I make a vow of any sort—"

"But you gave your word, and that's powerful enough," Leo interrupted, shaking his shoulders to the lively beat of the music on-screen.

"Seriously, can't you ever sit still?" Maia threw a wadded napkin at his head. She missed and the napkin hit his shoulder; Leo picked it up from where it had landed on the armrest and threw it back. Maia held up her hand to catch it, but instead, the napkin became caught in a gust of air and went dancing around the room.

When she dropped her hand, the ball fell into the waste basket across the room.

Maia sighed. "The truth is," she said. "I don't know how to give it up."

Reed cleared his throat. He sounded nervous when he said, "If you just stop tapping into your celestial power, it should disappear on its own."

Maia examined her hands. They didn't look any different since the ceremony at Little Diomede, when her powers had really begun to grow. They weren't glowing, nor had they become more graceful and slender. They were just thin hands, with veins crawling over fine bones and showing blue under her skin, a few freckles, and short, blunt nails.

"If I let these powers atrophy, how am I going to get home?" Maia asked. Then, "Oh, right . . . I don't have a home."

Everyone but Poppy looked away, avoiding eye contact with Maia and each other.

Maia continued, unsure now if she was talking to them or herself. "I can't just get on a bus or a plane, or even rent a car to get back to Portland. I don't have the money, and the vehicles wouldn't work with me on them, anyhow."

"Look," Reed said, finally glancing up from the swan he was folding. "We're sorry about dragging you into this. Honestly, we are. But if you can't use your powers and you don't have anything left in Portland, why don't you just get a job here and start a new life? We'll help. We can leave you some cash to get you started, but under no circumstances are you allowed to use your powers. The best thing to do is just let them fade away." He shrugged. "Then you can go back to your thrilling life."

Pulling the lever on the side of the recliner, Maia forced it into an upright position, the slam of the springs echoing in the room. Anger seared its way through her chest as she stood suddenly, but just as quickly, she was at a loss for words as blood rushed to her head, thundering in her ears as the room spun.

She blinked and waited until she was steady before leveling a glare at each of the *praeses*, her silent accusation thick.

"Go back to my 'thrilling' life?" she hissed, finally landing on Reed. "As what? I'm not even human anymore. I don't—hell, what the fuck am I?" No one met her gaze, and silence stretched the breadth of the room. Maia seethed. "So, the mighty Gaea *praeses*, who have the planet's greatest powers at their disposal, are just going to give up? Do nothing? That is not what I had in mind when I gave Blake up to buy us more time, but fine. Fantastic!" Throwing up her arms at the level of cowardice permeating the room, she stomped off to her bedroom in disgust, slamming the door behind her hard enough to rattle the frame and crack the wall.

She kicked off her shoes and peeled off her jeans and sweater as she pushed her way through the double French doors that led into the adjacent bathroom. The cool tile floor under her bare feet seemed to ebb the heat building inside her, and she sat at the edge of the Jacuzzi tub, turned on the hot water, and watched as the tub began to fill, mesmerized by the undulating steam that writhed and coiled upward, filling the bathroom and fogging the mirror with its hot breath. It dampened her skin in a sticky layer of humidity, and Maia finally turned on the cold water, removed the rest of her clothes, and brushed her teeth, waiting for the water to cool.

When she finally stepped in, shutting the water off, her feet and ankles reddened instantly. She had to lower herself into the bath an inch at a time, as the heat eagerly licked its way across her skin, burning even as the steam followed through with wet kisses to dull the pain. Sinking low, until just her head was above the surface, Maia closed her eyes. She wanted to communicate with Blake again.

For a moment, she thought she heard his voice trying to speak to her. Though she still felt him in her bones, he sounded far away, his words muffled and unclear, jolting her heart into a panic.

The more she focused, the more her body relaxed, becoming one with the water as the hazy view of a familiar garden rose up behind her closed lids. When it was finally clear, Maia took off down the path in a sprint, her eyelet dress swishing and bunching between her legs as she skidded around corners and jumped over low-lying plants. Everything was hazy in her peripheral view, as though her mind struggled to maintain the image of the dream, but otherwise, the exotic garden was the same. She had to search for only a few moments before she spotted what she was looking for.

The creature stood on its thin back legs, its front hooves planted against the trunk of a tree while its long neck stretched forward elegantly as it nibbled at the tree's leaves and mimosa-shaped flowers.

"Hey!" Maia slowed to an out-of-breath, cautious tiptoe as she drew nearer.

The gazelle turned its noble head in her direction and nodded for her to sit down. She placed herself on a nearby boulder, and it went back to its meal without speaking.

"I'm really glad I found you," she said. She twisted her hands in the fabric of her dress's hem, her emotions a tangle of overwhelming anxiety. There was so much to say, she wasn't sure where to start. "I said 'yes' like you told me to, but it's kind of opened a Pandora's Box for me, if you know what I mean?"

The gazelle dropped down to all fours and, after taking a few sips from the nearby brook, pranced over to her side and sat next to her, blinking its wise eyes at her slowly. "Tell me."

Maia started with the moment she'd said "yes" to the position of a Gaea *praeses*, and ended with the moment Blake left with Selene. She left no detail out, aside from her intimate moments with Blake. Those she glossed over as much as possible, feeling fiercely protective of them, as though the mere knowledge of them was something the gazelle could use against her. When she finished, the gazelle nodded thoughtfully. "I see you have found your team, and your *astrum*, but now, you have lost them all. I suppose, then, you are not the leader I thought you to be."

"What's that supposed to mean?" Her newest friend, rash anger—which had somehow overthrown her anxiety—welled up in her like a nettled cobra, ready to strike. "I never said I wanted to be a leader, and I can't make them do what they don't want to. If you haven't noticed, they're all a bit more powerful than I am!"

"Are they?" The gazelle answered coolly. "I believe they are wayward children who need guidance. Their mother has not maintained control over them, and now, they have turned against her."

"But Heidi isn't their mother! What about Blake? Doesn't everyone revolve around him? Don't they all answer to him?" Maia lifted her chin, defiance building as she met the gazelle's condescending gaze. She was tired of being treated like a child just because she was new to this world. She'd managed so far, and she knew how to hold her own. Besides, she'd survived worse. Her father's illness was but a mere scratch on the iceberg of problems her life had accumulated, problems she'd had to solve on her own. She may be young, but as they say, age is just a number. Survival is what truly matures you.

The gazelle cocked its head, answering both her verbal questions and internal statement. "Be that as it may, you must answer those questions on your own. No one is going to hand you the keys to the kingdom, my child."

"But why? Isn't it your job to help me? Whoever you are?" Maia braved a quick, accusing glance at the gazelle before returning to the little pile of dirt she'd idly begun to create, pushing the grains around absently as she waited for the gazelle to say something.

It sighed, exasperated, before standing and stretching its long legs, flicking its tail at nonexistent pests. At its full height, it was tall enough to look down on Maia, who remained seated on her rock, feeling like she was in time-out. She really had no time for an existential crisis, but perhaps she needed one. Before that day in her mother's garden, Maia had known who she was—as much as a nineteen-year-old who'd grown up faster than most could, anyway. She'd known what she liked and didn't, and what she wanted to do with her life. She'd been in enough situations to mold and shape her ideals into what was right and wrong. Memories of this life, her life, instead of ones from lives past, clamored for the attention of her tears. She didn't have time for them, either. Those lessons of abuse and betrayal at the hands of her over-religious grandparents and old boyfriends had taught her the most important lesson—trust no one. Be an island of one. She looked up at the gazelle's narrow face and thought she saw the light of the garden shimmering around its antlers, creating an odd halo that looked anything but angelic.

"My job is merely to guide you to greatness," the gazelle said. "However, if greatness is not already there, then my guidance is useless."

Maia scowled at the creature, and it almost looked as though it smiled in return.

"I will, however, give you one more hint. You possess all the powers of the other *praeses*, but you do not know how to use them. If you challenge Heidi alone, you will fail. It is up to you to convince them to give you use of their full powers."

Maia straightened. "But if I continue to use my powers, won't Heidi know? Won't she feel her own fading?"

The gazelle shook its head as it turned to walk back to the brook, leaping over the gurgling water and pausing on the other side. Without looking back, it replied, "As of now, Heidi thinks she has won, and is full of too much confidence to notice the absence of her power. Hard decisions are ahead, Maia Thompson. Sacrifices will need to be made." It glanced at her over its shoulder. "You still wonder if you are human. But what part of that humanity you have left are you willing to sacrifice to win?"

Before a stunned Maia could squeak out an answer, the gazelle had disappeared into the bush, and she felt the water of her bath, now cooled to a lukewarm temperature, lapping against her skin.

When she opened her heavy-lidded eyes again, her movements felt slow and mechanical. She operated in a haze, unplugging the drain, stepping out of the tub, wrapping a towel around her body. Only one sentence floated through her mind, repeating over and over: *"what part of that humanity you have left are you willing to sacrifice to win?"* So, she was still human, but how much was yet to be seen.

She padded into the cold bedroom, stopping when the mattress bumped into her shins. Sinking slowly onto the bed, her hands automatically fumbled for the covers to warm her damp body as she rolled over, staring unblinking at the patterned wallpaper, and tried to process her vision. It was as though her mind had stopped working and was stuck like a cracked disc, that one question permanently repeating, and no matter what else she tried to think of—Blake, the other *praeses*, her childhood full of nightmares, her parents, her home, her future—none of those thoughts could remain solid in her mind. They were continuously interrupted.

She'd barely had a moment to mourn the loss of her humanity, let alone anything, but she wasn't a monster. What would her sacrifice entail? The very word itself conjured thoughts of pain and torture. To sacrifice meant you had to give up something precious. Hadn't she done a lot of that already?

Maia's temple throbbed as a migraine teased the edges of her brain. She had nothing left to give. The older and incomplete memories of past lives rose to the surface of her mind like a Leviathan, attempting to drown her thoughts and heart in their ocean of shame, guilt, and abject fear. She bit her lip as hard as she could, tightened her fists until she felt her nails break skin. With a shudder, she sighed. She didn't have time for those old memories. They could stay buried in the unsustainable depths of her subconscious where they belonged.

Slowly, as she lay there, the flower pattern of the wallpaper grew hazy and her eyes fluttered closed. Drifting into exhaustion, she hoped for a reprieve from the question still swirling in her mind.

But even in sleep, it haunted her.

24

BLAKE TURNED ANOTHER thin parchment page of the original Shakespeare folio. Leisurely lounging on the library's couch, his ankles crossed before him, he let the words drift through his mind without reaching his heart. He had the entire works of Shakespeare memorized. He didn't need to read them—after all, he'd been the one to give the Bard a few of his ideas, working at The Globe together the way they had. But unless he was poring over some book or manuscript, Heidi was likely to prattle on incessantly.

What he really wanted was to reach Maia, but when their souls connected, he felt how deeply she breathed and how slow her heart beat. If she was sleeping, he didn't want to disturb her. He bit back his disappointment and dropped the communication attempt, focusing again on the tale of the Scottish king who let his deadly prediction-sparked ambition consume his life.

His eyes traveled across the lines and he turned another page, confident that although Heidi wasn't in the room, she was definitely watching him. He just needed time to think, time to understand what their options were, time to decide what, exactly, to tell Maia when they spoke next, because it was impossible to know how much time they would have.

It had surprised both Blake and Selene when Heidi had agreed to meet at her home—well, technically, *their* home. Prior to that, no one—not even Selene—had known where the home was located. Though it had been meant to be shared by Heidi and Blake, it was Heidi alone who occupied it. Partial to Scotland's ethereal countryside, Heidi had always been drawn to its rough and wild landscape. When she first came to Earth as a replacement, Scotland had been mostly barren of human inhabitants. Heidi had been there when the first castle had been built, and eventually—through a high-profile marriage of means and enough serfs—had built one of her own. For centuries, Heidi had lived the immortal way, cleverly maintaining her hold on home and land through servitors and barristers until humanity finally caught up with the idea that a woman could own property. Heidi loved attention and challenging the social norms, and being a single woman, living and owning one of Scotland's most historic castles, had definitely earned her notoriety and attention.

Blake shook his head. It was just like Heidi to prey on the prejudices of humanity, bending them to her will and becoming more powerful than their narrow comprehension could ever allow. Unfortunately, her tenacity in defying humanity hadn't extended to the decoration of her home. She'd gone with all the usual clichés, insisting on cluttering the walls and nearly every flat surface with any piece of macabre, medieval tapestry or accessory she could find.

Upon arriving, Selene and Blake had both been ushered into a sitting room by a tuxedoed butler, where they'd found Heidi reclining gracefully on an intricately carved fainting couch displaying black velvet cushions and the body of a swan carved into its back frame. Her dress was of the lightest cyan blue—chosen to match Blake's eyes, he was sure—with celestial scenes embroidered upon the hem and bell sleeves in silver thread. Her long, thick auburn hair was styled in artful curls that cascaded over her shoulder.

Selene had sunk immediately to her knees before the couch. "My lady, I have good news. The replacement has agreed to let her powers expire and not seek your throne, while the Sideralis has agreed to remain by your side in exchange—" The Luna guardian had faltered at the hard look in Heidi's eyes at the word "exchange." The Terra guardian hadn't once taken her eyes off Blake, from the moment he'd entered the room, but it was clear that she did not like having anyone manipulate her plans, either.

"Um." Selene had braced herself for whatever wrathful reaction Heidi was going to display next. "It's in exchange for you ceasing to harm the Earth, and agreeing not to punish your remaining *praeses*."

The silence that permeated the room was long and thick as Heidi deliberated, her eyes still fixated on Blake. She'd carefully noted his casual dark blue suit, and the way he'd left the collar of his shirt unbuttoned at the neck, how he leaned against a side table with his hands stuffed in his pockets. He looked fresh off the cover of *GQ magazine*, right down to his deliberately un-styled curls and the shadow of a close-trimmed beard.

"Is it true, then?" Heidi asked. "You're willing to finally rule by my side, where you belong?"

Swallowing his rising pride and anger, Blake had forced a half-hearted smile that didn't reach his eyes, but that he knew Heidi would take as a flirtatious one. Then he'd walked to her side, taken her hand, and, after swallowing a little bile, placed a small kiss on her knuckles.

"If you'll have me." He was glad he hadn't been human for centuries, or beads of sweat would have rested on his upper lip and his hands would have trembled. Not from fear or nervousness, but from concealing his disgust. It was worse now that he had tasted Maia's lips, and Heidi no longer scared him. He had faced far more evil in his many lives. What worried him was her unpredictable emotions and intentions. Those were what made her dangerous. She was a threat to Maia, and even though he knew Maia was a formidable foe, she was vulnerable without her lost memories. She would never remember how incredibly powerful she was.

A triumphant smile crept across Heidi's delicate features.

"Well, I . . ." Heidi fluttered her long lashes coquettishly, and almost looked flustered at her loss for words. Blake wasn't buying it, though, and finally, she used her free hand to shoo Selene away. "Fine," she said. "You go and tell the other traitors that all is forgiven, but only for now. Blake, dearest." She patted the empty ottoman in front of her couch, and Blake had struggled to contain a wince at the hated pet name. "Why don't you rest awhile and fill me in on everything?"

And that had been that. After Selene had scuttled from the room to send a message to Reed, Blake had spent the next four hours sitting on that stupid ottoman with beads from its embroidered design digging into his ass.

He still wondered, hours later, if he would have a permanent flower tattoo from that damn ottoman, and he irritably flicked another page in the folio, letting words he knew by heart wash over him in comfort. Remembering Macbeth's story made him very aware that things weren't that bad. Not yet, at least. Heidi had had very little interest in her replacement, and he intended to keep things that way. She'd asked only a few questions about Maia—whom she'd simply called "that girl"—and with Blake's convincing disinterest and short responses, she had quickly grown bored of the topic. Treating the entire series of events like water under the bridge, she'd switched to her most favorite subject instead—herself.

It had felt like half an eternity before Blake could finally get away, and when he did, he'd made a beeline for the library. It was soothing; he loved the ancient smells of the oak shelves, the bindings of the books, their old parchment pages, the leather and other materials that made up their covers. But what made the spot even sweeter was the wall almost entirely comprised of a single large window overlooking the North Sea. He missed his home in Australia, and when the sun hit the waters of the ocean, the glint of the rippling waves reminded him, if only for a moment, of the waters off the coast of his home.

He forgot the folio, letting the book slump over his stomach as he stared out at the churning sea. Clouds had clotted around the sun, turning the water into dark hues of blue and gray, with the occasional angry froth of flotsam. The wind tripped merrily by the window panes, making them rattle. Blake closed his eyes, not to sleep but to check on Maia, and when he realized his mate was still asleep, he began, again, to think about his home.

Blake smiled at the memories of swooping gulls diving for their breakfast and hot sand beneath his feet, of surfing the waves off Kirra Point, and the taste of home-brewed ale from an Esky cooler hidden beneath some rocks to stay cold. He was just about to head out to the beach in his half-memory, half-dream when the scratching of the wind at the window became too grating to ignore. At first, he thought it was only the tall grass outside, scraping against the glass, but then came the heavy thud of beating wings, and he figured he should check it out.

He opened his eyes slowly, peering around the room to make sure he was truly alone. Setting the folio aside, he went to the door and opened it, picking up the distant sounds of Heidi banging away on her piano on the opposite side of the house. Rolling his eyes at the Terra guardian's lack of musical talent, he softly closed the door and patted the thick wood, grateful that it acted as sufficient sound barrier to the wailing, gnashing sounds coming from Heidi's piano. He turned to the window.

A harrier hawk pranced in the air outside, brushing the window in its agitation. Blake slid the window's lock over and let the eager bird in through a small pane. Thankful to be out of the damp and cold, the bird ruffled and picked at its feathers, standing on one leg and allowing Blake to untie the tiny pouch attached to its ankle. The minute its leg was released, the bird resumed hopping about, searching for payment in the form of a mouse or two that could always be found hidden away in a bed of old parchment.

The tiny brown pouch Blake had removed was barely the size of a fingernail. He turned it inside out, and a single bronze light appeared, spinning as it hung in midair before dividing into smaller lights that filled the entire library. Every surface—everything but Blake and the tiny hawk—was dotted with the bronze beads, until they coalesced suddenly into the shimmering figure of a familiar man, detailed all the way down to his dark hair and quick eyes.

"Leo?" Blake asked, surprised. "How in the actual hell did you find this place?"

The figure paced with leonine grace around the couch and table. "Followed your scent, of course. You didn't think we'd lose track of you that easily, did you?" The Corocottas flashed a reassuring smile without breaking stride.

Feeling only slightly relieved, Blake asked, "Then why are you here?"

"What? Can't a guy check in on his best friend? See how he's holding up in prison?" Leo chuckled and winked in Blake's direction. "Just think of this as a conjugal visit, only without the conjugal stuff. You're on your own there, man."

"Leo." Blake rubbed his temples in exasperation. "It's not like I'm not pleased to see you, mate. Honestly, I am, but if there is no real emergency and if Maia's fine . . . she's fine, right?" The Corocottas nodded and Blake instinctually grabbed his friend's shoulder in an effort to hold him still, only to find his fingers slipping through the aura projection without finding purchase. He rolled his eyes at his forgetfulness. It'd been awhile since any of their group had needed to resort to this form of communication. Aura projection was fragile and unpredictable. The watered-down version of Leo, which was all this tiny piece of his aura would allow, made his vernacular even ditzier. Which, for Leo, was saying a lot. "If she's fine, then why are you here?"

"Remember Maia's cat?" Leo's image flickered.

"Her cat? You mean the fat orange tabby you sent on a mission?"

Leo grinned wolfishly, his only affirmation before he turned and resumed his careful stalking. A crunching noise in the corner of the room made the Corocottas pause for a moment. He looked around nervously, sniffing the air.

"That's just—"

"Clarence having a tasty snack?" Leo finished for him.

"Yeah, so about this cat?"

"Right. So, I sent the cat out to gather some intelligence for me. Pretty easy. Cats are excellent at that, you know, 'cause they're, like, the original ninjas. I mean, they can probably sneak up on you in the dark and kill you with just a whisker."

Blake raised an eyebrow, waiting for Leo to get to the point. "And what does a ninja kitty have to do with you being here?"

"Don't you get it, man?" The more excited the agitated Corocottas got, the faster his shape flickered. The air hummed with the projection's attempts at containing his energy. "Intelligence! I wasn't expecting much, but that cat got me the juiciest intelligence I've ever heard!"

"Ar'right, okay! I get it. Would you just—" Blake tried unsuccessfully to snatch at the edges of Leo's hoodie, flapping in the waves of crackling static energy, in the hopes he could anchor the other *praeses's* projection to his own aura. "Calm down, mate! I don't want Heidi to hear you!"

With a muffled thump of mixed energies, Leo's image landed on the couch, leaning back like a prince of leisure. "Aw, man, you're no fun! Hey, got anything to eat?"

"Leo, focus! What did the cat tell you that's so important?"

"Ha! Get this, dude. Nikki just found out how Maia can, you know." When Blake just stared at him, he drew a line across his throat. "To Heidi! You know, take her out. Poof, no more!" The projection began to giggle like a drunk sorority girl. Celestial energy had never been good at maintaining projections this long without causing some pretty eclectic effects.

Blake shushed his friend, and this time, when he touched the image, their collective auras met and he was able to hold his hand over Leo's mouth. He searched the room with his eyes, his heart racing, preparing his muscles to fight in case somebody had heard them.

The only thing that came close to that was Blake's own, "Agh!" when Leo licked his hand. Blake pulled away and wiped his palm on the Corocottas's shoulder.

"Really, mate? What the hell was that for?"

"Why'd you have to cover my mouth, bruh? Didn't you hear what I said?"

"Yes, I did, but you needn't shout," Blake whispered through clenched teeth.

"Why not? It's incredible!" Leo began bouncing on the couch cushion, obviously eager to get up and resume his pacing. Blake stopped him with a firm grip on his friend's forearm.

"That's fine," Blake in the calmest voice he could muster, while inwardly, hope over Leo's words lit a fuse of adrenaline that sparked through his veins. "But why don't you tell me exactly what you mean?"

"Maia knows who Poppy's *astrum* is, right?"

Blake nodded. "Yeah, apparently it's Maia's *Talis* guardian, Mac. When we saw him at the park, I didn't realize they were one and the same. I thought he was just another *praeses* replacement at the time."

"Exactly. And, apparently, good 'ole Mac isn't just any *Talis* warrior."

"What do you mean?" Blake's eyebrows bunched so much they nearly formed a single line across his worried forehead.

"He's . . ." Leo's pause was for dramatic effect, but even he looked around a moment before revealing in a hushed voice: "Camael."

"What?" If Blake had been in the middle of sipping a drink of water, Leo and a couple thousand-year-old books would have been drenched. Camael? An Ancient? This was an oh-shit moment if ever there was one. Blake chewed on the inside of his cheek, thinking. Camael was one of the original seven *Talis* warriors. Legend had it that the Source had birthed them and set them with the task of being the first harvesters of the supernovas. They were the only ones with knowledge of the true identity and location of the Source, and they also usually only guarded Council members. The knowledge they possessed meant that they never reincarnated, or were ever stationed anywhere. They chose where they went. Which also meant that they never had cause to take human form or spend time on Earth, or any system for that matter. Blake rubbed his forehead as he finished his last few thoughts. Leo's projection was waning; his time coming to a close.

"Groovy, eh?" Oblivious to Blake's shock, Leo wiggled free of Blake's slackened grip. Clapping his hands, he moonwalked about the sofa in a victory dance before resuming his pacing. "There's never been one of the Ancients here on Earth, not that I know of, and to make things weirder—" Leo guffawed. "Weirder." He scrunched his nose over the syllables as he played with the Rs. "Such a funny word . . ."

Blake ignored the Corocottas's erratic musings; it was only going to get worse from here on out. Instead, Blake paced alongside him, his nerves a sponge to the high-tuned, frenetic animal energy of his friend. He rubbed his hands together and tried sorting through his thoughts out loud.

"I can't believe it. This . . . this is incredible." He stopped. "But why is he guarding Maia? And how is he supposed to help us fight Heidi?"

"Well . . ." Leo's enthusiasm waned slightly. "See, that's the problem. The gang, the crew, the team, the posse, the—"

"Leo," Blake growled.

Leo didn't skip a beat. "—don't know exactly." He held up his hands as Blake's face clouded in frustration. "We do know that he has something that can help Maia. Unfortunately, he'll only give the mandate to her."

"This is a mandate, then?"

Leo nodded with certainty. "Of the highest order, if you know what I mean."

The Council. This entire thing smacked of their backdoor secrecy and all the shit that phrase entailed. Blake mirrored his friend's nod, scratching the stubble on his chin.

"All right," he said heavily. This changed things. "If you don't mind, I'd like to tell Maia about this myself. If, of course, you haven't already told her?"

"Nah, man! She's been out cold since I got the message and sent you this." He waved to his projection, still glowing slightly. "I'm sure she's probably still asleep."

"Good. And, Leo?" He looked into his friend's eyes, the unwavering loyalty between them unspoken. Even so, he said, "Thanks."

"Yeah, you got it." With that, and a sudden snap in the air, his friend disappeared.

Blake heard another frustrated tap on the glass. He let the hawk back outside and stood at the window, breathing in the fresh air off the ocean. The attempt at calming himself failed, though, and he turned away, plopping back down on the couch, his emotions torn in two. He was never one to sit quietly, which is why he had made the perfect Sideralis. He had just as much energy, if not more, than Leo, but it was fueled by something more—a destructive force that was both beautiful and dangerous. If he didn't control himself and the energy within, he could do more damage than Heidi could conjure on her best day. Nothing destroyed quicker than heat, and the beauty of light would have one staring, mesmerized, instead of fighting. Before he'd been chosen as the Sideralis, though, he'd been a *Talis* warrior, and his self-control and discipline was what made him one of the more successful. His passion on the battlefield, and restraint when off, had made him invaluable in the delicate political world of the vast universe. Humans had no idea what was out there, and their own political heckling was as adorable as a baby's coo in comparison.

Blake's fists clenched under the memories of tyrants and warlords, of calculating old beings. He had been in this *praeses* guardian role too long. He was a man of action, a man of war, whether he liked it or not. The Council had asked him to remain a *Talis* warrior, but he and Maia had wanted—needed—a change. The duties they shared had worn on them both.

His lips curled into a subtle smile. Shaking his head, the tension eased out of his shoulders as he leaned back, letting out a chuckle. The breeze continued to blow in through the window, playing with his unruly hair. He may not know why an Ancient had been tasked as her guard, and he may not have liked sitting quietly while she acted in his stead, but he had fought by that woman's side for eons. They had been *Talis* more than any other role. Heidi had no clue what she was up against. Neither did anyone else.

24

MAIA WOKE TO the sound of screaming.

She nearly fell out of bed as she fumbled to dislodge herself from the tangled sheets, but once on her feet, she raced to the door. The screaming came from the room Lana shared with Leo, and she almost collided with the Corocottas as he rounded the corner from the kitchenette, his face pale.

When they burst through the door, they found the water Nymph shivering and dripping in the middle of the bed. The sheets and pillows, even the mattress, were all equally soggy and waterlogged, and the carpet squelched under their feet. Water poured from Lana's eyes, lips, nose, ears. It even trickled from beneath her nails, and her curls were limp with the weight of it. Leo reached her first as Maia skidded to the bed, a step behind, her feet slipping beneath her until the bed's frame slammed into her knees.

Leo scooped the sobbing, drenched girl into his arms. Lana's own slipped as they curled around him, her slick fingers scrabbling for purchase against his bare skin. His drenched pajama bottoms whipped at his ankles as he hurried out into the living room, heading for the couch. Maia raced into the other rooms to gather more blankets and towels, stopping by the stove to quickly put the kettle on as her heart raced with fear and questions. By the time she returned, Leo had peeled away Lana's wet clothes and had her bundled in a blanket. A now wet tissue was balled in her hands, and tiny flakes of the delicate material clung to Lana's face where she had pressed it to stave off the tears. The Nymph clung to the tiny ball as she sobbed and shook, muttering to herself while rocking back and forth, her hazel eyes glassy with tears. Thankfully, the water had slowed to a meandering drip from her pores.

"What happened to her?" Maia was breathless, piling more blankets onto the still-shivering girl and rubbing a towel through her wet curls.

Leo shook his head. A sharpened canine pierced his lower lip, drawing blood as he clenched his jaw shut in barely controlled grief. "She hasn't been the same since Little Diomede," he whispered, eyes focused on his mate. "Nightmares every night, and she flinches at the sight of water. I've never seen her like this. Ever." His voice broke as he rubbed his hands up and down her arms, pulling her close to try to warm her. "Damn it, we need Blake." He shook his tousled head roughly, as if reminding himself why Blake couldn't be there. Maia watched in dumbstruck horror as his muscles crawled, agitated, under his skin. He was fighting the change, but occasionally, the short hair on his forearms would become thick and scaly before returning back to normal. Feathers would sprout along his fingers before receding to human digits, and he fought the growth of the claws that appeared immediately after. Maia half-expected a tail to wiggle out from beneath him, but he clutched Lana tighter, pressed his face against her wet hair, breathed her in, and squeezed his eyes shut.

Lana shivered violently. "Cold, so c-c-c-old." Her teeth chattered as Maia handed her a hot mug, and she kept her hands wrapped around the Nymph's to steady them so Lana could hold the drink without also wearing it.

A door slammed in the hallway, causing the walls to shake.

"What the hell? Ah, shit! What is this?" An angry Reed could be heard sloshing through the wet carpet. "It's every-where!"

Indeed, it was. Maia realized that the suite's entire carpet was now soaked through, as well as the couch and about half the blankets immediately surrounding Lana. Water still poured from the Nymph, and her agitation as she gasped and shook only increased the flow.

Reed's eyes settled on the sobbing girl. As he studied her, his lips slowly pressed into a thin line and his jaw clenched. "She's having an aversion to her element."

"You've seen this before?" Leo didn't take his eyes from Lana. He patiently wiped the tears from her cheeks and handed her more tissues. It was the first time Maia had seen him so attentive and focused. Now that he had reined in his instincts, he was entirely concerned for his partner, and nothing else.

Reed nodded and perched on top of the couch's back. "It's rare, but when a *praeses* experiences a traumatic event while using their element, it can cause an aversion. She's having a negative reaction to her own powers. The more upset she is, the less she'll be able to control her element."

"How do we fix it?" Maia asked, searching for a dry piece of blanket to cover Lana with.

Reed shook his head, rubbing the side of his nose in frustration. "We can't. We can temporarily stop her flow of magic by taking as much of her energy into ourselves as we can, but—"

"But what?" Leo growled.

The look on Reed's face was one of hopelessness. "It's dangerous."

"I don't care. What do I have to do?"

"Take her back to her source, in the Garden. Drain off the rest of her powers and hope that her tree can restore her. There's no guarantee, though. There's a chance her energy can't be restored."

Leo didn't hesitate. "Lay your hands on her. Please?"

He turned his eyes to Maia and Reed both, and neither of them had to stop to consider what he was asking. All three of them gently placed their hands on the shaking girl. The effect was immediate. Maia felt cold all over, as if water ran through her veins instead of blood. The pressure was nearly too much to bear, and Maia sucked in a breath as her lungs struggled for air, drowning against elemental will and aura. One moment, Maia felt like a geyser ready to erupt, and the next, Lana's shaking had subsided and she slumped lifelessly against Leo's chest, her energy significantly drained. The water stopped leaking from her body. Her beautiful caramel-colored skin was pale, and her curls covered her face in a limp mass.

Reed stood, opened the patio door, and called for Poppy. A hot gust of wind, smelling of desert sand and the heat of rocks baking in the sun, swept through the room, drying everything it touched, though not instantly. While the wind coursed through the hotel suite, Leo lifted a still-dripping Lana from the couch and carried her outside to the balcony's rail. Reed and Maia followed. She was worried for Lana, but also eager to see what Reed would do next. She wanted to learn more from him, since his strengths resembled her own abilities the most.

The Nepenthes curled his fingers and flicked his wrist, and just like that, he'd called forth the roots of the nearest surrounding trees. He nodded to Maia to do the same, and she mimicked his movements, pleased by the ease with which she carried out the deed. It wasn't long until the roots created a ramp from the balcony railing to the ground, arcing with a gentle slope. Leo carried Lana down, both nearly dry now thanks to Poppy's gentle wind. The Nymph snuggled her head against Leo's shoulder with a contented sigh, and Maia could have sworn she heard the happy rumble of a purr emanating from his chest.

At the bottom, he turned into a large chestnut stallion. With Lana perched on his back, her fingers loosely twisted in his mane, he took off at a canter.

Once they were gone, Maia asked, "Where is this garden they're going to?"

The roots had already begun to return home, soil rolling over them, tucking them back into their beds beneath the surface.

"Eden," Reed said. Though Maia was poised to unload a stack of questions, he held up his hand to cut her off. "Look, I don't have time to explain, and it doesn't matter, not right now. Here." He handed her a manila envelope he'd had folded and stashed in his back pocket.

"What's this?" She peeked inside to see several stacks of banknotes, along with her birth certificate, passport, and driver's license. "How—?"

"That should be enough to get you back on your feet." He turned on his heel, heading for his bedroom. The suite was nearly dry, and the hot wind had finally died down. Maia didn't want to let him get away with another quick escape, but Reed must have anticipated her following. As she neared the threshold of his room, his door met her nose.

Appalled at how quickly he'd shut her out, she rubbed at the sore appendage. She was considering knocking the door down when a familiar voice reverberated through her core.

"Maia? Are you awake?"

"Blake." The knots of anxiety around her heart loosened a fraction. *"Thank God."*

"What happened?"

"Lana had an aversion to her element."

"Shit. Did Leo take her back to the garden?"

"Yeah. Is she going to be okay?"

"Honestly, mia regina? I don't know. I've never seen it happen. I've only heard of it. It . . . usually doesn't end well."

"Great, just what we need." Maia groaned as she shuffled back to her room. She wanted to change, or cry, or do something productive. But a sudden thought made her pause. *"Can you see what I'm doing right now?"*

Blake chuckled. She felt it reverberate through her chest as if it were her own. *"Not unless you let me. Do I want to?"*

Maia blushed, but was relieved. She loved him, but she still needed to have some freedom, some privacy. Glad that Blake couldn't see what she was up to, she stuffed the manila envelope into a bag with the rest of her things before heading to the bathroom, determined to untangle the birds' nest that was her hair.

"*I was just curious. There is a lot about this whole soul mate thingy I still don't understand.*"

"'*Thingy,' huh?*" Blake's laugh deepened, its energy traveling and bringing warmth to the space between Maia's hips. Her heartbeat quickened, and Blake gave a little hum of satisfaction. "*The term 'soul mate' is the problem, I think. It's not really the best way to describe it. At least, not the way humans interpret it. It's much closer to the idea of Yin and Yang, and has more to do with the balance of our energies than the human concept of love. I'll explain more about it when I can, but right now, we have a more pressing matter.*"

Mixed feelings of disappointment and curiosity swept the rest of Maia's anxiety away. "*And what is that?*"

"*Remember Nikki?*"

"*My cat?*" Guilt colored Maia's tone as she realized she hadn't thought of the sweet creature in days. Not since the feline had become Leo's new best friend, actually.

"*Don't feel bad. She's been enjoying herself immensely, according to Leo.*"

"*Hey, I thought you couldn't read my mind?*"

"*I can't, but when your emotions are strong enough, I can feel them.*"

"*Oh.*" Maia felt slightly foolish as the handle of her hairbrush broke off in her hand. Frowning, she twisted her hair on top of her head and secured it in a messy bun instead. "*So, what's this pressing matter that has to do with my cat?*"

"*It has to do with Poppy's soul mate, actually. Nikki's the one who discovered it. He isn't human, Maia. He's Camael.*"

"*Cama-who?*"

"*Camael. It's a name humans associate with archangels, but*"—Blake snorted derisively—"*trust me, the* Talis *warriors are far from angels. They're more like bodyguards to those who hold positions of power.*"

Maia sighed as she returned to her bedroom. She hated not knowing, hated having everything constantly explained to her. "*I hate being such a late bloomer,*" she grumbled.

Blake chuckled in response. "*Trust me, I know the feeling. We'll get you all caught up soon. For now, all you need to know is that he needs to speak with you.*"

"*He does? Why?*" Maia zipped up the backpack, throwing it over her shoulder. The hotel suite was quiet as she made her way to the front door, pausing for a moment with her fingers on the door handle, turning back to Reed's closed bedroom. He'd made it clear that he didn't want to help her. Not anymore. She had no choice but to go it alone.

"*Because Camael is no ordinary* Talis. *He's an Ancient, one of the originals birthed by the Source. He's never been anything else, and this is the first time I've ever heard of one assuming a human vessel. Every replacement has a* Talis *warrior assigned to them, someone close to them their entire lives, but it has never been an Ancient. There is still a lot we don't know, but he might have something that can help us.*"

"*Something you don't know, huh? Welcome to the club. Membership two.*" Maia chuckled softly as she opened the suite's door and stepped out into the hall. "*What do you think it is?*"

"*We don't know. Apparently, he'll only speak to you about it.*"

She hesitated in the middle of the hallway. "*Are you sure? Shouldn't he take this up with Poppy? I still need to introduce them.*" The lobby of the hotel was chaotic, heavy with tourists.

She quickened her pace, dodging through the crowd as those closest to her dropped sparking phones with startled gasps, and tiny bursts of electricity and flame erupted from the television monitors on the walls.

Grimacing at the sudden display of damage, Maia shoved her way out the front entrance, fearful of touching anything else as she continued her discourse with Blake. *"I mean, I've known Mac for years. Why would he never mention this to me? Or does he not remember, like the rest of the human* praeses*?"*

"No, as a Talis *warrior, he'd most likely opt to keep the knowledge of his past and position. He wouldn't tell you about it, though. Not until you accepted your role as the Terra guardian and came to him for answers. Not all of the replacements become guardians of Earth, so it's often unnecessary to tell them about any of this."*

"And now that I'm expected to just let my powers wane, now what? Will he still talk to me? Or will he go back to just being my friend Mac?" As she neared the edge of the parking lot, the steaming hoods of vehicles popped open and headlights cracked. She winced and gave the them a wide berth.

"Mia regina, I've known you too long. Your powers will never wane. You're too clever for that."

Maia conceded a small smile of pride, her heart warming at his praise. *"Well, at least now I know what to do."* How she was going to get there was another matter, but she'd figure it out as she went.

"Good. Look, I hear Heidi calling me. But one more thing before I go."

Maia wondered if he was going to tell her to be safe, like an overprotective boyfriend. Or maybe just a worried one. Either way, the thought filled her with dread. She didn't need to be smothered, or hovered over.

"*I know Leo and Lana are gone, but Reed can help you get to Houston. That's where Mac is. I know he can be a jerk sometimes, but I trust him.*"

"*Right.*" Maia kept her tone cheerful. The last thing she needed was for Blake to know she was doing this solo. She stared up at the sky through the treetops, where the tips of the branches created a frame around the blue expanse. "*I'll let you know how it goes.*"

Neither of them needed to exchange their love verbally; at this point, using the simple L-word was inadequate. Instead, she felt Blake's affection as if it was woven into her heartbeat. A final surge of energy and warmth flowed through her as she let their connection dissolve.

Standing alone in a small copse of trees, she shook her hands out before swinging her arms across her chest and opening them wide. A casual observer might have thought she was preparing to climb one of the trees in front of her. Instead, Maia stretched her head from side to side and took a deep breath, closing her eyes tightly and hoping she could figure this out on her own. She concentrated first on the soft wind fluttering through the leaves of the trees. The last time she'd done this, she'd had the borrowed energy of the other guardians, and Poppy had been by her side to give her instructions on how to summon the winds.

This time, she was completely on her own, but at least she had taken that extra energy from Lana. The strength of its power buzzed in her veins and wrapped around her muscles.

She felt silly, standing beneath a tree she was certain dropped sap down the neck of her hoodie, but she held her arms out, the way Poppy had instructed her to, and concentrated on the air with all of its tiny particles, the breeze, the strong west wind, all the way up to the clouds hovering in the sky. But no matter how many times she ran through the exercises Poppy had taught her on her maiden voyage, or how hard she concentrated, she couldn't convince the wind to blow strong enough to pick her up. She got a few lifts out of the hood on her coat and a slight ruffle in her hair, but it wasn't enough. Feeling another sticky drop slide down her neck, she thrust her hand out in frustration, hitting the bark.

"Damn tree! I'd move if it would do any good, but your next of kin would just finish the job." She grumbled a few curses. "I feel like a freakin' pancake." Her tummy grumbled, and she answered with a grumble of her own. "And now I'm hungry. Perfect." She tried to move, but as predicted, there was always another tree to douse her with more sticky love.

The moment her palm met the bark on her third thump, she felt an energy pulse through her, like she'd gotten shocked with static.

"What?" she whispered, stunned for a moment. Placing her hand on the tree again, she stood still while the plant's energy pulsed through her veins.

Then, remembering her lessons with Reed, she knelt and plunged her hands deep into the soft, damp soil at her feet. Feeling more at home, she repeated Poppy's focus exercises, combined with Reed's controlled will and breathing. Within moments, the west wind she was looking for swarmed around her like a miniature cyclone, whipping her clothes and whistling by her ears. It gradually pulled enough moisture into the air to form another structure of clouds around her, and after planting the city of Houston firmly in her mind, she was off on the Tempest Express.

26

HOUSTON WAS EVERYTHING Portland was not, but that's what Maia liked about it. Her Aunt Madeline had a house in the Heights, and once Maia had become a teenager, she'd often been sent to take care of things while her aunt went on one of her many Caribbean excursions with the newest flavor of the month.

Depressingly, though, Houston was giving ode to the Pacific Northwest when Maia arrived. Low-hanging clouds and a slight chill in the air punctuated the late spring day. Apparently summer had not descended early here, the way it had in Portland.

Maia landed with a soft thump in her aunt's backyard, and she tiptoed to the nearest window to peer inside. No fresh vase of flowers graced the kitchen island, signaling that her eccentric aunt was indeed gone for some time. Satisfied, Maia turned and kicked through the thick grass to one of the overgrown garden's many benches. Throwing her hood up against the fresh pummel of rain, she plopped down on the soggy seat to think.

"Okay," she muttered, crossing her legs in an attempt to keep heat from leaking out of her body. "I need a plan." She groaned. She felt silly for talking to herself, but knew it was the only distraction available. This place was the closest she had to a home and her old life. She hadn't been close to her aunt, but the sheer nostalgia was enough to invite tears into her eyes.

Her stomach growled, reminding her that she'd missed breakfast, but going inside would be disastrous to her aunt's many electronics. The woman had a television in every stinking room, and even in some of the closets, so she wouldn't miss a moment of her cop dramas when they were on.

Yet Maia also knew that none of the fruits and vegetables in Aunt Madeline's garden would be ripe enough to eat, so she got up, pulled down the spare key hidden above the patio door, and let herself in. Walking through the mudroom and into the kitchen, she winced at the popping noises and small puffs of smoke that erupted from the phone on the counter and the fancy espresso machine built into the dark wood of the cabinets.

"Sorry," Maia mouthed to the rest of the electronics in the room. Lights blinked out, and more popping and buzzing followed her through the kitchen. Stepping softly, giving the imposing subzero fridge a wide berth, she made her way into the pantry, grabbed a box of her favorite cereal—she and Aunt Madeline had, fortunately, always shared similar great taste in cereal—and tiptoed back out through the kitchen, hoisting herself up onto a stool by the breakfast bar. Swinging side to side in the swivel seat, she popped the box open and began shoveling the sugary, puffy treats into her mouth, wishing for some milk to go with it. After stealing a few furtive glances at the fridge with its built-in television, then around at the handful of gadgets that hadn't survived her entrance, Maia decided to nix that idea.

She still needed a plan for what to do next. Pressing her fingertips to her forehead, she whispered, "Think, damn it!"

Shoveling more cereal into her mouth—because, let's be honest, sugar always makes one think better—she went over her current problem.

She started simple: she needed to find Mac and find out what sort of information he had for her. He was in Houston, according to Blake—Nikki?—but where, exactly? Her vision from the tunnel, of him at the hospital, didn't help; the Legacy Emanuel Medical Center was in Portland, and probably gone. Though, knowing Mac, he would have found a way to move his mother before the earthquake hit. Maia paused with her hand wrist-deep in the box and shook her head with an aggravated sigh. Feeling sticky, Maia set the cereal box aside, hopped off the stool, and rinsed her hands in the sink.

Even if I get to the right hospital, I could bring down every electronic in there. She growled in frustration, turned the tap off with her elbow, and ripped a paper towel from its ring with more force than necessary, earning herself three sheets instead of one. After spending a few minutes attempting to re-wrap the roll, she gave up and used all three to dry her hands.

Like a child throwing a tantrum, she slammed the used paper towels into the trash bin, watching the lid swing violently with satisfaction. It was short-lived. The aura of her frustration must have caught every gadget in the room, as sparks erupted and wires detached from their sockets, writhing like snakes as their energy flared. Maia threw her arms over her head, screaming as she ran down the hallway to the front door, chased by more explosions and sparks as every electronic in the house came alive. Fumbling with the three locks on the front door, she finally managed, after a few scathing curses, to wrench open the heavy oak slab. Slamming it behind her, she bolted down the porch stairs—only to run smack-dab into a breathing wall.

"Maia?"

She cringed with closed eyes. The instinct to cover her head, preparing for a blow, washed over her. She counted slowly back from ten, composing herself, and looked up into the familiar face of her old friend, who was keeping her from toppling over. Swallowing her confusion in favor of relief, she flung her arms around his neck. "Mac!"

"What are you doing here?"

"I could ask you the same question."

His eyes searched her face for the answer to an unasked question. Ignoring her query, he asked, "What happened to your family after the storm? I haven't been able to reach anyone. You, your parents . . . not even Hayley."

Maia's shoulders slumped, as though his words were sandbags settling on top of her. Feeling strangely as though she was trapped underwater, she gulped for air before answering. "They're dead."

Mac's face softened, the lines around his mouth deepening into a frown. Maia knew Mac was only supposed to be a few years older than her, but in his expression, she could see the eons of time that made him an Ancient. He had known so much grief, yet her comment still managed to elicit genuine sadness from him.

"I'm sorry," he said softly, wrapping her in a tight hug. Maia felt the strength of his aura, and it struck her own like a tuning fork. She suddenly wanted to fight, to yell, to wage war. It terrified her, this intensity she never knew she'd craved. Maia gasped as the hug squeezed more air from her lungs.

"You're going to be even sorrier when you've committed murder."

Instantly, Mac's vice grip was gone. "What?"

"Nothing." Maia coughed, stumbling back to the steps, sitting on the bottom one in hopes that she was still far enough away from the house to not cause damage. "You couldn't have done anything. And I heard your mother hasn't been well."

Mac joined her, but didn't sit. He stood over her, blocking some of the rain that still drizzled down. For the first time, Maia actually paid attention to his posture and how he carried himself. She'd never noticed the way he held his head so high, or the set of his shoulders, or how he always had a natural energy that kept him alert and ready to spring into action. Like a warrior. She'd always thought he was, perhaps, a natural athlete. Now, she knew the truth.

"Do you want to go inside to talk?" Mac motioned for the door as he made his way up the stairs. "You've got to be freezing out here."

"Yeah, I am." Maia rubbed her nose, feeling its cold tip, and twisted in her seat to look at his worried face. "But I can't. How did you know I'd be here?"

Mac made his way back down the steps, scratching his red curls under the gray beanie he wore before pulling it down tighter over his ears. He folded himself neatly onto the bottom step next to her.

He stared at her for a moment, taking in her dejected expression before answering. "Remember my big brother, Richie?"

"The 'purveyor of fine antiquities'?" Maia used one hand to make air quotes half-heartedly, but the thick sarcasm layering her words got her point across.

"Yeah." Mac chuckled. "That's him. He's kind of dating your aunt."

"Oh, right!" Maia squeezed her eyes, shuddering against the memory of Mac's brother, who was only twenty-five, and her aunt, who was fifty, meeting at a family wedding last winter. Her aunt went through so many boyfriends she always forgot who her most recent catch was. "You know how my family is. I hardly hear from or see anyone unless there's a big event. That wedding was almost a year ago, and it was the first time in almost seven years that I'd seen most of those people. I never know what's going on with anybody. Madeline and Ritchie." She shook her head, and then shuddered in disgust. "I can't believe they've lasted this long."

"I guess age really is just a number." Mac shrugged an indifferent shoulder.

"So, you're house sitting, then?"

"Yeah, they're in Europe for a few months, and Madeline said I could stay here while my mom is in the hospital. So . . ." He bumped his shoulder with hers.

"So?" She bumped back, enjoying their old camaraderie. This was the Mac she'd known her entire life. The one before Hayley had inserted her tall, Brazilian self between them. Or tried to. Idly, Maia wondered what had happened to Hayley. Had she survived the earthquake, too?

"What brings you here?" Mac prodded, bringing her mind back to the moment.

"Ah, yes." Maia stretched her legs out, crossing her ankles and leaning back, propping herself with her elbows on the step above her. Tilting her head back, she stuck her tongue out to catch a few rain drops, closing her eyes to enjoy the sky's tears on her face while she debated over how to bring up her mission.

Maia peeked at him with one eye, offering a coy smile. "I think you know."

He stared back for a few moments before looking away. He shook his head with a laugh. "I never could win at those staring contests."

"Pfft! And you call yourself an Ancient," Maia scoffed, straightening up again.

Just like that, Mac's smile was gone, his features turning to stone in the space of a blink. A strange light glimmered around the edges of his irises. "Never call me that," he said. His voice was so low, Maia almost didn't hear it, save for the bite of steel it was layered with.

Maia leaned back, raising her hands in surrender. "Whoa. Touchy much?"

Mac shook his head, his shoulders slumping. "Sorry. That title just reminds me too much of my many mistakes."

"Well," Maia said, placing a hand on his arm. "You could start by 'fessing up."

"There's nothing I can do to—"

"Don't play coy with me, Mac. You've been lying to me for as long as I've known you. I deserve to know the truth."

Mac winced at her words, and Maia was surprised by how hurt and bitter she was over that fact. It had taken her verbal acknowledgment of it for her emotions to catch up.

"Maia, you have to understand, I—"

She held up a hand, cutting him off. "Save it. We'll have time for that later. Right now, I need to know how to defeat Heidi, and you're going to tell me why."

"Don't you mean, how?"

"No, I want more than that. There's too much I don't know, and I'm not going to war against an infinitely powerful supernatural being without knowing what I need to know. So, 'fess up."

Mac smiled slightly as he rubbed at the sharp lines of his jaw. "What have your memories shown you?"

"Not enough." Maia's tense muscles relaxed slightly, relieved that she was finally about to get some answers. "Just pieces, mostly, about my birth in the nebula and my relationship with Blake."

Mac nodded. "I'm guessing you don't have memories about the others, then?"

"No."

"Well, that minimizes what I can tell you. As you grow more into your powers, your mind will be able to handle more information and memories. We aren't holding out on you to intentionally leave you in the dark. We just don't want—"

"Yeah, yeah. You don't want my head to explode." Maia waved a hand at him. "Blake already told me."

Mac smirked, and a wicked gleam danced through his eyes. "You shouldn't be too worried about that. You'd go so thoroughly mad beforehand that having your head erupt would be a dream come true. In fact, most people would open their own heads just to relieve the pressure, rather than actually wait for their domes to explode."

"Ha, ha. Very funny." Maia punched him on the arm, and he laughed. Maia couldn't help but smile; she'd missed his teasing.

"Here's what I can tell you. I assume Blake's mentioned the Source to you?"

Maia nodded. The rain had finally dissipated, but the humidity had not. Sticky sweat mixed with the moisture on her skin as her shirt stuck to her. She shivered despite feeling like she was wrapped in a hot, wet blanket.

Mac lifted his eyebrows. "Good. Then you also know that no one knows where it's located, or if it's a place, being, or thing."

"But if you were one of its original creations, don't you remember?"

Mac shook his head. "I remember crawling from the depths of a deep pool of—" He stopped, and his bright green eyes flickered over Maia's face, assessing her. Whatever he saw there made him change his choice of words. "It was a pool, and something was calling to me."

Maia realized then that if she wanted information, she would also have to choose her words carefully. "Who called to you? What were they saying?"

"I don't know. Of all my memories, only that one changes like the details of a dream. I can't be sure. I just remember coming upon a dying star and pulling the animus from it. I remember the creation of the first set of *praeses,* and I remember my Ancient siblings, but that's it." Mac pressed his eyes closed against the memories before blinking them open. "None of my siblings know anything more about the Source than I do, but that hasn't stopped the search to find it." He leveled a hard look at her. "By everyone."

"Everyone." Maia repeated his word, drawing it out the way he had, then looked down at her hands, resting in her lap, as she spoke her next words. She wasn't sure she wanted to see Mac's reaction to her next statement. "Let me guess. Whoever finds the Source can control it?"

"Yes." Mac's voice was rough, but Maia didn't want to read the emotion on his face. "That's the delusion, at least. Some have said they've come close and have actually seen it, but they all went mad shortly thereafter and found an end at their own hands."

Maia grimaced. Suddenly, the events of the past few days and everything she had learned clicked into place.

She gasped, looking up into Mac's face. His brows were drawn tightly over his eyes in a scowl that wavered between frustration and worry, almost as if he willed her to understand but feared that she would.

"Heidi. That's her play, isn't it? She wants to kill off her replacements and go after the Source. But that doesn't answer the question of what you're doing here and why you're guarding me . . ."

Mac rubbed his face roughly with both hands. "Unfortunately, that falls into the realm of things we can't discuss until you're no longer human."

Maia chewed on her lip. "Fine, but you do know how to stop her, right?"

Mac nodded curtly. "Yes." His fingers twitched as they rested on his knees, and the memory of his hand curling around the hilt of a gleaming broadsword flashed into Maia's mind, reminding her of the other important piece of news she needed to give Mac.

The clouds shifted as they sat in silence, and the sun peeked through, offering the tiniest bit of warmth.

"I found her, Mac."

Despite the knowing look Maia gave him, he still looked confused at her sudden change of topic. "Who? Heidi?"

"Poppy."

27

"CHECKMATE."

Selene chucked her rook across the room with a cry of frustration.

Blake chuckled as the attending butler walked stiffly to the corner of the sitting room, where the offending rook lay. The man retrieved the chess piece from the floor, looking as if bending over to pick it up for the umpteenth time was the most demeaning insult he could endure, and took his time returning it to the chess board. Blake had to admit, he was impressed that the butler set the piece down so gently, because he would have slammed it down hard enough to crack both the board and the table.

"You're getting better," he said to Selene, trying to calm the scowling Luna guardian as he reset the board. "Not everyone gets it right away."

"You began teaching me five years ago. I should be able to beat you by now." Selene glared at him, arms crossed.

"Well, if your goal is to beat me at chess, you should just give up now, considering I knew the bloke who invented the game." Blake finished his task, looking up at her with a satisfied smirk.

Selene's lower lip jutted out further. "You don't have to be so—"

"Selene!"

The Luna guardian winced as the harsh voice sliced at her, like a whip across her shoulders.

"What are you doing here?" Heidi demanded from the doorway.

"Oh, I—" Selene bit her lower lip as she shrugged and lowered her eyes, picking at the jewels on her sleeve. "I came back because . . . I have news for you?" She looked expectantly at the Terra guardian.

Heidi swept into the room, her long silk skirts scraping against the wood floor with a sound similar to that of a snake rustling through dead leaves.

"News?" Heidi positioned herself behind a cowering Selene, placing her hand on the girl's shoulder, her long fingernails pressing into the thin cloth of the Luna guardian's dress.

Blake attempted to feign interest in the chess board, moving the pieces around and battling a fake opponent. He'd been in discreet contact with the other *praeses*, but aside from Reed telling him that he'd lost Maia, and that Leo was still working on restoring Lana in the Garden, there wasn't any other news to relate. So what kind of information could

Selene have that would be worth suffering Heidi's wrath? He hoped she didn't know about Maia looking for Mac in Houston; he had no doubt that that was where his mate had gone, despite being alone.

Selene threw a pleading glance Blake's way before nervously licking her lips and pressing on. "It seems as though our contacts have lost the replacement."

"What do you mean 'lost'? And why should I care?" Heidi tightened her grip on Selene's shoulder, puncturing the fabric with her nails. The Luna guardian smothered a whimper as she attempted to escape, her face scrunched in pain.

"Heidi." Blake nodded to the small red spot welling up on Selene's shoulder, blooming across the thin silver lace of the Luna guardian's dress.

Sighing her frustration, Heidi released her grip before flouncing over to her chaise lounge, reclining and spreading the folds of her red dress in the most flattering way possible while gently tugging the bodice down.

Blake purposely averted his eyes, focusing on the chess board again. Every time he looked her way, Heidi tried to seduce him with ample cleavage and bare leg.

"So then, tell me"—Heidi sneered from her perch on the couch—"why should I care about what the replacement is doing? I shouldn't have to worry about her anymore. Unless . . ." Heidi tilted her head to the side, leveling a cold, calculating glare at the two praeses sitting before her. "Unless she has broken her word and is still pursuing my throne. Is that it? Has she gone back on her word?" she hissed. She picked up the closest items near her—a picture frame, and then a tiny paper weight—and threw both at Blake's head.

He ducked, and when she next flung a small, antique dagger, he caught it by the hilt, twirling it indifferently between his fingers as he dodged yet another few objects.

"You were sent here to distract me, weren't you?" Heidi shrieked, continuing her tantrum and wiping at the crocodile tears glistening against her bronzed cheeks. "You don't care about me at all, do you? You just wanted her to be able to make her move. Admit it! You don't love me. You never have. You—"

Blake stood and pulled a plum-colored pocket square from his blazer. He handed it to Heidi with a sigh. "No one is after your throne, Heidi. We all know the consequences of such an action, and none of us would ever do something like that. Just like we would never set our sights on the location of the Source, right?" He looked at her solemnly, hoping that dropping his latest theory in her lap would cause her to slip and reveal her plans. But all she did was wave the offending fabric away.

"You know that color clashes with this dress! And how do you know that horrible little bitch isn't after my throne?" she screeched indignantly, snatching a pearl-colored silk handkerchief out of the butler's hand when he offered it. Blake rolled his eyes as she dabbed delicately at her eyes. Not wanting Heidi to remember Selene's "news," he tried a different tactic to get the information he wanted.

"Solomon." He waved the pretentious butler over. "Our mistress is distressed. How about you get Agatha down at the spa to do a deep tissue massage? You'd like that, wouldn't you?" He placed a hovering hand on Heidi's knee; she trained her eyes on it as though every finger bore a large diamond she coveted. Without waiting for her answer, Blake continued, "I'll go down to the wine cellar and pick out something nice, and I'll meet you for lunch when you're finished. How does that sound?" He patted her knee in quick, staccato taps. Apparently, his touch and the promise of spending lunch with her was enough to switch Heidi from a raging Medusa to an obliging beauty queen. Still wearing an injured air, and sniffling as Solomon took her hand, she stood and began smoothing and adjusting her dress.

"Yes, okay. I think that would suit me very well." She patted her curls, currently twisted and pinned into an intricate updo, and made her way to the door. "I'll see you in a few hours?" She blinked her eyes at Blake, suddenly wide and much like a small child's.

Blake gave her a reassuring smile, and though he cringed inwardly, he even added a wink. "Wouldn't miss it."

Heidi simpered a little in a bid for more sympathy before stalking out the door without a single glance at Selene. Blake waited as Heidi and the butler's footsteps retreated down the hall, pressing a finger to his lips in warning to Selene, who'd been about to protest Heidi's exit.

Once he was sure they were gone, he dragged the beaded ottoman next to Selene's seat and, clasping his hands before him, set imploring eyes upon the Luna guardian. "Selene, what other news did you have for Heidi?"

"Oh, I shouldn't bother you with it," Selene said, her lips still wobbling after Heidi's tantrum. "It's really something that only concerns Heidi." She made to get up, but Blake grabbed her hand and pulled her down to her seat again.

"Heidi's really stressed right now. I think it would be best for *everyone* if you told me, and I'll tell her."

"W-well." Selene waffled in deliberation. "I don't know." Her lips twisted as she considered the implications of not giving the rest of her news directly to Heidi.

"Look." Blake lowered his voice. "We both know that Heidi isn't always gentle or grateful for news she hasn't generated herself. Being in the dark about anything is a major pet peeve of hers. You know this."

Selene's silvery eyebrows formed a rigid worry line across her forehead as she nodded.

"But if you tell me, then I can make sure that Heidi gets the message in a way that would be beneficial to everyone."

"How?" Selene implored. "She could hurt you, too."

"Yeah-nah, don't worry about me. She'd never hurt me. You know that. Think about how many times I've turned her down, and aside from throwing a few things and screaming, she hasn't done anything else of note."

At that, Selene winced. "That's true," she muttered bitterly.

"Now, what is this news? Come on, you can tell me." He attempted to give Selene his most comforting smile. Though it felt too stiff, it must have worked, because after releasing a shuddering breath, Selene spent only another moment chewing on her bottom lip before diving in.

"I heard a rumor that there's a powerful weapon the replacement can use to defeat Heidi. That's why she's missing. She's looking for it."

Blake swallowed thickly, trying not to give away what he knew. Right now, he needed to know what *she* knew. "And what is this weapon?"

"That's just it." Selene shook her head slowly. "No one is sure what it is, or where it's hidden."

Blake gave a subtle sigh of relief. "Well, like you said, it's probably just a rumor. Where did you hear it?"

Selene gulped, her uncertainty growing. "After you returned, Heidi sent out a declaration to any replacement residing on this planet, and any allied beings with the identity of her replacement. I think she was hoping those loyal to her would hunt the replacement down and take care of her. So they—"

"Wait a minute." Blake held up his hand before dropping it to his knee, suddenly feeling nauseous. "What do you mean, 'take care of her'?"

Selene answered him with a knowing look, staring at him with thinned lips until he finally brought himself to admit it.

Blake dropped his head in his hands, running his fingers through his messy curls as a new wave of worry crashed into him. "Ar'right," he said. "Heidi also has plenty of enemies, though, so this rumor is most likely just their wishful thinking that the replacement will actually be able to do something. Have you told Reed any of this?"

"Yes!" Selene perked up slightly, a timid smile flashing across her classic features. She seemed relieved at the thought of doing something, anything, right. "I told him just before I walked in here. I asked him if he'd heard of the rumors, and if there was any truth to them. He said that the replacement was no longer with them, and then—" Moisture welled up in the Luna guardian's eyes as she raised fingers to trembling lips. "He told me what happened to Lana." She blinked away a few tears, trying to get her emotions under control. "It's so awful!"

Blake frowned and patted Selene's hand, waiting patiently for her to continue. The Luna guardian was clearly very upset. She and Lana had been best friends for centuries. He wondered idly why Leo hadn't sought out his help, and why he hadn't tried to contact him again.

Selene took a shuddering breath, and with a little hiccup, began once more. "She had an aversion to her powers. Water was pouring out of her, drowning her from within. Reed said Leo took her to the Garden to see if her tree could restore her powers, but—" Selene sniffed, rubbing at her eyes. "He hasn't heard from them."

Blake smiled gently at her, then gave her a nod. "I'll contact them both to see if there's anything I can do." He worried at his inner cheek, looking for the right words to say, but knowing they would only be hollow sounds shaped by lips. "Thank you, Selene. I'll look into things and attempt to get more solid answers before I bring this to Heidi's attention."

Selene's silvery brows tented in further concern. "Oh, but shouldn't we tell her right away?"

"No." Blake stood, shaking the creases from his trousers and twisting to see what new damage the ottoman had given to his bum. He could feel the embroidery marks embedded in his skin. "She'd be angrier with us if we don't have all the facts. Going to her with pure speculation is no better than throwing gas on a fire. Trust me."

"Oh," Selene answered in a tiny voice.

"Selene," Blake looked back down at the tiny girl. She seemed so weak and defeated; she never used to be that way. "Why don't you go meet with Reed? It's been a while, and you don't need to be here right now. I'll take care of *everything*. Promise."

"But I want to . . . be here, that is." Selene's lower lip jutted out again, and Blake cringed, feeling as though he had just kicked a puppy.

"I know you do, but you've already risked enough just by gathering this information. Go spend time with Reed. It would do you both good."

"But won't Heidi be pleased?" Confusion clouded Selene's silvery features. "I mean, if I tell her, perhaps—"

"Selene." Blake's voice was firm. "The sooner you realize that Heidi is not your friend, the better off you'll be. She won't hesitate to shoot the messenger. You know that."

Selene protested again, but after a few moments, Blake convinced her to contact Reed and meet him at their flat in London.

"And, Selene?"

The Luna guardian paused with her fingers on the doorknob and glanced over her shoulder at the Sideralis. "I could also use yours and Reed's help with Leo and Lana. I don't know why Leo didn't come to me for help." Blake spread his hands wide and gave a slight shrug. "Can I count on your assistance?"

Selene's lips pressed into a thin line of determination before she nodded and left the room.

28

"POPPY?" MAC ASKED, his face pale as he said her name. He stared at Maia, open-mouthed.

"Yes, Poppy," Maia said. "She's the Tempest guardian. You didn't know?"

Mac's cheeks colored slightly, and he shook his head. "No. I only know about the *praeses* I've been chosen to protect, which is you. Besides, most *praeses* stay within the realm of their little cliques. They don't even know I'm here."

"Well, they do now." Maia stood, crossing her arms against the new breeze that had picked up, and began pacing along the short gravel walkway. "They know your real name, that you're Poppy's *astrum*, and that you know how I can defeat Heidi."

Maia stopped in front of Mac, shifting her weight from foot to foot. Mac nodded, still dazed, and rose as well, dusting off his jeans before motioning her to follow him.

"I think its best we continue this conversation on the road," he said as he walked around the side of the house, Maia trailing reluctantly behind.

"The road?" Curious, Maia watched as Mac approached a large lump covered with a dark green fabric. He peeled the cover off with a flourish, revealing a shiny black car nestled underneath, unlike any Maia had ever seen. It was clearly a refurbished classic, with its rounded cab, sloping back, and headlights on either side of the grill forming a dignified face. Remembering the gadgets in her aunt's house, Maia stepped back several paces, not wanting the gorgeous piece of machinery to spontaneously combust because of her. "What is it?"

Mac's grin widened at the awe in her voice. "It's a 1953 Jaguar XK 120 fixed-head Coupe."

"Come again?" Mac shrugged modestly while he opened the passenger door for her, waving her forward. Maia shook her head vehemently. "I can't. Anything electrical will blow up if I'm in it."

"Ah, but not this." Mac stroked the cab of the shining car lovingly. "This is something I've been working on for years. I haven't had a reason to use it until now."

"Okay, but aside from it being a really nice, really expensive-looking classic car, how does that explain how I'm supposed to ride in it?" Maia backed away another step, her hands held out in front of her as she attempted to ward off Mac's advance. He took her hand, anyway, and tugged her toward the car.

"Go on, get in. I swear it won't bite!" He motioned for her to get in again.

"Or blow up?" Maia asked nervously.

"Or blow up," Mac agreed.

Still hesitant, she climbed in and settled onto the slick leather seat.

Beaming, Mac shut the door and jogged around to the other side, sliding behind the wheel with a smile that seemed to split his face in two.

"This car," he said, reverently patting the dashboard as he pushed an innocuous black button, "does not run on human electricity, but on the same energy that runs through our veins. I completely redesigned the engine and all components to run off the celestial energy that *praeses* and other celestial beings possess."

"Wow," Maia breathed. The engine purred to life and Mac pulled smoothly from the driveway. "I know the basics of how celestial energy works, but I have a feeling I wouldn't understand its application here."

"Yeah, probably not," Mac agreed. "Let's just say that human science hasn't even scratched the surface of that energy field."

Maia ran her fingers along the walnut finish on the dashboard. "Why don't the other *praeses* know about this, and where does the energy come from?"

"Some is my own, but most is from the people here on Earth who are more in touch with their celestial energy. Creators, inventors, and the like."

Maia's brow furrowed as she tried to understand. "So you steal their energy?"

Mac pressed the gas pedal hard, and the car roared and shuddered in delight as it sped up enough to merge onto the main highway. "Well, when you say it like that . . ." He grinned at her again with a mischievous wink. In all the years she'd known him, she had never seen him so happy. When he'd gone off to college, she'd realized just how much she'd depended upon him. He was more than a glass half-full optimist, he was a realist, with a clear perspective of life. He'd always been a strong, guiding force in her life, balancing her, but never intruding, and when he left, she'd slumped into a terrible depression as things at home got worse.

She'd wanted to be strong on her own, and she'd had good intentions. But she'd also been vulnerable—adrift without his anchoring presence, never knowing the danger she was in.

Mac glanced at Maia before explaining. "Artists and visionaries throughout time have often had a history of mental illness. They're brilliant, and can create amazing things, but it often costs them much to do so. Their energies are imbalanced. The human vessel is not designed to handle an over-abundance of aura."

"So, you help them."

"Exactly. I'm their metaphysical Xanax."

Maia chuckled as she ran her fingers across the plump leather seats. She leaned back into the seat's embrace as Houston's concrete-and-billboard skyline shot past her on the highway. "Man, I wish I would have known about this sooner. You wouldn't believe what a nightmare travel has been. I dare say I'd have even sat in traffic again, just for the nostalgia of sitting in a car. I wasn't even sure how I was going to find you once I got here. I mean, I practically destroyed every electronic in my aunt's house, just in the pursuit of breakfast!"

Mac snorted. "I doubt she'll even notice."

Maia responded with a smile of her own. "How's your mom, by the way?"

"You know she's not actually my mom. Not really." Mac dipped his head for a brief moment, and it was clear to Maia that pushing him would get no answer. But he continued on his own, shaking off his black mood. "She's improving."

He looked relieved as Maia patted his shoulder. "Good. Now tell me about this weapon or grand plan for defeating Heidi."

"It's actually pretty simple. You're going to laugh at how simple it is—"

Maia burst out with a mocking, knee-slapping cackle, stopping only when Mac punched her arm lightly. "What? You said I'm going to laugh!"

Mac stuck his tongue out, but continued on as though he hadn't been interrupted. "Ever heard of the Tree of Life, or seen images of it?"

"Heard of it." Maia punched him back. "But don't know what it looks like."

"Fair enough." Mac pulled a small square of onionskin paper from the breast pocket of his shirt and handed it to Maia.

Unfolding the paper as delicately as possible, she asked, "Is it safe for me to be touching this? It looks like it's going to crumble if I even breathe on it. Much like your poetry book, actually."

Mac choked on his next words: "My poetry?"

Maia nodded as she gazed at the inky black image of a tree, whose twisted and knotted branches formed a protective circle around itself, until they reached down and connected with the roots.

"I have it in my bag, right here." She nudged the bulk of fabric at her feet. "Blake gave it to me so I'd be able to understand Poppy."

Mac squirmed. "We'll return to that topic in a minute, but first thing's first. That tree resides in the Garden of Eden. See how its branches connect with its roots?"

Maia nodded.

"It's symbiotic, a manifestation of the Source here on Earth. Kind of like a well of energy that feeds the Earth, and in return, is created by the Earth."

"M'kay." Maia's tone encouraged him to go on.

"The Source has always been about balance. The tree provides the balance the Earth needs to maintain the proper amount of both celestial and astral energy. It's the order of things. Things must die in order for new things to be created, including human vessels."

Maia pursed her lips as she shifted uncomfortably in her seat, letting the broken lines of the road before them hypnotize her as they rolled beneath the car. There wasn't much else to look at outside. They'd been in the part of Texas that was sparse brush and tumbleweeds for the better part of an hour. Maia rolled her eyes at the cliché. At least the air was dry here. Houston's constant humidity had made her feel as though she would never get dry, despite the coolness of the A/C licking at her bare skin.

"Why do you call humans 'vessels'? It seems kind of . . ." Different words skipped through her thoughts. Rude. Disrespectful. Uncaring. Weird.

"I know it sounds unkind, but you have to remember that being human is only an experience, one of many, for many of the beings the Source has created."

Maia's lip curled at his words.

"We aren't aliens, walking around in pod bodies. Although"—he rolled his head from side to side in thought—"that is one way of describing it, I suppose."

He quickly raised his hand to cut off her protest. "But we're getting off topic here. The tree—"

Maia frowned. "I'm afraid I don't follow."

A laborious sigh escaped him as he dug around in the middle console, finally pulling out a pack of cigarettes and a lighter. Maia stared at him, bewildered, as he lit one and took a long drag. The hard edges of his face relaxed as smoke escaped his lips and nostrils. He cracked his window open.

"You smoke?"

Mac shrugged, taking another drag.

"I thought that smell was from your mom."

Mac ignored her comment and continued as if her words had merely mingled with the smoke from his lungs, twisting and swirling in the air until they were sucked out the window. "The tree nurtures the soil it rests in, feeding its power to anything planted within a radius of about eight-hundred feet. That's where the weapon comes in. Each elemental *praeses*— that's you and your friends, by the way—has a smaller tree planted within that radius, which is what gives you access to your power. It also represents your status as a Gaea *praeses*. Without it, your choice would be to live on Earth as a human, or accept whatever assignment the Council gives you."

His smile was pained as those words left his lips. "To defeat Heidi, you need only replace her tree with your own. Once that happens, her soul will no longer be recognized by the Source as a Gaea *praeses*, and she will lose her power."

"Where am I supposed to find my tree, though? Do I just run down to the local nursery and pick up a random one?"

Mac snorted. "Hardly. It's located in Mount Hood National Forest."

"Really?" Maia sat up straighter. "It wasn't destroyed in the earthquake?"

A predatory grin slid over Mac's face, sending a chill down Maia's skin. She had never seen him look so dangerous. Ever.

"The eventual buckling of the Cascadia subduction zone was no secret, so there was no way I was going to hide your tree in Portland. Fortunately, the other side of the Cascades was never in any real danger."

"And that's where the park is. So, we're headed back . . ."

Mac stabbed the butt of the finished cigarette into his palm before he closed his hand, forming a fist. Maia watched in dumbfounded fascination as he blew onto his fist and opened his fingers one at a time. The cigarette was gone. Sure, it looked like a magic trick she had seen hundreds of times, but despite the conspiratorial wink Mac gave her as he showed her his empty palm, she knew that this was no illusion. As he rolled up the window, appearing more relaxed and calm than he had when Maia first ran into him, he picked up the question she had left hanging in the air. "It would seem so. Now, since we have a long road ahead, you can fill me in on how you know about me and Poppy."

Maia returned his smile with a timid one of her own. "Well, I met Poppy in New Zealand . . ."

29

HEIDI STOOD IN front of the closed door to the sitting room she'd left several hours ago. She ran her fingers along the edge of her cream-colored wraparound cardigan, then smoothed the skirt of her jade green jersey dress. She'd chosen the outfit precisely for its comfort, so she could prolong the relaxed state her recent massage had instilled. With closed eyes, she breathed in the scent of myrrh and jasmine that still wrapped her skin in harmonious comfort. She loved massages, not only because her favorite scents lingered for hours after, extending her feeling of calm, but because she loved the feeling of fluidity her body experienced. She often felt as though she was made of water and air rather than muscle and bone.

She pulled in another deep breath. Despite the heady scent of her skin and the looseness of her muscles, she could already feel a tiny pucker beginning to form between her eyes once more. The edges of her lips turned down slightly as she hesitated. The minute she opened the door, she knew all of the stress that had been blissfully rubbed away would return. The smell of sunshine that always lingered behind Blake would still be there, too, piercing her with the dagger of constant reminder, teasing her with what she couldn't have.

A tiny voice, deep within, whispered, "*What you couldn't have, or choose not to? I'm still here. I'm lost, but I'm here and waiting for you.*"

She swatted at the air, as if the voice within was a pesky fly she could shoo away.

Besides, she had more important worries—like the table. Solomon may have been the best butler for centuries, but he was atrocious at setting a proper table. Everything was always set in its designated place, and nothing was ever out of line, of course—the silverware always shone to perfection and the crystal always sparkled—but none of that was what irritated her. It was the floral arrangements that drove her mad. All that precise perfection was always ruined by his abhorrent choice in flowers.

The pucker between Heidi's eyes deepened, and she stretched her neck from side to side, hoping to diffuse the tension that threatened a mutinous tightening of her muscles. She kept her eyes closed as she took in another large breath, releasing it slowly as she rolled her shoulders back, readying herself for whatever awaited her. Lately, Solomon had been obsessed with a rare breed of tiny lavender tea roses.

Heidi grunted in an unladylike fashion, her eyes snapping open as a familiar twinge of annoyance sparked within her chest. *Lavender is such a stupid color.* She glared at the intricately carved door before her. Centaurs and fauns peered out between the trees portrayed on the slab of wood; their quizzical expressions caused a fresh ripple of irritation to flush her dark skin. *It's like mauve. Neither are appropriate for flowers.* She threw her hands in the air and slammed them into the door, pushing it open with a shake of her head.

She halted as soon as she stepped inside, letting the heavy door swing shut behind her with a muted *thwump*, and looked around in confusion.

The sitting room that she'd filled to the brim with rich fabrics, colors, and ancient medieval artifacts was now completely empty, and stark white. She had long ago painted the walls in rich tones of auburn and chestnut, but not a drop of color remained. Even the large fireplace sat completely empty and blindingly white. Heidi took a few cautious forward. Turning in a slow circle, she searched for anything familiar, but there was nothing to catch her eye save for an unfamiliar metal-and-ceramic table positioned in the center of the room. As she inched closer, she realized that it wasn't just any table, but rather an antique autopsy table. It looked brand new, even down to the bucket suspended beneath the table's drain.

Heidi swallowed thickly as the coldness of the metal and stone filled the distance between them, causing small bumps to appear along her arms and across her chest. She rubbed her arms absentmindedly, and tugged her cardigan tighter around her torso. For once, the supple softness of the sweater was not reassuring. Shivering, she stared, not at the table, but at the item placed upon it.

Colored the same crisp, clinical white as the room, a small box sat in the middle of the table, beneath a cluster of white poppies whose black centers gaped like empty mouths.

Heidi tasted blood, and only then realized that she had been chewing on her lip. She swallowed the coppery taste with a shudder before turning around and marching back toward the door. Only, instead of coming nearer, the door continued to get further and further away. She reached out her hand, pulling with all the supernatural strength she could muster, but to no avail.

Breathless, Heidi stared at her hand in disbelief. The wooden door should have answered her summons, yet it remained out of reach. She dropped her hand to her side with a frustrated scream, and then froze as she felt something cold and hard slam into her backside. Not wanting to turn around, she groped behind her until she felt the smooth, curved edge of the ceramic table. Letting out a yelp, Heidi clenched her eyes shut and pushed herself away.

The aura of death clung to the autopsy table. It radiated longing, regret, fear, and had burned her skin with cold, even through her layers of clothes. With the table no longer touching her, Heidi let out a sigh of relief that did nothing to loosen her stiff shoulders. She opened her eyes and felt relief give way to terror. She was facing the table.

The box was in her hands.

"No!" she yelled. "No, no, no, no . . ." But she couldn't keep her hands from removing the poppy-draped lid.

She never saw what the box contained—her vision suddenly black—but she could feel it. An aura that had only ever lurked in the darkest corners of her being before now. An energy that lurked within everyone. This new aura was dark, mysterious, seductive. Addicting. Her body slumped to the floor under the astral energy's pressure, and at first, she was frightened. The sounds and weight of the dark energy's despair, guilt, shame, and terror swept over her, an overwhelming burden. The world's darkness crushed her, bone by bone, and as her body shook with the sobs of the Earth's pain, threatening to tear her apart, her eyes snapped open with a suddenness that had her blinking away tears.

She was suspended in the middle of the room. The box and table were gone, but thin black strings attached to every vein she possessed stretched outward from her body, reaching to the opposing walls.

The threads were strong, but the muscles in her outstretched arms and shoulders soon screamed in agony at the strain. Time crept forward as she squirmed and wiggled, hoping to shift her weight somehow. She screamed and screamed, until her voice ran raw. No one came. Hours crawled by. Her arms grew numb, and the weight of her body made it hard to breathe. She panted and gasped for air, and a new terror filled her heart.

Was this how she died?

Then, as if someone had flipped a switch, the feeling of terror and anguish evaporated.

Heidi nervously eyed the hundreds of threads that had burrowed beneath her skin as an inky black substance crawled from the walls, seeping toward and into her veins.

A familiar voice echoed throughout the room. "I told you I would take care of you."

The erratic thud of Heidi's heart instantly settled. Calmness stole over her, more luxurious than any massage she'd ever had.

"What is all of this?" she asked, surprised that her voice had returned to normal. She wondered if the horrors of the past few hours had even happened. She couldn't be sure, but she also suddenly didn't care. She tried to twist her head to look for her new master, but the action tugged on the strings attached to her neck, pulling against her skin.

"Shh. Don't move, or you'll ruin my little operation."

Heidi smiled, her lips trembling with the pleasure of knowledge and clarity being transmitted to her through the substance now coursing through her blood.

"Although," the voice sighed. It filled the room, making it impossible for her to figure out where it came from. "I must say, I am quite disappointed in you. You don't really deserve this gift I'm bestowing upon you."

Despite the power and giddy happiness that Heidi was gladly drowning in, the disappointment of her master came crashing down, suffocating her strange high. "What do you mean? I've done everything you've asked, and—"

"Ah, but that's just it, isn't it?"

Tugging the strings brought pain; still, Heidi couldn't help but flinch at the steel in his voice.

"You've done everything I've asked, but you have taken no initiative to take care of the extras." The voice softened, returning to its low, velvety tones. It caressed her skin like the hands of a lover, and she shuddered in pleasure as it reached a place no man had touched in centuries. "How can I make you my queen if you can't take care of the unexpected? Nothing ever goes according to plan in war."

Heidi gasped through the waves of pleasure rippling through her body, latching on to only one word out of the many he'd spoken. "You want me to be your queen?"

His mocking laugh filled the room, but Heidi ignored it. Instead, she focused on the gleaming jewel of thought that she could be queen of not just Earth, but the entire universe.

"Of course. Why else would I enlist your help?" The strings sagged as the fluid holding dark energy halted its journey toward her veins. "I worry, though, that perhaps I am wasting my time, since you love another."

Without the fluid, Heidi's body began to tremble and ache with uncontrollable hunger. She wanted more of this new aura that was slowly corroding the celestial energy of her guardianship. Just a few moments of it swirling within her veins and she was addicted.

"No." She shook her head minutely, panicked eyes shooting about the white room in an unsuccessful attempt to find the dark figure. Her chest heaved as she struggled for her next breath. "You know I don't love Blake—that was just an infatuation!"

"What about your *astrum*?" The strings jerked taut again, but this time, they were harsh and pulled too tight, causing Heidi to shriek. "You've made no attempt to find him after all this time. Why?"

That was one question Heidi wasn't going to answer. Not even to him. Anger and rebellion burned in her gut as her disdain resurfaced. "I would think the fact that I have not searched for him for centuries would prove that I do not love him. If he doesn't want what I want, then I don't want him. Why do you question me?"

The sudden silence was palpable. Heidi thought she would suffocate from the lack of noise. She opened her mouth to call for him, her master and benefactor, but before she could draw her next breath, the strings attached to her snapped and disappeared entirely, sending her falling to the floor.

She landed lightly on her feet, and she had never felt stronger, more graceful, or more alive. She suddenly wondered how she had ever lived without whatever it was he had given her.

Heidi closed her eyes, reveling in the new sensations the astral energy gave her. She felt arms clamp around her shoulders, holding her from behind. Despite their earlier tension, she was no longer afraid of his quick temper or his threats. She felt stronger, more powerful than ever, and she relaxed into the embrace as her favorite voice whispered in her ear, his gentle cadences caressing each word: "I will give you one more chance to prove yourself worthy to be my queen." Heidi sighed as a dangerously satisfied smile tugged at her lips. "The Sideralis has information regarding the replacement, who is, in fact, his *astrum*."

Heidi stiffened.

"And he knows of her plans to destroy you. Selene would have told you hours ago, but you dismissed her. I want that information, Heidi, and I don't care how you get it."

She felt the gentle press of lips upon her neck, just below her ear, and her eyes fluttered. The sensation sent a tingle of warmth through her, charging her relaxed body into action. As a new plan of attack slowly formed in her mind, there was a loud *pop*, and she opened her eyes to see that the sitting room looked exactly as she'd left it. The old grandfather clock in the corner chimed a new hour, its brass pipes ringing with a pure and confident sound. Apparently, she hadn't been gone any longer than her massage had allowed.

Heidi grinned, surveying the room to find everything in its proper place, even Solomon's hated lavender tea roses.

Nothing was going to stop her now.

30

"*BLAKE?*" MAIA FELT his sigh of relief as their souls connected, and the way his heart relaxed at the sound of her voice.

"*Maia? Thank God, you're safe. I've been worried.*"

"*Why didn't you say something? I thought you could contact me any time?*" She had long since lost track of which state they were driving through—the scenery all started to blend together after a while—and had decided to try contacting Blake, pretending to sleep while Mac drove. Her relaxed posture tensed slightly as fear stabbed at her heart, and she quickly turned it into a nap-induced twitch, repositioning herself in the leather seat of the classic Jaguar.

"*I couldn't. You were closed off from me.*"

She panicked. "*What? How? I didn't mean to—*"

"*No worries*, mia regina." The warmth of his comforting voice caressed her core. "*I know you didn't mean to. This type of communication takes a lot of practice if you aren't used to it. Have you been talking to someone?*"

"*Mac. How did you know?*"

"*When externally conversing with someone, inner communication can get blocked without you even realizing.*"

"*Oh.*" Maia's body relaxed into the soft rocking of the car. "*So, what's the latest?*"

This time, she could feel a sense of foreboding and rebellion coming from Blake.

"*I'm in the wine cellar right now, picking out something for lunch with Heidi. Selene just tried to give her news about you meeting with Mac. Fortunately, she didn't have many details, so I was able to intercept her by convincing Heidi to go get a massage, and that I'd join her for lunch later.*"

Maia felt a small flicker of annoyance, but it was almost impossible to tell whether it belonged to her or to him.

"*A massage, huh? Must be nice.*"

She felt Blake's suggestive chuckle pool deep in her abdomen, and wondered if her face looked as red as it suddenly felt. Old dreams of him mixed with memories from another life, swirling through her head in a sensuous tangle. It was getting harder to distinguish the two. If Blake knew the effect he had on her, though, he didn't say, just continued with their original conversation.

"*I'm just glad it worked. I was prepared to start chucking every excuse I could think of at her, just to get her out of that room. Tell me, though, what's Mac's plan?*"

Grateful they'd turned to an easier topic, Maia smiled. "*It's simple, actually. Almost too easy. Mac hid my tree in a forest near*

Portland that fortunately escaped Heidi's destruction. He said all I need to do is retrieve it and replace Heidi's with my own."

"Perhaps that's why Camael was guarding you. Only an Ancient has that kind of power."

"I've peppered him with as many questions as I can, but we always—Blake?" Maia bolted upright. Her head throbbed suddenly, as though someone had slammed an ice pick through her skull. Fear and panic clawed through her chest as she pressed both palms to her forehead, the sharp pain radiating from her temples backward.

"Maia?" The car swerved slightly as Mac looked her way. "Maia, are you okay?"

"Yeah," she said uncertainly. As soon as the pain had appeared, it was gone, and she straightened, shaking. "I don't know what happened. I just got a weird headache—"

"Yeah, I'm not buying that for a minute. You were talking to someone, weren't you? What's going on?"

Maia's back pressed further into the seat as the car's speed increased. They were making exceptional time.

"I don't know." She rubbed her eyes hard, trying to reconnect with Blake without any success. "Something's very wrong, but I can't—" Blake didn't answer when she called. All she felt was a dark emptiness inside of her.

"We need to hurry," she finally said, refusing to look at Mac for fear he'd see how worried she was. "I think Heidi may be catching on."

Blake blinked into consciousness slowly, his vision hazy as he tried to focus on the blurred light. His head throbbed, and a warm, thick liquid ran down his temple. The only thing he could see was a dark, cold room around him. He hadn't been truly cold in a very long time. So long that he had forgotten what it felt like. But this he felt as more than just goose bumps on his bare skin; this was an ice that gnawed on his bones like a starved beast. He felt empty inside. Try as he might, he couldn't access the warmth that usually pulsed through his every fiber, nor could he find his connection with Maia.

He touched his temple with frozen fingertips, attempting to wipe away the blood dripping into his eyes, and winced. His vision cleared finally, and he recognized the castle's dungeon.

Looking up at the vaulted ceiling, he realized he was lying in the dungeon's only tower, and the only room with a source of light. Feeling a prickling in his backside, he lowered his gaze from the blackened stones of the oval room and noticed the molding straw he was curled up on. Rusting, fractured pieces of manacles still clung to the damp walls, and more than a century's worth of blood and gore, along with a few hapless skeletons, was scattered maliciously about, as if Heidi hadn't bothered to clean up in quite a while.

The room itself was chilly, but the coldness that permeated the walls seemed to be of a different nature altogether. It crept over his skin with razor-edged fingers, slicing his nerves raw as it snuck under the edges of his clothing. He still wore the wool-blend suit he'd put on for lunch, which offered at least a slight warmth, and a few weak rays of light hovered near the ceiling, casting a muted glow against the gray walls. Blake focused on it and tried to pull on its energy. But aside from the continued throbbing in his skull, nothing happened. His head felt heavy, foggy, and his eyelids were weighted slabs. Closing them felt better as his body slumped and shuddered against the cold wall.

He tried contacting Maia again with no success. It was as if he was human, feeling the hollow loneliness they all felt before finding their mates, and he realized with horror that if he couldn't pull power from the weak light, he had no way of getting a message to any of the other *praeses*, either.

Blake stuck his hands inside his jacket and rubbed them against his barely warm chest, trying to get some feeling back into the tips of his fingers. They'd already begun to turn blue.

Sharp, staccato taps echoed along the walls as footsteps neared. Blake knew only one person who could make that horrid sound. With a glance at the heavy wood door that barred his exit, he struggled to right himself.

The door's peephole slid back with a nerve-rubbing scrape.

"Heidi? What's going on?"

He couldn't see her, but he could smell the abrasive scent of her perfume emanating from just outside the door. He heard her excited breath, sending puffs of visible air into the room. Attempting to move his stiff joints, he struggled to his knees, but collapsed on the floor again with a strangled groan. The huff outside the door was one of barely suppressed anger, and he wondered if Selene had gone to spill her secrets, after all.

"Heidi?" he said, voice shuddering in the frosted air. "Please don't tell me you're about to walk in here covered in leather and studs, cracking a whip." He attempted a small chuckle that ended in a gurgle as he rolled back over into the hay.

Her laugh was short and brittle around the edges. "You wish." There was a pregnant pause where neither of them said a word, and Blake wished the suffocating darkness would do its worst and take him. His head swam with exhaustion and cold. His body felt drained, his celestial energy siphoned away by some unseen force.

"What do you want, Heidi?" Blake's voice was barely audible, his tongue swollen with dehydration. How long had he been down there?

"Nothing from you," Heidi shot back. "I've met someone. Someone with more power, who actually lo—who wants me." He could hear the Terra *praeses* rub her hands nervously down her shivering arms.

Blake struggled to keep the surprise and curiosity out of his voice as he chose his next words carefully. "I'm glad to hear that you're happy, but I don't understand." His body shuddered with coughs that made his brittle lungs feel as though they were being bulldozed. "Why does this new relationship of yours necessitate me being in here?"

"Don't play dumb with me, oh *Angel of Light*." Her voice dripped disdainfully over his translated title. "You know why you're being punished."

"Because . . . your new man wants to kill me so he can take my place in your heart? You know that only works with pack animals, right?"

Heidi's sigh was one of disgust, and she pointed a thin finger through the metal bars of the peephole. "You have no clue whom you disrespect, but I'm willing to make a case for your life if you tell me the truth about my replacement."

As though to show her noble intentions, she placed a key in the door's lock, turning it as fast as the rusty metal would allow. Sliding the heavy bolt back with a reverberating clang, she opened the rotting door. Blake winced as the loud noise scraped against his sensitive nerves. She stepped inside and shut the door behind her, but stayed close enough to it to give herself a quick escape, regardless of the fact that Blake could barely lift his eyelids, never mind a large slab of oak.

"I still don't understand." Blake rubbed his cold hand across his face, feeling more exhausted with every breath. He actually did understand; he just wasn't sure who had told her the truth she so desperately wanted from his lips, or how much she knew. His brain hurt too much to play the manipulative mind games of a spoiled woman. His only option, as he could see it, was to try and get her to reveal her hand first.

"Look." Blake craned his neck uncomfortably, trying to catch a glimpse of her face, but she was doing a remarkably good job of hiding in the room's many shadows. His stiff lips formed his lie, and he shivered as he said, "I know very little about her. We tracked her down in Portland, where she lost her parents in your earthquake. We convinced her to come with us."

Heidi ignored his rebuke about the earthquake. Standing unusually still, she replied, "To do what, exactly?"

Blake chewed on his next words thoughtfully before he spit them out. "To do exactly what we did."

"To manipulate me into lowering my guard, so that you could come here and plan to steal my throne?"

He was used to Heidi's constant injured air; she was the most high-maintenance woman in existence. But her last sentence overflowed with a genuine hurt Blake hadn't expected.

"No, of course not!" His attempt at determined defiance sounded more like a hoarse growl as another coughing fit shook his body.

"You failed to mention that this woman is your *astrum*."

Her words were like ice, and this time, Blake had no reply. He groaned, unsure of how Heidi could have possibly found out. He wanted to dispute it, and he tried to, but the

cold was shutting his body down. He was in a near-hypother-
mic state, and he knew Heidi could glimpse the truth of her
statement written all over his face.

She slinked into the tiny patch of light before him, placing one hand on her tilted hip and holding her head high.
"I am, however, willing to forgive your momentary lapse of
judgment, Blake, if you tell me now—honestly and truth-
fully—what she's really up to."

Uncontrollable tremors shuddered through his body,
but Blake still managed to arch one eyebrow in disdain. This
wasn't another of Heidi's silly tantrums; she was dangerous,
more so than she'd ever been. He didn't know how she'd come
to be this way, but he wasn't going to give Maia up.

He managed to slowly extend a bluish-purple middle
finger before collapsing once more against the cold stone wall.
This time, his eyes remained closed as the room's astral aura
filled his mind with images of Maia—ravaged, tortured, and
dying.

31

SELENE SIGHED, COMPLETELY content as she snuggled into Reed's warm embrace. She loved how her head fit perfectly in the nook of his shoulder and neck, and she would often press her cheek as far into his chest as she could manage, just to breathe in the scent of exotic spices that always seemed to emanate from him, along with the vibrating pulse of surrounding plants.

Reed set his finished glass of Pimm's Cup down so he could wrap his other arm around her, and Selene smiled, enjoying the way his body shifted slightly with each soft breath. Despite the full day they'd had, attempting to see every one of London's museums, they couldn't pass up a night ride on the London Eye. The energetic city, with its melting pot of people and sights, twinkled and flashed around them, setting off a hazy glow that bounced off the low-lying clouds. This was their favorite city; the only one they could compromise on. It had just enough nature mingled with modern industry to keep them both happy.

Selene had been elated when Reed agreed to meet her here. He was integral to her balance, as all *astrum* were to one another, and they had been kept apart for far too long.

"Reed?" Selene said softly, turning her head up to meet his curious gaze. "I am sorry, you know. For . . ."

She didn't finish her sentence, but she didn't need to. Neither of them had ever been verbose; it suited them well, for there were never any awkward silences to fill. She twined her fingers through his, lifting their joined hands to her lips to kiss each of his fingertips, offering the rest of her apology through physical contact, and it was enough. She was instantly forgiven—he could never hold a grudge against her—and he told her so by pressing his lips to her own.

This time, her sigh was tinged with sadness. She pulled away from him reluctantly, but not before running her fingers once over his face in their old personal salutation.

"I really don't want to ruin this moment, or this lovely evening, but I—I need to tell you something."

Reed nodded as he idly fiddled with a strand of her long hair.

"Remember the rumors I told you about, the ones that spoke of a weapon to defeat Heidi?"

Reed looked at her keenly then, letting the strand of hair fall as he dropped his hand to his lap. "We've heard the same rumors, but I haven't been able to find much truth to them."

"They're true."

"You're sure?" Reed straightened in his seat, his eyes searching her face for verification.

"Yes. There have been confirmed sightings of the replacement—"

"Maia," Reed interjected.

"Yes." Selene bobbed her head. "*Maia* has been seen with an old friend of hers. Someone she used to work with? Micah, or Mike? Max? I'm not sure." She fluttered a hand delicately before continuing. "Anyway, apparently he is the Ancient *Talis* warrior Camael!"

A slight crease appeared between Reed's thick eyebrows, but otherwise, his expression was carefully controlled. Selene hastily finished her Pimm's Cup as the pod they rode in came to rest at the bottom of the Ferris wheel, their night of romance decidedly over. "Not only that, but he really does have a weapon that can defeat Heidi. He'll only tell the replacement, though. They're being followed, and it looks as though they're headed to"—Selene lowered her voice to whisper in Reed's ear as he helped her from the pod—"what's left of Portland."

They slipped quietly into the crowd dispersing in all directions and headed toward the Westminster Bridge. They'd spent the entire day bouncing energy between themselves, and occasionally giving some away to the humans they came across that either had too little creative energy in their lives, or too much. It was a short-term solution—a failsafe to keep their celestial energy from interacting with nearby electronics—but it worked. A familiar feeling of déja vu, eye contact that seemed painful to break, and a brief nod of acknowledgment was often all it took to give someone a creative boost, or steal one away. Selene hoped they could pass off enough energy on their way to the Tube to be able to ride it up to their flat near Hampstead Heath without it breaking down.

As they walked, Reed picked up their dropped conversation, concern in his voice. "You didn't go to Heidi with this information, did you?"

"What?" Selene was momentarily stunned by the question. She picked at the pills on her favorite red sweater-dress, going out of her way to give a nearby puddle a childish splash with her black, equestrian-style boots. She looked up into Reed's eyes; they glanced at her often, even as he somehow always managed to avoid crashing into another pedestrian.

"Well, yes," she admitted. "Sort of. I almost did. But Blake was there, and he said that if I told him, then he would tell Heidi for me."

Reed sighed, and Selene felt a frisson of confusion. Was he relieved that she'd passed the message to Heidi, or that she'd told Blake, instead? Either way, the result should have been the same.

She grabbed Reed's arm as they were jostled down the stairs of the busy Westminster Tube station. "I don't think it worked, though."

"Why?"

They paused their hushed conversation for a moment, drowned out by the loud clacking and rushing *whoosh* of trains passing through the underground tunnels. The pair stood huddled together, leaning against a tiled pillar apart from the shifting crowds, waiting to board the next train. They didn't have long to wait; the next train arrived within moments with a squealing halt.

Selene chewed on her lower lip as they pushed their way inside and gripped the pole that represented the last two standing spots left on the packed train. Once the doors had closed and the train took off, Selene answered Reed's waiting question. "Well, not long after I left, I got word from one of our allies that Heidi had locked Blake up. Apparently, her plan is to torture him. She's cut off his celestial energy, forcing a wedge between him and Maia, in the hopes he'll give up Maia's whereabouts."

The sharp angles of Reed's face grew sharper in the glaring, white-yellow fluorescence of the train car. Fire kindled in his eyes, and his knuckles grew white as he gripped the pole tighter in anger. "That fu—" Reed's choice words describing Heidi's character were drowned out by the screaming of the Tube as it rumbled along a tight curve, whisking its many tired occupants away.

They rode the rest of the way in silence, their only communication the circular rubbing of thumbs against the outside of hands and the closeness of their bodies. Sure, they were crowded together by other swaying beings, bumping and jostling, and Reed's mind was somewhere else, no doubt worried about Blake, and maybe even Maia, but the constant circulation of energy between the Nepenthes and Luna guardian was still more intimate than any human surrounding them could bear to understand.

The situation wasn't perfect, but Selene took comfort in that small connection. No matter how divided in loyalties they were forced to be, they would always be connected.

When they finally arrived at their stop, they filed out of the Tube with the other passengers and made a quick walk out of the few blocks to their home. The foliage lining the fences and walkways tentatively reached out to Reed as they passed, discreetly caressing his shoulder, arm, any part of him it could touch. As always, Reed kept close to the surrounding plant life, touching and brushing up against it as he went. He held Selene tightly to his other side, as if she would disappear if he let go.

"*Reed. Reeeeeeed!*"

Reed's shoulders tensed. He pulled Selene even closer as he slowed his walk, listening for the voice.

"*Reed!*"

It was coming from the plants. He stopped abruptly beside a large ivy, looking up and down the deserted street.

"Reed?" Selene asked. "Is everyth—" He stopped her words with a slender finger; he held one up to his own lips, as well, motioning for them both to be quiet.

Selene nodded. Lowering both hands, but wrapping an arm tightly around his mate again, Reed turned toward the ivy. "You don't hear that, do you?" he whispered, scratching his head and staring at the silent plant.

"No," she whispered back, standing on her toes and staring around suspiciously. "What do you hear?"

Reed plunged his free hand into the ivy bush. "I think the plants are trying to talk to me."

"Don't they always talk to you?" Selene tightened her grip on him, staring at his face with wide eyes.

Reed nodded, but then recoiled from the bush as if he'd been bitten. He stared at his hand, carefully examining every slender digit and the lines on his palm.

"Reed," Selene squeaked. "Please, tell me what's going on."

"I think Maia's using the plants to send me a message."

Selene gasped, covering her mouth with her hand and shaking her head. "No! She couldn't possibly—how does she even know how to do that?"

Reed shook his head, the shock wearing off, leaving behind a familiar irritation that sank into his features. "I don't know, but I'll most certainly find out." He placed his hand within the ivy, and again, he heard Maia's voice.

"*Reed!*"

"*How are you sending me this message?*" he asked, impatience making his words sharp. "*Who taught you or gave you permission to use my energy?*" His thoughts passed through his body and into the ivy, where they were carried by the plant to the one Maia was touching. Judging from the distance, Reed could tell she was already on the outskirts of what used to be Portland, but the conversation flowed into him with the same perfect clarity he shared with Selene.

"*No one taught me anything!*" Maia shot back. "*Plants talk to me more than any other element. You know that. Jesus, I didn't think you were going to be so pissy about it, though I guess I should have known.*"

Reed took a deep breath in a pitiful attempt to control his guilt, and the annoyance that seemed to be waging war with his thoughts died down. Sighing, he expelled a bit of the irritation clouding his lungs, and responded. "*Fine. What do you want?*"

"*I think something bad's happened to Blake.*"

Her pain was clear in the tenor of the message, and he turned to look at Selene, his eyebrows forming a solid line of worry across his brow.

"*Can you tell me what you know?*"

"*Very little. We were in communication, you know—inwardly—and he was in Scotland with Heidi. He got interrupted, and then my head suddenly hurt, like I'd been hit with a pickaxe or something. I haven't been able to contact him since. I can still feel him, but it's a cold and sad feeling. He feels off, and I just don't*—" Her mounting anxiety was enough to drown her out. Reed could imagine her trying to swallow it down, trying to be strong. He may not have cared for her much, but even he was impressed with how well she'd kept herself together. Not many nineteen-year-olds still struggling to understand who they were could do that.

He unclenched his jaw. "*Selene told me*—" He cut himself off, deliberating over how best to break this news to her. His arm tightened instinctively around Selene, and, placing a soft kiss on her silver crown of hair, he told Maia in the only way he knew how. "*Heidi has him locked up. She's trying to get him to tell her what your plans are. I don't know how she's cut off his energy, though. I've never heard of that being done by another praeses before.*"

Reed waited patiently for Maia's answer, but the rustling of the ivy and nearby foliage was silent for several heartbeats. She was probably too upset to speak, and as he stood there waiting, he realized he didn't blame her. He didn't know what he would do if Selene were in Blake's place. Glancing over at his mate, he realized that he did know. Selene had been every bit as much Heidi's prisoner as Blake now was, and he'd done nothing. He'd failed her, just as he'd forced Maia to fail Blake. He shouldn't have advocated for her to uphold her promise to Heidi. No, he'd done more than advocate for it, he had facilitated it. Instead of helping her, he'd handed her, her old life as a human and walked away. Shame burned through him as the ivy began rustling again, as though it had a frightened rabbit ensnared in its twisted depths. Placing his hand back on the struggling plant, he heard Maia's voice.

"*How could she do that? He doesn't know anything! I mean, he knows a little, but not enough to give her any details. We have to think of something, Reed. Someone needs to go back and throw her off the scent. We need to get Blake out!'*

"Agreed. How soon can you get to Scotland?"

"Reed!" Selene slapped him on the arm, hard. He turned to her, shocked, and was surprised to see she looked enraged. Had he said that last bit out loud by accident?

Reed rubbed the offending arm, scowling at Selene. "What was that for?"

"You know you can't ask her to do that!"

"Wait, how did you—"

"Plants aren't the only means of communication, and Maia's not very good at this. But it doesn't matter. We should be the ones going!"

"What? Why?" Reed ignored the shivering bush next to him, pulling Selene in close as an old man walked by with his yapping Yorkie.

Selene lowered voice. "Because Maia needs to finish her task in securing the weapon. Heidi still thinks I'm on her side. I can return and talk to her, and while she's distracted, you can get Blake out."

Reed placed both hands on Selene's shoulders, looking into her dark eyes, trying to decipher her sincerity. He had never before questioned her intentions, but that was also before she'd cut him off. If she'd betrayed him once so easily, what was to keep her from doing it again? The romantic in him fought his denial—no, not his Selene, she would never. But she already had. And if she thought it would help him, she'd do it again. Still, while he no longer fully trusted Selene, he would gladly die by her side. Even if she was the one to place the knife in his back.

"It's dangerous," he finally said. "I won't be separated from you again, and if we're caught—" His concern was stopped as Selene wrapped her tiny arms around his neck and crushed her pink lips to his.

"We will never be separated again," Selene promised between desperate kisses. When she finally pulled away, her labored breaths matched his. She rubbed the small hairs at the nape of his neck before pressing her palms softly to either side of his face. "We have to do this, Reed. *I* have to do this."

Shutting his eyes, Reed gently placed his forehead against hers and nodded, kissing her once more, lightly. He placed his hand in the quivering ivy bush again.

"*Maia.*" He wasn't even sure what she had been saying when he interrupted her tirade. "*Maia, you secure the weapon. Selene will distract Heidi while I search for Blake. I think there's a good possibility Blake knows more than we think he does.*"

"*Okay,*" Maia sniffled. "*Thank you.*"

Reed nodded, knowing that she would feel it and understand. "*I'll send a message to the other* praeses, *ask them to meet you in Portland at the park. Ask them to help you.*"

"*You know about that?*"

"*Yeah. You're being watched, you know. And not all of them are going to be on your side. Be careful.*"

"*Have you heard from Lana and Leo? Is she okay?*"

"*I haven't heard anything. I'll try to reach them and let you know, but I suspect it may be some time before we can know for sure.*"

"*I'll look for your word, then.*"

Reed broke the connection and turned to a visibly grave Selene. He attempted a comforting smile. "Well, lovest, shall we?"

She returned his smile with a little peck on the cheek, and they hurried back to their flat. Once they'd reached the tiny garden, obscured from the view of passersby with tall

Italian Cypress hedges, Selene looked up to the sky. Reaching toward the heavens with a slender arm, she pulled a moonbeam down through the thick, low-lying clouds. When it reached her, she squeezed Reed's hand in farewell and shimmered into the moonlight.

Moments after she had safely disappeared, she reported back to him that she had arrived at Heidi's home. Only then did Reed follow her, wrapping his arms around the large Japanese maple residing in the middle of their garden. Pressing his body into the purple-red leaves, he gave his human form over to the humming energy of the plant and flowed quickly through the tree's veins, down to its roots, and onward to the large weeping willow he could feel placed just outside the castle's front door.

Stepping out from the tree as though walking through an unseen door, he joined Selene on the front steps. She pulled him into the alcove the castle's guards had once used to stay on watch, and in hurried whispers, they devised their plan.

32

LEO PACED BEFORE Lana's tree, carving a path in the soil beneath his bare feet. His mate lay curled up at the wide base of the bald cypress tree that represented her element. Heavy branches dipped forward, and long, needle-shaped leaves softly brushed against her exposed skin. He'd covered her with as much of the dark soil and leaves of her tree as he could, and now, he could only wait. Occasionally, a blue shimmer of light passed over her in waves, and she would glow faintly, but as soon as the energy receded, so did the Nymph. He could feel the hours passing as if the sands of time piled upon him, weighing him down with each precious, passing second.

She hadn't gotten much better, and the terrible truth he didn't want to believe was that she might not.

His loud roar shook the branches of the trees nearest him. Expressing his pain only tempered it in the moment, though; it returned as soon as the silence of the Garden did.

"My, my, she doesn't look so good."

"You!" Leo raced toward the lithe figure that suddenly stood over Lana, her hands on her hips as she straddled the prone Nymph, fake concern drawing her features down. "We give you the information you want, and this is what we get?" She raised her hand and Leo stopped short, heels digging into the earth as he struggled against invisible bonds. His nails had already extended into claws and his teeth had sharpened into preternatural points, but he wasn't going anywhere. The only thing that frustrated him more was that he couldn't understand how Heidi was suddenly capable of such a feat.

Her smile was one of triumph as she tilted her head to the side like a curious predator, watching her prey struggle before going in for the kill. It was a look Leo recognized, and he stilled, knowing it was useless to fight. He would lose.

"Are we done? Good. Now, you can listen or not, but I'm only going to say this once."

Her gaze shifted back to Lana. She lowered herself down until her knees dug into the supine figure beneath her and ran a dark finger along the girl's face, mocha caressing caramel.

Leo shuddered. It was such an innocent touch, but the malice was evident. He opened his mouth to protest, but nothing more than a whisper of air escaped. He clenched his jaw shut.

"Looks like your little water pixie doesn't have long. Fortunately, I have just the thing." She reached out and ripped several curls from the Nymph's head before slipping them into a small bottle she produced from the inside pocket of her blazer. She shook the small vial vigorously, and the liquid inside turned from black to a tropical blue. Then she reached out a second time and forced Lana's mouth open, gripping the Nymph's cheeks. Heidi poured the liquid down the girl's throat, and then squeezed her neck, massaging the fluid down. Once she was finished, she tossed the empty bottle to the side and stood.

Leo's heart dropped in confused dread. He'd never seen Heidi act so carelessly; she may have always had a horrible attitude, but she'd also always had the utmost respect for her position. She used to love the planet she protected.

Heidi pointed at Lana, who had yet to move as she rested between the Terra guardian's feet. "You've got forty-eight hours to bring me the replacement *and* the team. The *entire* team, Leo. I want them intact." She strode over to him until they were nearly nose to nose, her lips twitching as he snarled, shaking with the effort to attack this strange being wearing Heidi's skin. "If you don't, she'll die—slowly, and very pain-fully." She enunciated every word, lips spreading further in delight over his struggle. "If you're successful, she'll live. All I need to say is one word." She tapped a finger against his nose for emphasis. "Deliver them to the Core before your time's up, and Lana will live. It's that simple."

She disappeared in a frisson of energy, the air crackling and burning with her exit. Leo fell to all fours, clawed fingers digging deep into the soil, and he shuddered as the unnatural stench of the air invaded his senses. His eyes and nose stung, and he coughed, his hackles rising before the lactic acid built up in his muscles finally caused him to collapse. His cheek hit the soft earth beneath him, but thoughts of Lana forced him to stay conscious. He gave himself a mental shake and army crawled until he was nestled against her side. Her breathing had returned to normal, as had the feel of her skin, finally dry. She looked so peaceful, and delicate.

He sighed as he brushed a curl off her forehead, already knowing what he would do about Heidi's ultimatum. He ran a soft fingertip down the bridge of her nose and across her plump lips, twisted an arm around her and twined a leg around hers, drawing her close. He wished he could slice himself open, draw her inside, and protect her forever. He couldn't, though, and he wouldn't want his vibrant love to be so confined.

Planting a gentle kiss on her temple, he whispered a promise into her ear before slipping into the skin of a python and sliding away.

The "Core" was Heidi's throne room, and her only access to the powers of all the guardians combined. Normally, it gave her peace, but now, she stood before the pillar of crystal in the center of the room, staring at the projection it threw against the opposite wall. After dealing with the Corocottas and his Nymph, she'd returned to her seat of power to find the face of someone she had not seen in a thousand years gazing back at her, his features set in stark relief against the stone wall. The longer she stood there, the more her anger had tightened the muscles in her shoulders, causing them to rise. Who would dare to confront her like this?

A wave of her hand toward the stone wall and its mocking image did nothing. The projection remained. She closed her eyes and took a deep breath, focusing inward to draw from the energy that surrounded her. The roots of each *praeses*' tree coursed beneath the Core, a symbiotic relationship not unlike the one the Tree of Life shared with itself. From here, she could tap into the power of the other *praeses* without their permission, and she could feel each of the elements in turn: earth, fire, water, air—the pulse of life that ran through all plants and animals.

Tapping into the power of life, feeling it pulse and course through every fiber of her body, she raised her palms and held them before the image, throwing all the combined energy she could produce at it.

It didn't budge.

Astral energy coalesced at the base of her spine like an untamed dragon, and she reached for that next, a shiver running through her as she touched this new source of power. It frightened her every time she drew on it. She was playing with fire, and she knew she was eventually going to get burned. Drawing upon it would undo her balance, and imbalance brought consequences. She knew the dangers better than anyone, but the intoxicating strength that came with the power to destroy preyed upon her already weakened will.

The familiar face, with its crooked smile, continued to stare at her from its projection on the wall. Heidi repeatedly slammed her fists upon the crystal until her skin broke and bled. But nothing worked. The projection remained.

Finally, tears streaming down her face, she sank to the floor, leaned her back against the pillar, and stared at the face before her, one she knew so much better than her own.

She was a goddess of creation, but she couldn't create the answer to why she had been chosen as a Gaea *praeses*, while he had not.

A solitary tear slid down her cheek, tickling her chin as it rested on the precipice, contemplating its fall. Just like her.

She had fallen so far down this dark hole in search of the answer to her question—her one tiny, simple question. Heidi remained motionless, staring at the image. Her gaze found the contours of his jawline, the bridge of his nose, the tips of cheekbones that created the subtle ridge the deep-set brown eyes rested within. She traced his hairline with her eyes, as if her gaze were her fingertips, and another tear escaped across her lower lashes. She could almost feel the softness of his skin beneath her hand.

She pressed her eyes closed, allowing a few more rogue tears to escape. Their heat burned her eyes and skin. Opening her eyes again, she forced herself to stare at the one part of him she had so far avoided. His lips were slightly parted, and wit tilted the edges of his crooked smile. She wondered what charming remark might be on the tip of his tongue. Raising her hand to her own lips, she traced their outline and finally pressed a kiss against two fingers. For a brief moment, she felt warm again, like she hadn't felt in years. Imagining his lips pressed against hers, she sighed and breathed in his essence.

Heidi sighed once more, and the ache she had defended herself against for so long surged forward, mixing with the love she had denied. The image before her disappeared in a flicker and, just like that, she broke. The mounting yearning within her reached a crescendo, cresting and building even higher.

It escaped in a hollow wail as the rest of her body slumped to the floor.

33

MAIA REMOVED HER hands from the wild vine near the entrance to Mount Hood National Forest. The part of the forest that faced east had fortunately sustained very little damage when the Juan de Fuca plate decided to get a little too cozy with the North American, causing the Cascadia Fault to finally break. Like children standing in line for a water fountain, it had only taken one shove from a bully at the end of the line to start chaos. Heidi had been that bully.

Maia bit her lower lip, frustrated as she watched SUVs and station wagons bulging with families and camping gear coming and going from the parking lot. Misplaced anger boiled in her gut; she wanted to rage at them. How could they let daily life continue when destroyed homes and buildings lay in pieces over the smothered bones of entire families? Did these people not care that the earth had opened its maw and consumed everything that touched its soil? Maia hadn't seen images of the earthquake's aftermath, yet they still flashed through her memory as if she'd stood at ground zero. She could smell death. The decay of flesh, blood, bone, feathers, fur, and scales. She could smell the astringent aroma of dead plants as their leaves and petals were crushed, and the mustiness of the churned soil. The ravaged land on the other side of the mountains was as fresh to her senses as if it were a mere step away.

"You okay?" Mac's voiced tugged at her attention. "You look like you're ready to burn a hole into that family over there." He chuckled as he pulled two backpacks from the trunk of the car, stuffing them with supplies.

"I'm fine," she snapped, yanking the strap of the backpack he offered with a little too much force.

Mac's gaze grew wary, belaying the easygoing look on his face. "Right, yeah. When a woman says 'fine,' that's usually the signal to take cover and run. Dare I ask?" He grabbed a plastic pot and a large piece of burlap to wrap her tree in, settling them on the ground next to him.

Maia shook her head, trying to shake out her anger. She waved her hand at the crowds. "I just can't believe the nerve of those people. Entire families on the other side of this forest have lost everything, yet these Stepford freaks act like nothing ever happened. How can they be so . . . happy?"

Mac slammed the lid of the trunk closed and settled his piercing gaze upon her face. His sudden intensity made Maia take a step back. "So, you're telling me that you think these people should mourn the lost lives of people they don't know instead of living their own to the fullest, knowing that nature could take a shit on their home's welcome mat at any moment?"

"W-well . . ." Maia stammered. Mac slung the second, larger backpack over his shoulder and gathered up the pot and piece of burlap. "When you put it—yeah, okay. I guess."

Mac responded with a derisive snort as he turned on his heel and stalked in the other direction, heading for the nearest trail.

Maia's heart raced with embarrassment as she jogged to catch up. She didn't like this tension between herself and her oldest friend, so she pointed to the hatchet looped into his belt. "We aren't going all Paul Bunyan on my tree, are we?"

The edges of Mac's lips twitched. She was scratching the surface of his disappointment in her, but it didn't yet break. Maia huffed as she scurried over rocks and fallen branches, quickly out of breath where Mac easily cleared the foliage in single strides. Within the woods, he seemed twice his normal size, and an ancient power radiated from him. It was similar to the one she'd noticed in Blake, but this one was dangerous in a raw, erratic way. It was untamed and almost frightening to behold the longer Maia looked, as though his muscles itched with the desire to swing more than just a tiny hatchet.

Crystalline scenes of violence and bloodshed crowded her mind, and she swallowed back a gasp. Just like the other new images her mind had recently entertained, the scenes felt more like memories than pure imagination. Imagination was like wisps of smoke, fragile and changeable upon a whim. These were solid, firmly attached to remembrances of the smell of open veins and bowels, the pained screams of the dead mingled with the triumphant shouts of their killers, the sound of bones crushing. Stars swam before her eyes at the intensity, and Maia wavered in her steps, feeling light-headed.

Her hand caught the rough bark of a tree, her toe caught on a rock protruding from the path before her, and her lunch began crawling up her throat before her knees had even met the ground.

Mac grabbed her by the shoulders, gently easing her down to the mossy carpet of the forest floor. "Maia? Maia, what happened?"

She wiped the spit clinging beneath her lips with shaking fingers, her breath flowing in gasps as she tried to quell the violent tossing of her stomach. Squeezing her eyes shut, she gripped the trunk of the tree with trembling fingers, hoping the roughness of its bark upon her skin would bring her back to her senses. Her human conscience felt so small; it had been barely hanging on the past few days, and now, it finally surrendered in a gibbering mess. She felt it retreating further and further into its subconscious haven, knowing that soon, it would be gone completely. It couldn't seem to reconcile the fact that those deaths in her memories—imagined or not—had been done by her own hands. She looked down at those hands: one gripped her bent knee, holding her up, and the other splayed against the very-much-alive bark of a pine tree.

A jolt from the tree passed through her, and she gasped at the energy buzzing anew in her veins. "Mac," she said. "How do we know each other? Really and truly?"

Mac gripped her under her arms and helped her to her feet, right as a family of four turned the corner. He thrust a water bottle into her hands while he waved at the parents, who stared uncertainly at the strange couple huddled against the splintered tree trunk.

"She just got a little dehydrated," Mac explained, giving them a nod and an easy smile. The concern on their faces relaxed with new understanding, and Maia added a meek smile until they were out of view.

"Let's keep moving," Mac said, tugging on her arm. "We don't want to draw attention to ourselves."

Maia nodded as she drained the rest of the water in the bottle. "I saw things," she told him, following the path he made through the leaves. "Terrible things, Mac." She shut her eyes in a long blink, hoping to erase some of the images now branded onto the backs of her lids.

"You've done terrible things." Mac leveled a heavy gaze her way, a look of grim acceptance.

Maia's heart fell at his words.

"We all have," he muttered. They passed another couple in silence. Their golden retriever struggled to free himself from his leash, attempting to make a beeline for Maia.

Maia bit the inside of her cheek. It seemed, lately, that she could only occupy two ends of the emotional spectrum, anger and intense sorrow. Her feelings were a swinging pendulum. She wanted to ask Blake when it would end, but she couldn't reach him. She missed him. He brought out something more alive in her, as if he carried the best of her emotions within him.

And if she didn't succeed at this mission, she might lose him for good.

"Are you going to explain, or continue being vague?"

She could only see Mac's profile as he marched defiantly down the trail. His jaw tightened at her words. The sun was at its highest point in the sky now, filtering through the canopy of leaves and branches above them. Mac's copper hair glimmered like fire in the light, and he looked every bit the terrifying warrior she suspected he truly was.

As if reading her mind, he relaxed and gave in. "You still don't have all of your memories, do you? They're only coming back in pieces?"

"Right, and I don't know what kind of memories I just had. The battle that just raged through my brain was . . . I thought it was my imagination, but nothing I imagine comes to me so vividly, with sound and smell."

Mac made an abrupt left turn off the trail, and Maia followed. He said nothing until they came to a small brook running low through the forest. A rustling in the bushes next to the water's edge exposed an entire family of rabbits, their ears and noses twitching. Their wide, alert gazes gave them the appearance of being there solely to watch the show, and Maia imagined them with tiny 3D glasses and buckets of popcorn, needing a little levity after the barrage of horror she'd witnessed in her mind.

"I've known you and Blake from your births." Mac's sneakers squelched in the mud before he hopped onto the first rock that marked the jagged path across. He didn't look over his shoulder, or even offer a hand to Maia, and for a moment, she was astonished at his rudeness. He'd always been a model gentleman, but something about him had been slowly changing, emerging ever since she'd revealed that she knew who he was—and, for that matter, who she was.

He was halfway across the brook before he turned back to look at her, wordlessly asking if she was going to come or not. With wobbly, slipping steps, Maia hurried to catch up.

Mac shook his head at her. "I miss the *Talis*, Maia." He sounded disappointed and, deep within, she felt something echo the sentiment.

She remembered what Blake had told her about the *Talis* warriors, how they were akin to guardian angels or minor gods, but there had been little by way of description when it came to their duties and powers. And yet, the very thought or mention of them excited her in a way she couldn't comprehend. She wasn't naturally inclined to violence or fighting, but the idea of protecting power from scavengers and thieves had spoken to her much the way the Earth's energy sang to her senses. Shock rippled through her as logic finally put two-and-two together.

"Wait, are you saying that I wasn't always a Gaea *praeses*? That I was a *Talis* warrior once, too? I thought celestial beings were only created as—I don't know—the different species, or races, or whatever they're considered. Were you not always assigned as my guardian? And what do you mean you've known us since birth?" Her questions tumbled out of her in a jumble, clacking together messily, much like the pebbles being tossed about by the water below.

"Long story short, the Source created many different species. Why, no one knows. We aren't even sure of the purposes they all hold. Regardless, a few—and I mean a very few—were created with the ability to occupy more than one role. For instance, Poppy was an *Eros* when the two of you were born. She was very skilled at that job, too," Mac said softly. "It's one she's always sought to return to." His lips tightened into a thin line as they picked their way up a rock-strewn incline that soon became steep enough they needed their hands to help them climb.

"How does that explain the battle I just relived, though?" Maia dug her fingertips into the dirt of the low cliff. The damp soil beneath her nails and the sharp tang of the earth that tickled her nose with every breath calmed her immensely, a reaction she was slowly getting used to.

"Well, because, as you've already guessed, you were once a warrior. You and Blake helped guard the Council. Hence your *Talis* memories."

"Ah, yes." Maia hoisted herself up over the ridge of a large boulder, until she was flat on her tummy, staring at the tops of Mac's shoes; he was already up and scanning the horizon. She grimaced and hoped she'd been a lot more athletic when she'd been a warrior. "The good 'ole 'council' trope. Every team adventure story needs one, yes?"

Mac raised an eyebrow at her scathing remark as Maia climbed to her feet and brushed the dust off her stomach. "Remember what I told you about the artists I borrow celestial energy from, for the car?"

"Sure."

"Many are storytellers in one medium or another. Where do you think their stories come from? It wouldn't be a trope if it wasn't true."

Maia conceded with a shrug. "I guess it's the same as stereotypes that won't die."

Mac nodded. "Along with rumors, fairy tales, and myth. They only remain because of that small kernel of truth."

"And the battle I saw?"

"Is what happens when there's an imbalance in the universe that causes all-out war."

"So, space wars essentially." Maia wrinkled her nose, swatting at an overly friendly set of leaves getting cozy with her cheek as she passed. "First soul mates, then councils, and now space wars. My life has turned into an episode of *Star Trek*. Awesome."

Mac shrugged as he pulled a bottle of water from his backpack. "There's that signature Maia sarcasm." He smiled. "I was starting to worry you'd gone a bit soft."

He chuckled as Maia waved her middle finger in his direction with a smirk, but her response died on her lips as she noticed a new energy pulsing through her veins, tugging at her. It had been subtly egging her on for a while now, she realized, but she'd been too focused on her questions to notice.

The woods were eerily quiet. No sounds came from nearby animals, no breeze rustled the leaves.

Absolute silence.

Mac looked at Maia and nodded, encouraging her. She focused on the tug of energy, following it until she stood before a very large cedar tree.

This was it. She looked back at Mac, and he nodded again in confirmation. Having already removed his hatchet, he crossed to her side and began chopping at the tree's lowest branch.

Again and again, the woods filled with the sound of blade meeting wood, and nothing else. Maia watched, transfixed, as Mac stripped away the cedar's outer bark, revealing a hidden hollow at its core. Inside sat a sapling unlike anything Maia had ever seen. It was beautiful, with velvety soft leaves that emanated a vivid, light green glow, its tiny trunk and branches pure white with paper-thin bark, like a birch.

Stepping forward carefully, Maia reached trembling fingers out to the plant, caressing its leaves and branches. Her proximity to it sent shots of adrenaline and peace pulsing through her veins, and a shaky breath of wonder escaped her as she wordlessly took the spade Mac offered. While he prepared the plastic pot with soil and fertilizer, she gently dug the sapling from its tiny home. Once free, she transplanted it into its pot, tucking in its delicate roots with fresh soil and placing it in the piece of burlap, where she stabilized it with cushions of rolled cloth before tying the burlap closed and placing the entire thing inside her open backpack.

At first, Maia hadn't given much thought to the unearthly stillness around them; she was too enamored with the tiny sapling hidden inside the large cedar. But as they finished the sapling's retrieval and stood, the silence around them grew suffocating.

Until, right before Mac gathered the final tool, Maia heard the crack of a twig underfoot—coming from behind her.

34

HEIDI STARED DISDAINFULLY at the still figure by her feet. The aureate skin of the once proud and mighty Sideralis was leeched of color, his muscular arms looked skeletal as they wound around his knees, and his honey-blond curls hung limply around his face, where his features pinched in pain. But he wasn't dead. Yet.

Heidi's lip curled as she poked a steel-capped toe at the emaciated form, but quickly stumbled back as she felt a sharp pulse of energy shoot through her.

Not knowing how long he would last under the effects of dark energy, she steeled herself against the rising bile in her stomach. She had no other choice. It was the only way to find the information she sought. She flexed her shaking fists open and closed a few times, then bent down and pressed her fingertips to Blake's temples.

Closing her eyes, she reached out with her mind until she found the barriers of Blake's consciousness. She had only ever heard about entering a soul's private space before, and there was absolutely nothing she could have done to prepare herself for the reality of achieving it. Usually, entering a soul's private space—the subconscious—was by invitation only, and the soul had to be in good health to be able to sustain it. Once inside, the invader could walk through whatever home the soul had created for itself, each unique room representing a different life the soul had lived, all of its memories and knowledge stored safely away in the room's furnishings. The most valuable of these were often stored in the shape of an object the soul treasured, and would pulse with a beckoning glow.

The crumbled, charred ruin of a castle that Heidi found was not what she'd expected, however. The draining of energy and his time away from Maia had ravaged Blake's soul, leaving it unfit to defend itself, its landscape destroyed and unrecognizable.

Frustrated, Heidi stepped over the rubble, hoping desperately to find the information she sought. Some of the rooms she passed were barred by debris; others had doors hanging off their hinges that she could push aside and peer into with ease. The first few rooms she saw consisted of a warrior's training room, its walls fitted with every type of weapon needed for a multitude of fighting styles; there was a room that overflowed with star and planetary charts, and the corresponding tools one would need to study the skies; and there was a beautiful temple that paid homage not to any religion, but to the practice of maintaining one's soul. Each room had memories that beckoned, softly glowing, but she knew they weren't what she was looking for. She was going to have to dig deeper to find what she wanted. Blake would have hidden the information well, probably in a favorite room, but which one?

A section of the roof cracked and fell, showering her in debris as she ducked. She had to hurry. When Blake's soul died, this place would collapse and completely disintegrate, like the ancient cities before time restarted.

The ground shuddered, and Heidi ran. The hallway crumbled around her and large paintings slid off the walls, the shattering of their bodies echoing like wails of mourning. She skittered around a sharp corner to escape them and stumbled into a new room that was undoubtedly the largest she'd seen so far.

Her lips curled into a triumphant smile. She should have known the library would be his favorite.

It was vast, unlike any she'd ever seen, with shelves upon shelves of ancient tomes and modern novels. Not being very sentimental toward books, Heidi scrambled over the lush leather chairs, ignoring overturned shelves, the shredded remains of feathered throw pillows and cozy blankets, and the demolished shards of precious memories in the form of artful sculptures and knickknacks. Her true prize lay glimmering and locked away behind glass, hidden among a large section of rare and precious memory books. She thrust her fist through the panel, disregarding the sharp glass that scraped against the skin of her hand and wrist as she grabbed the brightest folio, the strength of its light indicating that it contained the most precious information. Tucking the leather-bound book into her bodice, she gathered her long skirts. The building shuddered violently around her and, after regaining her balance, she dashed from the room, down the long corridors, and out the front entrance to where she began. Not looking back at the debris, she pulled herself back into her own body.

With shaking fingers, she released Blake's temples, and sat back before fingering the edge of the book hidden in her bodice, wincing at the pain in her hand and wrist, and the way her skin glistened with dripping blood. A polite tap sounded on the door behind her.

Without turning around, she demanded, "What?"

Solomon's haughty voice drifted toward her from outside the cell. "A visitor for you, madam."

Heidi quickly twitched the sleeves of her dress, pulling them down to cover her hands before she stood and turned, stalking like a graceful cat toward the austere butler waiting for her at the dungeon's door.

"No one of importance knows about this place," she snapped.

Solomon was one of the few who didn't flinch at the sharp steel in her voice; as always, his features remained stoic and impassive. It was the only reason he'd lasted so long in her employment.

As he followed Heidi down the dim hallway and up the stairs, his bored look descended into further indifference. "Selene is here to see you."

"As I said, nobody of importance." Heidi gathered her skirts in her fists as she climbed the steep stairs, her heels clacking on the stone floor. "What does the little twit want now?"

"She said she has information for you." Solomon had the train of Heidi's dress pinched delicately between his fingers. When they reached the multi-level dungeon's final landing, he dropped it with a gentle flourish, the fabric flowing artfully to the floor with a much-practiced motion. They continued through the twisting halls of the dungeon in silence, until they reached the front hallway. Seeing the glimmer of candle-light slipping out beneath the cracks of the door to her sitting room, Heidi hesitated, suddenly overcome with a mixture of dread and irritation at needing to deal with the Luna guard-ian's flighty antics.

"Fine," Heidi grumbled. Snatching the pocket scarf out of Solomon's jacket, she wrapped her hand and wrist, slapping the butler's fingers away as he attempted to bind the wound for her. Shooting him another sneer at his request to tend to her properly, she elbowed him out of the way and slammed through the door of her sitting room.

The Luna guardian stood firmly in the middle of the room, her thin shoulders set back and her chin lifted in the kind of defiance she'd never dared show before. She looked like she was prepared to fight.

Heidi raised her eyebrows in surprise, slightly taken aback by Selene's rigid posture, but turned to the right side of the room, where an old, small chest lay on one of the side tables, beneath the room's only window.

"What do you want?" she finally muttered.

"I have information for you." Selene's voice was surpris-ingly strong, a challenge for Heidi to do her worst.

Heidi smiled slightly. She pulled a key off her person and unlocked the box. "I doubt it will be of much use, but what is it?"

"You wanted to know about the replacement, didn't you? I have the information you sought." Selene's voice dripped with the saccharine sweetness of a spoiled brat who had lever-age at her disposal.

Heidi quietly slid the pulsing book out of her bodice and plunged it into the deep chest to better hide its glow-ing energy. "Do you?" she asked lightly. She slowly flipped through the pages of the book until she had reached the end. "Go on, then."

"Maia is looking for a way to destroy you, and she has found a weapon hidden in a sanctuary in the Appalachian Mountains."

Heidi read the last entry quickly, her heart pounding as the words she read contradicted every one of those spoken by her strongest ally amongst the *praeses*. "Is that so?"

Reed cringed when he heard Heidi slam through the doors of the sitting room like a category five hurricane. He'd hidden inside a medieval sarcophagus that decorated the main hallway; the stench of death and decay rankled his nose. Heidi had morbid tastes. He'd noticed that the most brutal weapons and devices of medieval torture were displayed proudly throughout the castle, and every piece of fabric—curtains, rugs, even lace doilies—was blood red or black in color.

Once Solomon had retreated, his mutters about scarring and stained carpets fading with his footsteps, Reed slowly eased the stone lid off his hiding place. Slipping out, he peered between a crack in one of the door jams, sending a silent message of courage to his mate. He was proud of her strength. Years of abuse at the hand of her best friend hadn't silenced her, though he knew by the strain in her words that this interaction and play on strength was difficult.

Sliding along the hallway with his back to the wall, Reed probed the stone—smooth and softened by time—with his fingers, searching for a way into the dungeons. Selene had told him that she'd seen Solomon open a camouflaged door with an unconscious Blake thrown over his shoulder. There was a loose rock in the wall, inside one of the decorative carvings that, when pushed, would reveal the door. Selene had blushed when she described its location as being "on the private area of a female's likeness," but she'd refused to be any more specific than that.

Reed's fingers settled on a small, wobbly stone representing the exposed nipple of a frolicking nymph, and after he'd pressed it, he watched with wary excitement as a door swung slowly open. He froze for a moment, and when no sounds of alarm were issued, he released a soft breath. His heart remained calm and steady during the brief, but tense moment, even as excitement buzzed through his veins and made the hairs on the back of his neck stand up in warning. Getting caught wasn't an option. Licking his lips, he cautiously stepped through the doorway, letting it slide to a soft close behind him.

The complicated nature of the twisting corridors and stairs leading down to the dungeon amazed him. Selene didn't know where, exactly, Blake was being held, but she was convinced he was the only one down there—an opinion reaffirmed by the sheer deathly quiet of the underground maze. The dank limestone corridors seemed endless, with multiple rooms containing only a small peephole to peer through. The lighting wasn't good enough to see into them completely, and the air was filled with the musty, intermingled scent of rust, mold, and rat droppings.

Reed rubbed his earlobe in thought, peering down the long hall. A large rat raced toward him, keeping close to the wall, and Reed stepped out of the way, wishing for once that Leo was around. The Corocottas's extra senses would have come in handy, and he felt a slight twinge of guilt at having not tried to reach Leo once more before he and Selene left on their little adventure.

Rolling his neck from side to side, dispelling the dark thoughts threatening to distract him, Reed turned once more to examine the halls. Time was of the essence, but he couldn't risk calling out, and he didn't have enough time to check each cell individually. Trying a different tactic, he closed his eyes and took a deep breath, sending a gentle pulse of energy down the corridors, through the entire dungeon. If there was another *praeses* down there, he hoped the pulse would bounce back with their energy, and that he could follow the echo. The problem was that he couldn't send it out too far or too strong, or Heidi and any other *praeses* in the house would feel it, too.

Reed stood very still for a few moments after he sent out the pulse, but felt nothing in return. He ran down the corridor with soft steps, pausing every few feet to try again, and again. Finally, he came to what looked like a dead end, and still there had been no answer.

Swallowing a groan of frustration and shaking his head, he ran his fingers through his thick hair. When he and Selene had made their plan, it had seemed too easy, which was part of the problem. Things were bound to go wrong. He'd given Selene strict instructions to leave the castle after she delivered her message and return to their flat in London. He would meet her there with Blake, and they'd wait until they could figure out what to do next, knowing that their every step would, from there on, be watched. Without Lana and Leo's help, they would be outnumbered. Poppy was too unpredictable to count on, much like the forces she controlled, and right now, she was most likely following Maia, waiting for the right time to approach her lost *astrum*.

In the middle of his pacing, Reed kicked at a stone that had fallen from the decaying wall, forgetting that he was only wearing a pair of thin sneakers and not steel-toed boots. The stone hardly moved, and he clamped his hand over his mouth to stifle the shout crawling from his lips into a muffled groan of pain. Every curse word in every language he knew flashed through his mind as he clenched his teeth, hopping around on one foot.

Fighting the moroseness of defeat, Reed sagged against the wall. He had to come up with a better alternative, and fast. But before he could start on plan *B*, the wall behind him shifted under his weight and his body gave way to the gravity of an empty space. He had no time to stifle a shocked yelp as he tumbled down a short flight of slick stone steps to land with an undignified "oompf" at the bottom.

"The Appalachian Mountains, you say?" Heidi closed the lid of the chest, locking it and storing the key back in its hidden pocket within her sleeve.

"Yes."

Heidi faced Selene, then, matching her steady gaze and cocking her head curiously. "Very well." She smiled, and when Selene's bottom lip began to tremble with nervous uncertainty, her smile grew over bared teeth.

Within two snaps of her fingers, Solomon came rushing into the room with a steaming bowl of water, some ointments, and strips of bandages on a large silver tray. Without taking her eyes from Selene, Heidi shoved away her butler's renewed attempts at bandaging her hand. Instead, she issued a directive.

"Please send a team to retrieve both the replacement, Maia, and whichever *praeses* may be aiding her attempts to secure a weapon against me. Also"—she slapped the butler's hands away again, her cold eyes still locked on the Luna guardian—"tell them to secure the weapon and bring it to me. I believe they will find both it and the replacement at Mount Hood National Forest."

Selene's silvery skin instantly turned chalky as she burst forward, stopping a few steps away from Heidi, not daring to touch her. "Oregon? I-I said the Appalachians. If you go to Oregon, you'll miss them!"

Finally, Heidi turned to Solomon. "Escort Selene to her new living quarters. I believe her room should be available, now."

Solomon placed the tray of medical equipment on a nearby credenza and grabbed the Luna guardian by the arm, dragging her from the room as Selene screamed. "No! Heidi, you're making a mistake. Don't do this! Please!" The tapestries and weapons hanging on the walls began to lift, peeling eerily away from the wall as unseen fingers plucked at their edges. The flowers elevated out of their vases, scattering about the room as the jewel-encrusted silk throw pillows and down blanket from the chaise lounge also began to rise. Soon, every object in the room floated as Selene's fear reversed gravity.

One glare from Heidi and the airborne items plummeted back to the floor. Selene gulped. She tried desperately to kick Solomon in the shins, but her struggled efforts only earned her a backhanded slap across the face from the stalwart butler before he dragged her limp body from the room.

Heidi waggled her fingers at their retreating forms, then poured herself a glass of wine from the decanter by her chaise lounge. Spreading her skirts elegantly, she reclined, delicately fluffing her hair and taking tiny sips of the Merlot as she waited to share her good news.

He would be arriving any minute, and he was never late.

35

"MAC? MAIA?"

Maia jumped, dropping the spade, her heart racing as though she'd just been caught stealing the crown jewels. She looked to Mac, and saw his confused face flush red before she turned around and was swept into a giant hug.

"Sam?" Maia gasped, struggling out of the veterinary assistant's too-tight grip. She rubbed her arms after Sam released her, wondering if she would have bruises later. Had the woman always been so strong?

Standing behind his wife was Dr. Connor, and Maia moved toward the shy veterinarian with an extended hand. "Dr. Connor, hi. I didn't see you there."

She'd only met him a few times, and though he was one of the most brilliant vets in the Pacific Northwest, she'd never been comfortable with the way his curious eyes traveled over her features, as though she was a creature to be inspected, sliced open, studied. His gaze was more intense this afternoon, and Maia felt a brief flash of fear as she let her extended—and ignored—hand fall to her side, wondering if he knew what she was, if he could somehow sense it.

"What are you guys doing up here?" Sam peered curiously at the sapling inside Maia's open backpack, her eyes flitting to the empty shell of the cedar behind them. "Was that tree inside that other tree?"

"Yeah, it was," Maia said warily. Changing the subject, she asked, "What happened to you guys after the quake?" She glanced to Mac for help, but his expression was unreadable. His gaze flew from Sam to Dr. Connor with quick, untraceable speed, almost calculating as he stared at the couple.

Maia stepped on Mac's foot to pull him out of his thoughts. He shifted slightly, but his iron grip on the hatchet didn't loosen.

"So?" Sam looked at them both, her husband's posture mirroring Mac's perfectly. She didn't even bother answering Maia's question. "What are you guys going to do with it?"

Maia stepped back. An odd feeling settled in the pit of her stomach as a cold, dark energy settled around them. Behind her, Mac removed what looked like a hunting knife from a sheath buried in the waistband of his pants, and when he flicked his wrist, it grew into a gleaming broadsword, humming with its own celestial energy.

"Beliel," he hissed. "It's been a long time." His sword sang as he deftly twisted his wrist, flicking the blade through the air.

"Who's Beliel?" Maia asked. She took another step back as Sam's lips stretched into a smirk. She looked from Sam, leaning casually against a tree in the suddenly too-small woods, to Dr. Connor, whose hands were balled into tight fists. Finally, her gaze landed on Mac, who looked ready for war.

He pointed the sword at Sam's throat, pressing its tip against her skin.

"Woah, slow down! Jesus, Mac, watch where you point that thing!" She pulled on his extended arm, but it didn't budge. Maia gasped as a line of red trickled down Sam's neck, staining the neckline of her white tee.

"Hand over the weapon, Camael." Sam's voice was strange, too calm and unnatural. There wasn't time to wonder over it, though, because from the depths of the woods came figures, all of them dressed as ordinary citizens, but each carrying archaic weapons, some stained with dried blood, some still dripping from fresh kills.

Maia spun around. They were surrounded.

"And what?" Mac sneered, nonplussed. "No one will get hurt?"

"I never said that," Sam retorted. Dr. Connor's head tilted to the side, the angle too sharp and crooked, as if he was a lizard eyeing a particularly juicy bug. His eyes widened, pupils bleeding their color into his corneas, and as the whites of his eyes became completely engulfed, his small smile stretched into a curve much too wide for his face.

Maia froze, both fixated and disgusted by his strange transformation, but the whir and shift of weapons slicing through the air, wielded by testy owners, created an unsettling buzz in her veins. It was as if the sound called to her. An echo of the cries of battle in her memories from before.

A sudden whistle sliced the silence, and Maia spun—too late. A whip embedded with tiny needles wrapped itself around Mac's outstretched arm. He grunted, switching the blade to his other hand, and grabbed the whip further down its line, blood seeping through the gaps of his fingers as the tiny points bit into his hand. With a quick jerk of the line, the man on the other end of the whip flew forward, landing at Mac's feet. Mac grabbed him and twisted his neck, dropping him after the sudden *crack* of breaking bones. A dark shadow emerged from the body, screaming as the shell sank to the ground.

Maia's cry of shock was drowned out as the scene around her erupted into bedlam.

"Maia!" Mac's sword hissed through the air, severing a man's head. "Get up that tree!"

The specter's death-scream tolled, jolting Maia out of her thoughts and into movement. Narrowly dodging Sam's outstretched hand, she decided the nearby tree was a good idea, and she started to scrabble up as Mac held his own. He whirled and fought, cutting back his opponents as they advanced like ants, wounds opening on his body as weapons snuck by his defenses.

Maia watched from above, awed at her childhood friend, as a proud smile crept across her features. Mac was a badass—who knew?

Several more bodies fell. More screams rent the too-quiet atmosphere, and while more men and women poured through the trees, it was impossible to see Sam through the carnage. The call to battle still buzzed in Maia's veins, vibrating, warming her muscles and speeding the beat of her heart. It was an instinct to fight, but she clamped down on it, trying to smother it with deep breaths, gripping the branches to either side of her in the hope that the rough bark splintering into her palms would snap her out of this nightmare.

She blinked her eyes furiously as she shook her head. Images of Sam's kind smile mixed with images of her violent sneer. Maia hoped that she could somehow make all the pieces swimming around in her mind fit together, like one of those impossible kiddie games where you had to tilt the board to get all the balls into each of their little holes. *Why would Sam and Dr. Connor do this? What happened to them?*

Tears threatened to spill over the threshold of her eyes as a rock of betrayal bloomed in the center of her throat. Another scream tore through the air and her eyes shot open, the sounds of the fight below shaking her back into her horrid reality.

She refused to give in to the instincts her old memories served, despite her twitching muscles. She still had a job to do. Giving herself a mental shake, Maia squared her shoulders and turned her attention to the sapling, reaching her hand into her bag to grope around the tree's many limbs. The climb didn't seem to have damaged it, but she checked the branches thoroughly, glancing down every few seconds to search for the once affable Sam. There was still no sign of her.

Maia probed the sapling further. Once her fingers had brushed against the intact leaves, she let out a great exhale of relief, relaxing slightly. She closed the bag as far as it would go and settled it back on her shoulders.

The branch she stood on shook violently. Maia scrambled to grip the one above her for balance as she pivoted, her feet nearly slipping off her delicate perch as a rough voice reached her.

"Hand me the weapon, Maia." Sam's voice sounded like sandpaper, grinding and crunching over gravel. She was crouched nearby, balancing impossibly on a very thin branch from a neighboring tree that had poked its nosy business into Maia's hiding place, its foliage so intertwined it was impossible to tell the two trees apart.

Trying to ignore the sadness clouding her heart, Maia stepped away and hoped her voice didn't betray her fear. "What happened to your voice?" she yelled back, searching for an escape route and finding none. "Did you catch a cold, or something?"

Sam's lip curled as black smoke seeped from between her gritted teeth. She leaned forward, threat in her posture as she tilted at an impossible angle, and yet still remained impeccably balanced.

Maia inched backward, toward the trunk of her tree, hoping to climb to the other side. "Sam, please," she said, voice uncertain as the lump in her throat grew. "What's going on? You've known me since I was ten. You brought us dinners when my dad was in chemo—" Maia's voice choked and stumbled, but she pushed on. "What's happening? Who are you?"

"Shut up!" Sam screeched. She continued to advance upon Maia, using her legs to push down on the branch Maia stood on, bouncing it menacingly as she moved. "Hand over the weapon."

Despite the shaking limbs of the tree and the scuffle still playing out below, Maia managed to carefully maneuver herself several branches away, until the tree's trunk was between herself and Sam. Her right cheek was scraped bloody and her hands were raw. Maia leaned one shoulder against the tree and looked up, relieved at having escaped Sam again and searching for some winged animal she could call on for help.

She relaxed too soon. Several sharp nails plunged into her shoulder, and Maia's scream was drowned out by the rise of several more death cries from below. The fingers dug and tore at her skin, pulling her in one direction while yanking at her backpack from the other, trying to rip it right off her back.

Maia didn't want to look behind her; she didn't see want to see what kind of creature had attached itself to her back. Grabbing a solid branch next to her, she twisted her body from side to side, swinging down to the branch below and silently cursing her lack of coordination as her fingers slipped. She snatched once more at another branch, her fingers and nails bloody, but missed again and fell through the thick tangle of branches and leaves, the thin fingers of the limbs scratching and tearing at her clothes and skin as she sailed by.

Her descent stopped violently when the backpack caught on the edge of a branch, causing her shoulders to jerk back against the straps of the bag, and she dangled like a ragdoll, her breath short.

Hanging dangerously far above the ground, Maia twisted and tugged, trying to disentangle herself. Sam's derisive laughter grew louder as she moved closer, the sound heightening Maia's anxious attempt to escape. Out of the corner of her eye, she spied Mac. He was still trying to defend himself, despite holding a gushing wound on his left side.

"Mac!" Maia gasped, as a blow to the back of his head finally downed him, but her screams were swallowed by the wind that rushed through the trees like a steam engine. Under its strong breath, the tree holding her shook even harder, and the straps of her bag finally slipped.

Maia fell, barely registering the crack of her ribs and the sound her wrist made when she landed on it.

Then the pain exploded, radiating through every nerve as she closed her eyes and grit her teeth. She didn't see what happened next, but the death cries were louder, mingled with screams of rage and frustration, followed by the savage roar of a bear. She didn't move when gentle hands wrapped around her still form and picked her up. Her body was sore all over, but she felt the bag still strapped to her back, and felt a moment of relief when she felt the subtle, but healthy, energy of her sapling pulsing against her spine.

She wanted to open her eyes, but something cool and wet touched her forehead lightly, and suddenly she was dreaming of waves crashing gently on a warm and sandy beach.

36

REED FLIPPED TO his stomach and army crawled across the damp floor to press himself against the wall. He kept still, certain someone would come rushing out to investigate the racket he'd made. Clenching his teeth, he willed his pounding heart to slow as he rubbed the back of his sore neck.

Nobody came. Reed's fingers brushed against wood, and though he came away with a few splinters, he also realized he was lying in front of a door. He sent out a pulse of energy, and when it bounced back, it carried an extra pulse so faint he wasn't sure it was real. Picking himself up off the grimy floor, he turned in a slow circle. The room he stood in was nothing more than a small corridor set between the stairs and door.

Disappointed that he still hadn't found Blake, Reed slowly eased his way back up the stairs, confident that if an alarm had been raised, someone would have been down by now. Yet, when he reached the fifth step, he paused, shuddering at the strange prickly feeling that walked up and down his spine. The stairway and corridor he stood in was cold. Not freezing-temperature cold, either. It was the ice of death, the chill of loneliness, the emptiness of despair. The kind of cold felt in the pit of one's stomach and the farthest reaches of one's soul. Hesitating before he took another step up, he shook his head in confusion. His teeth began to chatter, but intuition gnawed at his fraying nerves, driving him back down the stairs like a possessed man until he once more stood before the large wooden door.

He shoved back the rusty bolt, shocked at how easily it moved along its bearings. The metal stuck slightly in a few places, but it took only seconds to fully slide it away and push the door open.

He didn't need to squint in the weak moonlight to see the huddled figure on the floor, cast aside like a broken doll. The familiar suit was enough to confirm the victim's identity.

Reed rushed to the huddled figure's side. Touching him gingerly on a thin shoulder, he rolled the body toward him, the pale yet familiar face sending first a burst of fear that he was too late, then a surge of anger that had him grinding his teeth until his jaw ached. Blake was hardly recognizable in this cold and frail state. Gently, Reed pushed a small amount of energy into his body.

He held his breath, but nothing happened. He offered a little more, having to force the energy through Blake's skin. After a few tries, Blake's eyes finally fluttered open to ice-blue cracks, a look of confusion followed by disappointment in his sharp eyes.

"Sorry, man," Reed whispered, pushing a little more energy into the Sideralis. It wasn't enough, but it was all he could spare. He helped his friend sit up and let him rest against his shoulder. "I'm not a pretty princess kissing you awake."

Blake wheezed out a short laugh. "Yeah-nah, mate. But I'm ruddy glad you made it."

Reed wanted to ask what happened, why the room was so depressingly cold, but a new commotion outside caused the friends to huddle together and scoot further into the shadows.

The loud arguing between a young woman and a bored-sounding older man came closer, and when the door to the cell burst open, Heidi's butler barreled through the door clutching a squirming Selene.

"Get your hands off her!" Reed instantly jumped up to rescue his mate, cringing when he heard Blake's body slump to the ground behind him. He pulled a sobbing Selene into a tight embrace, then pushed her behind him, settling back into a fighting stance with raised fists.

"Fool," the weary butler hissed. His voice was no more than a whisper, but he glared first at Selene, then Reed. "If you don't stop making such a commotion, I'll never be able to get you out of here!"

Surprised, Reed lowered his fists slowly, while Selene peered around his shoulder. Even Blake managed to push himself up on his elbow, his wide eyes staring at the butler's sudden outburst.

"But . . . why? You work for Heidi. Why would you help us? Who are you?" Selene asked.

"A *Talis*, and that is all you need to know." He waggled a finger at the Luna guardian, as though she was nothing more than a naughty child in need of reprimanding. Passing them, he knelt down beside the weakened Sideralis, pulling a vial out of his pocket and offering it to Blake.

"Hold on." Reed rushed over, placing a hand on Blake's to stop him from tipping the shining orange contents of the vial into his mouth. "How do we know we can trust him? He's the one who brought you down here!"

"Indeed," the butler said, looking toward the stairs nervously. "And that is something I must apologize for. I had no idea what the Terra guardian's plans were, and until you two showed up, I didn't know how I could help." He motioned to the vial in Blake's hand. "However, if our esteemed leader would kindly drink the celestial energy, he should be back on his feet quite soon."

Blake threw back the contents of the vial before Reed could protest, and the effect was instantaneous. He didn't look quite back to normal, but color returned to his skin and he was finally able to stand on his own.

"Well, I definitely feel better." Blake leaned heavily on Reed's shoulder as the Nepenthes pulled his friend's arm across his back. He shivered. "Still cold, though."

"Yes." Solomon nodded, his expression grave as he dropped his eyes, his thin lips forming an even thinner line beneath his otherwise haughty features. "She poured astral energy into both you and this room, draining you of nearly all your celestial energy."

"Astral energy?" asked Reed. "How the hell did she get so unbalanced?"

The butler shook his head. "I am unsure. I only know that the only way to reverse its effects is pure celestial energy. I have already summoned Raphael, and she has agreed to meet you at your house in London."

"The Great Healer?" Selene gasped, her tiny hand covering her mouth.

"She is a good friend of mine." Solomon smiled. "Now, Selene, I believe it is a full moon tonight?"

Selene nodded. "Yes, I can take all three of us back to London. But what about the others? Shouldn't we try to contact them, warn them?"

Solomon pulled Blake's free arm across his own shoulders and helped Reed pull him to the center of the room, right below the moonlight streaming through the room's only opening to the outside. "I am afraid it is too late for your friends. Heidi has suspected that Portland held the key for some time. She already had a team standing by, waiting for her order. They will have acted immediately."

Blake tried to straighten, pulling on his assistants to get them to move faster. "We need to get there," he said, already out of breath.

"Blake," Reed said. "Let's get you back to the house, first. When we get there, we'll send out some messages to get news on Maia. I'm sure she's fine." He wrapped his arm around Selene when she took Solomon's place, and she wrapped her other arm around Blake. The three of them stood huddled in the center of the room, the moon's silver light casting them in a ghostly glow.

"There is no need for messages," Solomon said. "The team was instructed to retrieve both her and the weapon. She has the weapon, and she will be meeting Heidi at the Garden of Eden shortly."

Blake's eyes widened with alarm, but before he could utter another word, Selene pulled on a moonbeam and whisked them away.

Heidi was pouring herself a third glass of wine when she felt the concentration of astral energy enter the room, making it feel empty, oblique, final. Her irritation flickered to life once more.

"You said you would be here within the hour, and it's been at least four. What took you so—"

The dark figure in front of her when she turned was not who she'd been expecting, but before she could gather herself and continue, her visitor said, "Sorry to disappoint you, mistress." The words hissed off the cloaked figure's tongue like water thrown onto a fire, complete with black smoke that permeated the room. Heidi coughed, and the figure continued, "Our lord is busy, but I have been sent to report that your message was received, and that the replacement has been found."

"Well," Heidi sputtered, "I should assume so. I told you exactly where she would be. Have you captured her, then?" Heidi tried to wave the thick smoke away, but it filled the room so densely she could no longer see the cloaked figure before her. As she was quickly learning, the effects of astral energy differed depending on who wielded it, and she was not overly fond of some methods.

"Our lord wishes you to meet him in the Garden. This will be your last chance to kill the replacement, once and for all."

"Fine, yes, what—" Another cough. "Whatever. Although, I can't see why he doesn't just do it himself, if you have her in custody. Where is he, anyway? Why is he not here?"

No answer. The only sound in the room was that of Heidi dry heaving as the thick smoke tickled her lungs and curled in her stomach.

"Fine, fine." Her shoulders shuddered violently. She held her stomach, feeling like she was going to be sick. "Tell him I'm leaving instantly."

The words had hardly left her mouth when the room cleared, as though someone had opened a window and sucked the air out. Only a slight burnt odor remained.

Shrugging in indifference, Heidi snapped her fingers for Solomon, but nothing happened. Raising an annoyed eyebrow at his tardiness, she snapped her fingers once more.

Still nothing.

With a labored sigh, she swung her legs to the floor, readjusted her skirts, and made for the door of the sitting room. Swinging the door open with such force the entire panel slid off its hinges, she was struck with her third surprise of the day.

Heidi blinked at the unassuming figure before her. "I did not call for you. Where's Solomon?"

"Pardon, my lady." Agatha, Heidi's masseuse and lady's maid, dipped into a deep curtsy. "Solomon has asked that I prepare you for your meeting tonight." Agatha paused for a moment, her shoulders rising as Heidi tapped her foot in annoyance. She visibly braced herself as she uttered the last bit of Solomon's instructions. "He said he will join us as soon as he has escorted the Luna guardian to her chambers and ensures that she will not leave."

After another hard look, Heidi accepted Agatha's explanation. Selene would surely have put up a fight once she regained consciousness; Solomon likely had his hands full trying to keep her in her cell. She tossed her dark curls with a victimized sigh and began walking toward her bedchamber, little Agatha trailing behind. The terrazzo floors of the hall-way cracked under each of her steps, the walls blackened with smoke, and anything made of paper curled at the edges, as if burned. Yet not a flicker of fire, nor the ocher of embers, could be seen.

37

MAIA BLINKED HER bleary eyes open. Her lids felt heavy, like lead, and her vision took several moments to focus. But even when the blurred shapes in front of her finally cleared, she still wasn't sure what she looked at.

The floor was hard, but warm. She lay on her side, and as she lifted her head, she could see a strange podium that looked to be made of rock, two large, throne-like chairs against the far wall behind it. Large, jagged crystals that stuck violently out of the floor bordered the circular room, a dark, smoky matter swirling inside each. As Maia pulled herself into an upright position, they moved closer, almost as though they wanted to be near her.

Wondering if she was dreaming, Maia blinked a few more times, but her surroundings remained the same. She rubbed her gritty eyes, and even gave herself a pinch on the arm. Nothing happened, though, and when the steady *clip-clop* of tiny hooves echoed through the room, she realized that she was very much awake.

The gazelle appeared from behind the podium, and Maia couldn't understand how the slender pillar of rock had hidden the creature from view. It came to a stop before her, dropping its head down gracefully until its face was level with hers. It gave her forehead a quick lick, and then stepped away again.

Feeling slightly more awake after the startling show of affection, Maia was surprised at how easily her body moved as she followed the gazelle to the thrones. She vaguely recalled that she should be in pain. Shouldn't she? They stared at the impressive chairs for a few silent moments before the creature spoke in its calm, wise voice.

"That one"—it nodded toward the throne that looked like it was made of smooth white branches, fur, and exotic plants—"is yours."

"It's what?" Maia asked, doing a double take. Her nerves shot adrenaline straight to her heart and it kicked up, beating in double-time, while sweat coated her palms. She rubbed them against the grain of her jeans. Everything, *everything* was happening too fast. Her mind whirled. How much time had passed since the earthquake? Had it been days? A week? More? She wasn't sure. Everything felt tumbled together, and she'd been knocked unconscious so many times she couldn't even remember when she'd last had a normal night's sleep.

Ignoring her question, the gazelle inclined its head toward the other throne, made of some kind of dull rock with intricate grooves carved into it. "That one, there, is reserved for the Sideralis."

"Blake," Maia breathed, her heart suddenly calming, returning to a normal pace. She was slowly getting used to the peace she felt at his mention, where even the sound of his name could settle her nerves. As little as she technically knew him, he was magnetic, addicting. She felt as though she could do anything if he was around to help. Memories—indistinct flashes and blurs of color—of the past lives they'd spent together flitted through her mind, and she wished she could catch even just one. She wanted to sit with it, examine it from all sides, much the way she would when scouting a location for photos. Not for the first time, she missed her camera, and for old time's sake, she made a square with fingers from both hands, giving the thrones and this strange room a new perspective. One she wished she could capture and hold on to for eternity.

The gazelle's bemused glance had turned almost to defiance when she uttered Blake's name. "The Sideralis is ruler of the guardians. His word is final and supreme. You understand?"

"If you say so," she replied, the creature's change in attitude catching her off guard. Blake exuded authority, sure, and she'd come to realize that he often made final decisions for the group, but he was no dictator. He always accepted the opinions and concerns of his fellow guardians, almost as though he was serving them.

"You have no qualms about obeying the Sideralis?" The gazelle's wide eyes were suddenly hard, challenging her to object.

"I trust him," Maia said, without hesitation. It was as if a deeper part of her was answering, a part that had more understanding of the situation than she really did. "He knows what he's doing. I don't, but he still asks for my input, and he respects me. He makes it easy to follow his lead, because I was involved in the process."

The gazelle cocked its head, looking once more at the throne in question. "But when you have learned how to be the Terra guardian, you will rebel. You will want to do things on your own."

The gazelle spoke as though it was already fact. Maia bristled at the notion. "I will not turn into Heidi."

"Will you not?" It asked, its voice dangerously steady, like the calm before the storm. "What if he was not the Sideralis, but another?"

"I'm not sure what you mean. Why wouldn't he be?" Sudden panic rose in Maia's chest, determined to crawl its way from her mouth in hysterics. She quickly tamped it down, clutching white-knuckled fists at her sides.

Ignoring her question, the gazelle turned and trotted to the podium, gazing at it with a secretive smile. "Have you decided, yet, what you are willing to sacrifice?"

"About that." Maia scuffed the ground nervously with her sneakered toe. "I'm still undecided. Humanity is . . . it's what separates us from every other creature on Earth. I'm not sure if I'm ready to go down that road."

The gazelle sighed, as though Maia were a child it was tired of explaining a very simple concept to. "When you become a guardian, you will no longer be fully human. Yet you will not be fully *praeses*, either. You are in between." It seemed to chew on the last two words for a bit, drawing them out.

Maia scrunched her eyebrows, still confused. "Okay, so I'm giving up—"

"A *piece* of your humanity, child." If the gazelle had had hands, it probably would have thrown them up in exasperation. Instead, it tossed its head a few times. "It is up to you to decide which piece."

"Oh." Maia exhaled, nodding a few times before asking, "When do I have to make this sacrifice?"

"You must make your choice when you officially take over your role as a Gaea *praeses*, during the transfer. If you don't, the choice will be made for you." The gazelle shivered, its whole body shuddering at the thought. "Believe me, Maia, you do not want the choice to be made for you."

"Who are you?" Maia asked. She blurted it out without meaning to, and knew she was probably going to get a vague answer, if any, in reply.

The gazelle did not disappoint. "You and I will officially meet, face to face, once you have successfully completed the transition and become the new Terra guardian."

Maia's lips twitched, and she raised her eyebrows. "Scared?"

But if she was hoping to challenge the gazelle into re-vealing its true identity, she was sorely mistaken. The gazelle merely laughed. "You'll find out soon enough, Maia. Besides," it said, looking at her slyly, "we don't want to ruin the sur-prise. It might affect your victory."

"But—"

The gazelle was gone. Not exactly a normal exit, either. One minute it stood before her, a patronizing look on its an-gular face, and the next, it was gone.

Maia's strength disappeared as well, and she slumped against the wall, suddenly tired and weak, as though she'd been drugged. She slid down to the ground, landing on her side in the same position she'd been in when she first woke in this strange room. Her right arm and wrist ached with a dullness that quickly became sharp and insistent, and her eyelids closed as she spiraled deeper into the pressure of unnatural sleep.

Every time she'd visited the gazelle, and even when she'd had the vision of Mac, the darkness had been the same: so thick, she felt suffocated, trapped, like she couldn't move no matter what she tried. This time, something was different. The pain in her arm was mirrored in her heart, as well. Her heart felt heavy, straining as though it would explode with grief, the pressure so strong she wanted to scream and cry to release the pain. Yet no tears came, no relief.

She thought of her mother, her short blonde hair turning slowly white, and the cream cardigan she'd always wrapped around her body. She thought of the way Beth used to sing when doing chores about the house, and the way she'd had the most comfortable shoulder to cry on, how she'd always given the best advice. She thought of her father as he wrapped his arms lovingly around his wife, his green eyes sparkling with mischief under his favorite Mariner's baseball cap. Maia desperately missed their long talks about the exotic places they would visit when he got better. That was the extraordinary thing about him, and one of the things she'd loved most—he never felt sorry for his circumstances, nor allowed anyone else to feel sorry for him.

Her parents' smiling faces looked back at her from in front of their old home, whole and complete, as it was before the destruction of the earthquake, and the desolation she had somehow kept at bay since her time at the cabin returned in a rush, drowning her in its undertow. A soundless scream escaped her open lips as she fought for her next breath, and the ever-present darkness pulled her under once more.

38

WHEN THE DARKNESS and grief threatened to crush her into a powder fine enough to be blown away by the lightest of breaths, Maia began crying out for Blake—in her mind or out loud, she wasn't sure—hoping he could hear her, asking him to hold on to her pain for just a little longer. She wasn't ready for it yet, not all at once.

She felt tears running down her face, and her body shuddered with sobs as she regained consciousness. Her nose ran, and she was surprised when she managed to lift an uninjured arm to pat around in the dark for a tissue. She really had no idea what damage her body had sustained in the fight. All she'd done was cower and run in fear, while Mac had done the dirty work. Guilt weighed her heart down further at the thought. What if she had given in to her urge to fight? Would it have made a difference?

She sniffled as the last shuddering sob left her frame, and she patted at her damp cheeks with the back of her hand. A tissue was thrust into her fingers, and she quickly covered her nose and face with soft fluff. When she was done wiping the tears and snot from her face, she bit back her embarrassment, wondering who was sitting beside her bed, watching her latest emotional meltdown.

Admittedly, she was disappointed by the face that greeted her as she opened her eyes and looked up, but she was happy, too, for the troubled smile from familiar features she hadn't thought she'd see again.

"Lana!" Maia bolted upright, throwing both arms around the Nymph. Her lips were dry as she spoke, and she felt the skin rip as she peeled them apart.

"*Ma petite*, how're you feeling?" Lana gently pushed her back onto the pillow, her cool hands gently squeezing Maia's shoulders.

"I don't know. My arm hurts." She looked down at the throbbing limb, shocked to see that it was only wrapped in a light bandage, as though she'd merely sprained it.

Lana was smiling when Maia looked at her again. "The Great Healer was here, but has already left to attend to another patient. Fortunately, she said your arm will be fully functional in about . . ." She paused, twisting in her seat to look at the digital clock on the dresser at the far side of the room. "An hour and fifteen more minutes. Which is pretty good, considering you broke several major bones."

Maia looked warily at her immobilized arm, not daring to move it. In fact, it almost felt like a phantom limb, there and yet not there, and she couldn't work out which was the truth. She knew it was there, of course, but she couldn't feel it.

"What about you?" she asked. "What happened? The last time I saw you, you were—"

"I was very much near death." Lana nodded. She sighed, her smile weakening, wilting the corners of her lips as tears edged their way to the tips of her lashes. She sucked in her plump lips, as if she could bite back her emotion, and glanced at the white railing that acted as a fourth wall to the room, separating the loft from the beige carpet beyond.

"Leo said it was touch and go for awhile, but I finally pulled through." Her smile grew, and she looked down, remembering a private moment before glancing at Maia once more. "*Mon amour* said that my tree healed me, and that I was strong enough. I've always been strong enough." Her last sentence was a barely audible whisper.

Maia placed her hand over Lana's and squeezed. The look on Lana's face when she thought about Leo only made the hole in Maia's chest feel that much wider.

Lana smiled again before worry creased her dark brow once more. She turned to look at the twin bed next to Maia's. "Mac, on the other hand, will be taking a little longer to heal. He sustained a lot of damage in that fight."

Following her gaze, Maia finally took in the rest of her surroundings. The opposing wall from the loft railing had one large window that looked out onto many acres of countryside and forest, and the two solid walls were mostly bare save for a few impersonal, hotel-like pictures decorating the striped wallpaper. Aside from the dresser and a couple of nightstands with lamps, the room was empty.

Mac lay in the bed next to hers, heavily bandaged, Poppy curled up next to him. She gently stroked his face while crooning sad poems of redeemed love in his ear. Every so often, he muttered along with her, repeating favorite phrases. Their two imperfect voices, cracked with the joy of their reunion as it mingled with the heartache of being apart for so long, was the most beautiful sound Maia had ever heard. Her tears returned in a rush, and she furiously blinked them back. Witnessing the carnal cavorting of Leo and Lana was nothing compared to the intimacy that laced the whispered words between two long-lost lovers.

Mac gazed up at Poppy in adoration, his eyes greedily roaming over her features, as if she were nothing more than a mirage he was desperate to memorize, and Maia was struck by how solid Poppy looked, more so than ever before.

With a slight shiver, Maia swallowed thickly and looked back at Lana, determined to give the lovers as much privacy as she could. "Who is the Great Healer?"

"Oh," Lana said, her voice softening in reverence. "She's another of the Ancients, Camael's sister."

"Sister?" Maia rubbed her cracked lips thoughtfully. She never knew Mac had a sister. He'd only ever talked about his brother.

"*Oui, chére.*" She reached for a pitcher on the nightstand and poured Maia a glass of ice water. After wrapping Maia's fingers firmly around the glass to ensure she had it in hand, she let go, her own hands hovering to catch it should it fall. "I take it he still has much to explain to you?"

Maia nodded, grateful for the icy water sliding down her parched throat. It coated the inside of her stomach and ran sweet relief through her veins. She finished the glass quickly.

"I do not envy you, your choices to be made." As Lana spoke, she switched the empty glass for a stick of honey pomegranate lip balm. Reveling in the calming scent, Maia applied it generously to her chapped lips. "But I have heard great things about you, Maia. You're a survivor. No matter what happens, you turn it into a success."

Maia smiled meekly and returned the lip balm with a murmured, "Thanks." Slightly embarrassed at praise she couldn't quantify, she opened her mouth to change the subject, wanting to know what had happened during the rescue, but an overexcited golden retriever bounded around the corner, noticeably Leo even with his pink tongue lolling out of the side of his mouth.

Lana giggled as the dog pranced over, licked her face, and then placed his big head—complete with beseeching puppy expression—on the covers of the bed, eyes roving back and forth between Maia's face and her hand.

Maia grinned as she rubbed the dog's head, relieved to feel the crushing weight of the grief in her chest lift slightly as the soft golden fur glided under her fingers. Leo smiled and licked her palm, and when she moved her hand to scratch behind his ears, he closed his eyes in contented peace. The sorrow and an almost overwhelming sense of loneliness still rattled in the depths of her heart like shards of glass, and Maia was sure that if she wasn't careful, they would slice her open from the inside, but for now, they would have to rest. Taking a deep breath, she imagined building a thick wall between herself and emotions that, right now, would only distract her. She needed answers. The restlessness of her curiosity and impatience was equally as uncomfortable as her sorrow.

"I need to know what happened," she said. "And what's going on."

The dog licked her fingers once more, before giving way to Leo's tall figure, wearing a dark green V-neck t-shirt and gray jeans. He tucked his black hair behind his ears and gave

Lana a quick nuzzle to her neck, nipping playfully at her ear. For once, Maia's discomfort at their open display of carnal affection veered toward jealousy, and longing.

Finally, Leo looked up at her and said, "After Lana was returned to health, we left the Garden—"

"Reed didn't expl—" Maia interrupted. Leo leveled a look of irritated impatience at her and she mouthed a quick apology, mentally adding the notion to her list of questions that was mounting daily. She could have written an entire encyclopedia on everything she still didn't understand about this strange new world.

"We heard you were in Portland, near the park by Mt. Hood," Leo continued.

Lana nodded, her tight ringlets quivering with the motion. "We didn't realize you were in so much in danger. We knew you would be with Camael"—she paused, looking back at the bed behind her—"um, Mac, but we didn't know you would be attacked like that."

"Yeah." Leo rubbed his hands against his face. He looked and sounded exhausted, and Maia wondered at his uncharacteristic stillness. He wasn't even pacing. "How the *terrarum exstinctors* managed to find you is baffling. Plus—"

"Wait." Maia bristled at the new piece of information being so casually slung her way. "What are *terrarum exstinctors*?"

"Destroyers of worlds." Leo's tone was offhand, flippant, as if he had just called a new species of flower she'd pointed out a "dandelion." He didn't meet her eyes. Instead, he glanced over his shoulder at Mac, who was struggling to rise against Poppy's insistence he lie down. She pushed on his shoulder gently, admonishing him in hushed whispers. He responded by covering her lips with his, pressing countless kisses against them.

Leo smiled at them, but Maia kept her gaze averted. When the Corocottas looked back at her, his brow was crinkled with concern once more. "I haven't the slightest clue as to why they would attack you in the first place."

"Seriously," Maia gritted out through clenched teeth. Her fingers had curled around clumps of the quilt draped over her as fury mounted within, mixing with adrenaline. She struggled against the both of them, feeling as though she wanted to run until she collapsed. "For fuck's sake, you guys need to level with me already, and start being more specific. First it was this garden place, and now these world destroyers? I'm tired of always being left in the dark with only half-truths and pieces of information!"

"The *terrarum exstinctors*," came a hoarse voice from the bed beside her, "are our opposing equals."

"Come again?"

Mac gave Maia a patient smile, the kind she'd always struggled not to find condescending.

"As *praeses*, we have more celestial energy than other beings because it's our job to create. We have some astral energy as well, because sometimes destruction is needed in order for life to come forth. Our mates see to it that the balance of our energies is maintained, because too much of one or the other would induce madness."

"Right, I remember you telling me that." For the first time, Maia noticed that the restless rage that had been shaking through her limbs had completely quieted, and she realized, as Mac gave her a knowing nod, that his redundancy was serving a different task.

"Good, I'm glad you remember, because the *terrarum exstinctors* do the opposite of what we do. They have more astral energy than other beings because their job is to destroy worlds and galaxies when their time comes. They also have celestial energy and mates to maintain balance. After all, destruction takes a bit of creativity. But they are, in essence, our mirrors."

Maia rubbed at her temple as she tried to absorb what Mac was saying, fighting off a new wave of long-forgotten memories. She didn't have time to sort through visions of dying stars and planets.

Lana chimed in as she began changing the wrappings of Maia's bandaged wrists. "But why would they attack Maia? Many of them were human. They've never interfered with our work before."

Mac shook his head, and then winced, to which Poppy responded with more coos and kisses. He gave her an indulgent smile before answering. "I don't know. They were being led by Beliel."

"Beliel?" Lana sucked in a breath, while Leo hissed at the name.

"You never did explain who Beliel was." Maia looked back and forth between their faces, each contorted in fear or fury or concern. "You mean Sam?"

"Yes," Mac sighed. "I don't know how I missed who she was, or how she was able to hide her dark energy for so long, but Maia—" He looked angry with himself for a moment, gritting his teeth and swallowing his own rage. "If Beliel is here, then this changes things."

"This changes a whole lot of things," Leo spat. "Is there any chance they're here for the Core?"

"But why?" demanded Lana.

"Guys?" Maia's tone issued a clear warning.

"It's the throne room belonging to the Sideralis and the Terra guardian, located in the Earth's core," Lana answered. Waving her hands about, she then described, in detail, the interior of the exact room Maia had just visited, except for one thing.

"What if . . ." She trailed off, swallowing another panicked feeling before continuing on. "What if the Sideralis's throne doesn't have any color running through the designs? What if it's just one solid color?"

Lana looked at her strangely, her skin paling as she turned to Leo. "Well, that would only happen if the Sideralis was dead, which isn't possible. There has to be one, always. Otherwise, the sun won't rise, and life on Earth would eventually cease to exist."

Leo narrowed his eyes, peering at Maia with a suspicion more befitting to Reed. "Why do you ask?"

"Well," Maia said, flexing her damaged fingers, testing the work of the Great Healer and the mobility of Lana's new bandaging job. "Before I woke up here, I had a vision, or something, and I was in that room. The Core, the one you spoke of." When only uneasy silence met her, she threw Lana a pleading look.

"Alone?" Mac looked at her strangely, too, but his was more a look of concerned thoughtfulness, as though there was some puzzle he attempted to put together.

"No," Maia admitted, lowering her eyes and picking idly at the worn quilt she was tucked under. "I've been having these visions." She glanced quickly at Lana, Leo, and Poppy before returning to her careful examination of the quilt. "Other than the one I had about Mac, I mean. I've been—" She hesitated, wondering if they were going to think she was crazy before realizing that those cards were no longer on the table. She sighed, and her words came bubbling out of her in a rush. "I've been visiting a strange garden, talking to this gazelle who said he—or she, I'm not sure which—was my guide during this transition. He, um, *it* has been giving me advice. Well, more like vague nudging. Nothing that damn creature says ever makes any sense." She suddenly felt the same strong sense of annoyance she'd often felt since this whole nightmare began, as if she was missing something because somebody was intentionally keeping it from her.

"A gazelle?" Leo asked incredulously as he stood and began his usual pacing behind Lana.

Maia flicked her gaze up at the many pairs of eyes staring back at her, feeling completely hollowed out on the inside, before looking down at her injured arm and flexing her aching wrist.

"Well," Mac said. He was sitting up further than before, now that Poppy had stuffed a pile of pillows under his head. "It seems likely that the garden in your vision was the Garden of Eden. It's where Lana was taken to heal, and where you're going to need to go next. You need to replace Heidi's tree with your own in order for the transition of guardianship to be complete."

He looked like he wanted to say more, but a sharp tapping noise caught everyone's attention. They looked out through the open slats of the window's blinds to see a hummingbird with an iridescent teal body and red chest zipping back in forth in the air. The little bird would zoom up to the window, tap furiously on it with its beak for a few seconds, and then zip away before returning to the window again.

Leo squeezed Lana's shoulder and went over to the window. Drawing up the blinds, he opened the glass and pushed the screen out far enough for the hummingbird to zip through. The bird's frenzied entrance was followed by a gust of strong wind that kicked the floral curtains about wildly and pushed a few of the smaller pictures askew. The tiny bird flew about the room in a sense of panic for a few seconds and then, hovering right next to Leo's ear, whispered some kind of message.

Leo's face hardened, his teeth grinding and jaw locked. Once the bird finished, Leo nodded once, and the bird disappeared out the window as fast as it had come. He closed the window and drew the blinds down, taking his time. Very slowly, he came to sit next to Maia and Lana on the bed, his eyes blank as though in a trance.

Lana touched his hands, which were gripping his knees so tight his fingertips were white with exertion. "*Mon coeur?*"

He jerked back slightly at her touch, but then grabbed both of her hands, seemingly holding on for dear life.

"What's the news?" Lana whispered, but Leo's lips were drawn in a tight white line, and he puffed out his cheeks to keep the tirade of angry words from spilling out.

"Heidi has enacted her revenge." Everyone's head whipped around to look at the source of the timid voice, who was sitting calmly next to Mac, looking just as solid as they were, aside from a slight blurring around the edges of her frame where the air of the room swirled and frolicked in her aura. Nobody said a word, shock settling in at the realization that the once-ghostly wraith had finally found her true voice. Mac beamed at her, stroking her slender white arm lovingly.

Poppy continued, oblivious to their reaction. "She has unleashed several natural disasters around the world, hoping to distract the guardians with her destruction. Tornadoes, tsunamis, hurricanes, earthquakes . . . they have become a means to an end for her."

Leo let out a huge breath, clenching his eyes tightly while nodding, agreeing with Poppy's explanation; it must have been the same thing the hummingbird told him. The next words out of her mouth, though, surprised them all.

"She is preparing to meet you at the Garden, Maia. She is counting on us abandoning you. She is counting on you being alone."

"That's not going to happen," Mac said. He tried sitting up further, but quickly slumped down on the pillows again, clutching at his side as he winced in pain. Poppy smoothed his auburn curls from his sweaty forehead and patted his chest, letting her hand rest there, discouraging him from attempting to rise again.

Mac placed his large freckled hand over her small one, then looked at Maia. "You already know how to use Poppy and Reed's power," he said, breathless from his exertion. "As well as your own." He then looked at Lana and Leo, who both seemed torn between fleeing the room and remaining where they were. "Leo, Lana, as soon as Maia's arm is functioning, you need to teach her how to use your powers as well. She'll need full permission from every *praeses* to use their powers during this confrontation. Poppy?"

Poppy nodded, and her hair—no longer transparent, but golden and fair—tumbled and tossed over her shoulders with her enthusiasm. "She already has my permission." She smiled, and Maia noticed for the first time that the Ariel had an adorable set of dimples embedded in the rosy cheeks of her milky skin.

Maia returned Poppy's smile gratefully, the shock of her new speech pattern still causing her eyes to widen. Not knowing what else to say, she stuttered a simple, "Thanks, Poppy." Dropping her eyes from the girl's gaze, Maia kicked the covers off the bed, wincing as her still healing ribs sounded their displeasure, glad that for once no one had tried to change her clothes for her, despite the flecks and pieces of bark and leaves that filled the sheets. She looked to the other *praeses*. "By the way, where exactly are we?"

"Upstate Montana, close to the Canadian border," Leo said. He stood, twisting his neck back and forth in order to work out the kinks. "When I was human, my family owned this land. Selene and I are Siksiska, of the Blackfoot Indian tribe. We grew up here."

"Oh." Maia glanced out at the large stretch of nature cutting across the very blue sky. Her fingers itched to hold her camera again, and her curiosity burned to ask Leo more about his tribe. But instead, she asked, "Speaking of Selene, has anyone heard from her? And what about Blake and Reed? I don't know why, but I can't contact Blake." The cold loneliness that had haunted her since Blake left threatened to take over the longer she stayed still. To keep it at bay, she hopped up and began shoving her feet into her sneakers, which had been placed thoughtfully at the foot of the bed.

Poppy rose with all the fluid grace of a dancer. "While you train, I will find out what has happened and let you know."

Maia threw her arms around her warm neck and squeezed her tight. "Thank you, Poppy," she said, knowing that at least the Tempest guardian understood the pain she was in. Poppy returned the gesture and, after giving Poppy one last squeeze, Maia followed Lana and Leo down the stairs, through the cozy house, and out into the expansive front lawn, complete with its own sizeable lake.

But even as she trailed behind the Nymph and Corocottas, Maia couldn't help but feel like there was still something she was missing. The news Poppy had relayed was tragic, certainly, but Leo's reaction to whatever the hummingbird had said had seemed personal. And he'd never actually told them what message the bird gave. A heavy feeling of dread settled over her heart. Whatever Leo was withholding, she was certain it wasn't good. And she was equally certain she would find out. She just hoped that she would be strong enough when she did.

39

THE GREAT HEALER was already waiting when Reed and Selene entered their London home, half-carrying and half-dragging a very weak Blake. She helped them carry him upstairs and laid him on the guest bed, and then, after many offers to help, she shooed them unceremoniously away and closed the door gently, but firmly in their face.

Several hours later, Raphael descended the stairs, finding Reed and Selene waiting for her in the living room, settled on their favorite couch, the latest fashion magazine resting in Selene's lap, and a first edition copy of Hemingway's *For Whom the Bell Tolls* in Reed's. Both *praeses* turned eager, hopeful gazes her way, but the news she had to give them was only partly good.

"He is going to need much rest," she said, her voice warm and gentle.

Reed and Selene only stared at her, waiting.

Clasping her hands delicately in front of her, Raphael continued, "Solomon told me what happened to him, but do you two know?"

They both shook their heads, concern creeping around the edges of their hope.

"Well, then," Raphael sighed. She walked to the large wingback chair by the fireplace and looked it up and down. Sniffing slightly, she wiped the seat off with a handkerchief, and then folded herself into the navy blue chair with more grace than any dancer could ever be capable of.

She crossed her legs, smoothing nonexistent wrinkles from the fabric of her ivory cotton dress while Reed and Selene leaned forward. She met their eyes and said bluntly, "Blake was poisoned with astral energy."

Selene let out a little gasp, which Raphael ignored, soldiering on. "Fortunately for him, the affects will soon wear off. I have restored his body with celestial energy, and given him the sun's energy in liquid form."

"Wait a minute, how—"

Raphael lifted a hand to interrupt Reed's questions. "Please, Reed, let me finish."

Reed hesitated, but he nodded and leaned back on the couch, only his tapping foot belaying his impatience.

"You may not remember all the way back to your initiation ceremony, but when you were chosen to replace your previous guardians, you were offered a cup that contained the energy of your element in liquid form. This is only given to those who have been chosen, because, under normal circumstances, the former guardian no longer exists to hand their power over. Maia's case is an exception. She slowly earns the Earth's energy because the Earth is leaving Heidi of its own accord, turning instead to Maia."

Selene's mouth formed a small *O*, but no sound came out.

"Giving Blake more of his element's energy in liquid form restores his connection to it, and therefore his ability to heal himself. But though his body shall make a full recovery, I am afraid his soul is a different matter."

Selene finally found her voice, but only enough to whisper, "What do you mean?"

"Something is missing, my dear child." Raphael's cold tone was not directed at the two *praeses* before her, thought it caused them to flinch, but at the atrocity done to the Sideralis. "I asked Solomon if he could tell me anything about it, but my mate was unsure. He believes Heidi might have taken a piece of his soul. He saw her rummaging around inside his subconscious."

Selene's skin paled further, while Reed bounced to his feet, pacing erratically enough to please even Leo, had he been there.

"The only one who has even the slightest chance of fixing him is Maia."

Before anyone could respond, a large *bang* shook the house. Lightning tore its way through the sky, its repeated flashes blinking through the house with unnatural frequency. Seconds later came the rain, but not the usual drizzle London experienced; rather, this was a deluge of massive proportions that threatened to chip its way through the stone walls. Large pieces of hail bounced off the already shuddering windowpanes, and when one golf ball-sized piece finally broke through, the guardians and warrior sprang into action.

Raphael leaped from her chair. Grabbing Selene and Reed by the arms, she pulled them into an alcove below the stairs, where she laid out her plan.

"I will take Blake into the cellar for safety," she said. "It looks as though Heidi has gone on the offensive, and I can guarantee this is not the only disaster affecting the globe right now. You two—" She paused and pointed at each of them as wind ripped through the house, tearing decorations from the walls and knocking over furniture with a series of deafening crashes. "Get to the Garden immediately. Solomon said that is where Heidi will be headed."

No further argument was needed. Reed nodded and took a frightened Selene in his arms. He looked up, out the house's shattered top window, then back at her. Understanding his question, Selene nodded. She closed her eyes, gripped Reed's arms tighter, and in a blink, they were gone.

Raphael dashed upstairs. Tearing the rubble out of the way, she managed to shove open the door, pushing aside an overturned wardrobe that had barred it.

Blake was already halfway out of bed, stunned as he stared at the shattered vials littering the floor. He looked up when Raphael entered the room, and when the *Talis* warrior beckoned, he hopped weakly over the shattered glass and accepted her help as she guided him to the wine cellar.

Plopping down on an old pile of blankets, he gratefully took the vial Raphael offered to him, and downed the contents without question.

Looking at the handsome boy who already seemed to be almost back to full strength, Raphael felt the anger of what had been done to him stab into her, settling deep in her stomach.

Solomon couldn't be sure what had been stolen, but Raphael had a good idea what it was. Heidi's violation of Blake's soul disgusted her, and though she tried to be indifferent toward the guardians, she had to put those notions aside. She had to believe that Maia would succeed.

Otherwise, there would be no saving the Sideralis.

40

MAIA WAS THE first to land at the Garden's gate, startled that she was even able to find it. A few seconds later, the soft thud of several pairs of feet landed nearby, and she looked over her shoulder at the couples standing behind her. For once, she was thankful for the pain of emptiness knifing its way through her chest; it made her angry, and as long as her anger drove away the nervous butterflies, she would welcome it.

Turning back to the Garden's gate, Maia whistled. Made of wrought gold filigree shaped like the symbols Maia had seen in Blake's notebook, it was overrun by climbing roses and honeysuckle that only served to make it even more beautiful. Two ancient *Talis* warriors stood before it, broadswords held aloft and crossing, creating a barred entrance to the Garden. Their armor, forged by beings who'd crafted it with celestial energy, appeared to be alive. Each plate swirled with a constant, shimmering color that resembled mother-of-pearl, and thin chain mail of the same living element clung to their bodies, moving and shifting with them.

"I can't believe this has been here all this time," Maia said. She felt as though she could stand there for eternity, just staring at the majestic gate and its guards. If it hadn't been for the increasing celestial energy controlling every cell in her body, she never would have even seen the Garden, located between the Tigris and Euphrates Rivers at the mouth of the Persian Gulf.

Mac cleared his throat loudly. He took a few limping steps forward and held up his right hand, scooting the sleeve of his jacket up to reveal his wrist to the guards.

Maia didn't see the guards look, but they slowly drew back their swords just the same.

Mac let his hand fall back to his side, where his sleeve slid back down. No matter how far Maia craned her neck to see, she couldn't catch a glimpse of whatever mark was on his arm. But before her curiosity could overwhelm her enough to ask, the gates opened and a familiar scene captured her attention.

The exotic plants and winding paths before her were the same ones from her visions. Same colors, same sounds of the wind brushing through the leaves. She had been here before, and as she walked through the gates, the others fell in line behind her. She didn't have a particular part of the garden in mind; she just meandered through the paths, watching as the foliage welcomed her like an old friend. The Garden itself was far more delightful in person than it had been in her visions. The air was filled with the delicious smells of the surrounding foliage, and curious animals soon began popping out of the various trees and bushes, as if to welcome her to their humble home. Though her companions trailed behind her in a morbidly silent fashion, Maia couldn't help but smile in wonder at this nearly anthropomorphic garden.

After only a few minutes of walking, Maia realized that the Garden was much larger than her visions had shown, which made it all the more surprising when they soon came upon a familiar creek. Turning to her companions, she slung the bag carrying her sapling off her shoulder and plopped down under the familiar, fluffy-blossomed tree.

"This is where I met the gazelle," she said. "I haven't seen him yet, though." She was disappointed that he hadn't been waiting for them, for she'd felt certain he was going to be there to show them the way. Her nervousness—which had first been offset by her anger, then her excitement—was quickly resurfacing. She plucked at the light green shirt she wore, and gave the hair piled atop her head in a messy bun a good scrunching ruffle. Anything to keep herself busy.

A pack of wolves had joined them, small at first, but slowly growing as Leo busied himself talking to them. A few smaller animals—a rabbit, a squirrel, and a dove—made their way to where Maia sat, sniffing at her quizzically and attempting to root around in her bag. Nearby, Lana ran her hands through the water of the brook with a satisfied grin on her face. She made the stream rise, run in waves, and form a small tide pool, all with a few flicks of her fingers.

"It doesn't make much sense," Mac said, standing with his arms crossed as he leaned against a sturdy oak for support. "This gazelle business." His reddish eyebrows were knit into a solid line over his eyes, and despite the carefree dance Poppy was engaging in with the wind she'd whipped up, drawing increasingly darker clouds across the horizon, Mac's frown looked like it had been permanently chiseled into his handsome features.

Maia opened her mouth to defend the gazelle, annoying though it was, when Leo's head popped back up after his conversation with the wolves. "These guys are telling me the gazelles rarely leave the mountains, or their valleys."

"Well, how far away are the mountains?" Maia hopped to her feet and stood on her toes, attempting to see into the horizon, but her view was obstructed by Poppy's gathering thunderstorm.

"Three days' walk." Leo tilted his head back and let loose a howl worthy of any alpha. The pack darted back into the brush.

Maia slumped, dejected. "Fan-fucking-tastic. So I guess they haven't seen one around here, lately?"

Leo shook his head, smirking at her language. He walked over and pulled a feisty little rabbit out of the front pocket of her backpack, where the critter had been happily feasting on a granola bar.

"Well—" Maia started, but was interrupted by the crunch of gravel on the path behind them.

Mac whirled around, fists clenched, and Leo wasted no time slipping into the form of a mountain lion, teeth bared and ready. But when two familiar faces emerged around the bend, Mac sagged back against the tree.

Leo remained as a lion, pacing around Reed and Selene, softly brushing his sleek body against them until they moved to stand next to each other. Seemingly satisfied with the arrangement, he flicked his tail at the two *praeses* and plopped down on his haunches in front of them, a low growl rumbling in his throat.

Maia sighed, exhaling her relief and resisting the urge to hug the two of them.

Reed gave Leo an exaggerated roll of his eyes as he stepped forward and gave Maia a light, but comforting one-armed hug. Selene followed with an encouraging smile and a much warmer embrace, and despite this being only their second meeting, any doubt Maia had had about the Luna guardian's loyalty was instantly dashed, along with her doubts about Reed. While she'd never mentioned it to anyone, she'd had a nagging feeling that if Selene had remained on Heidi's side, Reed wouldn't have hesitated to follow.

Selene pulled back with a timid smile that failed to hide the grief or ease the tight lines near her eyes. "Blake—"

A large ripping noise echoed through the peaceful moment, and Selene screamed as she was suddenly yanked backward into the air, a stunned Maia holding on to her arms for dear life.

Maia thought they would land in the thorn-filled rose-bush they had been standing near, but instead, they sailed right over the top. As they lifted higher above the trees, her panic doubled. Maia struggled against the sharp wind stinging her eyes, forcing herself to look around, to see where she was going and what she was about to land on.

They didn't travel very far before they were flung mercilessly back to the ground in a small, oval-shaped field.

A new voice squealed in delight. The sound was followed by a shriek of pain as Selene was ripped out of Maia's grasp and dragged across the field by her hair, where she was slammed against a large rock. Maia looked up to see a tall, bronze-skinned woman whose terrifyingly beautiful face was morphed by fear and rage, and needed nothing more to recognize her. This, she knew, was Heidi.

Heidi, evidently believing the Luna guardian could be frightened into submission, snapped her fingers. Instead of cowering further in fear, Selene crawled away on all fours. Throwing her hands up in disgust, Heidi grabbed Selene by her calf while simultaneously bending to retrieve a stone the size of a baseball. She slammed the stone across Selene's temple, and as the Luna guardian slumped against the rock, her pale hair becoming soaked with red, Heidi began pulling at the vines looped above the boulder, seemingly oblivious to Maia's weak attempts to stand.

Heidi snapped her fingers a few more times in irritation, and finally, the vines moved, albeit sluggishly. They wrapped themselves around and around Selene's still body, pinning her arms firmly to her torso.

By the time Maia had managed to pull her slightly dizzy self off the ground, gasping for air, Heidi had begun to march toward her. Looking like a fierce warrior, her sienna-brown hair was pulled back in braids, and an armored vest much like the ones the guards at the gate wore gleamed across her chest. She carried a wicked-looking broadsword made of the same gold-like metal, but with her bare arms exposed—aside from the armored guards on her forearms—she didn't look as though she planned to do much fighting.

As Heidi's black-leather clad legs strode closer, Maia dropped into a crouch. She buried her hands into the earth, her mind skipping erratically through the countless elemental exercises she had done with Poppy, Lana, and Leo only a few hours ago. Without the others there with her, she could only use a small portion of their powers, not very effectively and only because they'd given her permission. Until they arrived, her best strength lay in the earth and plants. As she pressed her own energy into the cool earth, begging it to crack open and buy her some time, she sincerely hoped she wouldn't be alone for long.

Before Heidi was within striking range with her sword, the earth beneath her quivered, then split, and she stumbled back as she tried to avoid it.

She glared at Maia with wide eyes. "You!" she bellowed, fury perverting her features, and she rushed forward again.

Maia pivoted as she stood and, gathering the air about her, threw the dirt she had clumped into her hands. A small tornado of soil formed, kicking up a substantial amount of grass, twigs, and pebbles. It met Heidi head-on, and she was knocked back, screeching and spitting mud while Maia ran toward the tree line. Catching sight of a large black bear crashing through the woods in front of her, Maia cupped her hands around her mouth and called to the creature, begging it to protect her. Instantly, the animal raised itself on its hind legs and returned the request with his own growled response. Behind her, Maia heard Heidi catching up, screaming obscenities, urging the bear to kill Maia instead.

The bear hesitated. Maia panicked, unsure whether the creature would listen to her or the current Terra guardian, but Leo's dark hair revealed his shape streaking through the trees, coming up behind the bear with his own call of encouragement to the giant creature. Maia smiled, relieved. The bear was back on the home team.

Despite knowing the animal was on her side, she skidded to a stop two feet away from the towering mass of fur and flesh and pivoted again, rushing toward a new target. On the southern tip of the field, twenty feet from where she and Selene had initially landed, Mac, Lana, and Poppy were working feverishly to dig up a tall tree that looked as though it had seen better days. Despite the robust health of every plant in the Garden, this one was grisly, with brown leaves, soggy and molding bark, and strange black ooze seeping through every crack in its surface, emitting an odor that reeked of decaying flesh and gasoline. But even though it looked as though it would fall over if someone so much as coughed delicately upon it, its roots ran deep, and it was going to require intensive digging to remove it.

Maia pumped her arms harder, willing her legs to carry her faster and ignoring the sharp stitch that had lodged itself in her side. Despite the bear's efforts, Heidi had noticed the attempted removal of her tree, and she pilfered one of Poppy's growing thunderstorms. Pushing it over Maia's head, Heidi saw to it that the needle sharp shards of ice pierced her skin as they came down, and were thick enough to obscure her vision. Maia ran, only to be caught up by several opposing winds that worked to hold her in place. There were shouts all around her as the other guardians attempted to guide her, urging her with suggestions, but the wind and ice smothered her senses.

Raising her arms in front of her face for protection, she opened her eyes just in time to see a flash of light flickering across the ground. The immediate explosion from the sky above awoke an instinct that pitched her body to the left and, dropping to the ground, she rolled until she felt dry earth, and popped back up.

Pointing her finger toward the dark cloud, she swirled it around in a circle, drawing the energy of the next growing bolt of lightning until she felt the ions shiver in their eagerness to be released. Looking ahead, she noticed Poppy, with a satisfied smirk, had stopped digging, and that her brown eyes were fixed on something behind Maia.

Maia grinned back and spun around, flinging the lightning in the direction of Poppy's gaze. It hit Heidi square on her breastplate, sending her flying backward several feet. Knowing Heidi was going to continue attacking the minute she recovered from the shock of being hit, Maia braced herself and went on the offensive.

41

HEIDI WAS STILL struggling to stand when Maia rushed her, wishing she was close enough to the water to mount another surprise attack. Maia mused that a good drowning might keep the Terra guardian quiet for a bit.

Besides, she could have used a drink herself.

Before she could get close—visions of a drowning, gurgling Heidi dancing in her head—she was suddenly lifted off the ground once more. This time, she didn't move anywhere, but was suspended upside-down, as if by an invisible giant who had grabbed her ankle and took joy in dangling her above the field. Maia yelped, and scrambled to tuck the edge of her shirt into the waistband of her jeans before twisting around wildly, flailing her arms in a windmill.

The cackling that erupted from below pointed her to the source. Tilting her head back in order to look directly beneath her, she saw Heidi's sneering figure standing triumphantly with fists on her hips, her breastplate strewn across the ground in pieces. It hadn't sustained any damage from the lightning bolt, but Maia realized that it must have been so heavy and bulky that it had kept Heidi from recovering quickly.

Heidi had one scraped arm raised, her hand curled in a fist, as though she was holding something. It took Maia only a second to realize that something was her.

The attack on her and Selene had happened so quickly that she never got a good look at Heidi. But now, staring down at her enemy's upturned face, she realized that it was strangely—painfully—familiar.

"Hayley?" she choked. Confusion lanced through her. It couldn't be. Hayley had been her friend. Her best friend. The tall Brazilian had also been spectacularly uninterested in being environmentally conscious, despite working at Tryon Creek State Park. And yet . . .

As Heidi opened her mouth, no doubt to say something unpleasant, she was abruptly lifted into the air with a shriek. Only, she wasn't only hanging upside-down like Maia; she was bouncing back and forth.

"*Tsk, tsk*, Heidi!" said a sweet, but clearly irritated voice below, as Maia was gently returned to the ground. "You never asked for my permission to use the gravity of my moon. In fact"—Selene touched a slender white finger to her chin and said—"you never do."

A stream of curses vile enough to curdle cheese erupted from Heidi's mouth, and they mingled with her shrieks as she continued to bounce with the lightest flicker of Selene's forefinger.

"Ask?" Heidi shouted between bounces and screams. "Bitch, you answer to *me*! Put. Me. Down!"

Selene giggled despite the obscenities being thrown her way as Heidi flailed about, and Maia's initial feeling of justice soon gave way to an uncomfortable tension. Heidi may have deserved a taste of her own medicine, but Selene's enjoyment blurred the line between abuser and victim. Yet, Maia didn't have the heart to deny Selene this tiny moment of revenge. She understood, and she also understood how dangerous the Luna guardian could truly be.

Reed appeared behind his mate. He stood with arms crossed, chuckling softly at the tableau before him. Pride shone in his dark eyes as smug satisfaction appeared in his grin.

After a few moments, Maia nodded at Heidi's suspended form. "Selene, Reed, may I have permission to use your powers to deal with this? Please."

"Yes," they chimed together.

Maia gave them both a grateful smile, tilting her head in a bow of acknowledgment. "Thank you."

Touching her fingertip to Selene's extended one, she took on the gravitational pull the moon guardian was using. Flipping Heidi's form around, she ceased the bouncing, pinning the Terra guardian to the closest tree instead, using its strong arms to hold her against its wide body.

Heidi struggled wildly, scratching at the thick branches wrapped around her torso until they pinned her hands to the side of the trunk. She hissed at the tree's blatant refusal to bend to her will.

Maia squinted at the squirming form before her, tilting her head first one way, then another. With a growing feeling of dread, she asked again, "Hayley?"

The words were barely a whisper on her lips, but Heidi still heard them. Ceasing her attempts to escape, Heidi screwed her lips into a smug smile before closing her eyes and relaxing. Her dark skin lightened a few shades, fading from rich mocha to russet brown. Her hair straightened from its natural curl, and her features rearranged just slightly, until it was Maia's best friend in the tree's embrace, not her enemy.

A strangled noise escaped Maia's throat as the pain of betrayal welled behind her eyes. Heidi laughed as she let the façade drop and her true form reappeared. Maia scrunched her eyes tight, fighting the tears as the last person she'd had left from her previous life was torn away from her. She really was an island of one. Everyone she'd loved was now either dead, or had been nothing but a lie.

"How did she . . . ?" Mac was suddenly beside her, and she gave a little start at his voice. His face bore the same furrowed lines of confusion hers had moments before.

"You didn't know?"

Mac scoffed. "Are you kidding? It was my bloody job to protect you. From her!"

Heidi rolled her eyes at the two of them as she resumed her struggles against the tree. "And such an excellent job you were doing, too." She clucked her tongue at them, but her dark eyes were elsewhere, constantly moving as they searched for something. Maia tried to follow her darting gaze, but to no avail.

"Do you realize how many times I could have killed her?" Heidi continued. "Good God, man. I honestly have no idea why you, of all people, were put in charge of her."

Mac stiffened at her words.

Heidi continued with a nod. "Especially given your history."

Maia looked up at Mac's tense jaw, hovering inches above her to the right. She was just about to ask—her sea of questions was no longer holding at her command—when she was struck in the chest and sent flying thirty feet behind her. She fell, coming to a skidding stop, and landed in a crouch. Her body heaved with a labored breath that stung as it traveled through her bruised chest. She had barely a moment before she heard a thunder that didn't come from the sky, and she looked behind her to see a herd of creatures bearing down on her, pouring from the woods. The strange stampede of gorillas, rhinoceros, bison, and zebras tore at the soil beneath their feet and hooves as they charged with wild eyes and flared nostrils. Above the sound of their charge, a strange chanting filled the air, mixed with words and the sounds of the animals nearly upon her, yet beneath the strange orchestra was a command.

"Maia, run!"

Screaming filled her ears as she finally unlocked her knees and picked up her feet to flee.

The stampede gained on her, churning the earth with hooves and talons, and Poppy appeared above her. Just as the tusk of a passing rhinoceros slashed across Maia's back, she felt Poppy's wind lift her above the melee. The cool rush of air was a welcome relief, even as Maia became more and more aware of the sting of her wound. She dreaded the moment her nerves awakened and became aware of the injury; all logic would disperse, and she needed to think *now*.

Poppy quickly enveloped them in the loud sanctum of a tornado's eye, obscuring Maia's vision as the whirling clouds dismissed any audible sound from below. The Tempest guardian's petticoats remained untouched in the strong wind, and Maia only felt a light pressure against her body as wind and debris whipped around her.

Poppy's eyes were completely clouded over, and her lips moved quickly as she stretched her palms flat against the tornado's eye. Her shoulders bore the strain of controlling the storm and keeping Maia safe, and concentration creased her brow. Maia instantly mirrored her, and with an effort of will, she added another layer of protection from the howling winds.

Poppy's eyes cleared as a result, enough for Maia to see the gray irises once more, and she smiled in gratitude. The pressure had eased on them both, and the noise had decreased a few decibels, but there was still no doubt as to their location.

"What's happening?" Maia shouted. "How did Heidi do that?"

Poppy shook her head and passed a hand over one side of their protective wall, giving the torrent surrounding them some transparency as she moved the twister to a safe place. "I don't know," she said. "There's no way she should be able to control the wildlife to that extent, not without—" A dark look crossed her face as a shiver of fear shook her delicate shoulders. "No, it couldn't be," she muttered, chin creased in worry.

"Couldn't be, what?" Maia asked.

Poppy looked up, her eyes glowing with mingled indignation and hurt as her nose blushed against the threat of tears. With a wave of her hand, she and Maia landed in front of an astonished Leo. The animals were already retreating into the forest, where a few rebellious bellows earned a rebuke from their Corocottas.

"You," Poppy breathed. Her tiny fists were balled at her sides, her face flush with emotion. "You gave her permission,"

Poppy whispered. Her voice shook with the effort to control her anger.

Leo couldn't meet Poppy's eyes and guilt tugged his shoulders into a slump. Lana, who had been helping with the removal of Heidi's tree, turned to him with dirt-smudged cheeks and shovel in hand. "Leo?"

Mac and Reed joined them, a squirming Heidi between them.

"What's she talking about?" Lana demanded.

Leo shook his head, stuffing his hands in his pockets, determination hardening his features.

"He made a bargain," said Heidi, addressing Lana with a haughty tilt of her head and a satisfied smile of triumph. "For your life."

A growl rumbled deep within Leo's chest as he whirled to face her. "A bargain and a threat are not the same."

Heidi attempted a shrug between the strong grips of her captors. "Nuance. She was dying, regardless."

Leo opened his mouth, but Lana beat him to it.

"You helped her?"

"Oh, it was more than help." Heidi's chipper tone was overeager in her insistence. "Go on, Leo, tell them how long you've been feeding me information."

Ignoring the provocation, Leo gripped Lana's shoulders. The Nymph flinched at his touch.

"Lovest," he said, pleading, as his hands fell to his sides. He dipped his dark head toward hers. "I had no choice. You would be dead right now if I hadn't."

Lana stepped back, crossing her arms as if to keep herself from reaching out to him. Still, her body leaned in his direction; the pain of pulling away was evident in every stiff line of her stance.

Maia clenched her jaw, debating over what to say as adrenaline coursed through her, making everything, even her emotions, numb. But logic told her two things. One, Leo had done what he did out of love for his mate. And two, he could no longer be trusted.

Steeling herself against the hurt and betrayal she felt, she knew there was only one course of action to take. "Leo." She stepped forward. "You're going to answer for this, but right now, we need to finish what we came here for. Mac?"

Without preamble, Mac lifted his free hand, and with a flick of his wrist and a few muttered words, invisible bonds gathered Leo's hands and feet. The Corocottas fell to his knees in submission, his head hanging in shame. Tiny sparks of energy could be seen hovering near his bound limbs. Lana gasped, clamping a hand over her mouth as she dropped the shovel with a muted *thud* in the damp earth; her other arm wrapped around her waist, as if she could somehow hold herself together. Leo didn't fight. He didn't struggle. He just clenched his jaw against his instincts to change. His skin rippled and morphed a few times, and his teeth grew in number and sharpness. He glanced at Lana briefly, at the tears in her eyes as she struggled to stay away from him. He shuddered, once, before he shut his eyes and curled into himself.

The pain of both *praeses* mirrored Maia's own, and she swallowed thickly before looking away, scanning the group before her. Her voice choked on the words that left her mouth, words her soul already had the answer to:

"What's happened to Blake?"

42

THE RUSTLE OF leaves underfoot made Maia turn, her
hands open, palms down, as she settled into a half-crouch.
The steady pulse of life beneath her feet had settled into
rhythm with her heartbeat, and she felt the vitality of the
Earth's energy flow through her veins. She had little doubt
that, if needed, the earth would answer her summons.

The two figures advancing upon her, however, changed
her impulse. It was Blake, slumped against the lithe frame
of a tall woman robed in white whose hair was a scarlet red.
Maia expected an overwhelming sense of relief and peace to
flood her, finally calming her volatile emotions and soothing
her frayed nerves. Instead, alarm bells went off as her senses

painfully sharpened. She felt as if someone had driven red-hot needles into her nerve endings, and she struggled not to collapse with the pain. Breathing heavily through clenched teeth, and with balled fists at her side, she looked at her mate again. Something was wrong. The pain subsided into a manageable ache, and Maia rushed forward.

"Blake?" She draped his free arm over her shoulder, and his face turned toward her . . . that face. She would recognize the lines of his brow and the curve of his jaw anywhere. But his eyes, the ocean-blue ones that used to haunt her dreams and now graced them instead, were vacant of recognition.

He gazed at her with a furrowed brow. "Who are you?"

Maia's heart dropped. Blake had a great sense of humor, but he wouldn't be cracking jokes now. Would he?

She frowned at him, but he had stopped looking at her and was instead staring at the small circle of *praeses* as Maia and his rescuer helped him shuffle by. Reed and Mac were busy retying Heidi to a tree with vines that were clearly no longer under her command; Reed was muttering something about the use of poisonous plants when Blake interrupted.

"What's happened here?" He looked at Leo's prostrate figure, the grief-stricken Lana, and the somber Poppy hovering nearby. "Leo?"

Nausea tightened Maia's stomach as she followed the other woman's lead, passing the tense group. Blake remembered them; he remembered them all—except her. As reality struck her, another flame of hot pain convulsed around her heart, burning her chest. She bit her tongue and tasted copper as she and the woman stopped before a large Desert Willow. The magnificent tree bowed slightly in the light breeze, its pink blossoms nodding a welcome to their Sideralis.

"We must lay him down here," the woman said.

Maia blinked dumbly a few times, until finally, some of the pieces clicked into place. "Oh . . . right." She nodded, helping Blake to sit, and gently pushed on his chest as he continued to address and question the others of the group. Not once did he spare a glance for her.

"Blake," the woman said. "You are unwell. You need to rest." Her voice held a motherly command.

"Raphael, I can't . . ."

He wasn't allowed to finish. Raphael waved a hand over his eyes, and as he slumped to the side, Maia caught his head, gently lowering it to the ground. She smoothed the golden curls from his forehead—they were softer than down feathers—and as she touched the worried crease of his face, the lines smoothed under her fingers.

"What happened to him? Why doesn't he know me?" Her voice cracked.

Raphael put a comforting hand on Maia's shoulder. "I restored his connection to his element, but he has lost most of his celestial energy. Let his tree heal him. Come." She tenderly smoothed Maia's hair away from her neck, twisting the loose strands in her fingers and tucking them back into the disheveled bun atop Maia's head. The gesture was so motherly and kind that Maia choked on the grief the memory awoke. Would there be no end to this?

As if to answer Maia's unspoken thought, Raphael took her by the hand and led her to the others, where they continued to dig up Heidi's tree. "We will set these things right," Raphael said. "The pain will heal. Never forget your strength, Maia. You have a tree to plant, a role to assume."

Maia nodded, her jaw clenched against the tears threatening to break through her careful defense. Restlessness crawled its way up her spine, and she couldn't help but look back at

Blake's sleeping form, at what she'd thought she'd gained and now . . . lost?

Why? Why her? She didn't want any of this; she never did. She wanted . . .

Maia dropped to the ground. She dug her fingers into the cold soil as her knees sank into the grass. The pulse of energy she felt pushed back against the pain threatening to drown her. It felt like a cooling aloe to the charred emotional mess the last few weeks had wrought. She felt stronger.

Yes . . . yes, she did want this. She could do this. She wasn't an island of one, not anymore. She looked up at the faces of those surrounding her, and each one was encouraging, hopeful, supportive. Even the pain etched in the corners of Leo's often happy lips spoke volumes.

This was her army, her team, her family.

Lightning cracked across the sky, illuminating the valley in overexposed light. Each *praeses* stepped back, away from Heidi's blackened tree, forming a semicircle before it. Heidi, with a cold and blank stare, looked on from her temporary prison. If she was truly cognizant of what was happening, she gave no indication.

Poppy raised her hand, and sparks of energy danced between her fingers as lightning reached down from the sky, licking her fingertips. Thunder bellowed and echoed in the valley, causing trees and boulders to tremble. Reed extended his hands forward, fingers curled and palms to the sky. As he pulled his palms closer to his body, the soil around the base of Heidi's tree responded in kind, pulling away, exposing the deepest parts of the tree's roots. A flick of Poppy's finger threw a string of electricity at the thickest cluster of roots, still stubbornly holding on. The roots were singed in half, and each time Poppy's lightning severed one, a scream of agony rose into the air. It wasn't until the fourth or fifth scream that Maia tore her transfixed gaze from the root to see Heidi writhing against her bonds, black smoke emerging from her fingertips, her lips, pouring from her eyes.

The valley echoed with the crackle of energy, the booming of thunder, and the piercing wails of a dying entity, but Maia felt numb as she watched Heidi's tree be pulled from the earth and cast aside.

Maia blinked, and the valley was suddenly quiet. The air was acrid and thick with smoke that burned Maia's lungs, and she coughed through the pain, grateful for the distraction against the conflicting emotions warring through her soul.

A gentle breeze blew through the clearing, taking the smoke with it, and Maia was greeted by the sight of her friends, beckoning her toward the freshly dug hole that now held her Magnolia sapling. As she patted the soil around the base of her tree, the Earth's reserved calm returned to settle like a balm over her fragile nerves. Once her tree was planted, she sat, hands wrist-deep in the soil, refusing to stand for fear of the new feelings that now stabilized her dissipating. As a compromise, she removed her shoes and socks, pressing her feet firmly into the grass and soil before shifting her gravity until she was standing.

"Maia." Raphael smiled at her. "I would like to—"

A strange haze flooded Maia's mind, drowning out the Great Healer's words. Maia blinked furiously, shaking her head, and swayed on her feet before squinting at Raphael's moving lips, still unable to hear a sound.

A voice echoed across her mind, calling out a name, but it wasn't her name, and it wasn't Blake's voice. Another soul called to her, but whether it was from memory or something more, she couldn't tell. A strange cold sliced through her skull, and she dug her fingers into her hair, gripping her scalp as she cried out, stumbling forward.

By the time she could open her eyes once more, she was standing inches away from Heidi. The other woman hung limp against the cedar trunk of her prison, the vines the only thing holding her up. Steam from beads of sweat trailing down her exposed skin rose into the air, cloaking the former Terra gaurdian in her grief.

A clamor of voices coalesced behind her, excited and frightened all at once. She felt the heat of their advancement, but held out a hand to stop them as she searched Heidi's face, looking for an answer.

"Who's Alistair?"

Heidi's brows pitched up in surprise, and her nostrils flared.

The voice echoed in Maia's mind again. She felt mad as hysteria gripped her lungs, pushing her breaths to be shorter, harder, as she struggled to understand what the voice wanted.

"He wants to know why?" She forced her words through shallow breaths. "Why haven't you sought him? Did you think he forgot?"

Heidi whimpered beneath her gag. A tear traveled down her cheek as she shut her eyes, shaking her head and straining against the vines that restrained her.

Mac was beside her. "Maia? What do you know?" She felt his gaze on her, and her skin prickled with instinct as her muscles tightened in defense, anticipating action. Yet her eyes never left Heidi's sallow face.

"You should have chosen him," Maia whispered, her voice monotone with shock. She knew the pain these two souls were in. She felt it intimately, but she wasn't sure how. She hadn't chosen this; she didn't have the will for this form of suicide. She couldn't fathom why anyone would choose to be torn asunder. "You should have chosen him."

Finally, the voice dissipated and the fog clouding her mind retreated. Maia swallowed thickly and took a step back. The raw grief etched into the sagging lines of Heidi's shoulders and slumped head echoed Maia's pain.

She turned back to the group and took a shuddering breath, attempting to regain her composure by restoring the mental wall she could tuck her emotions behind. "I heard Heidi's *astrum*," she explained. "He's been searching for her, but he was unable to find her because he was still an invoked human. I guess he isn't any longer, and he's become aware of her betrayal. He wanted to know why."

Raphael nodded in understanding as she glanced at Blake's shimmering form beneath his tree. The sun's energy radiated through him, visibly healing and restoring his broken body.

"I will take her before the Council," Raphael said. "They have much to answer for in not protecting these souls. Alistair isn't the only one with questions on how three sets of mates" —she nodded first at Heidi, then Maia and Blake, and finally at Poppy and Mac—"could have been separated. It's unprecedented."

"But there must be some explanation," Reed said, his fingers lost in the ends of Selene's silvery locks as his arm draped over her shoulder. "The last time so much destruction was wrought against the *praeses*, a battle ensued over the source of celestial energy. That's why the Council was formed."

Mac's eyes narrowed. "You think someone is going after the Source again? After so many lives were lost?"

Reed shrugged as though they were merely discussing the weather.

"Heidi wasn't acting alone," Selene added.

"How do you know?" asked Poppy. Her question was followed by a warm wind that kicked through the leaves and licked at the edges of her dress. Mac grabbed her hand and the wind settled, but Maia felt a sprinkle of water splash her cheek. Soon, a fine drizzle added mist to the clearing and the freshly planted sapling.

Selene shoved at a damp strand of hair sticking to her cheek, and the drizzle faded as Poppy fought for control. "She often received a strange visitor. A man, but I never saw him, only heard his voice. She was careful to keep their meetings private."

"And what did they speak of?" Raphael pressed.

Selene shook her head as Reed squeezed her shoulder in support. "I'm sorry. I don't know. I tried listening in a few times, but . . ." She shook her head once more, as if the movement would jar the information to the forefront of her mind. "It was so strange. Their voices were unclear, as though deliberately concealed against eavesdropping."

Raphael's shoulders tensed as a frown broke across her noble features. "Astral energy, the energy of destruction. That is the only answer."

"Perhaps it's *him*."

Maia jumped at the sound of Leo's voice. He and Lana had been so quiet, standing slightly separated from the rest of them. Maia had almost forgotten they were still there.

Mac glanced at the shamed Corocottas, who dropped his gaze from the *Talis* warrior the moment their eyes met. Mac's hardened gaze remained on the man for a few moments longer before glancing at Raphael with a slight nod. "Perhaps. However, there's still something else we need to deal with first." His eyes shifted from his sister to Maia.

"What does Leo mean?" Maia asked.

Raphael smiled gravely, a slight tilt to her head. "There is much to discuss, but first—have you chosen?"

Maia knew the answer to this question, and before the words left her lips, she felt the cord of control slip from her as she finally let go. The control she had always harbored and maintained, her security and her anchor; she no longer needed this crutch of humanity. Her ego cried out as she gave it up, sacrificing what she'd always thought was her strongest quality, the part of her that had carried her through her worst times, but had also restrained her from her best.

And it was easy, like exhaling. The moment she felt the control slip away, the people before her, the many plants, the animals scurrying across the forest floor to greet her, even the weak sunlight filtering through shade above, all faded from her sight.

43

THIS TIME, THERE were no grainy eyelids to groggily blink open. In this vision—or whatever it was—her eyes flew open and she felt fresh, awake, stronger than before. She sat in the Terra guardian's throne in the Core, dressed in a beautiful emerald gown made of a mixture of velvet and chiffon, intertwined delicately into full A-line skirt. The small cap-sleeved bodice was comprised of deep jade satin ribbons that wove in and out of a mixture of glistening raven and peacock feathers. Nothing so exquisite had ever touched her skin.

The throne upon which she sat looked different, as well. It was no longer a pale mix of sticks, plants, and furs, but consisted now of geo-rock crystals, with tiny waterfalls that leaked through the gems below the armrest into a thin, rectangular pool that ran halfway 'round the chair. The armrests and back were coated with the softest moss she'd ever felt, and Maia's favorite flowers—magnolia, honeysuckle, wisteria, jasmine—draped over the back, filling the room with their sweet, intoxicating aroma. There was even a soft, cashmere pillow that rested against Maia's back, and a multicolored woven rug under her feet, every thread and string spun from the hairs of creatures who had given them freely and without pain to their new Terra queen.

Maia looked at the chair next to her, eager to share this new experience with her mate, but her heart fell when she realized it was not Blake who sat beside her. Another man sat there, and instead of the Sideralis's warmth and passion, a vacuum of coldness emanated from him. Not the chill of winter, just an emptiness that couldn't be explained. He had dark hair, cut short, and chiseled features with a fine, slightly crooked Grecian nose, and his eyes were a very dark, wintry blue. Yet his smile was warm and carefree as he stretched in the Sideralis's throne.

"This is nice!" His voice was deep and cultured, without hint of an obvious accent. His dark gray suit was well tailored, proof that he not only appreciated, but demanded luxury. It was a trait mirrored in the way he rubbed his hands longingly over the armrest of Blake's throne, as though it were a long-lost friend.

"But, you know," he continued, "I never cared for the fiery look." He waved one hand carelessly through the air. "I'd much rather something more classic, more elegant." He tapped a tapered nail on the armrest and watched in smug satisfaction as new colors flowed through the geometric patterns of the throne.

Maia watched in horror as a dark red color, not quite black and not quite purple, mixed occasionally with a putrid green, flowing like sickly blood through the veins of the rock.

"Who are you?" Maia demanded. She shoved his hand off the armrest. "And what are you doing to Blake's—" She couldn't quite choke the word "throne" out. It still sounded far too silly.

The man grinned wider. "Don't you remember me, love, after all we've been through?" He pointed to the top of his head as the twisted antlers of the gazelle stretched out of his skull.

"That was you?" Maia cringed further into her throne. Bile rose in her throat as her heart picked up its tempo. Her palms were suddenly sweaty, and her skin prickled with heat. The anxiety she was sure she'd banished surged through her chest once more. "But I thought—"

"You thought what?" With a lick of his lips, the man no longer looked carefree and happy. He looked ready to tear the world to bloody shreds with a single gnash of his teeth. The edges of his form flickered strangely, as though his very shadow could not sit still.

Maia clamped her lips into a thin line.

The man relaxed, but the cold flint in his gaze remained.

"I'm sorry I wasn't able to properly introduce myself, but I did promise that when the time came, I would." Barely waiting for Maia to respond, he gave her a mock bow and sailed on. "I am your new lord and master, Aevum."

Maia raised a brow in question. The man sighed, obviously annoyed, as he ran his forefinger languidly across his top lip until it settled into the philtrum beneath his nose. "They never talk about me," he muttered. His voice was soft as he addressed the air before him. "When will they learn?"

Maia's typical urge to plunge forward, to steer the conversation and mold it to her will, was thankfully absent. She sat patiently, waiting for him to reveal himself, knowing he would if she gave him time. The sudden realization that she *had* time, more time than if she was human, more than she could have ever comprehended, settled into her bones with comfort.

Aevum flicked a glance in her direction, his eyes appraising before he nodded and returned his gaze to the cave's opposite wall. "Fine," he groused. "I am the keeper, and guardian, of Time. Every one of you answers to *me*."

Even from where she sat, Maia could feel the roots of her tree in the Garden, growing as they stretched further into the soil. She had gained memories and knowledge along with her power, not in a rush—she would have gone mad—but slowly, subtly. Certain words and sounds were keys to unlocking more pieces.

At the man's declaration, another well of knowledge was made known to her, and she could feel from its dark depths that this one was quite deep.

His real name was Luca, and he was the Aevum *praeses*, the *praeses* of time, just as he'd claimed, but time is a destructive force, always ending. Nobody could gain or make more, and thus his station also made him lord and master of death, time's ultimate harbinger. Suddenly, the empty coldness that radiated from him made sense. He was near pure astral energy, and if there was any strength of creation within him, it was but a pinprick of light, lost in the vastness of his night.

Images preceded her newfound knowledge, and her heart grew heavy. "I know you," Maia breathed. She felt as if the air had just been wrung out of her lungs.

"Indeed." He spoke as if she was a great tolerance he was allowing, waving a dismissive hand in her direction.

"What do you want?" The question was a necessary evil, and Maia feared its answer, even as she knew it.

"A trifle," he replied. "You. The entire universe." Luca shrugged, examining his nails closely, as if there was no greater importance in the world. "Since Heidi stole the part of Blake's soul that held his love and *astrum* memories of you—purely by accident, mind you—he is not going to be able to survive long." Ignoring the terror that settled in Maia's eyes and face, he continued, reaching out and patting her arm none too gently. "But, my dear, since you will have me as your new king and mate, soon enough you will be spared his depressing and brooding moods. Otherwise, I'm afraid you will not last long, either."

"So," Maia choked out, surprised she had any voice left at all. Shock was wreaking havoc on her mind as riotous feelings struggled to catch up. "You're just going to wait around until, what, Blake—" She bit her lower lip, too hard, and welcomed the superficial pain. She couldn't imagine a world or universe without Blake. She couldn't even allow the word to be expressed.

"Oh no, no, no! Of course not!" Luca chuckled softly beside her. The sound burrowed under her skin like maggots.

Before Maia could feel relieved, Luca burst her bubble of hope. "I'm offering you a chance to reclaim your place by my side, where you've always belonged. *You* are going to put him out of his misery." He held up a finger. "And *you* are going to bring me the rest of the Gaea *praeses*. They must see my way of matters if they are to survive."

"Why would I do that?" Maia asked.

"Because Leo and Lana have been summoned to appear before the Council."

Another blow, adding more weight to Maia's already heavy heart. "Lana didn't do anything wrong."

Luca smirked. "You, my dear, have much to learn. She is his mate, and as such, she is complicit in everything he does."

Maia scoffed. "Let me guess, guilty by association."

Luca nodded as he continued to rub the armrests, settling deeper into the chair. "Good, it looks like you do know something, after all."

Maia weighed her options quickly, but the words left her mouth nearly without volition. "Then I guess you'll have to teach me."

Luca steepled his fingers beneath his chin as his gaze traveled over the room. A secretive smile cut across the angular lines of his chin.

"Lesson one," he said. "Did anyone ever tell you that you are not an only child?"

44

Maia woke with a start. It took her a few seconds, but the crashing sound of waves, the cawing of seagulls, and the salty breeze that licked its way deliciously over her damp skin was not part of some fantastic dream. Though it would have been a well-deserved fantastic dream after the nightmare she had just suffered. She shook her head against the soft pillow it lay upon, and carefully peeled away the crisp white sheet that stuck indelicately to her body. The old rickety ceiling fan wasn't turning—broken, probably—and the cool breeze from the cracked window was not enough to dry her perspiring skin.

Maia ambled over to the window and mindlessly grabbed the bottom of the sash before glancing looked down at her body to make sure she was still dressed. A breeze tickled parts of her skin that shouldn't be exposed, and she realized with annoyed relief that she was dressed, but in a very large and loose cotton t-shirt. She wore nothing underneath, and despite the thin nature of the fabric, she was glad she was petite enough for the shirt to brush against the tops of her knees.

Noticing the low hum of murmuring voices outside, she lifted the window sash all the way up. Pressing her face against the musty screen, she saw Reed, Selene, Poppy, and Mac, all sitting in wicker deck chairs on the house's wraparound porch. They were clustered around a small table, sipping on cans of beer. Maia would have been content to watch them, finally in a moment of relaxation and friendly banter, but Selene happened to glance up and notice her peering out of the screen. With a shy smile, she peeled herself from Reed's embrace and approached. Her pale skin and hair were at odds with the tropical climate.

"I hope we didn't wake you," she said, her gaze wary.

"You didn't," Maia said quietly, shaking her head, wondering if she should mention her vision. "I hate that I've been passing out so much. I'm sure it looks quite—"

"Don't say weak." A touch of repulsion colored Selene's tone briefly before she forced another smile. Steeling herself to try again, Selene offered, "You are not weak. Never think that. To be quite honest, we all go through the same experience. It's jarring when you make the transition from human to Gaea." She shook her head. "It's cruel, really."

Maia picked at the flaking paint on the sill. "I really have a lot to learn. And so many questions, still."

"Why don't you come sit with us, then? Have a drink."

"I would if I had clothes," Maia picked at her hem, not wanting to know who had dressed her this time. "And . . . I hope you guys have something stronger than beer."

Selene smiled. "Your clothes were ruined, from everything that happened." She blushed and looked away awkwardly, but then she straightened and looked Maia in the eyes. "I have another dress in that closet that you can borrow." She nodded to the small door behind Maia. "It should fit. As for the drink . . ." She rotated her own can around in her hand, tilting it gently back and forth to get a good look at the label. "Well, its strength will do you little good. You aren't human anymore. There are many things you won't experience the same." Her voice dropped toward the end, carrying an edge of sadness and loss.

Maia shrugged. Acceptance was her only boon. "I see."

Selene smiled, turning slightly to look over her shoulder at the small group behind her. She kept her gaze on Reed, and his eyes flickered toward her even as he continued his conversation with Poppy. The Luna guardian sighed, the sound getting lost in a gentle breeze that played with the strands of the wind chime hanging from the edge of the porch. The tinkling melody danced through her next words. "Humans may not have our elemental powers, but they are blessed with a child-like ignorance that allows, well . . ."

She left her thought incomplete as she turned around and drifted back to her seat, where she promptly placed her chin on Reed's arm. He grabbed her hand, greeting her return with a gentle kiss to her forehead, not missing even a beat of his conversation.

Maia stared for a moment at the tableau before her before pressing her eyelids closed for a moment. Another memory surfaced, and she finally recognized it for what it was: another piece of her past. The same four souls before her were seated again in conversation, but in a different time, a different realm.

And she knew the thought that Selene did not complete. Yes, as mundane as humans thought their lives were, the power they often dreamt of in legends and myth were nothing compared to the power of discovery and wonder that they had.

For when one knows all, when one has experienced everything, they begin to miss the intoxicating buzz of impassioned excitement, of doing or learning something for the first time.

Maia closed the window and curtains, and went to the closet, retrieving the dress Selene had offered. She changed quickly into the cotton spaghetti-strapped dress and swallowed thickly; the dress's gentle blue color reminded her of Blake's eyes.

She let a single tear roll down her cheek as she tucked a strand of hair behind her ears and smoothed her dress. *That was it*, she told herself. *No more pity parties, no more crying.* She squared her shoulders and wrenched the bedroom door open, not even noticing, for the first time, the details of her surroundings. As she passed through the halls of the little beach house, Maia focused only on the door that led outside.

She was no longer in control; she no longer needed to be. She had relinquished that piece of her humanity, and the sensation of being tossed about by the waves of destiny was positively dizzying. She should have had Blake as her anchor, but in many ways he was gone. She wasn't even sure how to find him again, and she still had so many memories to uncover, so many answers to retrieve.

Her grief and sorrow were still there. But at least now, they were supported by a resolution.

She would fight for Blake's soul, and she would find this lost sibling she supposedly had. She had her army, but what was more, she had the support of many. Each of them, like Alistair, called to her. They needed her, and she needed them.

Now, she was ready for battle.

ABOUT THE AUTHOR

Carly Eldridge is a fantasy writer who calls New York City home; where the vitality of the metropolis, with its rich history and culture, provides an unending source of inspiration. She can often be found exploring the city, in awe of its always surprising display of art, beauty, and raw American grit.